Deliver Us From Evil

Peter T. King

ROBERTS RINEHART PUBLISHERS

Published by Roberts Rinehart Publishers
A member of the Rowman & Littlefield Publishing Group
4720 Boston Way
Lanham, MD 20706

Distributed by National Book Network

Library of Congress Control Number: 2002100759

ISBN 1-57098-419-0 (cloth: alk. paper)

∞™ The paper used in this publication meets the minimum requirements of American National Standard for Information Sciences—Permanence of Paper for Printed Library Materials, ANSI/NISO Z39.48-1992.
Manufactured in the United States of America.

To
Rosemary, Sean, and Erin for still putting up with me.

"Deliver us from evil, now and at the hour of our death."

—From the Lord's Prayer

Glossary

Gerry Adams—President of Sinn Fein, a member of the British Parliament from West Belfast, and the acknowledged political leader of the republican movement.

Bertie Ahern—Prime minister (Taoiseach) of Ireland, elected in 1997.

Tony Blair—British prime minister, elected in 1997.

Bill Clinton—President of the United States, 1993–2001.

Democratic Unionist Party (DUP)—Fundamentalist Protestant party in Northern Ireland supporting continued British rule. It opposed the Good Friday Agreement and is characterized by extreme anti-Catholic rhetoric.

Garda Síochána (Gardai)—Police force in the Republic of Ireland.

Good Friday Agreement—Peace accord signed in April 1998 establishing new governmental institutions in Northern Ireland, creating cross-border governmental bodies for Northern Ireland and the Irish Republic, and reforming the Northern Irish criminal-justice system.

John Hume—Leader of the SDLP and member of the British Parliament.

Ireland—The nation comprising the twenty-six counties on the island of Ireland that are not part of Northern Ireland. It received autonomy as a Free State in 1921 following the Irish war of independence and declared itself a republic in 1949.

Irish Republican Army (IRA)—Outlawed paramilitary force that waged armed struggle to end British rule in the north of Ireland. It has maintained a ceasefire since 1997.

Tony Lake—President Clinton's national security advisor (1993–1997).

Loyalists—Supporters of continued British rule in Northern Ireland. They are predominantly Protestant and supported paramilitary forces such as the UDA and the UVF.

Seamus Mallon—Prominent member of the SDLP, elected Deputy First Minister of the new Northern Ireland Executive (1998–2001). Also a member of the British Parliament.

Peter Mandelson—British secretary of state for Northern Ireland 1999–2001.

Patrick Mayhew—British secretary of state for Northern Ireland 1991–1997.

Martin McGuinness—Vice president of Sinn Fein, acknowledged leader of the republican movement in Derry City. Elected minister of education in the new Northern Ireland Executive in 1999. Also a member of the British Parliament.

MI5—British security service authorized to counter internal threats of espionage and terrorism against Britain. It is the British equivalent of the FBI.

MI6—British intelligence service set up to gather worldwide intelligence data. It is the British equivalent of the CIA.

Marjorie "Mo" Mowlam—British secretary of state for Northern Ireland 1997–1999.

Nationalists—Opponents of British rule in the north of Ireland. They are predominantly Catholic.

Northern Ireland—The six northeastern counties of Ireland still under British jurisdiction. They were partitioned from the rest of the country in 1921 following the Irish war of independence. Because republicans do not recognize the legitimacy of the state of Northern Ireland, they refer to it as "the north of Ireland."

Ian Paisley—Free Presbyterian minister who heads the Democratic Unionist Party (DUP) and is a member of the British Parliament.

Progressive Unionist Party (PUP)—Protestant working-class party affiliated with the Ulster Volunteer Force (UVF).

Real IRA—Dissident paramilitary group that broke from the IRA after the IRA resumed its ceasefire in 1997. Opposed the Good Friday Agreement and is responsible for such atrocities as the Omagh bombing of August 1998.

Republicans—Nationalists who supported the IRA.

Royal Ulster Constabulary (RUC)—Northern Ireland police force strongly opposed by Catholics. Reformed and restructured following the Good Friday Agreement, it is now known as the Police Service of Northern Ireland.

Sinn Fein ("Ourselves Alone")—The political arm of the republican movement. It supported the IRA's armed struggle against British rule.

Social Democratic and Labour Party (SDLP)—A predominantly Catholic and middle-class political party in Northern Ireland favoring the reunification of Ireland. It opposed the IRA.

David Trimble—Leader of the Ulster Unionist Party, elected First Minister of the new Northern Ireland Executive in 1998. Also a member of the British Parliament.

Ulster Defense Association (UDA)—Loyalist paramilitary force supporting continued British rule.

Ulster Democratic Party (UDP)—Protestant working-class party affiliated with the Ulster Defense Association (UDA).

Ulster Unionist Party (UUP)—Predominantly Protestant and middle-class party in Northern Ireland supporting continued British rule.

Ulster Volunteer Force (UVF)—Outlawed loyalist paramilitary force supporting continued British rule.

Unionists—Supporters of continued British rule in Northern Ireland. They are predominantly Protestant and not allied with paramilitary forces.

Author's Note

Deliver Us From Evil is a work of fiction set in the past and in the future. The events it describes prior to 2001—particularly America's role in the Irish peace process and the impeachment of President Clinton—are based on fact. Events occurring in the future are necessarily based on speculation, conjecture, and surmise.

The Good Friday Agreement of 1998 provided the people of Ireland—north and south, Protestant and Catholic—with the first-ever framework for a genuine peace. This historic accord was the culmination of years of diplomatic machinations and tortuous negotiations. It would not have been possible without unprecedented American involvement. This involvement began with President Clinton granting Gerry Adams a visa in 1994 and continued through the President's phone calls to the central players in Belfast in the early morning hours of Good Friday 1998.

Despite complications and delays the Good Friday Agreement is being implemented and it is working. The IRA is putting its weapons beyond use, the British Army is steadily reducing its presence in Northern Ireland, and the police are being reformed and restructured. Most significantly, the Northern Ireland political institutions designed by the Agreement to protect the rights and aspirations of both communities are in place and gaining increased acceptance among Catholics and Protestants.

But there are still forces in play—whether they are renegade paramilitaries or government agents—who for entirely contradictory reasons do not want the Agreement to succeed. *Deliver Us From Evil* attempts to show who these forces might be and how close they might come to success.

Predicting the future is a necessarily daunting venture. The tragic events of September 11th—the destruction of the Twin Towers and the attack on the Pentagon—demonstrated just how daunting. In just a moment, our lives and our world were changed forever. But the death and carnage of that day also demonstrate the necessity of anticipating threats to freedom and peace. And that is what I have attempted in *Deliver Us From Evil.*

Prologue

Sunnyside, New York
Arpil 8

It was the moment Frank McGrath had been dreading for almost twenty-five years. He had lived with the terror that it would end like this—a gun pressed against his temple, just above his right ear.

But not here. Not on a dreary, damp night in a dark alley in Sunnyside, Queens. Maybe on Belfast's mean streets. Or somewhere in England. But not in New York.

And the gunman. Frank always thought it would be one of the poor bastards he'd betrayed, not a man he'd been told he should trust. The man who was to protect him from the executioners.

He knew it was over. No one would hear him if he screamed. Besides, he'd been running and hiding for too long.

As a curious calm came over him, Frank McGrath thought of those friends he had betrayed, praying they would forgive him for being an informer.

And he thought of Vera.

The gun roared, blasting a bullet through Frank McGrath's skull. Pieces of brain and shattered bone exploded everywhere.

And blood poured onto the hard concrete ground where Frank McGrath's corpse now lay in a lifeless heap.

CHAPTER ONE

Wantagh, New York
April 11

Congressman Sean Cross sat in a rear booth in the nearly empty Lighthouse Diner. He watched as the middle-aged waitress, friendly but tired, walked slowly toward him.

"There's another guy on the way," he said. "The rain's probably slowing him down."

"You going to order, or do you want to wait?"

"I'll go ahead and order. Could you bring me a coffee and toasted English?"

"Sure, Congressman, it'll be up in a few minutes."

Cross glanced at his watch. Ten minutes before midnight. Looking out the rain-soaked window, he saw the glare of headlights turning off Sunrise Highway and into the parking lot. *Must be Jack*, he thought.

Sean Cross had been in Congress for more years than he'd ever expected. The Long Island Republican was running for re-election again this year. The September primary was still five months off, with the general election eight weeks after that.

Cross never took an election for granted and always campaigned hard, but this year he was in his best political shape ever. He hadn't anticipated much trouble at all—until two hours ago, when he'd gotten a call from Howard Briggs, a homicide detective with the NYPD.

"Here's your order," said the waitress. "I brought your friend along, too. He doesn't look so happy."

Jack Pender slid into the other side of the booth. Wiping the rain from his face and drying his eyeglasses, he sighed with feigned exasperation. "For Christ's sake, it's pouring out and I'm supposed to be retired. This better be important, dragging my ass out on a night like this."

"Why don't you order something," said Cross. "Maybe your mood'll improve."

"Same as him," Pender said to the waitress. "So what's this about? Why the dramatic midnight meeting? Did your favorable rating drop below 70 percent?" he asked, grinning sarcastically.

"Actually, Jack, this is pretty serious shit."

Pender stopped smiling. He looked at Cross intently.

Jack Pender had been a fixture in Nassau County Republican politics for four decades. He'd started out as a beat reporter in the early 1960s but, after a few years made the jump into local government, becoming a key advisor and political operative for a succession of town supervisors and county executives. Then in the early 1980s he went to Washington with Congressman Michael Ashe, who represented Nassau County. Pender was Ashe's chief of staff, and chief political troubleshooter. Ashe gave him a number of particularly sensitive missions. In 1984, Pender was sent to Northern Ireland to observe a celebrated trial of major IRA figures. Jack's subsequent report was a scathing exposé of Britain's reliance on paid informers, known as "supergrasses," and was credited with promoting the collapse of the supergrass system. When Ashe retired from Congress in 1992 and was succeeded by Cross, Jack stepped in as Sean's chief of staff. Retired now and playing a lot of golf, Jack still helped out on Cross's campaigns and was always available to dispense advice as a political wise man.

"Remember Howard Briggs?" asked Cross.

"Sure. The city cop that used to guard Gerry Adams when he was in town. Is he still on the job?"

"Yeah. He's a detective now, in homicide. He called about two hours ago to tip me off."

"About what?"

"Frank McGrath."

"Frank McGrath. Holy Christ. There's a name from the past. What the fuck did he do?"

"Whatever he did, he's not doing it anymore. They found him dead in an alleyway in Sunnyside, off Skillman Avenue."

"This *is* serious shit."

"He had one bullet in the head, and both his kneecaps were blown off."

"Jesus!"

"It gets worse. The cops found the gun he was shot with and they've traced it to the IRA."

"The IRA! Fuck me."

It had been more than two decades, but Jack Pender remembered Frank McGrath all too well. McGrath had been the supergrass in the trial Jack observed in Belfast. During the trial, McGrath was shown to have been an alcoholic, a habitual liar, and a psychopath who robbed and brutalized old ladies. His testimony was the only evidence the government had, and it was riddled with inconsistencies, contradictions, and outright lies. Yet thirty-four out of thirty-five IRA men had been convicted on it. That was because the fix was in. There'd been no jury, just a unionist judge who was a former British Army officer. He found them guilty and sentenced them to hundreds of years in jail.

But this time the Brits had gone too far. There was immediate outrage, particularly in the United States. Jack's report helped fuel it. In the end, the pressure proved too much. The Appeals Court threw out the conviction, calling McGrath's testimony "bizarre" and "contradictory." That ruling effectively ended the Brits' reliance on supergrasses. As for Frank McGrath, he had been promised financial security, a new identity, and guaranteed protection for the rest of his life. Anyone who remembered McGrath assumed he'd gotten plastic surgery and been relocated to England so he could live anonymously and safely. Instead he was lying in a New York City morgue.

* * *

"Did Howard give you any details?" asked Jack. "And how're they so sure it was an IRA gun? Those guys've been out of business for a few years now."

"Apparently, the body was found two days ago in a dumpster behind the Shamrock Bar. McGrath had a British passport on him with an alias—Edward Barrington. The cops contacted the British Consulate about the passport, and the FBI got involved. The cops also passed along the ballistics information on the bullets they took from McGrath's body."

"And the Brits got back to them?"

"Yeah, about nine o'clock. They said Barrington was McGrath, and the bullets came from the same gun that killed another IRA informant in London about a month ago."

"So maybe the IRA isn't out of business after all."

"I don't know. I can't believe it was them. Not after all this time. Christ, the war's over and McGrath's been out of the picture for more than twenty years. And with the Homeland Security Office working so closely with British intelligence against terrorism, the IRA would have to know how vulnerable they'd be. Why risk everything over a jerk like McGrath?"

"Maybe it's some IRA nutcase who hasn't heard the war's over."

"This is way too sophisticated an operation for one guy. To track McGrath down and knock off the other guy in London—that's pretty heavy-duty shit."

"Let's get to the basics. The story's too late for tomorrow's papers, but it'll be all over radio and television by morning. After that, the shit's going to hit the fan. This isn't going to help you in the primary."

"No shit," said Cross with a grim smile. "I guess I'll never get this fucking Irish issue behind me."

"Not after you got the State Department to let all those former IRA guys into the country last month."

"Jesus, Jack, they had nothing to do with McGrath."

"Try explaining that in a thirty-second commercial."

"That's what I need you for."

* * *

Sean Cross had been involved in the Irish issue in one way or another for almost thirty years. First as a town councilman and then as county comptroller, he had traveled to Northern Ireland time after time. He was there during the hunger strikes. He was a member of the International Tribunal that denounced the Brits' use of plastic bullets. And he was an observer at the supergrass trials. During all that time, he was an unapologetic advocate for Sinn Fein and developed a close friendship with Gerry Adams. He infuriated not just the Brits but the Anglophiles in the State Department when he said that the Irish Republican Army was a legitimate force that had to be part of any peace negotiations.

In 1992, Cross was elected to Congress. When he arrived in Washington, he found that the British Embassy had gotten there ahead of him, telling Republican leaders how radical he was, and how he hung out with terrorists. But after a while that didn't matter much. Bill Clinton granted Gerry Adams a visa in 1994, and the IRA called a ceasefire. The Irish issue became mainstream. Cross found himself invited to dinners at the British and Irish embassies and accompanying the president on trips to Ireland and Northern Ireland. Cross, however, had drawn heavy criticism from Republicans who felt that he was working too closely with Clinton—especially when he was one of only five Republicans to vote against Clinton's impeachment in 1998. Since then, his Republican primary opponents always accused him of selling out to Clinton over Ireland. Fortunately for Cross, the charges only resonated with the hard-core cadre of Clinton haters and he won each primary with a comfortable majority.

For the past few years, Ireland had been a back-burner issue. The horrific attacks on the World Trade Center and the Pentagon in 2001 had focused world attention on Islamic terrorism. The successful allied war effort which overthrew the Taliban in Afghanistan, crushed the bin Laden terror network, and deposed Saddam Hussein in Iraq brought the United States and Britain closer than at any time since World War II. And in Ireland British prime minister Tony Blair, coasting through his third term, had withdrawn all British troops from the North. The regional Northern

Ireland government set up in Belfast after the 1998 Good Friday Agreement was, after some fits and starts, solidly in place and working ever more closely with the Irish government in Dublin. Sinn Fein, the only all-Ireland party, was completing its transformation from pariah to major political player. It held three seats in Northern Ireland's ruling Executive and was a key partner in the Irish coalition government in Dublin, where it held two cabinet seats. The IRA and the loyalist paramilitary forces had not only maintained their ceasefires but, according to all intelligence reports, disbanded as well. And, in perhaps the most startling turnabout, Gerry Adams was awarded the Nobel Peace Prize for brokering a peace accord in East Timor. In the United States, a Republican president was continuing the bipartisan Irish policy which Clinton had initiated more than a decade before.

Cross himself had been low-key on the Irish issue until three months ago, when he used his seniority on the International Relations Committee to pressure a reluctant State Department to grant visas to five ex-IRA men who had served time for killing British soldiers in the mid-1980s. Cross saw the visa denials as a last gasp from the unreconstructed Anglophiles who still operated from the dark corners of the State Department. The five men, from East Tyrone, had been part of a particularly effective IRA unit that had carried out devastating attacks against British forces throughout the early 1980s. Sniper fire, land mines, rockets—this Tyrone unit did it all and did it well. In 1986 they ambushed an elite British commando force on an isolated country road. The firefight was brief but brutal. When it was over, eight Brits were dead and three severely wounded. The Brits launched an all-out manhunt, capturing five members of the unit. They each were sentenced to prison terms exceeding three hundred years.

Now, however, in the wake of the Good Friday Agreement, which called for the release of all paramilitary prisoners, they had been out of jail for years and were living nondescript, law-abiding lives in Tyrone, traveling freely throughout the six counties and the Republic. Earlier this year the Tyrone Society in New York had invited them to be honored guests at the Society's annual St. Patrick's

Day dinner. This was too much for the Foggy Bottom bureaucrats, who, with the help of their allies in the Justice Department, turned down the visa applications of the Tyrone Five, as they came to be called.

"You couldn't keep your mouth shut, could you?" said Jack. "Once the State Department denied those visas, it was like they were waving a red flag in front of you."

"Come on, for Christ's sake. They knew they were wrong. One press release and a phone call and they folded like a cheap accordion."

"And it's not bad enough you get five murderers their visas, then you have to introduce them at the Towerview Ballroom in front of five hundred screaming micks, getting your picture all over the papers."

"What can I tell you?" replied Cross. "It was a slow news day."

"Well I can guarantee you it's not going to be slow again for quite a while. This shit is only just beginning."

"I can hardly wait," smiled Cross ruefully.

CHAPTER TWO

Westbury, New York
April 12

Puffing on one of his trademark cigars, Joe Mondero leaned across his massive oak desk and grinned broadly at Sean Cross, who was seated on a leather couch in Mondero's office at the fortress-like Nassau County Republican Headquarters in Westbury.

"Sometimes I think you Irish guys are more trouble than you're worth," said Mondero.

"Sometimes I think you might be right. But you Italians aren't always such bargains yourselves," Cross replied with a smile. "Seriously, though, I appreciate your seeing me on such short notice."

"Hey, it was the least I could do. It's not every day one of my candidates is clever enough to get his name tied to an execution-style killing."

Joe Mondero had been chairman of the Nassau County Republican Committee since the early '80s. Friend and foe agreed that despite an occaisional setback Nassau Republicans had the best political organization in the country. More than two thousand committeemen and women attended to such unglamorous but essential grassroots tasks as collecting signatures for nominating petitions, getting out the vote for primaries and general elections, and, perhaps most importantly, serving as the eyes and ears of the organization. Seventy-three executive leaders, representing the various communities throughout Nassau, constituted the organization's ruling body. Mondero presided over that executive committee. Supporters said he was a strong leader. Detractors labeled him a hard-line boss running the American version of a pre-Glasnost politburo. Either way, very few ventured to cross Mondero or his machine.

"So, what's going on?" asked Mondero. "When you called this morning, I didn't know what you were talking about. But then I heard it on the radio. With your name tagged on at the end."

"Joe, all I can tell you is what I know, which isn't much."

"That's usually the case with you," Mondero interrupted.

"Thanks for the vote of confidence. Anyway, here's the story. The guy who was murdered is Frank McGrath. He was an IRA informer in the 1980s. The British used him to put away more than thirty guys. People like Michael Ashe attacked the Brits for relying on McGrath, who was a real head case—"

"Sounds like the kind of guy we should run for Congress."

"No, he wasn't that bad," rejoined Cross. "Anyway, the criticism came from everywhere, and finally the Brits gave up and the IRA guys were released."

"What happened to McGrath?"

"As far as anyone knew, he went into the British version of the witness protection program."

"What about the guy that got whacked in London?"

"Barry Kilpatrick. Another informer. He was found dead last month. The same gun was used in both cases. Ballistics tests trace it to an IRA killing going back ten years. That's how they're connecting the IRA and McGrath."

"How are you supposed to be involved?"

"First of all, I'm not involved. Even though Barclay Spencer is going to try his best to throw me in the middle—make people think I had something to do with it, even if they're not sure exactly what."

Barclay Spencer was the ultimate Republican partisan. A wealthy investment banker, he'd run two primaries against Cross, assailing him for his "obsession with foreign causes while ignoring the needs of real Americans here on Long Island." Despite pouring more than $2 million of his personal fortune into the campaigns and enlisting the support of some particularly vocal right-wing talk-radio hosts, Barclay garnered less than 20 percent of the votes in both races. Just two weeks ago, he had announced he'd be a candidate again in this year's primary.

"Spencer has something out already?" asked Mondero.

"Yeah, and I've got to give the son of a bitch credit. The story about McGrath broke on the radio at seven this morning. When I was driving over here just now, I heard Spencer's statement on the nine o'clock news. He must've gotten a press release out within an hour."

"What's he saying?"

"Basically, that I have serious questions to answer. McGrath was a hero who put his life on the line to expose terrorism, and I was his sworn enemy. The State Department tried to keep IRA murderers out of the country, and I abused my influence to get them in. One month after these murderers get their visas because of me, this anti-terrorist hero is found shot to death less than a mile from the ballroom where I welcomed the IRA murderers to America."

"Where do we go from here?"

"Joe, I want you to know that I didn't have the slightest—"

"Will you stop it! We've been friends for more than thirty years. I *know* you had nothing to do with it."

"Thanks. I just didn't want you to think I was taking your help for granted. The main thing is to let everyone know that you and the organization are with me all the way. Get the word out to the troops, let them know there's a tough primary ahead."

"Done!"

"So from now through September, I'll be in full campaign mode, going to all the dinners, parades, barbecues—everything that's going on in the district when I don't have to be in Washington for votes."

"Just keep me up to date so we have as much coordination as possible."

"Absolutely."

"I'll also talk to the union guys, especially the building trades. And the cops and firefighters. They're great at getting out the vote."

"That'll be a big help."

"Forget the politics for a minute. I'm sure we'll knock that fuck Spencer on his ass. What I really want to know is, do you have any idea what the hell happened?"

"No, and that annoys the shit out of me. It just doesn't add up."

"And you're supposed to be the Irish expert."

"Yeah, I'm a real fucking genius. Anyway, I'll be talking to some cops and FBI agents I know. Maybe they'll have something for me. Also, I've been able to get Jack Pender out of retirement."

"Pender! Jesus, I thought it would take World War III to get him off the golf course. But he should be a big help. You going back to Washington next week?"

"No. There's another week in the recess. I don't have to be there until a week from next Monday."

"Anything special planned in the meantime?"

"Yeah, but you won't believe it. Next Thursday and Friday there's a conference out at Notre Dame. It was planned over a year ago. It's called 'The New Ireland—North and South: A Study in Conflict Resolution.'"

"Your sense of timing is extraordinary."

"At least they won't have any trouble filling the house."

"Who's going to be there?"

"Just about every major leader from Northern Ireland over the past ten years—Trimble, Hume, Mallon, Adams . . ."

"Gerry Adams?"

"Yeah. He and I are scheduled to speak on Friday morning."

"That should get attention."

"It'll give me a chance to speak to him face-to-face. The phone, especially with something like this, is too risky. Mary Rose and I are having dinner with him on Thursday night."

"Mary Rose, now there's a saint. Is she looking forward to it?"

"Sure. She loves going back to Notre Dame. After all, that's where she met me."

"Have a safe trip, and remember to stay in touch on everything you do."

"Thanks a lot, Joe."

CHAPTER THREE

University of Notre Dame
Late April

Atop the Administration Building in the center of the Notre Dame campus, the famed Golden Dome glistened in the midday Indiana sun.

Mary Rose gazed up at it. "At least there's some stability in our crazy lives. Anyway, it's great to be back home."

In many ways Notre Dame was home to Sean and Mary Rose. They had met here at South Bend more than forty years ago when he was a law student and she was attending St. Mary's, the women's college next to the Notre Dame campus.

Attending Notre Dame had been a defining life experience for Cross. As a kid growing up in Sunnyside—an Irish working-class neighborhood in Queens—he had revered Notre Dame. To Sean Cross and other Irish Catholics of his generation, the "Fighting Irish" personified the way they wanted to see themselves—tough and smart and able to overcome the odds. Rooting for Notre Dame's football team was an article of faith. Later, when Cross was attending St. Francis College in Brooklyn by day and loading trucks and freight cars at the Railroad Express terminal on Tenth Avenue in Manhattan by night, he was able to put aside enough money to go to law school in New York. He applied to Notre Dame not because he thought he had any real chance of being accepted but just so he could say that he'd given it a shot. When the acceptance letter arrived, Cross couldn't believe it. His mother and father were ecstatic.

Once it sunk in that he had, in fact, been accepted, Cross's immediate concern was money. Travel, room, and board would make Notre Dame at least twice as expensive as a local law school. But his father, a New York City cop, said they'd find a way to scrape the money together. Sean was off to Notre Dame that fall. And for the next three years, between student loans and family savings, all the bills were paid.

Notre Dame exceeded Cross's expectations. The law school's philosophy was a rough mixture of high idealism and hard reality. This blue-collar Catholicism ideally suited the students, who were overwhelmingly working-class and Catholic. Very few had parents who had attended college. Though Cross and the others were unaware of it at the time, Notre Dame was lending intellectual reinforcement to their neighborhood values and providing the ability to break free from the Catholic ghettos and make a mark in modern American society.

Mary Rose's background was a little different. Her entire family—mother, father, brothers, and sister—had all attended either Notre Dame or St. Mary's. She was born and raised in Atlanta, which at the time boasted so few Catholics that the Church classified it as a mission—something like Red China or the Congo. When Sean and Mary Rose met at a law-school party during his first semester, their accents clashed so badly (youse and y'all) they thought they'd need an interpreter. Somehow, though, they hit it off. They were married during Sean's third year and moved to New York after his graduation. They had two children—Danny and Kara—who also graduated from Notre Dame.

Over the years, they always found excuses to revisit the campus and its tranquil environs.

"What time is Gerry coming in from Chicago?" Mary Rose asked.

"About five thirty," said Sean. "He'll meet us at the University Club at seven thirty."

"Think he'll be able to tell you much about McGrath?"

"Probably not—except, hopefully, to rule out the IRA."

"Will that be enough to calm down the New York media?"

"I wouldn't count on it. This is too good a story for them to let up on."

The McGrath murder and the possible connection of a congressman, no matter how tenuous or remote, had dominated New York news for the past week. The print dailies, talk-radio, and the evening news were addressing the story with varying degrees of hysteria, intensity, and concern.

Fueled by Barclay Spencer's incessant press releases and news conferences, the *New York American* published a brutal editorial in Monday's paper:

SEAN CROSS: U.S. CONGRESSMAN OR IRA HIT MAN?

For too many years Congressman Cross has tried to have it both ways. By day he portrays himself as an Irish peacemaker. In the shadows of the evening and dark of night, however, he associates with and advances the cause of the most brutal terrorists in the world today. The cowardly murder of Frank McGrath not only brings the IRA's terrorist campaign to the streets of New York, it exposes the so-called Irish peace process for the sham that it really is and focuses a spotlight on the troubling conduct of a United States congressman.

By executing Frank McGrath in our city, as well as Barry Kilpatrick in London, the IRA has demonstrated, as this newspaper has argued all along, that it has not turned over all its armaments and has no desire to abide by the norms of a democratic society.

By using his considerable influence as a senior member of the House International Relations Committee to browbeat the secretary of state and the attorney general into overruling their career officials and allowing convicted IRA murderers into our country just weeks before McGrath's execution was carried out, Representative Cross has raised the most serious questions about his moral capacity to continue in the United States Congress.

While there is no clear evidence as yet that any of the infamous "Tyrone Five" actually pulled the trigger or that Congressman Cross was aware of what his IRA friends were up to, these issues should never even have come up. Quite frankly, we expect more of a congressman—particularly a congressman who made such a show of supporting the war against Islamic terrorists in the wake of the attack on the World Trade Center. Maybe it's time for the voters of the Third Congressional District to send the message that they believe Irish terrorists are as evil as Islamic terrorists and no longer want their congressman's office to be used as a haven for terrorists of any sort. They can best do that by electing a new congressman.

"I guess the *American* won't be endorsing you any time soon," Mary Rose said wryly as they walked toward the Huddle, the venerable campus hamburger haunt.

"Christ, no. They didn't hold anything back. Spencer should put them on his campaign payroll."

"But *Newsday* was great."

"Yeah," said Cross, "thank God for *Newsday*."

"I never thought I'd hear you say that."

"I never thought I'd be saying it."

Cross and *Newsday* had been sparring partners during his early terms in Congress. On domestic issues like abortion and affirmative action, he was too conservative for *Newsday*. On foreign policy, though acknowledging Cross was knowledgeable and a firm internationalist, at least some of the editors thought his Irish agenda evidenced a certain irresponsible streak. The policy differences were only accentuated by Cross's compulsion to launch scud-missile-type missives in response to any *Newsday* criticism.

But gradually the hostilities diminished. Cross delivered for Long Island on projects like beach restoration and mass transit. He became a strong advocate for the Northeast, assailing Newt Gingrich and the Republican House leaders as "barefoot hillbillies." He worked with Bill Clinton in bringing about the Good Friday Agreement and withstood the full fury of his party to vote against Clinton's impeachment. During the war against al Qaeda, Cross was an unyielding supporter of the American–British alliance. Somewhere along the way, *Newsday* and Cross decided that it made sense to emphasize what they agreed on and respect their differences. It seemed to work for both sides. Certainly, it did for Cross. *Newsday* had endorsed him in his recent primaries and general elections.

Yesterday's *Newsday* editorial was a welcome respite from the venomous attacks of the *American* and the talk-radio wackos.

REP. CROSS DESERVES FAIRNESS NOT SLANDER

Last week's brutal murder of Frank McGrath was a tragic reminder of just how difficult it is to write the closing chapter of an age-old conflict. McGrath's killers must be tracked down, with no stone left unturned. Simple justice and the future of the Irish peace process require no less. Simple justice also demands the immediate cessation of the vicious innuendoes and baseless allegations being made from too many quarters against Congressman Sean Cross.

Indeed, the charges against Rep. Cross so casually tossed about by elements of the media and political aspirants defy elemental logic and basic decency. Stripped of their wild rhetoric, the allegations against Rep. Cross are based entirely on his long-standing relationship with the Irish republican movement and his recent successful efforts to secure visas for convicted IRA killers.

As to the first, it was precisely his contacts with Sinn Fein and the IRA that enabled Cross to play such a key role in bringing about the historic Good Friday Agreement. Because of that agreement, recent years have seen the development of democratic structures in Northern Ireland, growing cooperation between the north and the south, the release of hundreds of prisoners, and an almost total absence of political violence. In other words, after almost thirty years of brutal warfare, Northern Ireland is making the transition to a normal society.

As to the visa fight, though we question Cross's political judgment in making it such a high-profile encounter, the bottom line is that he was legally right—the "Tyrone Five" were entitled to their visas. Moreover, there is absolutely no evidence or reason to suggest that any of these men was in any way involved in McGrath's murder.

For the sake of justice and the Irish peace process, we urge the NYPD to continue giving this investigation its highest priority. And for the sake of the continued effectiveness of Congressman Cross, we advise that in the future he show some discretion before rallying to the defense of convicted murderers. He has been around long enough to know that being technically correct is not always the same as being right. Appearances count in politics and diplomacy. And as Congressman Cross should now realize all too well, unfair perceptions can become reality.

Cross and Mary Rose were finishing their lunch when George McCreedy came through the Huddle's side door and ambled toward their table.

"George, it's great to see you. How's everything?" said Cross, standing up to shake McCreedy's hand.

"Not so bad, Sean. I just finished up my speech at the conference. How're you keeping?"

"Nothing to complain about," said Sean. "You remember my wife, Mary Rose."

"I do indeed. She was at the Shankill Festival last year. I never forget a beautiful woman."

"That's enough for me. I'm out of here," said Mary Rose, smiling widely. "I'm going to walk over to St. Mary's and let you two figure out how to save Ireland."

"*Northern* Ireland," said McCreedy with a loud laugh. "You Fenians can worry about the rest of the place."

George McCreedy was renowned in loyalist paramilitary lore. As a Belfast commander in the Ulster Volunteer Force in the 1980s he was fearless and ruthless, orchestrating repeated shooting raids and bombing attacks in Catholic neighborhoods. Yet McCreedy was different from many of his fellow loyalists. He was never sectarian or bigoted against Catholics. Nor was he ever particularly pro-British. Certainly, he never trusted the Brits. He knew they were using his people—the poverty-level Presbyterians of the Shankill Road—and would cut them loose whenever it served Britain's purpose. To George, Catholics and Protestants were adversaries thrown against each other by cruel forces of history. He was fighting not to kill Catholics but to protect his people.

McCreedy was arrested in the mid-1980s and convicted for blowing up a furniture store on the Falls Road. No one doubted he had done it, but there was strong suspicion in UVF circles that George had been set up: the Brits had double agents throughout the UVF. In the weeks before McCreedy was locked up, the Brits had lifted dozens of prominent Belfast republicans in one more attempt to break the IRA. By sending away a figure as prominent as George McCreedy, the Brits were giving the appearance of being at least somewhat evenhanded.

George wasn't angered by his fate. Nor was he particularly surprised at how the Brits had turned on him. He'd always expected it, just not so soon. But at least he was alive and able to think and to plan. During his five years in Long Kesh prison, McCreedy became convinced that the fighting had to end. Poor Presbyterians were being killed fighting a dirty war for bigoted upper-class unionists who never shed a drop of blood or lost a loved one.

But McCreedy knew all too well that the war wouldn't end overnight. Political structures had to be put in place that would offer an alternative to war and protect poor and working-class Protestants. McCreedy also knew that for any of this to have a chance of working, contact had to be made with the republican movement. The British and Irish governments couldn't get it done; mainstream unionist politicians like Molyneaux and Paisley couldn't or didn't want to get it done. It was time for the IRA, the UVF, and the UDA—those actually doing the fighting—to find some common ground.

George was well aware that Gerry Adams and Sinn Fein were at least ten years ahead of the loyalists in building a political base. So throughout the early 1990s McCreedy proceeded on dual tracks—making the Progressive Unionist Party the political voice of loyalism and meeting clandestinely with local IRA commanders. While it became nowhere near as powerful as Sinn Fein, the PUP became strong enough so that when the IRA called its ceasefire in August 1994, McCreedy was able to convince the UVF and UDA to do the same.

Throughout the years of tumultuous negotiations leading to the Good Friday Agreement, McCreedy was an unswerving advocate for peace and loyalism. Again and again he'd say, "The war is over." At the same time, he would demand that any agreement protect the rights of loyalists to maintain their unique identity—an Ulster Britishness that he was never able to precisely define. He was a strong supporter of the Good Friday Agreement, and though the PUP never won many seats in the Northern Ireland Assembly, he became one of the most effective voices in that new body. His invitation to the Notre Dame conference was a recognition of that effectiveness.

* * *

"My Presbyterian grandfather must be turning over in his grave at the very thought of me actually walking about this Roman Catholic fortress," said George with a smile as he sat down across from Sean.

"Maybe this exposure to hallowed Catholic ground will help save your UVF soul," answered Sean.

"Well, I'll need all the assistance I can get in that regard, especially since Dr. Paisley isn't about to give me much help."

Just then, one of George's student escorts brought him a cup of tea.

"Is there anything else you need?" the student asked.

"No, Tommy, you've been very kind indeed. Just don't go too far away. I'd like you to keep your eyes open in case the distinguished congressman starts shooting at me. From what I've read lately, he's been known to do that."

"You shouldn't believe everything you read," replied Sean. "But before we get to that, how's the conference going?"

"Very well. This morning was the opening act, if you will. I shared top billing with Harry McNicoll," said George, referring to the former UDA commander who headed the Ulster Democratic Party.

"How was the crowd?"

"It looked like every seat was taken—mostly students, but a good bit of media as well."

"What was the thrust of your speech?"

"Basically, that Catholics and Protestants in Northern Ireland don't exactly love each other, but they've finally come to realize they have to work together."

"Did you get many questions?"

"I did indeed. And they sounded very knowledgeable. The students were curious about job opportunities and discrimination, and also about the police. Then at the end a few asked about McGrath."

"What did you tell them?"

"Pretty much the same I'm going to tell you—that I'd be very surprised if the IRA killed Frank McGrath."

"Do you have any idea, then, what the hell might've happened?"

The middle-aged McCreedy stroked his white mustache and looked at Cross for a long moment before asking, "Will you be seeing Gerry tonight?"

"Yeah, we're having dinner."

"I'm sure he'll tell you the IRA had nothing to do with it. And I'm sure he's right. Why the fuck would they? Everything's going their way."

"Well . . ."

"And don't get any ideas that my side did it either. Believe me, that shit is over. Besides," he laughed, "we're not that clever."

"Okay, if the IRA didn't do it and you guys didn't do it, who did? Could it've been some local IRA unit?"

"Listen, I'm not about to defend the IRA. I'll leave that to Gerry. Despite what you romantic Irish-Americans think of them, I know there are some mean, vicious bastards in the IRA—or whatever's left of it. But this was a major operation. I doubt the IRA at its peak could have carried it out, never mind some half-assed faction."

"So what you're telling me is you've got no idea."

"What I'm telling you, Sean, is that I don't have a fucking clue."

It was shortly after 5:00 P.M. Sean was back at the hotel, talking on the phone to Jack Pender.

"So Spencer was really knocking the shit out of me?"

"Yeah, Campbell had him on for almost the full hour between four and five," said Jack. *The Mike Campbell Show* was the highest-rated talk-radio show in New York.

"Was there anything new?"

"No. It was pretty much the same shit, except for one thing. He claimed that since everyone knows you're so close to the cops, there should be an independent investigation or the Homeland Security Office should handle it."

"Did Campbell take him seriously?"

"Campbell takes anything seriously that undermines you. But nobody else will. Spencer didn't even suggest who would do the investigation, unless maybe he wants to bring Ken Starr out of retirement, and Homeland will give the cops any help they need. But they'd never take it over from the NYPD."

"Give Spencer some credit. It's not a bad PR stunt to call for something, especially if you know it's never going to happen."

"Yeah. It'll help him keep the story alive a while longer."

"How were the calls?"

"About 50-50. It seems like the *Newsday* editorial helped. A few of them mentioned it."

"Anything else going on?"

"I have a meeting with Mondero and the union guys at headquarters in the morning. Joe's going to have some of the Town of Hempstead leaders there, too. He told me this afternoon that he intends to come out strong for you. He wants to let these guys know what the story is, that he's supporting you all the way."

"That's important. We can't have any of the organization guys getting panicky and defecting to Spencer."

"Suppose they want to defect because they think you're a pain in the ass—sorta like I do?"

"I can't imagine that," Sean replied, laughing.

"I'm sure you can't. Anyway, give my best to Gerry tonight and check in tomorrow. I'll let you know how the meeting went."

"Okay. Take care of yourself."

As Sean was putting down the phone, Mary Rose came into the room. "Anything going on?" she asked.

"I was just talking with Jack. There was the usual talk-radio nonsense. And Gerry called from Chicago. He still expects to be checking in about five thirty. I told him we'd meet in the lobby just before seven thirty and walk over to the University Club together."

Sean Cross and Gerry Adams had known each other for a quarter of a century. The first time they'd met was in Belfast at the funeral of IRA hunger striker Kieran Doherty in 1981. Cross had been struck by the respect that Adams—who had not yet turned thirty-three—commanded from hard-core republicans who were very much his senior. It wasn't until the mid-1980s, however, that Cross had the opportunity to speak with Adams at length. By then Adams had become president of Sinn Fein and been elected to the

British Parliament, a seat he did not take, refusing to swear allegiance to the Crown. He had also barely survived an assassination attempt by loyalist gunmen, the bullets just missing his heart.

During the conversations, held at the Sinn Fein Press Centre on Sevastapol Street just off the lower Falls or at Connolly House in Andersonstown, Adams laid out his ideas as to where the republican movement should be going. Without ever actually saying it, he clearly implied that the war had reached a stalemate. After almost two decades, it had become obvious that the Brits, even with the most sophisticated weapons and counterinsurgency tactics, could not defeat the IRA. Similarly, the IRA had to accept that despite its reputation as the most effective guerilla force in the world, it would never be able to drive the British Army out of Ireland.

Adams saw the pragmatic and moral imperative of seeking a political settlement. But he knew how long it would take and how frustrating it would be. And he also knew there was no assurance of success. The Brits couldn't be trusted. What they really wanted was surrender. So the IRA would have to remain an effective fighting force, able to carry out the occasional spectacular operation to rally their own people and keep the fear of God in the Brits. At the same time, Sinn Fein would have to expand its political base, necessitating the reallocation of scarce republican resources and incurring the ire of IRA hard-liners who quite rightly realized that any money spent on politics meant fewer weapons.

Adams was definitely on the high wire. But, working with other like-minded leaders in the movement, among them Martin McGuinness of Derry, he painstakingly got the job done. Sinn Fein's vote in local elections steadily increased, and he was overwhelmingly re-elected to Parliament, still refusing to take his seat.

Perhaps most importantly, Adams and McGuinness did what no Sinn Fein leaders had ever done—they reached beyond their base. Sinn Fein, "Ourselves Alone," is by definition an insular party. Its strength was that it would not allow itself to be tainted by outsiders. That was also its weakness. Adams saw this and reached out to John Hume of the nationalist but nonviolent Social Democratic and Labour Party (SDLP) to seek common ground. He also reached out to pro-nationalist politicians in the Irish Republic.

These approaches led to the establishment of secret lines of communication, not just with the Irish government, but, more significantly, with the British government itself.

Still, Adams and Sinn Fein were very much isolated. Because of repeated threats, he stayed in a different house almost every night and traveled in a lead-lined car. His voice was banned on radio and television throughout the United Kingdom and even the Republic. But perhaps most damaging to his efforts, he couldn't visit the United States. Adams strongly believed that if the United States could be persuaded to become an honest broker among the parties, the dynamics of the Irish conflict would be changed forever. The issue would be internationalized. No longer could the Brits portray it as an internal issue of law and order. To have any chance of success, Adams would have to show the flag on American soil, mobilizing Irish Americans and making his case through the American media. But time and time again the Reagan and Bush State Departments denied him a visa.

All this changed when Bill Clinton reversed American policy, defied the Brits, and granted Adams a visa in February 1994. It was only a forty-eight-hour visa, but its impact would be felt for years. Hordes of media gathered at Kennedy Airport for Adams's arrival, and Cross was the first to greet him publicly. Adams handled all the shouted questions—rude, friendly, and ignorant—with wit and charm. Though thoroughly jet-lagged, he won rave reviews for his appearance on *Larry King* that evening. The following day was a blur of events—an early-morning news conference with Cross and other New York area congressmen, a meeting with Cardinal O'Connor, a major address to a foreign-policy think tank, and a monster rally that evening at New York's Sheraton Hotel on Seventh Avenue. Everywhere he went, the media were tripping over themselves in pursuit. One cynic was heard to comment, "Yesterday he was a murderer. Today he's a cross between the Pope and Elvis."

The reverberations were enormous. Downing Street and the Foreign Office realized the "special relationship" which had linked American and British foreign policies for so long was forever altered. The IRA hard-liners were made to realize that the power equation had been dramatically shifted and that diplomacy might indeed work. Adams had done what he needed to. By August the IRA called its ceasefire.

In the years since, there had been countless trips to the United States, meetings at the White House and on Capitol Hill, the implementing of the Good Friday Agreement, and the general recognition that Gerry Adams was a certified player on the world stage.

Tonight they were seated at a corner table in the University Club. A large window to the side; an impressive portrait of Ara Parseghian, the legendary Notre Dame football coach, behind them.

"So, Gerry, how's the trip so far?"

"Just grand, Sean. The crowd in Boston was very good indeed. And today's in Chicago seemed even larger. Wouldn't you say so, Richard?"

"I would. I'm absolutely amazed that the American people haven't tired of you by now. God knows I did—years ago," quipped Richard McCauley, Sinn Fein's longtime press officer.

"Ah, Richard, smart people can never get too much of a good thing," answered Adams. "So, Mary Rose, tell me, how does it feel to be married to a gunman?"

"It all depends upon what newspaper I read," she answered.

The waitress brought them their drinks. "Are you ready to order, or are you still waiting for someone?" she asked.

"Professor Rice is going to join us, but he probably won't be here for a while," replied Cross, "so we might as well go ahead."

After they had placed their orders, the conversation went on uninterrupted.

"How's the situation on the ground, Gerry?" asked Cross.

"Politically we're doing fairly well. In the north, politics is less along sectarian lines than it was even six months ago. There's a number of issues you'll see Catholics and Protestants working together on. In the south, being involved in government gives us a new dimension and different responsibilities. It's a bit of an educational process for us; we're finding it can be tougher on the inside. But we're quick learners, you know."

"That's certainly debatable," answered Cross. "Anyway, what do you make of Kilpatrick and McGrath?"

"Well, I was slagging you about it, but believe me, we know how serious this is for you. It's serious for us, too. Let me tell you straightaway that these were not IRA operations. It would serve no purpose."

"That's what McCreedy told me earlier today."

"Ah, yes, George would know. And fair play to him and his loyalists, they wouldn't be doing that sort of thing anymore either."

"Could it be one of the guys Kilpatrick or McGrath turned on—or maybe some relative of theirs?"

"Not operations this clever. Not without someone in the republican movement hearing about it."

"Where does that leave us?"

"It leaves me thinking that someone's messing about. Someone who's trying to bring the peace process down and has the means to be effective."

"The Brits?" asked Cross.

"Certainly not Blair. The last thing he'd want to do is to come back into Ireland. It took them over eight hundred years to get out."

Just then, Professor Charles Rice, the conference chairman, walked over to the table, warmly greeted everyone, and sat down.

Charlie Rice was one of those Irish-Americans the Brits found baffling: extremely intelligent, a Marine, very right-wing conservative—all qualities that should have made him an avid Thatcherite. Instead, he was an outspoken opponent of British rule, an officer in a number of Irish-American organizations, and the author of a best-selling tome skewering Britain's Irish policy. Now in his seventies and semi-retired, Charlie Rice had been teaching at Notre Dame Law School for more than thirty-five years. He had put even more years into the Irish cause. He was delighted to welcome Gerry Adams back to Notre Dame.

The pleasantries concluded, Cross asked, "So, Charlie, how did the conference go today?"

"Very well. I heard you met with McCreedy. He and McNicoll did a great job explaining where the loyalists are coming from. They really have an endearing type of gritty honesty."

"Ah, yes," injected Adams, "they're sound as a bell."

"This afternoon we had the unionists," continued Rice. "William Carson and Roger Thompson."

"How were they?" asked Cross.

"Not bad, but very begrudging. Even after all these years, they only go forward because they have to—not because they want to.

"Did they say anything about McGrath and Kilpatrick?" asked Adams.

"Not really. A reporter from the student paper asked about it, and Carson vaguely implied that someone somehow affiliated with the IRA might have had a hand in it. But it was obvious he knew he was reaching. He didn't pursue it. Do you have any ideas, Gerry?"

Adams told Rice everything he'd told Cross. Rice listened intently. When Adams was finished, Rice was silent for a long moment. Then he said, "I'm just guessing, and I have nothing specific to base this on, but I wonder if besides checking into the Brits, we should also take a look at our own government."

"Who did you have in mind?" inquired Cross.

"FBI, Justice, Immigration—a lot of those guys invested an awful lot of years going after the IRA. And now, as they see it, the IRA is running the show."

"Charlie, your theory's as good as any. I don't think we can rule anything out," said Adams.

"Sean, how close can you get to the investigation?" asked McCauley.

"I know some of the cops on the case. In fact, Howard Briggs, Gerry's old bodyguard, is the one who tipped me off in the first place. I'm sure they'll leak me some of what they find. But they'll have to be careful. And I have some other sources. I'll pursue them as well."

"Gerry, Sean—you guys all set for tomorrow morning?" asked Rice. "It'll be just the two of you, discussing whether or not America has a continuing role in Ireland."

"Ready as I'll ever be," said Adams. "It's Sean I'm worried about."

"I can appreciate that," said Rice.

"I'm sure it will be in the Notre Dame highlight film," said Cross with an ironic smile.

"I can see it now," said Rice, "the pantheon of Notre Dame heroes—Rockne, Parseghian, Adams and Cross!"

They all laughed and wished each other good night.

It was shortly before 9:00 a.m. Sean and Mary Rose were walking across the bright, sunlit campus with Gerry and Richard. They passed the Huddle and approached the mosaic-covered fourteen-story Memorial Library where the conference was being held.

"Now with your third visit, you're a real Notre Dame veteran," said Cross to Adams. "They might make you coach of the football team."

"I suppose some would say I could qualify as the Fighting Irish," laughed Adams.

When they reached the auditorium, it was filled nearly to capacity. Cross noticed that the crowd—as was always the case when Adams spoke in the United States—recognized the bearded Sinn Fein leader and looked to him with anticipation.

Mary Rose and Richard were shown to their seats while a student escorted Sean and Gerry to the stage. Each would speak for fifteen minutes, Adams first, Cross to follow. Questions from the audience would be taken for up to an hour.

Adams began by recounting, briefly but starkly, the oppression that Catholics in the north had suffered under British rule and unionist domination—the brutality, the discrimination, the third-class citizenship. He did so with much poignancy but no whining. What's done is done. Speaking in a deep, deliberate voice, he expressed his clear belief that the progress of the past decade toward equality—and, yes, toward reunification—would not have been possible without the United States. Clinton's intervention and leadership, George Mitchell's patience and persistence, and Congress's prodding had been indispensable.

—But much remains to be done. In our part of the world at least, the United States is still the moral center. American influence keeps the parties honest. So, too, American investment provides jobs and opportunities. Ultimately, we'll have to make our own way, and America's role must necessarily diminish. But the wounds are still too raw, the divisions too deep, for us to do it alone just yet.

By your presence here today, you are showing the Irish people that they are not alone, that religion can be a powerful force uniting people of different faiths in a common quest for justice and peace.—

After Adams concluded his remarks to sustained applause, Cross stepped up to the microphone.

—For too long the United States ignored British misrule in Ireland. In many ways, we were an acquiescent accomplice. Too many in the Irish-American and Catholic communities were silent for too long. But the past is gone, hopefully forever. The future holds great challenge, but enormous opportunity as well. There are good people on all sides—republicans such as Gerry Adams, and loyalists such as George McCreedy and Harry McNicoll, whom you heard here yesterday. But there are also those—including some in government—who still want the peace process to fail. Having done so much to bring about the recent peace in Ireland, the United States cannot now retreat. To do so would only encourage the forces of darkness.—

The statements concluded, Fr. Armstrong, the university's vice president, opened the floor to questions.

—Charlie Milone, graduate student. Is the reformed police service being accepted in nationalist communities?

Adams. The situation has certainly improved from what we had with the RUC, but much remains to be done. More nationalists are needed in policy-making positions.—

—Lou Bianchi, philosophy major. Can the Republicans be counted on to continue American involvement in Ireland?

Cross. Clinton made Ireland an integral part of American foreign policy, very much like Israel. The Republican administration has continued that. Our Irish involvement has bipartisan support.—

The questions ran more than half an hour, covering the adjustment of former prisoners into society, the extent of cross-border contact and cooperation, the role of religious institutions, and the creation of an independent judiciary. With just minutes to go, there was time for one final question.

—John Coyle, *Chicago Journal.* Congressman Cross, would you update us on the status of the investigation into Frank McGrath's murder and what possible role you may have had in that murder?

The audience erupted with loud murmurs and scattered booing.

Cross. The New York City Police Department is doing its usual professional job. It is also cooperating closely with the FBI and Scotland Yard. Any involvement of mine in this tragedy exists solely in the minds of political opportunists, conspiracy theorists, and ignorant reporters.—

After a moment's hesitation, the audience applauded.

Adams. I realize this question was not addressed to me, but I feel compelled to respond. No one with any knowledge of the situation in Ireland would think for even a second of mentioning Sean Cross in the same breath as this terrible crime. They *would* realize, however, that someone or some group wants very much to disrupt the peace process and has the capacity to do just that. That should be the concern, not the ludicrous charges against Congressman Cross.—

The audience broke into loud applause.

In his hotel room that afternoon, Cross called Jack Pender and filled him in on the conference.

"So Gerry's left already?" asked Jack.

"He's off to Albany for a speech tonight, and tomorrow he'll be going back to Ireland," answered Cross, lying down on the bed and propping his head on two pillows.

"Are you catching the five o'clock flight?"

"We're leaving for the airport right after I hang up. Mary Rose is just finishing packing. So how was the meeting at headquarters?"

"Very good. Great, actually. Mondero let them know he's with you all the way and expects them to be as well."

"How'd they react?"

"The executive leaders were good. They know their job. The union guys were terrific, though. Tom Ward was there from the Operating Engineers and Jack Quinn from the Carpenters. And Michael Boyle from the Firefighters. They're going to go the whole nine yards—phone banks, mailings, fund-raising—everything."

"What's Spencer been up to?"

"He held a news conference this morning at the press room in Mineola. Same old shit. I doubt he'll get much coverage. I didn't get any press calls on it."

"I'm sure he'll think of something new by next week."

"Don't help him out by saying something wacky. What's on for the weekend?"

"I've got Little League parades in the morning—Seaford and Massapequa—and a Knights of Columbus dinner in Oceanside tomorrow night."

"How about Sunday?"

"Two American Legion breakfasts, in Wantagh and Manhasset."

"That should keep you running."

"Yeah, and then there's a cocktail party in Island Park in the afternoon."

"Is D'Amato going to be there?"

"I assume so. I've never been to anything in Island Park when he isn't."

"Well, you're going to enough events to get a feel for what kind of impact the murder is having."

Cross laughed. "Christ, when you put it that way, it can't be good."

"You know what I mean—parents, veterans, loyal Republicans—you should be able to get a sense of whether the issue is sticking. When are you going back to D.C.?"

"Sunday night. We go back in session Monday afternoon."

"Should be interesting. I'm sure your distinguished colleagues are looking forward to welcoming back a notorious murder suspect."

CHAPTER FOUR

Washington, D.C.
The Last Week in April

By Monday morning, Sean Cross was back at his desk in his fourth-floor office in the Cannon Building. Behind him was a large window affording a clear, unobstructed view of the Capitol. Reviewing his schedule for the week, he saw the agenda wasn't too heavy. A Financial Services Committee hearing on interest rates. A subcommittee hearing on money laundering. And an International Relations Committee hearing on African trade. There were also meetings with lobbyists and interest groups—investment bankers, life-insurance companies, the Teamsters, and a nurses' association.

His phone messages, letters and e-mails from the previous week were stored in a red folder. A few touched on the usual hot-button issues—Social Security, abortion, and gun control. Maybe about thirty in all. Sorted separately were the communications that had come in on McGrath's murder. These numbered about a hundred, the overwhelming majority hostile to Cross. *Most people only write when they're pissed off,* Cross mused. He also noted that almost half came from outside his district.

Cross could see that awareness of the McGrath situation was growing. At each event he'd been to over the weekend people had mentioned it to him. Most were quizzical rather than hostile—except for the guy who'd heckled him from the sidewalk during the Little League parade in Massapequa. Cross knew his district pretty well. And he'd been around long enough not to panic when something went wrong. The McGrath issue would give Spencer attention he wouldn't otherwise have gotten, but it shouldn't be enough to turn the election around. Not unless Cross overreacted. Or something new came out.

Tom O'Connell, Cross's amiable but highly efficient chief of staff, came into the office to discuss the status of mass transit legislation Cross was pushing, then brought up a trip to London that Sid Gordon, chairman of the International Relations Committee, had scheduled for the following week.

"Sean, this just came up, but I really think you should consider going."

"What's it all about?" asked Cross.

"The NATO foreign ministers' meeting on terrorism that was scheduled six months ago. Apparently, the secretary of state just decided it would be a good idea to have a congressional presence with her, so she called Sid Gordon on Friday and asked if he'd put a delegation together."

"So, they're asking me?"

"Yeah, Gordon's chief counsel called this morning and said Sid would like you to go, especially since you're slated to chair the European subcommittee in the next session."

"How many are going?"

"They're trying to get five—three R's and two Dems."

"What's the schedule?"

"You'll leave Andrews Saturday afternoon and get into London early Sunday morning. There's a formal welcoming dinner on Sunday night, meetings all day Monday, and then a reception Monday night. You should be back late Tuesday afternoon."

"Do I miss any votes?"

"You shouldn't. There's nothing Monday, and the first vote Tuesday isn't scheduled until six o'clock."

"What are the pluses?"

"The main thing is that it puts you on the world stage against terrorism and takes you away from back-alley murders and all that crazy shit. It'll also show you're on good terms with the Brits, which wouldn't be the case if they thought you were killing off their informers."

"I think you're right. I don't see any minuses at all; tell them I'll go."

That afternoon Cross and O'Connell were on the phone with Jack Pender.

"I think we should get hold of John O'Laughlin," said Cross, referring to his longtime pollster.

"You want to do a poll now?" asked Pender.

"Yeah," said O'Connell, "we should get a baseline so we'll be able to gauge between now and the primary if any of Spencer's shit is sticking with the voters."

"Well, you have the money," replied Pender. "I'll call O'Laughlin this afternoon. He should be able to wrap it up in a day or two. What's happening with the London trip?"

"Gordon was able to get four members plus himself," said O'Connell, "so everything is a go. The committee'll be putting out the press release tomorrow."

"Any chance you'll be able to see Tony Blair while you're there?" asked Jack. "That'd be a great PR shot."

"I don't think so. It'll be mainly Foreign Office types. Blair'll be at the banquet on Sunday, but that'll be a big fucking production. I probably won't get near him."

"No matter. It's still good you're going," said Jack. "It's all part of your rehabilitation—slow but steady."

Late Wednesday morning, Cross was leaning back in his chair in the Financial Services Committee hearing room on the first floor of the Rayburn Building, trying to look attentive and make sense of the Federal Reserve chairman's testimony. Interest rates. Money supply. Exchange rates. Inflation. Trade deficits. Industrial capacity. Productivity. *Jesus,* Cross thought, *the world is getting more confusing every day.* Just then his beeper went off. It was his press secretary, Kevin Finnerty. Cross called Finnerty from the phone behind his chair.

"Kevin, it's Sean. What's up?"

"You'd better get back to the office as soon as you can. There's a story breaking out of London."

"I'm on the way."

Cross looked around the committee room, trying to appear nonchalant. *There are more than enough members of Congress here to keep the Fed chairman company*, he thought. *The world economy should be able to survive for an hour or so without me.* He ducked out and headed for the Cannon Building.

Opening the door to his suite of offices, Cross walked through the reception area and into his private office. O'Connell and Finnerty were waiting for him, their faces grim.

"You look like a couple of pallbearers," said Cross. "Whatever you have to tell me can't be any worse than that shit I was listening to on interest rates. So what's the story?"

"Unfortunately, you're not going to be as welcome in London as we thought you'd be," said O'Connell.

"I just got a call from the *Daily Telegraph* in London giving you the chance to comment on a story they're running tomorrow," said Finnerty.

"Like I said, what's the story?" said Cross, sitting down at his desk and leaning forward on his elbows.

"It's about the Codel you took to Dublin three years ago," said Finnerty. Cross had been part of the congressional delegation led by Chairman Sid Gordon. "Apparently, someone told them that one afternoon when the rest of the delegation was attending meetings in Dublin, you snuck off on your own to meet with Seamus McCoy in the back of some pub in Dundalk."

Cross smiled grimly. "Okay, I can fill in the rest of the story. McCoy is part of the Real IRA, which set off the bomb in Newry two years ago, killing all those civilians. So that means that somehow I'm tied to the McGrath murder *and* the Newry bombing."

"I think what they're saying," injected Finnerty, "is that you keep showing up in strange places."

Cross thought for a moment. "Let's get everything straight," he said, "so we're all talking from the same page. I did meet with Seamus McCoy three years ago. I first met him about twenty years ago in Derry. And I saw him off and on after that. Then the Good Friday Agreement was signed, and I didn't hear from him until three years ago when I was in Dublin and he sent a message asking to see me."

"Did he say what about?" asked O'Connell.

"No, but I figured he wanted to make the case for the Real IRA and tell me why the Good Friday Agreement was no good."

"Is that how it went?"

"Pretty much. It was nothing I hadn't heard before. He just couldn't accept that the war was over."

"What did you tell him?"

"That I was totally behind Adams and McGuinness, and, except for a few head cases, so was Irish America. I was polite to the guy, but I told him the Real IRA had no support—none whatsoever—in the United States."

"What should I tell the *Telegraph*?" asked Finnerty.

"Don't tell them shit," answered Cross. "Just give them 'No comment.' First of all, they're out to fuck me. They're a pro-unionist rag, and I have nothing to gain by telling them anything. They'll just distort it. But more importantly, I want to see how much they actually know—because the real issue here is where they got this story in the first place."

"Couldn't it have come from McCoy himself?" asked Finnerty.

"Yeah, if he hadn't blown himself up with one of his bombs a year ago."

"I guess that does rule him out," said O'Connell. "I must say, though, you sure hang out with a great class of people."

"Forget the jokes for a minute," Cross replied, "and think about this: I didn't even know about the London trip until two days ago. But already someone's managed to leak a story about a secret meeting I had three years ago with a guy who's dead. That's pretty good turnaround time."

"You're right," said O'Connell. "Whoever we're up against knows what they're doing."

Voting on the House floor ended just after eight that evening. As was often the case, Cross walked over to the Dubliner Restaurant on North Capitol Street with Dick O'Neill, a Democratic congressman from Massachusetts. O'Neill had been active on the Irish issue for many years. The two men preferred the Dubliner to the more upscale, lobbyist-laden eating establishments on Capitol Hill.

The Dubliner had good food, good beer, good prices, and good atmosphere. You could take off your jacket, loosen your tie, and unwind. Cross and O'Neill entered the Dubliner through the lobby of the adjacent Phoenix Park Hotel, which was under the same ownership. Danny Coleman, the avuncular proprietor, led them to a table in the rear room, known as the "snug." The waitress came by and took their order, returning with pints of Harp and their staple order of shepherd's pie.

"You've been taking some heavy shots," said O'Neill, sipping his beer.

"It's not as bad as it looks," answered Cross. "But there's more on the way tomorrow."

"Any idea who hit McGrath?"

"No. I saw Gerry last week, and George McCreedy. They don't know a thing. But they did rule out the IRA and the loyalists."

"What do the cops say?"

"They tell me they're not getting anywhere either."

Cross then told O'Neill about the story that was going to break in tomorrow's *Telegraph*.

O'Neill paused, considering. "You're right. On their own, none of these stories should hurt you. But there could be a cumulative effect. And no offense to you or your brilliant political career, but this could really screw up the peace process."

"Any thoughts?" asked Cross.

"See what you can find out when you're in London, and then maybe we'll have to reactivate the Ad Hoc Committee."

From the time of its founding by Bronx congressman Mario Biaggi in the late 1970s, the Ad Hoc Committee had pushed a strong Sinn Fein, pro-republican agenda. Cross and O'Neill had co-chaired the committee since 1995. Though the Ad Hoc Committee had no official jurisdiction or staff, it made an impact. Conducting hearings, holding press conferences, and issuing statements, the committee played a particularly prominent role in the lead-up to the Good Friday Accord and again during implementation of the agreement. During the past few years, the committee had been decidedly low-key—not because Cross and O'Neill had lost interest in any way but because so much progress was being made through mainstream committees and ordinary channels.

"It'll be like the old days," said Cross. "We'll be on the outside, throwing rocks."

O'Neill smiled and shook his head. "Sean, this just proves that you're destined to remain a fringe player. You're just not the type who'll ever make it with the establishment. Too bad you're dragging the rest of us down with you."

In his apartment three blocks from the Cannon Building, Sean Cross was jarred from his sleep by the telephone. Prying open his eyes, he could see the morning sun peeking through the blinds. He glanced at the clock. It was just after six.

Getting out of bed, he lumbered toward the phone and picked it up on the fourth or fifth ring. It was Kevin Finnerty.

"Sean. I hate to bother you, but BBC just called me. The *Telegraph* put you on page one."

"Aw, Christ. What does it say?"

"I just got it off the Internet. I'll read it to you."

Cross sat down on a chair, holding the phone to his ear. He rubbed his eyes and forehead as he listened to Finnerty.

"The headline is 'U.S. CONGRESSMAN MET SECRETLY WITH IRA BOMBER—WILL ATTEND NATO PARLEY.'"

"That's a great start," said Cross. "Let me hear the rest."

"'This Sunday evening United States Congressman Sean Cross will be in London dining in the sumptuous splendor of the Hilton Hotel. His dining companions will include Prime Minister Blair, foreign ministers, defense ministers, NATO generals, parliamentarians, and fellow congressmen. They will be denouncing Islamic terrorism.

"'This lavish setting and panoply of dignitaries will be a far cry from another meeting which Congressman Cross so willingly attended with an Irish terrorist in the back of a ramshackle pub in Dundalk, Ireland, just three years ago.

"'The *Daily Telegraph* has learned from the most reliable sources that, on the afternoon of July 8 three years ago, Congressman Cross met secretly with Seamus McCoy, the notorious IRA terrorist who died at his own hands last year when one of his bombs prematurely detonated. McCoy was a leader in an IRA splinter group, the so-called "Real IRA," which lists among its achievements such atrocities as the 1998 car bombing in Omagh, which killed twenty-nine civilians, and the devastating bomb attack in Newry just two years ago, which claimed eighteen civilians.

"'According to our sources, Congressman Cross arrived in Dublin on July 7 as part of an official delegation led by Congressman Sid Gordon, chairman of the prestigious International Relations Committee. The purpose of the delegation's visit was to participate in a three-day series of interparliamentary meetings with Irish leaders, including the Taioseach, the foreign minister, and senior members of the Dail.

"'The itinerary for July 8 included a luncheon hosted by the Foreign Affairs Ministry at Iveagh House on St. Stephen's Green. Congressman Cross, however, failed to attend this luncheon. Instead, following a delegation meeting that morning with Liz O'Donnell, the leader of the Progressive Democrats, Mr. Cross surreptitiously broke away from his congressional colleagues and returned to the Berkeley Court Hotel in Ballsbridge, where he changed from his suit into a dark sweater and jeans. He then went by taxi to Connolly Station and took the 11:00 A.M. train to Dundalk. At Dundalk, Mr. Cross was met by two men who drove him to Donovan's Pub, on the very outskirts of the city. The automobile left Mr. Cross at the rear entrance, and he then met alone in the back room with McCoy. The meeting lasted about ninety minutes. While it is not known what the two men discussed, it is known that less than one month later, in early August, the Real IRA began planning the Newry bombing, which took place the following year.

"'Congressman Cross has failed to deny any of the facts set forth in this story. Just yesterday in Washington, D.C., Mr. Cross's press officer, Kevin Finnerty, refused to comment when given the opportunity to refute these allegations.'"

"Christ, they really got a lot of detail," said Cross.

"What should I tell the BBC?"

"They've always been pretty fair with me, but I don't think I should say anything yet. Tell them I can't make any comment because it involves official congressional business—whatever the hell that means," said Cross. "At least it'll buy me some time."

Hanging up the phone, Cross walked over to the window and opened the blinds. This had all begun just two weeks ago. Events were moving fast, he thought. Much faster than he'd anticipated. And he was at least a step behind. He still had no end game, but he knew he had to stop the momentum.

Half an hour later, Cross climbed the stairs to the fourth floor of the Cannon Building. The hallway was empty. He unlocked the office door and put on the lights. It was just after seven o'clock. He removed a file folder from the lower right drawer of his desk and immediately found the number he needed. Cross looked up at the clock. It was a few minutes past noon in London. He picked up the phone and dialed the overseas number on his private line, connecting to another private line in the Foreign and Commonwealth Office.

The phone had barely rung when Cross heard a familiar voice at the other end. "Ellis here."

"Sir Leonard, it's Cross."

"I thought you might ring."

"Very clairvoyant of you."

"Just practical."

"I'll be over on Sunday and Monday."

"So I've read. Should we get together?"

"I think so."

"I agree. Monday noon?"

"Sounds fine. What's the location?"

"The usual."

"That'll be okay?"

"Trust me."

"See you then."

Cross put the file back at the bottom of the lower drawer. Then he called Jack Pender at home. It took six rings before Pender answered. His voice betrayed his tiredness.

"The one good thing I used to be able to say about you was that you never wanted to work early in the morning."

"For Christ's sake, will you stop pissing and moaning. I'm trying to make you part of history."

"Thanks. You've no idea how much that means to me. I guess the *Telegraph* story wasn't good, or you wouldn't be bothering me so early."

"In substance the story was pretty much what I thought it would be. But the details—they have every last goddammed one. We're not dealing with amateurs or freelance wackos here."

"You want to start firing back?"

"I have to do something. I'm fighting on two fronts—Ireland and the primary."

"What do you have in mind?"

"I just called my friend in the Foreign Office. I'm going to meet him in London."

"That's a good start. He may have something for you."

"I also want to get together with O'Laughlin as soon as possible. When'll he have the numbers?"

"He finished the polling last night, so the overnights should be ready by noon," answered Pender. "I'll have him fax them to us as soon as they're done."

"How about the complete poll?"

"He'll have it by tonight. When do you want to meet with him?"

"As soon as possible. Do you think John can get out to Long Island tomorrow?"

"Let me ask him, but I think he probably can. When are you flying back to New York?"

"Voting should be over by early evening, maybe six or seven o'clock. So I'll catch the shuttle home tonight. I'll be available all day tomorrow, but I've got to be back in D.C. on Saturday for the London trip."

"You're a busy man."

"More like a moving target."

"What's the rest of today's battle plan?"

"The American media will pick up the *Telegraph* story. I have to make sure Sid Gordon is ready to stick with me if he gets any questions about whether I should be kept on the Codel."

"Do you expect any problems?"

"No, I just don't want him to be blindsided."

"Anything else?"

"I'm going to ask Dick O'Neill to circulate a statement of support in the House and get as many members' signatures as possible—hopefully, forty or fifty, Republicans and Democrats. Then I'll have to talk to the media myself."

"What can you say?"

"The usual. That I met with McCoy to advance the peace process, to let him know the Real IRA had no support. I think just saying something is important. I don't want it to seem like I'm in a bunker."

"Did you make a report of the meeting at the time?"

"Just to Jake Barton at the National Security Council, and that wasn't in writing. We met one-on-one at the White House."

"Will the NSC back you up on that?"

"I don't see why not."

"Looks like you have a busy day ahead of you. If nothing else, it'll keep you occupied."

"Remember, an idle mind is the devil's workshop."

Cross spent the rest of the morning on the phone. And he was pleased with the results. Sid Gordon was with him all the way—"You're staying on this Codel no matter what anyone says!" The same with Dick O'Neill, who offered to circulate the letter right away, adding, "I want to assure you no one on our side is going to use this against you."

Just after noon O'Laughlin faxed the first poll numbers. At face value, they looked good. Cross's favorable rating was 60; his unfavorable only 19. His numbers against a potential Democrat in the general election were equally encouraging—58 percent for, 24 percent against, 18 percent undecided. It was the Republican primary numbers that were more worrisome—Cross 51 percent, Spencer 15 percent, undecided 34 percent. To the untrained eye a thirty-six-point lead might look like a cinch. But Cross knew better. He knew the danger signs. He was a longtime incumbent and there was a good economy, but barely half the Republicans were willing to commit to him. Moreover, primary turnout is small—maybe 12 to 15 percent of registered Republicans—and hostile, angry voters come out in disproportionately large numbers. Cross spent the afternoon voting on the House floor and fielding media calls in his office. It seemed that every reporter in New York—print, television, and radio—was on the story. Their questions were virtually identical, as were Cross's answers.

—Is it true you met with a known IRA bomber?

Of course I did. It would have been irresponsible not to.—

—How can it be responsible for a member of Congress to meet with a murderer?

Nothing could be more responsible than to tell a man of violence who is seeking support that he has none.—

—If your actions were so responsible, why did you keep them a secret?

Just because the media didn't know about my meeting doesn't mean that influential people were unaware of it. I fully advised the NSC.—

—How will this affect your primary race against Barclay Spencer?

That's for the Republican voters of the Third Congressional District to decide. Fortunately, they've shown the good judgment to reject Mr. Spencer in the past. I'm confident they'll do so again.—

After passing the Agriculture Appropriations Bill on virtually a straight party-line vote, the House recessed at six forty-five until Tuesday. Cross immediately left for Reagan National Airport with O'Connell, who was coming to New York for the meeting with O'Laughlin. They caught the seven-thirty Delta Shuttle to LaGuardia. After dropping O'Connell off in Westbury, Cross made it home to Seaford before ten o'clock. Mary Rose was still up, sitting at the dining room table, paying bills.

"How was your day?" he asked.

"Everything was fine until I turned on the *Mike Campbell Show* on the way home from work. My God, that man hates you."

"Don't pay any attention to him."

"What can I tell you? I was stuck in traffic and thought I'd just listen for a minute or two. But he launched into such a tirade, I left it on. Before I knew it, he'd gotten to me, and I've been upset ever since."

"At least it took your mind off the traffic."

Cross arrived at Domenico's, an Italian restaurant in a small shopping center just off Hempstead Turnpike in Levittown, shortly before noon. The manager met him at the door and led him to a corner table in a side room. O'Laughlin and Pender were already there, the volumes containing the poll results already spread out on the table.

"I'll make sure you have privacy," said the manager.

"Thanks, Rocco, I appreciate that," replied Cross.

Cross sat down and O'Laughlin handed him his copy of the poll results. The volume contained well over three hundred pages and tens of thousands of numbers. O'Connell joined them a few minutes later and was handed a copy as well. Angelo, the waiter, took their orders. Pasta and a coke for McLaughlin. Meatball hero and a coke for Cross. Sausage hero and a ginger ale for O'Connell. Veal parmigiana hero, mozzarella sticks and a diet coke for Pender.

"This certainly goes against stereotype," said O'Laughlin. "Four micks, and nobody's ordered a drink."

"I never drink during the day," said Cross. "Even a beer—especially when I'm meeting with you. I don't want you confusing me with all these numbers. Why don't you start?"

"Okay. The bottom line is that you're in good shape. But there are potential problems. From these numbers, it doesn't look as if there's any way you can lose the general election, but you've got to keep your eye on the primary."

"What are the trouble points?" asked Pender.

O'Laughlin took the poll in his hands, and for the next fifteen minutes turned one page to the other, flipping back and forth, all the time synchronizing and harmonizing the numbers—like a conductor with his orchestra. The key to O'Laughlin's polls was the cross-tabs—demographic breakdowns not just by party or ideology but by age, religion, nationality, gender, and income level, as well as every variation within those subsets. Cross was constantly amazed by how a one-night sampling of three hundred voters could so accurately assess the thinking of more than a quarter million. It could also spot and project trends—trends the voters themselves might not realize they were trending toward.

Sipping his Coke, O'Laughlin continued.

"Forty percent of the voters are aware of the McGrath story. The poll was taken before the McCoy story broke. Of that 40 percent, only 3 percent said they'd vote against you because of it. However, among Republicans most likely to vote in a primary, 60 percent have heard about McGrath and 5 percent would vote against you because of that. Most significantly, another 9 percent who previously supported you are now undecided. That's why your primary numbers are down to 51 percent. And your slippage is pretty much across the board, even though you're holding slightly more steady among Irish and Italian Catholics. Once the McCoy story begins to sink in, you'll drop below 50 percent. I don't care how many years have gone by—no one's forgotten the Twin Towers. And they're scared stiff of anything even remotely close to terrorism. On the positive side, Spencer himself has no support. The only reason people will vote for him is because he's against you."

O'Laughlin stopped his dissertation to take a bite of his lunch. The others had begun eating at least five minutes before.

"Besides countering the McGrath and McCoy stories, is there anything Sean can do to get his numbers back up?" asked O'Connell.

"He may not be able to pull them up," answered O'Laughlin. "But he can break the fall by appealing to the Republican base. Remember, we'll be lucky if there's a 15 percent turnout, and those 15 percent will be hard-core."

"What do you suggest?" asked Cross.

"Hit hard on gut issues—taxes, crime, strong defense. Make sure you get yourself seen with the president. He's very popular with Republicans."

"What do I do about Spencer?" asked Cross.

"Try to ignore him. Like I said, he's really not a factor," answered O'Laughlin. "The person you're running against is yourself."

"Toughest opponent Sean's ever had," cracked Pender.

"It's important to stay on offense," said O'Laughlin. "I like the coverage you got last night and today. You can't afford to let yourself appear defensive or apologetic."

"That's what Al D'Amato told me," said Cross.

"Christ, if anyone knows about staying on offense, it's him," said Pender.

"Yeah, I saw him in Island Park last Sunday at the Republican Club cocktail party," said Cross. "He told me to rip the heart out of anyone that comes after me on this. Accuse them of being anti-Catholic. Take no prisoners."

"The D'Amato school of politics," said O'Laughlin, laughing. "We miss that in New York, the gentle touch."

CHAPTER FIVE

Early May

The following afternoon, Sean Cross was back in his Washington apartment, reviewing the NATO briefing that the State Department and the International Relations Committee had prepared for the Codel. The plane was scheduled to leave at five. Kevin Finnerty came by at three twenty-five to drive Cross to Andrews Air Force Base in Virginia. With the roads filled with cars of people taking advantage of the clear spring afternoon, the drive took longer than usual, but they still arrived in plenty of time for Sean to make the five o'clock flight to London. After being cleared through various checkpoints, Finnerty dropped Cross at the Distinguished Visitors Lounge, where the delegation and support staff were gathering. Like Cross, they were all dressed casually. He was wearing a sports jacket, polo shirt, and khakis.

Cross was warmly greeted by Sid Gordon, who, besides his official status as Codel Chairman, always appropriated the role of official greeter. Gordon's district was north of New York City. He was a Korean War veteran now serving his thirty-fourth year in Congress. As chairman of the International Relations Committee, he was a strong internationalist, with particular interest in NATO, Israel, and Ireland—the latter two accommodating the wishes of his most vocal constituents. Though he was Jewish, with no trace of Irish ancestry, Gordon was extremely helpful to Cross on the Irish issue, often providing cover when the more timorous were ducking.

"Sid, I really appreciate you sticking by me when the McCoy story broke," said Cross.

"Come on, Sean. That's the least I could do. It's obvious someone's out to get you."

Cross sat down next to Congressman Vito O'Leary, who represented Staten Island and western Brooklyn.

"Christ, I hope they put you through a metal detector," said O'Leary. "God only knows what you might do."

"What I'd like to do is give everyone a break and drop a bomb on Staten Island."

"You're just jealous because you're living out there in no-man's land instead of God's country."

Though he was only in his early forties, Vito O'Leary had been a congressman for ten years. He and Cross had a solid relationship and tried to help each other politically whenever possible. Though not as much an internationalist as Cross or Gordon, O'Leary had a real interest in the Atlantic alliance, which is why Gordon had selected him for the delegation.

"I know it's easy for me to say," said O'Leary, "but I don't think these IRA charges are going to hurt you that much. Once you strip away the bullshit, there's nothing there."

"I agree. My only real concern is if it gets out of control between now and the primary," answered Cross.

"Just let me know if there's anything I can do."

"Thanks, Vito."

Cross and O'Leary were joined by two Democrats on the delegation—David Arce from St. Louis and Tim Haskell from Chicago. Both were centrist Democrats who served on the International Relations Committee. Cross considered them to be regular guys, easy to get along with.

They were discussing NATO's political divisions when Sid Gordon's voice boomed from the center of the room. "Okay, everybody. It's time to roll out."

Getting to their feet, the four congressmen followed Gordon through the glass door and out onto the runway, where the blue and white C-32A waited. Emblazoned on its side was UNITED STATES

OF AMERICA. At the foot of the stairway and again at the plane's door, they were greeted by the Air Force personnel who would accompany them.

On board the spacious plane, the congressmen headed for their designated seats. Gordon, as chairman, was given the front seat. An announcement was made to put their watches ahead five hours. Looking about the plane, Cross said to O'Leary, "this sure beats the shuttle."

Twenty minutes later, the plane was off the runway and into the air. Flight time to London would be a little more than seven hours. Cross and O'Leary engaged in casual conversation and banter and read over the day's newspapers until dinner was served about an hour into the flight. Cross finished the main course but passed on the dessert and coffee. He wanted to be sure he'd get some sleep. After the steward removed his tray, Cross swallowed two sleeping pills, pushed his chair back, and closed his eyes.

The next thing he knew, a steward was serving breakfast. Cross looked at his watch. He'd slept for four hours. They would be landing in about an hour.

Beginning his descent into London, the pilot announced that the temperature there was about 51 degrees Fahrenheit and it was drizzling. As the plane landed and taxied to a reserved area of Heathrow Airport, Cross moved into the center aisle, where he stood fourth in a line headed by Gordon and the assistant secretary of state, Farrell Lynch. Secretary of State Constance Reese was already in London. At a signal from the ground, they filed from the plane down the staircase, where they were greeted by Steve Madonna, the U.S. ambassador to Britain, and escorted directly to a bus waiting for them on the runway.

It was early morning and traffic was light on the way into London. The bus turned onto Portman Square, stopping at the front entrance to the Churchill Inter-Continental Hotel. The Churchill was an imposing, modern structure with more than five hundred rooms. Because of its location and facilities, it was the hotel of choice for American diplomats and congressional leaders. As the congressmen stepped from the bus, an official from the American embassy directed them to the seventh floor, where the delegation would be staying.

When the elevator door opened, Cross realized straightaway that the secretary of state was staying on that floor—two Marines were stationed directly opposite the bank of elevators. Cross and the delegation moved past them into the control room—a large suite taken over by the Air Force as the base of operations during the trip. They were handed their room keys and given an updated schedule. The first meeting was at ten twenty, a briefing from the secretary of state.

Secretary of State Constance Reese was an extraordinarily able foreign-policy expert. Almost as important in this media-driven age, she was a strikingly attractive African-American woman in her mid-forties who seemingly was born for television. On substance and charisma she was the superstar of the administration. Perhaps the most politically attuned secretary of state since Henry Kissinger, she knew the importance of engaging Congress in formulating foreign policy, which was why she'd asked Sid Gordon to put together a delegation and why she was so enthusiastically welcoming each of the congressmen to her briefing.

The briefing lasted only about twenty minutes, but it was enough for Secretary Reese to make her points.

> —NATO is the bedrock of our anti-terrorism policy. The alliance is as strong as it was when we destroyed al Qaeda. The cooperation is terrific. Especially the intelligence sharing. Of the major NATO powers, Britain is the most reliable, France the most troublesome. Tony Blair has been particularly pro-American.—

After answering some routine questions and exchanging political pleasantries, Secretary Reese was off to Whitehall for a one-on-one meeting with the British foreign minister. She would next see the delegation at the formal banquet that evening.

The rest of the morning and afternoon consisted of the usual meetings and briefings typical of Codels.

- A meeting with Ambassador Madonna at the American Embassy at Grosvenor Square on the state of Anglo-American relations. They were never better.
- A briefing back at the hotel from Tom Curtin, our NATO Ambassador, on NATO's political cohesiveness. The cohesion was good but could be a lot better.
- A meeting with Admiral Dyckman, the Commander, Chief Naval Forces in Europe, CINCNAVEUR, at the Navy Headquarters Building in Grosvenor Square on NATO's military readiness. It couldn't be better.

During a two-hour late afternoon break, Cross and O'Leary walked a few blocks to attend mass at St. Teresa's and did a little sightseeing. When Cross returned to his room, there were a number of messages from the British media. Obviously, they wanted to speak to him about the McCoy story, and probably McGrath as well. His usual instinct was to talk with the media. It was a lot easier than ducking them. But this time it would serve no purpose. If anything, it would only divert attention from the NATO meetings and rub the American delegation—both the secretary of state and the congressmen—the wrong way. Besides, he had to get dressed for that evening's formal banquet at the London Hilton.

At six thirty the five Codel members climbed into their bus for the short drive to the Hilton. Located on Park Lane in fashionable Mayfair, it overlooked Hyde Park and was just minutes away from Buckingham Palace and Harrods. When they arrived, the cocktail reception was already under way. Hundreds of diplomats, military brass, and parliamentarians were milling about. Scanning the room, Cross was gratified to see Secretary Reese had attracted considerable attention. Apparently, Tony Blair would not be arriving until the dinner actually began. For now the American secretary of state was the star attraction.

Cross was sipping a straight Scotch and talking with Sid Gordon and a member of the Polish delegation when Michael Birmingham, a British Labour M.P., came by to say hello. After a few minutes of small talk, he told Cross, "Don't let that story in the *Telegraph* get you down. You're among friends here."

Cross smiled. "Thank you very much. I appreciate the kind words."

That was the only mention of McGrath or McCoy until later that evening. Cross was seated at table 32 with two American military officers and parliamentarians from Denmark, Italy, and Germany. Tony Blair had just concluded his speech—the main address of the evening—and Cross, along with everyone else in the room, was according him a standing ovation. Just as Cross was about to take his seat, a man in his mid-forties appeared beside him.

"Congressman Cross, I'm Geoffrey Howell, from the prime minister's office. Would you mind greatly coming with me to the rear of the room for a brief chat?"

"No problem," answered Cross, following Howell to the very back of the room, about twenty feet from the closest table.

"Congressman, I'll be brief, but I would ask that you keep this conversation in total confidence—just between the two of us."

"Sure. What's on your mind?"

"You should know the prime minister is as concerned as you are about the murder of Frank McGrath. We've analyzed all our police and intelligence reports and are certain the IRA is not responsible. We also want you to know we had absolutely nothing to do with that dreadful story in the *Telegraph*."

"I never thought you did. But it's very decent of you to say so directly. What do you think's going on?"

"Someone is attempting to disrupt the peace process. And we can only hope no one on the republican side takes the bait."

"I'm sure they won't. But I'll do what I can to reassure them."

"Thank you very much indeed. You can be sure we'll be watching this carefully. All of us have too much invested to lose everything now."

"I couldn't agree more."

The five Codel members and four staff assistants from the International Relations Committee began their Monday morning with breakfast at Clementine's on the first floor of the Churchill.

The consensus was that the conference was going surprisingly well. Secretary Reese was getting rave reviews, and Tony Blair's speech had been decidedly pro-American. Moreover, a strong feeling of cooperation among the member nations had permeated every meeting they'd attended.

Following breakfast, the congressmen went again to the American Embassy, where they received a series of military and political briefings that lasted until eleven thirty. Next on the agenda was a luncheon hosted by the British Foreign Office at the Atrium Restaurant, located just across from the Parliament Building.

Cross, however, would not be attending. He'd be meeting with Sir Leonard Ellis. To forestall any concern or incident, Cross had informed Gordon of his plans, saying he had a private meeting to attend. Gordon had asked no questions and told Cross there'd be no problem.

As the other members of the delegation filed into the bus, Cross walked to the corner of Grosvenor Square and hailed a taxi.

"The Garrick Club, please. At 14 Garrick Street, just off Trafalgar Square," said Cross as he eased himself into the backseat of the taxi.

"Very well, sir," said the driver.

Sean Cross had first met Leonard Ellis more than a decade earlier, when the career diplomat was assigned to the British Embassy in Washington. Ellis's actual title was diplomatic officer, but his power and clout extended far beyond his official job description. Soon after Ellis's arrival at the embassy, it became obvious to Cross, O'Neill, and others close to the Irish issue that Ellis had been sent to Washington for a purpose. The IRA ceasefire was in its second year. Bill Clinton had made it clear he was going to pursue his own Irish policy and not be controlled by the Brits. British Embassy officials, long used to having their own way on the Irish issue, proved stunningly inept in adapting to this new era. For more than a year they opposed extensions of Gerry Adams's visa, apparently not realizing they'd long since lost that battle. Rather than working with congressional activists such as Gordon, Cross, and O'Neill, they still relied on their weakened allies in the State Department.

The Foreign Office and the people around John Major finally recognized that the power equation had changed. The United States was going to stay involved in the Irish issue for the long haul. Rather than resisting, the British would have to engage the White House and Congress. This would be a dramatic reversal of British policy, and Leonard Ellis was selected for the mission. It was not his first sensitive posting. NATO during the nuclear freeze debate, the European Community during currency disputes, and Hong Kong during those first, tense negotiations with China were just several of his prior assignments. He also had direct access to John Major. And as Cross got to know him better, he learned Ellis was no stranger to the British Intelligence Services, MI5 and MI6.

Within a month of his arrival in Washington, Ellis journeyed to Capitol Hill to meet with the Ad Hoc Committee. This was unprecedented. For almost two decades the British Embassy had branded the committee as a pariah—at best, a dupe of the IRA, at worst, a willing accomplice. Now Ellis sat across the table from them, stressing how essential it was that they work together.

This contact only increased over the next several years. Cross and the other activists were invited to the embassy for dinners with visiting British dignitaries. At these dinners the food was copious, the drink plentiful, and the conversation animated. Never was there even a hint from Ellis that he resented American involvement, nor any indication this involvement constituted interference in an internal British matter. No, to listen to Leonard Ellis, Her Majesty's Government welcomed this American interest, particularly the interest of dedicated Irish Americans. Whenever there was a crisis in the north, Ellis would come to the Hill, set forth his government's position, try to answer all questions, and earnestly ask for advice and input.

Ellis also developed a strong personal working relationship with Cross. They exchanged private phone numbers and used them whenever developments merited. The calls were particularly frequent when the IRA broke the first ceasefire in January 1996. Ellis would reveal Britain's actual policy versus the public posture. In turn, Cross would convey not just the thinking of congressional activists but what he thought to be the true positions of Sinn Fein and the IRA as well.

Cross viewed his relationship with Ellis as both direct and complicated. In exchanging information, Cross never lied, never misled Ellis. And he strongly believed Ellis acted similarly. They did not, however, tell each other the entire truth. To Cross, it was selective intelligence—not the whole story, but very helpful nonetheless. Cross considered Ellis a friend, but it was a friendship limited by the reality that their positions could become adversarial at a moment's notice.

As the Good Friday Agreement was reached and then, however haltingly, implemented, Ellis left Washington. He was appointed ambassador, first to Spain and then France. He was also knighted for his years of service. For the past two years he'd been in London in the Foreign and Commonwealth Office, where he served as a master foreign-policy strategist. Over the years, Cross maintained contact with Ellis and stopped by to see him whenever he was in London. He particularly looked forward to today's meeting.

The Garrick Club was quintessentially British, exactly as Cross remembered it—majestic staircase, handsome portraits hanging from dark, wood-paneled walls, exquisitely detailed woodwork.

As Cross stepped through the front door, a very proper manager approached him.

"Congressman Cross?"

"Yes, sir."

"Sir Leonard is awaiting you. Please follow me, if you will."

"Thank you."

Cross followed the manager up the staircase and down a hallway, which led to a large dining room, now half full. Seated beneath a towering portrait of the Duke of Wellington was Sir Leonard Ellis.

As Cross walked toward him, right hand extended, Sir Leonard stood up, reached out his hand, and said warmly, "Sean, my friend, it's a pleasure. A very great pleasure."

"It's great to see you again, Sir Leonard. You're looking well."

"As are you. Now sit down."

In his mid-sixties, Leonard Ellis did look remarkably fit. Trim, with ramrod-straight posture, a full head of white hair, horn-rimmed glasses, and a well-tailored suit, he was the ultimate Brit statesman.

Sir Leonard summoned the very efficient waiter and ordered himself another martini. Cross violated his almost ironclad role of never drinking during the day and ordered a Scotch.

"So, how is your visit coming along?" asked Sir Leonard.

"Actually, very well. I don't expect anything dramatic to come out of it, just the determination to keep Islamic terrorists on the run. That has to count for something."

"It does indeed."

"And to give credit where it's due, the prime minister was very much on target last night. He really has taken the Labour Party a long way."

"Yes. Difficult to imagine that this is the same party that used to advocate unilateral disarmament." Sir Leonard sipped at his martini. "I was reading the morning papers just now. It appears you've been able to avoid further scrutiny."

Cross smiled. "I was glad to see that myself."

"Well, what do you make of it all?" asked Ellis, getting straight to the point.

"The murders and the story in the *Telegraph*?"

"Indeed."

"I was hoping you could help me," said Cross, sampling his Scotch.

"Perhaps we can help each other."

"Well, I don't know much," said Cross, "but I'll go first. I'm certain the IRA had nothing to do with McGrath."

"I imagine you're correct."

"As for the *Telegraph* story, that was troubling. The implications and conclusions were way off base, but the actual facts were disturbingly accurate. That means that not only was someone following me two years ago, but whoever it was, was able to get the story into the *Telegraph* last week on less than a day's notice.

"That was disturbing."

"Not just for me," Cross emphasized, "but for the entire peace process. One of your top informers is killed in London. Another is killed in New York. And then intelligence material is leaked to the press. Obviously, someone powerful wants to disrupt the peace process."

Ellis had been listening with his usual stoic reserve until he heard the word "intelligence." Cross detected the slightest tensing of Sir Leonard's jaw.

"This entire sequence of events is extremely unsettling. I understand you've been advised of the level of concern at Number 10," said Ellis, referring to the prime minister's staff at 10 Downing Street.

"Yes, I spoke with Geoffrey Howell yesterday evening."

"Regarding any 'intelligence,' that, of course, was never my field. MI5 and MI6 operate in spheres totally separate from mine. I'm as sure as I can be, however, that the intelligence services would not have any hand in this. It would be in direct violation of the PM's policies. While I admit our record in this regard hasn't been perfect—especially with regard to Ireland—that's all in the past. There's a new crowd running things today."

"That's what they say about the IRA Army Council," Cross said with a smile.

"Did you have to choose such an odious comparison?"

"I'm afraid the IRA might be even more offended," said Cross.

Ellis laughed and took another sip of his martini.

"Sir Leonard, I have to say I was surprised you wanted to meet here at the club. We are pretty obvious."

"There's really not much of an alternative. Whoever's following you seems to be able to do it anywhere. We're better off here than on a park bench, wearing trench coats and dark glasses, don't you agree?"

"So it's safe for us to talk?"

"Quite, so long as we don't shout. I can't vouch for everyone here, but I can tell you there are no bugs or listening devices. I suppose we're as secure here as we can be anywhere."

"Fair enough. This is your turf. So, then, is there a chance this could be a rogue MI5 or MI6 operation that the guys at the top aren't aware of?"

"That's always a possibility. And believe me, we're looking at that. Of course, everything in that world is shadows and mirrors, so it's often quite difficult to sort out just what's happening."

"I can imagine," said Cross, believing quite surely that Ellis knew a bit more about that world than he was letting on.

"I do think, however," Sir Leonard continued, "that whoever is behind this, you were not a target at the outset."

"What do you mean?"

"Whoever shot Kilpatrick and McGrath was trying to, as you say, disrupt the process. They wanted to provoke the paramilitaries, create confusion. Believe me, with all due respect, I doubt they had your campaign in mind. You were an unintended victim. Collateral damage. Of course, once your opponent—Spencer, is it?—opened fire, so to speak, they saw an opportunity not just to damage you, but to create more confusion."

"I'm such a lucky guy."

They paused as the waiter brought them their meals. Ellis ordered another martini. Cross, who had taken only infrequent sips of his Scotch, politely declined another. As Ellis began eating, Cross asked the next question. He wanted to return to the possibility of British intelligence involvement.

"Doesn't the excruciating detail of my meeting with McCoy point to someone in MI5 or MI6? Who else would have that level of surveillance expertise?" asked Cross.

"Your point is well taken. And I assure you that line of inquiry will be pursued. But it isn't the only possibility."

"What do you mean?"

"Well, this did transpire in the Republic, and the Gardai's Special Branch can't be ruled out," replied Ellis, referring to the intelligence unit of the Irish police.

"Doesn't that seem unlikely? I don't know of any instance where the Gardai worked with the *Telegraph* or any of your other tabloids."

"You're probably right. I just don't believe anyone should be ruled out. Another very real possibility, however, is that it was one of McCoy's mates."

"In the Real IRA?"

"Precisely."

"Would any of them have the know-how to work that cleverly and quickly with the *Telegraph*?"

"Probably not. But that doesn't rule it out. It just means that they didn't do it alone."

"So there could have been collusion of some sort between the Real IRA and your group?" said Cross, realizing that his probing was pressing the outer limits of their friendship.

Ellis paused for a moment, looked calmly at Cross, and answered. "As you and I should know as well as anyone, anything is possible," said Ellis, taking his fork and placing a piece of lamb into his mouth, politely but firmly making it clear he'd said all he was going to say about MI5 or MI6.

Cross took his cue.

"Whoever's behind this, do you think they believe they've been successful?" asked Cross.

"Quite frankly, no. And I don't know how they could've expected to be. Apparently, what they were hoping for was that the loyalists would think the IRA killed Kilpatrick and McGrath. And then the UVF or UDA would retaliate. Maybe five or ten years ago that would have worked. But not now. Besides, why the hell would loyalist paramilitaries care about two IRA informers?"

"Could this be it, then?"

"If we're lucky, yes. But with the effort they've made up to now, it's hard to believe they'll just pack up and quit."

The conversation moved briefly to matters less sinister than murder, conspiracy, and the shredding of the peace process, but Cross soon returned to the subject foremost in his mind. "I've been thinking over what you were saying about the Real IRA. They might well be involved."

"I don't know anything for sure, but, yes, at the very least, I believe their possible involvement should be looked into."

"What do your people tell you about the Real IRA?" asked Cross. "My understanding was that they had no structure left at all."

"Let's be honest—they never had much support to begin with. Nor did they have many members. And what backing they did have, they lost after the Omagh bombing in '98. The disaster in Newry two years ago decimated them altogether. What's left are some stragglers—essentially freelancers."

"So if it is the Real IRA, it's probably just a few malcontents."

"I would say so," answered Ellis.

Cross shook his head slowly. "I find it hard to believe that a handful of psychopaths would have been able to track down Kilpatrick and McGrath without outside help."

"That's why this is all so difficult to figure out."

"Sir Leonard, it's been a pleasure, but I should be getting back to the hotel. There're still some meetings scheduled, and I should at least make an appearance."

"It's been marvelous getting together. Let's be sure to stay in touch on this."

"I'll let you know if I hear anything," said Cross.

"Likewise, my good friend."

The C-32A landed at Andrews Air Force Base just after five on Tuesday afternoon. The flight had been smooth, and Cross had managed a few hours' sleep over the Atlantic.

When Cross came down the steps, he was greeted by Tom O'Connell, ready to drive him back to Capitol Hill.

"How'd the trip go?" O'Connell asked.

"Fine. No problems at all."

"Did you learn anything?"

"I didn't get any answers, but I might've gotten some leads. When's the first vote?"

"Not until six thirty."

"Great. Anything going on I should know about?"

"Not really. But Bill Clinton called."

"Clinton?"

"Actually, his office. About two hours ago. He's in L.A. for a speech at some foreign-policy dinner. They asked if you could call back at about eight o'clock."

"Did they say what it was about?"

"No. But I assume it's all this Irish shit."

By five past eight, Cross was back at his office in the Cannon Building, having cast three routine votes on the House floor. It was time to return Clinton's call.

"Do you have his number?" Cross asked O'Connell.

"His secretary said he'd be in his hotel room now, getting ready for his speech."

"Will you place the call?"

"Sure."

Almost five minutes later, O'Connell called Cross on the intercom and said, "Clinton's secretary is on the line."

"Hi, this is Sean Cross."

"Congressman Cross, President Clinton will be with you in a moment."

"Sean."

"Mr. President, how are you, sir?"

"I'm doing fine, but you must be exhausted from your trip. How'd it go?"

"It went well. Whatever differences there are within NATO, the bottom line is that the alliance is solid when it comes to fighting terrorism and they still look to us for leadership."

"Good. That's pretty much what I intend to say in my speech tonight. How was Tony?" Clinton asked.

"Terrific. He gave the main speech, of course, and he couldn't have been more pro-American."

"I'm not surprised. He was the one NATO leader I could always count on."

"For Ireland as well."

"Yeah, and that brings me to the main reason I wanted to talk to you. Man, you're really getting the shit knocked out of you. What's going on?"

"I wish I knew. The more I look, the more confusing it gets. I've been talking to the New York cops, and they have no leads. When I was in London, I spoke to Geoffrey Howell—"

"Tony's guy?"

"Yeah, and with Leonard Ellis—"

"From the embassy?"

"Yeah, that's the one."

"Shit, he shows up everywhere."

"He certainly does. Anyway, Howell assured me the Blair government had nothing to do with any of this, including the story in the *Telegraph*."

"That was a real hatchet job."

"The scariest part was that most of the details were right on target."

"I believe Howell. You can be sure Tony and his people wouldn't go near something like this. But still, this has to be an inside job. Someone, somewhere in government."

"I asked Ellis whether he thought it could be MI5 or MI6."

"What did he say?"

"Basically, that he didn't know."

"But he didn't rule it out?"

"No."

"How's the primary going?"

"I'm still ahead. But there's been some slippage, and some of my numbers are getting soft."

"Christ, people wouldn't vote for that dumb son of a bitch who's running against you, would they?"

"It's not so much that they're voting for him as voting against me. As my pollster says, I'm running against myself. And not doing too well."

Clinton laughed. "Listen, I'd like to get together with you so we can talk all this over. Maybe we could have dinner."

"Great. What do you have in mind?"

"I'm going over to Europe next week. I'll be talking with Tony in London, and I'll see what I can find out. I'll be back in New York the following week."

"Do you want to have dinner then?"

"Yeah, I'll have my office let you know when I'm free."

"Where should we go?"

"I'll leave it up to you. How about one of those Irish places on the East Side?"

"Great, I'll line one up for us."

"Sean, just one thing."

"Yes, Mr. President?"

"Try to make sure there's no gun deals going down while I'm there. I am a former president, you know."

CHAPTER SIX

April 1992–June 1995

When Sean Cross was elected to Congress in 1992, the last person he expected to become friendly with was Bill Clinton. Cross had strongly supported George Bush's re-election bid and saw Clinton as too liberal on most issues. Moreover, even though they were close in age—Cross was just two years Clinton's senior—Cross saw Clinton as part of an entirely different generation, one for which he had contempt. The '60s generation, privileged and pampered, had prided itself in always blaming America first and had turned its back on patriotism, on respect for the military, and on so many of the other neighborhood values Cross had been raised on.

But it was ironic that Cross opposed Clinton so strongly. Because Clinton had been the first presidential candidate in American history who promised to pursue an independent policy on Ireland, a policy free of British interference and control.

Clinton first detailed his Irish agenda on April 5, 1992, at Manhattan's Sheraton Centre Hotel just two days before the New York presidential primary. A group of the state's Irish-American leaders had scheduled a meeting with Clinton and Jerry Brown, the former governor of California. They were the two remaining Democratic candidates. The meeting was held in a small room that held about thirty people. Cross, then the Nassau County Comptroller, was the only Republican to attend. The candidates were scheduled to speak separately, Clinton at about seven o'clock, Brown shortly after his arrival at ten.

At a few minutes past seven, Clinton entered through a door at the front of the room. Without hesitating, he walked toward the third seat from the left in the front row where he shook hands with Paul O'Dwyer, the venerable white-maned warrior of New York Democratic politics. *Great move*, Cross thought. *And well planned.* Clinton shook a few more hands before sitting down behind the candidates' table. There was a lone microphone in front of him.

Clinton made a brief opening statement before answering questions from a panel of four. Cross noted right away that Clinton was different. There were no references to shamrocks or green ties. Nor was there any ritualistic denouncing of terrorism. Instead, he told of being a student at Oxford in 1969 and visiting Ireland during the start of the Troubles. He spoke of America's obligation to denounce human rights violations—even when the offending nation was our closest ally. He said that as president he would appoint a special envoy to help mediate a solution to the Irish struggle. In answer to the burning question of Gerry Adams's visa application, Clinton stated he'd grant the visa as he would to any other elected official.

Cross was struck not so much by Clinton's answers—though he certainly agreed with them—as he was by Clinton's obvious ease and familiarity in addressing an issue that rendered many politicians tongue-tied and caused most others to fall back on timeworn clichés.

Cross was still the Nassau County Comptroller. Congressman Ashe, however, had confided to him he wouldn't run for re-election that year. Ashe intended to make his announcement in mid-June. Cross was already planning his strategy to secure the Republican nomination. He was poised to move as quickly as possible after Ashe went public. Only Ashe, Mary Rose and Pender were aware of the game plan. It was essential that between now and June Cross do nothing to generate any opposition or cause any controversy within the Republican Party. Now, as he stood near the back of the room and watched just about everyone in the room lining up to get their photo taken shaking hands with Clinton, Cross realized the last thing he needed was to get caught in one of those pictures. So he hung back until the photo shoot was finished and, as Clinton was heading towards the back door, Cross gave him a quick handshake and said "Good job, Governor." Clinton thanked him, smiled and walked on—not having the foggiest idea who the Comptroller of Nassau County was.

During the two-hour interval between Clinton's departure and Brown's arrival, Cross went downstairs to the coffee shop. With him were Mickey Brannigan, a longtime New York reporter and Pulitzer Prize winner; Frank Doolan, an Irish-born lawyer who had represented defendants in a number of celebrated IRA gunrunning cases; and Paul O'Dwyer.

The four sat down at a corner table, and a waitress brought them coffee. Adhering to New York's Irish-American protocol, no one spoke before the patriarch O'Dwyer.

Usually stoic, O'Dwyer was clearly moved. After sipping his brewed decaf he said, "I never heard a candidate who knew more about Ireland." Brannigan, who preferred causticity to sentiment, nodded deferentially toward O'Dwyer, then gruffly interjected, "The goddamned Irish. If they don't vote for Clinton, they don't deserve anything. Fuck 'em."

Doolan, now in his sixties, was O'Dwyer's nephew and had immigrated to New York as a teenager. "That was some performance Clinton gave," he said. "John Major and the rest of the Brits'll be absolutely raging when they hear about it."

"They've probably heard about it already," said Brannigan. "I bet they had a fucking informer in the room."

"Mickey, this has been a good night for us," said O'Dwyer with a gentle smile. "Why don't you let yourself enjoy it."

Cross, slowly stirring a spoon in his coffee cup, added, "Obviously, Clinton knows what he's talking about. If he means just half of it and gets elected, the world will turn upside down for the Brits."

Jerry Brown didn't show up until midnight, and he might as well never have bothered. His speech was perfunctory—a few jokes about the Jesuits and the standard call for an end to Irish violence. He gave the clear impression he thought he was doing everyone a favor by being there. So as the room emptied onto 7th Avenue in the early morning hours of April 6, Jerry Brown was already forgotten. The talk was all of Bill Clinton.

Clinton went on to win the New York primary, the Democratic nomination, and the presidency. But the first months of the Clinton Administration were dispiriting to the Irish-American activists who had allowed their hopes to be raised. No special envoy was appointed. As ambassador to Ireland Clinton chose Jean Kennedy Smith, who had never demonstrated any interest in the Irish issue and whose only apparent qualification was that she was Ted Kennedy's sister. The first evidence of clear betrayal, however, came in April 1993. Gerry Adams, who had lost his re-election bid to Parliament, went to the American consulate in Belfast and applied for a visa. His application was perfunctorily rejected.

But what of Clinton's campaign pledge to grant Adams a visa? Clinton argued at a Rose Garden news conference he hadn't broken his word because Adams was no longer a member of Parliament, and therefore no longer an elected official.

Talking on the phone to Brannigan that afternoon, Cross was furious. "That fucking liar. What bullshit!"

"Let's face it," answered Brannigan. "That prick took us to the cleaners. Someday we'll fucking learn."

The situation only worsened that October when New York City mayor David Dinkins, in the midst of an unsuccessful re-election campaign, wrote to Clinton, asking him to reconsider Adams's visa request.

To Cross, Clinton's response couldn't have been more devastating, and it only compounded Irish America's sense of betrayal. In his letter, Clinton adopted the traditional State Department and Brit line about Adams's "involvement" in terrorist activity. Not unexpectedly, the Foreign Office was relieved. The unionists were ecstatic. The special relationship would endure.

As for Gerry Adams, Clinton was imperiling his effort to lead the republican movement from armed resistance to politics. But just when prospects seemed at their bleakest, the administration began re-examining its policy. At first the change was imperceptible; very quickly it became irreversible.

Days after Clinton denied the Adams visa, Tony Lake, head of the National Security Council, requested a meeting with the Ad Hoc Committee. This was unprecedented. Since its inception in the late seventies, numerous administrations, and the British government, had refused even to acknowledge the committee's existence because of its Sinn Fein sympathies. The meeting was scheduled for early evening. It would be in the White House Situation Room. Then, on the morning of the meeting, word came that Lake had come down with influenza and the meeting would most likely have to be postponed. In mid-afternoon the meeting was back on—but the venue was changed to a fourth floor conference room on the House side of the Capitol. The time was moved back to six o'clock.

When Cross entered the meeting room, it was ten to six. Sid Gordon and Tom Manton, the veteran congressman from Queens, were already there. Within minutes Dick O'Neill and Hamilton Fish and many of the other stalwarts who had pushed forward on the Irish issue over the years joined them. It was a few minutes past six when Tony Lake arrived, accompanied by his chief assistant, Nancy Soderberg. He was congested, running a fever and looked terrible. A laconic New Englander, the owlish, bespectacled Lake was understated but firm. He opened by saying he'd been at home in bed all day but decided to go ahead with the meeting because he felt it was so significant. While making no commitment, Lake emphasized the importance which the President attached to the Irish issue. The end of the Cold War offered the opportunity to address previously intractable conflicts—Northern Ireland possibly being one of them. Though he didn't precisely say it, Lake clearly implied that the decisions and statements of the previous ten months were not an accurate indicator of what the Clinton Irish policy would actually be.

Cross was most encouraged by what Lake did not say. There were no references to terrorism or IRA atrocities or men of violence. Instead, Lake spoke entirely in geopolitical and diplomatic terms. Cross realized that simply by addressing the Irish struggle in such a way, Clinton and Lake would be internationalizing an issue that the British always insisted was entirely internal. That by itself would be a seismic shift in policy. But Cross's inherent sense of Irish fatalism put a brake on his expectations. After all, hadn't candidate Clinton said pretty much the same thing more than a year and half ago? On the other hand, this meeting had to mean something and as they exchanged a firm handshake, Cross committed to Lake that he would work with him as closely as possible and not allow any partisan differences to divide them.

At the same time Tony Lake was re-evaluating America's Irish policy in Washington, Jean Kennedy Smith was asserting herself in Ireland. From the moment she had taken over as ambassador in the summer of 1993, and removed the career foreign service officer who had been running the Embassy in Dublin because of his resistance to her peace initiatives, Kennedy Smith had been shaping events in a manner and to an extent Cross had never anticipated. Now she was meeting with John Hume and Taoiseach Albert Reynolds and concluding that Gerry Adams was committed to pursuing a political solution and should be granted a visa.

Events began to cascade. In December the Brits had to admit they'd been meeting secretly with Sinn Fein for a number of years. Then on January 14 Gerry Adams traveled to the embassy in Dublin, rather then the consulate in Belfast, to submit another visa request. Ambassador Kennedy Smith sent a cable recommending approval of the visa. What followed was a political and diplomatic hailstorm. The State Department opposed the visa. The Justice Department opposed the visa. The British Embassy opposed the visa. And Tom Foley, the Speaker of the House, opposed the visa. But this time the counterattack was overwhelming. Ted Kennedy and Chris Dodd circulated a letter of support from the Senate. Sid Gordon, Dick O'Neill, and Cross did the same in the House. The Irish government used its diplomatic muscle. Even the *New York Times* broke ranks with the Brits and urged approval.

Finally, on Sunday morning, January 31, Clinton issued an order granting Adams a visa waiver allowing him into the United States. The waiver limited the visa to forty-eight hours and restricted Adams to a twenty-five-mile radius from Manhattan. But to Cross the restrictions were irrelevant. Gerry Adams would be admitted into the United States. And that was all that mattered.

Adams's visit was a complete success. He rallied Irish Americans and united them more than any Irish leader since Eamon DeValera had barnstormed America in 1919. But the full ramifications of Adams's visa extended beyond Irish America. Clinton had delivered a severe body blow to career diplomats in the British Foreign Office and Anglophiles in the State Department. He'd also sent a clear message to the IRA that if it was serious about seeking a just resolution, it no longer had to stand alone.

The next several months were frenetic. The British persisted in refighting the battle against Adams. The Irish government, led by Albert Reynolds, accelerated its contacts with Sinn Fein. The Clinton administration pressed forward on all fronts. Clinton made it clear to the Brits that he would not reverse his policy on the Adams visa and that the United States stood ready to make its diplomatic resources available to bring all parties to the table. The message to the IRA was that the United States would not wait forever for a ceasefire to be called. Cross and the Ad Hoc Committee kept the pressure on the Brits, particularly Sir Patrick Mayhew, the British Northern Ireland secretary.

By late August it seemed an IRA ceasefire was imminent. Then, on August 31, it became a reality. The IRA declared a "complete cessation of military operations." Cross was overjoyed. So much so that he almost refused to believe it was actually happening. After twenty-five years. After so much tragedy. And so much suffering. But it was happening. And it could not have happened without Bill Clinton and the visa he gave to Gerry Adams.

Cross spent all day August 31st at his local office in Massapequa Park fielding phone calls and doing radio and television interviews.

—Yes, this is an historic day for Ireland.

—Yes, I believe it can lead to a lasting peace. But the British must respond and engage Sinn Fein in negotiations.

—No, the IRA is not trying to sucker the British or anyone else.

—Yes, President Clinton's role was pivotal.

In late afternoon, just after five o'clock, the last reporter had left and Cross telephoned Mickey Brannigan. He reached Brannigan as he was leaving the newsroom. They shared their joy over the ceasefire and agreed how important it was that the Brits move quickly and respond to the ceasefire. Cross then said, "Let's face it Mickey, we were wrong, fucking wrong."

"What do you mean?"

"Clinton. We thought he was bullshitting us on Ireland."

"You're right. He fucking delivered big time. Either Clinton's got incredible guts or he's fucking crazy."

"Mickey, why not give the guy a break and just say he's got guts?"

"Okay. He's got guts. Are you happy?"

"Yeah."

Within weeks the UDA and UVF called ceasefires. The Brits, though, still appeared to be floundering, not certain how to react or what to do. Then in late September, Gerry Adams was back in America. This time it was a full-fledged tour and visit—Boston, Detroit, Hollywood, New York, Philadelphia, and Washington, D.C. And he was lionized at every stop along the way. Political heavyweights like Ted Kennedy, civil rights leaders such as Rosa Parks, and an array of movie stars all wanted to see and be seen with Adams.

Adams capped off the trip with a triumphant visit to Washington, where he and Richard McAuley used Cross's congressional office as their base of operations. The four days on Capitol Hill were a kaleidoscope of photo opportunities and serious discussions. There were the meetings in the Senate with George Mitchell and Bob Dole. The lunch in the Senate dining room with Al D'Amato. The cordial get-together with House Speaker Tom Foley, who had fought so hard against the visa. The reception sponsored by the Ad Hoc Committee where more than a hundred members of Congress dutifully stood in line to get their picture taken with Gerry Adams. *Like kids waiting to meet Santa Claus,* thought Cross. And though Adams wasn't invited to the White House, he did have a well-publicized telephone conversation with Vice President Al Gore. By all accounts the visit was a tremendous diplomatic success for Adams and Sinn Fein.

Adams next visited Washington in December. This time, besides stopping by Capitol Hill, he was scheduled to go to the White House to meet Tony Lake—another direct hit at the Brits, who were still refusing to meet with Sinn Fein even though the IRA ceasefire was in its fourth month.

On the Sunday evening that he arrived, Adams met with Cross and Mary Rose in the rear room of the Dubliner. Notre Dame Law Professor Lanny Bonenberger and his wife Barbara, who were in town for a legal seminar, stopped by the table to say hello. After about twenty minutes of casual conversation, Adams expressed his concern that the Brits were not responding to the ceasefire. He'd convinced the IRA to go the political route, and the Brits were stonewalling. Sometimes, Adams confided, he would wake up in the middle of the night wondering if he were doing the right thing. But despite it all, he was still confident. And that was because of America's role. "Clinton," he said, "is the only one who can make the Brits move."

Clinton's role was now more vital than ever because Albert Reynolds, the Irish prime minister who had sided with Adams, was going to have to step down because of a sex scandal involving a pedophile priest. It had nothing to do with Reynolds personally but someone in his government had delayed the prosecution of the priest and Reynolds would have to take the bullet. *Leave it to the Irish*, thought Cross. *This couldn't come at a worse time*. Adams was hopeful Reynolds could hang on, at least for a while. In any event it was important that his party, Fianna Fail, remain in power. That would keep the nationalist alliance intact.

Cross had come to Washington that week for two reasons: Republican leadership elections the following morning, and the White House Christmas party Monday night. The previous month the Republicans had captured control of both houses of Congress for the first time in forty years, and they were ready to coronate Newt Gingrich as Speaker of the House.

Cross was up early Monday morning and out of the apartment by eight. Even though the result of the Speaker's race was preordained, there would be a number of contested leadership battles, and Cross knew they'd go on for most of the day.

Mary Rose was still half asleep when the phone rang at about eight thirty. It was Dermot Gallagher, the Irish ambassador to the United States, desperate to reach Gerry Adams. Rummaging through Sean's papers, she quickly found Gerry's room number at the Phoenix Park Hotel and passed it along.

As soon as Gallagher got hold of Adams, he connected him with Albert Reynolds in Brussels. Reynolds wanted Adams to know he was resigning immediately. He'd lost control of the political situation. More importantly, Fianna Fail had lost control as well. The next Taioseach would be the Fine Gael leader, John Bruton. Reynolds did not have to elaborate. Adams knew straightaway what this meant. John Bruton was the most pro-unionist politician in the Irish Republic. To Adams this meant one thing: Bill Clinton had now become indispensable.

Sean and Mary Rose arrived at the east entrance of the White House that evening just before seven o'clock for the annual Christmas party. The setting for the ball, which the president hosted for the Congress, was typically festive and joyful. At the same time, however, the atmosphere was decidedly awkward as Democrats and Republicans eyed each other warily. Democrats who just weeks ago had been powerful chairmen presiding autocratically over their congressional fiefdoms were now unceremoniously relegated to minority status. And they were at the mercy of the very Republicans they'd lorded it over for four decades. As they walked past one another offering subdued greetings, there was only one thing on which they could all agree. The Republicans had seized control of Congress because of Bill Clinton's unpopularity, and the Democrats knew it. Clinton had just flown in that evening from a series of European meetings and the word was that he was exhausted. To his jet lag would now be added the indignity of standing in a seemingly endless receiving line and shaking the hands of so many of the very Republicans who had climbed to power over his political carcass.

It was about eight thirty when Cross and Mary Rose came through the receiving line and wished the president a merry Christmas. As Cross always did when he had time with Clinton, no matter how fleeting, he thanked him for "what you've done for Ireland." The frozen smile the president had affixed to his face for the difficult evening thawed momentarily. "We have to stay on this," Clinton replied, his left hand gripping Cross's right forearm and drawing him closer. "We have to make this work."

Despite the president's show of support, Cross became increasingly concerned over the next several months that the seismic power shift in Congress and the president's weakened political state were combining to short-circuit Clinton's Irish policy. Newt Gingrich, who now bestrode Washington like a colossus, had never demonstrated any interest in Ireland. Indeed, he had previously pointed to Margaret Thatcher as an ideological guru and political role model. And the Brits, ever alert to shifting political fortunes, were launching a renewed public relations offensive on Capitol Hill, the White House, Foggy Bottom, and the Washington press corps.

On February 22, 1995, the lines were drawn. Gerry Adams applied for a new visa. He wanted to be in the United States for St. Patrick's week. He also formally requested permission to raise funds for Sinn Fein. Circumstances were leading inexorably toward a political and diplomatic firestorm.

Newt Gingrich was holding the annual Speaker's St. Patrick's Day luncheon in the Capitol on Thursday, March 16. The president was hosting a St. Patrick's Day party at the White House the following evening. So there it was in one shot—the Speaker's lunch, the president's party, and the fund-raising issue. *Christ,* Cross thought, *it's the Irish trifecta. If we win, we win big. If we lose, we're fucked.*

Cross moved quickly. He sent a letter to Gingrich, urging him to invite Adams to the Speaker's lunch. And followed up with phone calls to Gingrich's top foreign-policy advisors. Then he and the other Ad Hoc co-chairmen—Sid Gordon, Dick O'Neill, and Tom Manton—sent a letter to Clinton, supporting Adams's request to raise money and asking the president to invite him to the White House party.

The initial signs were not promising. Gingrich was not showing up on the House floor and didn't return any of Cross's repeated phone calls. Worse, the word from Cross's diplomatic sources was that Lake and Soderberg were recommending that the president limit Adams's visa to a visit—no fund-raising and no invitation to the White House.

Cross's fears were confirmed on Friday afternoon, March 3. The House had just completed its final vote for the week, and Cross was walking off the House floor when Jim Walsh, chairman of the Friends of Ireland Committee, stopped him and said, "I just got the word. Newt's not inviting Gerry to lunch."

"Shit. Did he say why?"

"Nothing in particular. Someone must have convinced him it wouldn't look good."

"This is bad."

"I know."

Cross hurried to his office and placed a phone call to Gingrich, who was on his way to the airport. The Speaker returned his call in minutes by car phone.

"Sean, I understand you called."

"Jim Walsh just told me you're not inviting Adams."

"That's right."

"I think it's a big mistake."

"The British disagree."

"The British!" shouted Cross, barely controlling his anger. "Fuck them! What the hell do they have to do with it? St. Patrick's isn't their holiday. It's for the Irish."

"Listen, I'm sorry, but that's the way it's going to be. I've made my decision."

"Newt," said Cross, lowering his voice, "I don't want to make this a personal issue. But if Adams isn't there, I won't be either. I'm not going to make a production out of it or call for a boycott or anything, but I just can't be part of something like this."

"You do what you have to. But I think you'd be making a mistake. I hope you'll reconsider."

"I'll think it over. But I don't see any way around it."

The Brits could taste victory. Sir Patrick Mayhew, Major's secretary of state for Northern Ireland, was making the Washington rounds. The White House, State and Justice. By the time Mayhew got to Capitol Hill for his meeting with Sid Gordon and the International Relations Committee, he didn't bother to hide his confidence. The meeting was held in Room 2173, the private conference room on the first floor of the Rayburn Building. Mayhew sat back in the large chair reserved for distinguished guests, sipping a cup of tea and nibbling on strawberries. Cross had always found the patrician Mayhew difficult to deal with. Today he was particularly haughty and dismissive:

—The British government—indeed, the British people—simply cannot conceive of the president of the United States shaking hands with or even meeting with a terrorist.

—The British government cannot begin any type of talks with Sinn Fein until the IRA begins to decommission it weapons.

—Her Majesty's government is confident the president of the United States would never undermine the common struggle against international terrorism by allowing terrorists like Sinn Fein to raise money on American soil.

It was clear to Cross that Mayhew thought the fix was in, that there was no need to win over anyone in Congress. Clinton was going to deny Adams's request. When Mayhew got up to leave, he was smiling broadly, looking every inch the winner.

The following day, voting was concluded by early evening. The only event on Cross's schedule was a fund-raiser for fellow New York congressman Gary Ackerman at the Carpenters' Hall on the Senate side of the Capitol.

After putting in an appearance, Cross headed back to the office to prepare for an upcoming Banking Committee hearing. Walking out into the night, he was met by an angry, driving rain. Luckily, he was able to get a taxi and within minutes was in the dry confines of the Cannon Building. Entering his office suite, Cross was greeted by Tom O'Connell, who was working late on defense bills.

"How was Gary's event?"

"Great. The food was terrific and he had a big turnout."

"You getting ready for Banking?"

"Yeah. I've got to go over that derivatives shit so I can at least sound like I know what I'm talking about."

"I'll be sticking around another few hours if you need me."

"Thanks."

Cross walked into his private office and began reading through the mound of documents assembled for him. After about an hour of intermittent concentration and incomplete comprehension, Cross heard his intercom ring. When he picked it up, O'Connell said, "There's a Patrick Maloney calling for you. Sounds like an Irish guy."

Patrick Maloney. Cross knew him well but had no idea he was in the country. Maloney was a career Irish diplomat, an acknowledged expert on the nuances and intricacies of Northern Ireland. Cross also knew, however, that Maloney's activities often extended beyond the role of traditional diplomat. When Irish governmental policy still prohibited contact with Sinn Fein, successive prime ministers assigned Maloney to establish clandestine contact with the republican movement. He was equally successful in making contact with the loyalists, including the UDA and UVF. Cross knew Maloney wouldn't be calling him unexpectedly unless something was up.

"Pat, how are you?"

"Very well. I'm calling from a pay phone," Maloney said tersely. "Can you take down a number?"

"Yeah. Go ahead."

"Call Niall O'Dowd at 212-729-8927. He has good news about the president. He's waiting for your call right now."

Niall O'Dowd was the publisher of the *Irish Voice.* A Tipperary native, O'Dowd had established himself as a player in New York's Irish-American community over the past decade. More importantly, he'd played a significant role in bringing about the IRA ceasefire, working closely with Sinn Fein and the White House.

Cross immediately dialed the number Maloney had given him. O'Dowd answered on the second ring. Cross could hear the excitement in his voice.

"Sean, great news!"

"What's happening?"

"You'll never believe it. It's more than we could ever have hoped for. The president's giving us everything on Gerry's visa—fund-raising and the White House party."

"Jesus Christ, Niall. This is terrific. What happened?"

"Apparently, everyone—the State Department, the Justice Department, and the NSC—was against it. The papers were prepared for Clinton to sign and put on his desk this morning. For whatever reason, he put if off. Then this afternoon he was playing golf with Chris Dodd, and Chris made the pitch for Gerry. Clinton thought it over, went back to the White House, and said he wanted it done. Sinn Fein can fund-raise and Gerry will be celebrating St. Patrick's Day at the White House."

"Jesus, Niall, we can *all* celebrate. And thank God for Chris. When's all this going to happen?"

"Tomorrow morning at eleven."

"I hope to God nothing goes wrong between now and then."

"Let's say our prayers."

As he hung up the phone, Cross decided to do more than pray. He rang O'Connell on the intercom and said, "Call the White House switchboard right away and tell them I'd like to speak to the president."

Cross looked up at the clock. It was nine forty-five. He doubted he'd get through to the President, especially at this late hour.

A few minutes later, O'Connell came into Cross's office and said, "The operator told me Clinton's at a dinner, but he'll call you when he gets back. For what it's worth, they probably say that to everyone."

"I might as well hang out for a while and see what happens."

"Okay. I'll be inside."

For the next hour, Cross skimmed through the banking materials, occasionally forcing himself to concentrate but usually finding his mind drifting to Clinton and Adams and the visa.

At about five past eleven, Cross heard the phone ring. Seconds later O'Connell put his head in the door, saying, "It's the president for you."

Cross picked up the receiver. "Hello."

"Congressman Cross," said the White House operator, "the president is on the line."

"Mr. President, I appreciate your calling. I've heard you'll be making a decision on Ireland, and I want you to know how much I appreciate it. I also want you to know that this isn't a Republican or

Democratic issue, and I'll stand by you on it. And so will other Republicans."

"Thank you, Sean. I think I'm doing the right thing. And it's important that as many of us stand together as possible. These are new times. There's a real opportunity to move forward here. And considering all the suffering that's gone on, I don't think the risks are really that great."

"I agree with you completely, Mr. President."

"Thank you man."

"Thank *you* for what you're doing."

Putting the phone down and leaning back in his chair, Cross realized that neither he nor Clinton had mentioned the visa or any particulars whatsoever. They'd spoken elliptically, but he was sure there was no misunderstanding. Tomorrow, he thought, would be one hell of a day.

It was just after eleven o'clock on Wednesday morning, March 8th. Sean Cross was at the Capitol, seated at a conference table in Room S-230, the majority leader's office just off the Senate chamber. Cross had been there for the past hour, along with six senators and two other congressmen. At the head of the table was Bob Dole. The purpose of the meeting was to plan and coordinate Dole's 1996 presidential campaign against Bill Clinton.

Cross's beeper went off just after eleven, telling him to call the office. Cross excused himself, walked to the rear of the room, and dialed. O'Connell answered the phone.

"Susan Brophy just called from the White House. She needs to talk to you right away."

Brophy worked in the Legislative Affairs office. An experienced Boston politician, her official job was to lobby Congress on Clinton's legislative program. Unofficially, she spent a lot of time lobbying Clinton on the Irish issue. Brophy and Cross had become close friends and, despite their philosophical differences over most of Clinton's agenda, trusted one another implicitly.

Cross dialed Brophy's number. "Susan, this is Sean," he said in a low voice.

"He did it. Clinton signed the order. Gerry gets everything. Is the guy amazing or what?"

"He sure delivers. Do the Brits know yet?"

"They were informed about an hour ago."

"And?"

"The shit's flying."

The repercussions were immediate. The British Embassy in Washington was apoplectic. The British media and Conservative back-benchers railed against Clinton. At 10 Downing Street, John Major ignored a hand-delivered letter from Clinton and refused even to take his phone calls. British-American relations were at their lowest ebb since the Brits burned the White House during the War of 1812.

On Capitol Hill, Cross received a phone call from Gingrich's office curtly informing him that "of course Mr. Adams would now be invited for the Speaker's lunch." Cross put out a press release stating that "Bill Clinton has done more for peace in Ireland than any president in American history." After distributing it to the media, he faxed a copy to Susan Brophy.

Adams wasted no time taking full advantage of his opportunity. By the end of the week, he and Richard McAuley were in New York, meeting with close supporters and making numerous appearances. That Saturday Adams and McAuley had dinner with Cross and Mary Rose and their daughter Kara, who was home from Notre Dame for the weekend. It was a moment of great diplomatic triumph, yet Adams was subdued. He knew it would serve no long-term purpose to needlessly antagonize the Brits. Nor did he want to say or do anything that would diminish John Hume's stature. At the same time, of course, he had to aggressively pursue the republican agenda.

"Sean, you and I have had this conversation before," said Adams, "but it's becoming critical that we get talks started with the Brits."

"The visa decision should strengthen your hand."

"It should indeed, but I truly don't know if it's enough to push them to the table."

"Do you think the Brits have a game plan?"

"They're a tough lot to figure even in the best of times, but no, I don't think they've devised a real strategy yet. Obviously, they don't want the ceasefire to end. But they don't want to engage us, unless, of course, they absolutely have to. And they don't feel they're at that point yet."

It was about ten minutes before noon on Thursday morning, March 16. The sun was shining brightly and the temperature was comfortably crisp. The sound of bagpipes filled the air as Sean Cross stood on the sidewalk on the House side of the Capitol, waiting for Gerry Adams to arrive. Adams and McAuley were flying in from New York that morning. Cross wanted to make sure Adams got into the Speaker's lunch without undue confusion. Directly across Capitol Plaza, herded into a roped-off grassy area known as the House Triangle, were the more than fifty still photographers and television camera crews who were there to capture the arrival of the major players: Bill Clinton, Irish prime minister Bruton, John Hume, and, of course, Gerry Adams. Scores of reporters were there as well. Many of the media were from Ireland and Britain. All were straining anxiously as they looked toward the north entrance on the Senate side of the Capitol, where the motorcades of the president and prime minister would enter and work their way toward the House. The atmosphere was electric. A burly African-American Capitol Hill cop turned to Cross and said "I've been here for twenty years and I've never seen a St. Patrick's Day like this."

Moments later Cross heard the wail of sirens and waves of applause from the throng of spectators opposite the Capitol Building. The presidential motorcade was arriving. The vans filled with machine-gun-carrying Secret Service agents and the bulletproofed black limousines pulled up just south of the House steps. Secret Service agents opened the door of the limousine with the gold presidential seal, and Clinton stepped out. He turned and waved to the crowd, which cheered loudly as the photographers' cameras clicked furiously. Turning, Clinton was officially welcomed by Gingrich and Walsh. Clinton then looked over and made eye contact with Cross, who smiled and waved. Clinton walked away from Gingrich to shake Cross's hand.

"Happy St. Patrick's Day, Mr. President," said Cross.

"Same to you, my friend. Susan showed me your statement supporting my decision. That was great. I really appreciate it."

"That was the least I could do."

"But let me tell you," said Clinton, dropping his voice to a whisper and pulling Cross closer, "I'm catching more shit because of you Irish."

"I know."

"But fuck it. I don't care," said Clinton, smiling and shrugging his shoulders. "See you inside."

By noon all the big names had arrived—John Bruton, John Hume, Ted Kennedy, Chris Dodd, Jean Kennedy Smith. All except Gerry Adams. Cross looked anxiously around the plaza, but there was no sign of Adams or McAuley. Then at about ten minutes past twelve, Cross saw O'Connell waving from Independence Avenue. Adams and McAuley were with him. Sean made his way over and shook hands with them.

"I was starting to worry," said Cross. "I didn't know where the hell you were."

"Traffic's all fucked up," said O'Connell. "The Secret Service and the cops have cordoned everything off. We finally parked back on D Street and walked."

"As long as you're here. Well, Gerry, are you ready to make your grand entrance? The photographers and camera crews have been waiting all morning."

"Then we shouldn't keep them waiting any longer," said Adams.

Adams and Cross then strode purposefully through the Plaza—past the concrete barriers that had been erected in the 1980's to protect against Libyan sponsored car bomb attacks; past Capitol Hill cops who smiled toward Adams; and past the array of media to their right. Reaching the top of the House steps, they entered the second floor of the Capitol through the revolving glass door. Once inside they walked past the bank of elevators and turned right at the hallway just in front of the entrance of the House Chamber. At the end of the hallway they turned left into another hallway. Down on their right was the Rayburn Room, H-207, where the Speaker's lunch would soon begin.

For the next ten minutes or so, the approximately eighty guests milled about, greeting and talking animatedly with one another.

Many of the men were sporting green ties, the women green dresses. A harpist played Irish music while liquor flowed. Most eyes were on Adams, who was accepting greetings from numerous senators and congressmen.

During this time, the president was always at least twenty or thirty feet from Adams, speaking primarily with Bruton and Hume. Several times, though, Cross noticed Clinton glancing furtively toward Adams. The White House had let it be known that there would be no photos of the two men together. Adams didn't argue. Members of the media were allowed into the room for a five-minute photo op. As the cameras clicked, Adams kept his end of the deal and made no effort to position himself into a picture with Clinton.

Their five minutes up, the reporters and photographers were escorted from the room, the doors closed behind them. The guests then proceeded to their assigned tables. Clinton's included Bruton, Gingrich, Hume, and Jim Walsh. Adams and Cross were seated about five feet away at table 3, along with Susan Brophy and Tom Delay of Texas. Senator Pat Moynihan was also assigned to table 3 but when he saw Adams sitting there, turned on his heel and found another table at the furthest end of the room.

After several minutes, Adams asked, "Sean, what's the protocol? When do I officially meet Clinton?"

"Should be any minute now," answered Cross.

"It's Gingrich's lunch," said Brophy. "Let me ask Annette Larson how they want to do this."

As Brophy went up to speak with Larson, Gingrich's staff assistant in charge of the event, the waiters took away the salad and served the main course of corned beef and cabbage. Brophy returned to the table, looking somber. Leaning over, she whispered in Cross's ear, "This is fucked up. She says Gerry can't meet Clinton."

"Why not?" said Cross, barely believing what he was hearing.

"Larson said the Irish Embassy doesn't want him to."

Adams leaned in and asked, "What's the problem?"

"Gingrich's people are saying the Irish Embassy doesn't want you and Clinton to meet."

"What do we do?" asked Adams, looking very calm, but fiercely determined.

"Let me talk to Dermot Gallagher and see if I can find out what the hell's going on," said Cross.

Cross walked to Gallagher's table and told the ambassador what Larson had said.

"Sean, that's not the case," said Gallagher.

"Are you sure the embassy hasn't vetoed it?"

"I am the embassy, and I'm saying we haven't," Gallagher shot back.

"Thank you, Dermot."

Cross and Brophy then sought out Tony Blankley, Gingrich's press secretary and media guru. Blankley said it wasn't actually the Irish Embassy that had opposed the handshake and meeting but the Irish Department of Foreign Affairs. Cross said nothing but thought to himself, *This is getting fucking ridiculous.*

Just then Cross saw Clinton summon Brophy with his right hand. Cross walked to the far side of the room, where Sean O'Huiginn, head of the Anglo-Irish division of Foreign Affairs Department, was seated. Cross recounted the story to O'Huiginn.

"It isn't true," said O'Huiginn.

Feeling his blood pressure rise, Cross headed for Blankley. On the way he was stopped by Brophy.

"What did Clinton want?" asked Cross.

"He asked, 'When am I going to meet this guy?' "

"What did you tell him?"

"The same thing we're telling Gerry—we're working on it."

Cross and Brophy confronted Blankley, who was standing in the center of the room.

"Tony, I spoke to Gallagher and I spoke to O'Huiginn, and they don't know anything about this," said Cross.

"Well, then, I guess there's been a breakdown in communication," Blankley replied condescendingly.

"Well, the fact remains that the president is here and he wants to meet Adams. If they want to shake hands with each other, how are you going to stop them?" asked Cross.

"That's just the way it's going to be," said Blankley.

Before Cross could reply, Jean Kennedy Smith interjected. She had overheard the last part of the conversation. "This is the craziest thing I've ever heard of," she said.

Cross went back to the table to tell Adams what was happening. Looking around the room, Cross realized almost no one in the room was aware of the major diplomatic war being fought around them. Except for the protagonists, the rest were merrily eating their corned beef, drinking their Irish whiskey and enjoying the music of the harp. They couldn't be happier. To them it was a perfect Irish party.

Adams listened carefully as Cross and Brophy told him what was happening. Pausing for a moment to sort it all out, Adams said with the barest hint of a half-smile:

"How about if I just get up and leave—walk out the door?"

"Jesus, Gerry, don't do that. Believe me, I'm as mad as you are at this shit Gingrich is pulling. He thinks he's undermining Clinton by not letting the two of you shake hands. But it's not over."

With that Cross and Brophy got up from the table, got hold of Jean Kennedy Smith and cornered Blankley.

"Tony, this is bullshit you're pulling," said Cross, "and it's going to be a disaster."

Before Blankley could reply, Jean Kennedy Smith interjected, "There's media from all over the world right outside that door. How do you think they're going to react if they find out the Speaker wouldn't let the president of the United States shake hands with Gerry Adams?"

"How will the media know?" asked Blankley.

"We'll make sure they do," replied Kennedy Smith with a cold stare.

"Tony you *have* to make this work," said Cross.

About two minutes later Blankley came to table 3, leaned over between Adams and Cross, and said, "Here's what we're going to do. John Hume is going to come over here. He'll bring Mr. Adams up to meet the president." Blankley then turned to Cross and said bluntly, "But you can't come."

"Fine," replied Cross.

And then the elaborately orchestrated meeting began. John Hume got up and walked over to Adams, escorting him back to the president's table. Bill Clinton stood up, put his left arm on Hume's shoulder, extended his right hand, and shook hands with Adams. The room exploded in applause, virtually everyone thinking this was the way it had been planned all along.

Gingrich then got up, shook hands with Adams, and joined the conversation. Clinton looked toward Cross, who gave the president a thumbs-up. Cross saw Clinton whisper to Gingrich. After a few moments Gingrich left the table and walked toward Cross.

"The president wants you to come up," said Gingrich before adding sarcastically "and I guess that's appropriate."

When Cross arrived at the head table, Clinton was animatedly detailing for Adams the diplomatic and political abuse he was taking from the Brits. As Clinton spoke, Adams listened silently, a bemused smile on his face. When Clinton concluded, Adams hesitated slightly before replying with perfect timing, "Now you know, Mr. President. You've found out in the last two weeks what I've had to live with for forty-seven years."

After a few more minutes of light conversation and banter, a look of steel-like determination came over Clinton's face. Looking Adams directly in the eye, he shook his fist and said: "We're going to make this work. We're going to make this work!"

The Irish issue remained on Washington's front burner over the next several months. In April John Major arrived for a series of awkwardly formal meetings with Clinton. Though nothing significant was achieved, the frozen relationship between the two leaders did seem to thaw a bit. Major also traveled to Capitol Hill to meet with the members of the International Relations Committee and the Armed Services Committee.

Cross arrived early at Room H-130. The room was nearly empty, and he took a seat at the long rectangular conference table almost directly across from the seat reserved for Major. This would be Cross's first meeting with Major. Sean had no intention, however, of confronting him. Instead he would find common ground, praise Major for creating the climate that made the cease-fire possible, assure him concerned Americans wanted to work with all sides to bring about a just resolution of the conflict. This was not the time for one-upmanship. The stakes were too high. The only goal was to get the Brits and Sinn Fein to the table.

When Major and his entourage arrived about twenty minutes later, the room was overflowing with congressmen. Once everyone was seated, Sid Gordon officially welcomed Major and then asked the congressmen to introduce themselves. Cross was looking forward to showing just how diplomatic he could be. The first nine introductions went without incident, noncontroversy apparently being the order of the day. Then it was Jack Barnett's turn. Barnett was a Republican congressman from Florida and, as far as Cross was aware, had never spoken a word on Ireland. Until now.

"Mr. Prime Minister," intoned Barnett, "my name is Jack Barnett, and I want to welcome you here today. Also, on behalf of the people of the United States, I want to apologize for the actions of our president in granting a visa to a known terrorist and inviting him to the White House."

Dead silence filled the room. Major looked surprised. He said nothing but nodded toward Barnett.

Fuck, thought Cross. *What the hell did he do that for?* Cross knew he had to say something. Diplomacy would have to wait.

"Mr. Prime Minister, I'm Sean Cross from New York, and I am *not* here to apologize for the president of the United States."

Again, there was silence. Major merely said, "Very well."

Major began his prepared remarks by recognizing the "historic special relationship between our two countries" and then spoke of Bosnia, NATO, and trade policy before turning to Ireland. He expressed willingness to have talks that included Sinn Fein but stated that this could only come about after IRA decommissioning had begun. Major repeated this point in various forms over the next five minutes.

Observing Major closely, however, Cross was struck by his unassuming manner. There was none of Mayhew's patrician pomposity or arrogance. So when Gordon recognized Cross to ask a question, Cross employed the more conciliatory tone he had planned on using from the start, telling Major how close it appeared the parties really were and how tragic it would be if this opportunity for peace were lost. Major replied that his government would do all it could, but the IRA and Sinn Fein had to take concrete steps to generate trust. Major was not changing his position, but neither was he being confrontational or caustic.

When the meeting concluded, Gordon assembled Major and the congressmen for the obligatory group photo. As the House photographer was lining everyone up, Major turned, shook hands with Cross, and said, "Maybe we can make this work. I think it can be done."

"Thank you, Mr. Prime Minister," replied Cross. "I truly believe you're close, and I'm convinced Sinn Fein wants it to work as well."

"Let's hope for the best," said Major.

CHAPTER SEVEN

Mid-May

On Monday morning, Sean Cross was in his district office in Massapequa Park. Before catching the twelve-thirty shuttle to Washington, he had letters to sign, a meeting with the business agent from the Ironworkers local, and photos with two Korean War veterans receiving long-overdue service decorations.

Just as Cross was about to head into the conference room for his meeting with John Ninivaggi from the Ironworkers, Anne Kelly, who ran the district office, called out, "Sean, Howard Briggs is on the phone." Cross closed the door to his private office and picked up the receiver.

"Howard, this is Sean."

"Another stiff's turned up."

"What?"

"You know Professor Ronald Williamson?"

"Sure, he's the Paisley guy who teaches at Columbia. I've debated him a few times."

"You won't be debating him anymore. He's dead. Shot behind the ear."

"Christ almighty."

"We found him this morning. About seven o'clock. In a parked car on Fifty-first Street, right across from St. Patrick's."

"Any details?'

"It was a stolen car. Must've been left there during the night. It was just west of Madison, in front of the cathedral gift shop."

"Any chance it was a robbery?"

"No. His wallet was still in his pocket, with three hundred dollars in it. He had a Rolex watch on. This was an assassination."

"Where was the body?"

"In the back of the car, on the floor. He was wearing a suit and tie. There wasn't much blood; we think he was shot near his apartment, then dumped in the car."

"Where did he live?"

"Upper West Side—Eighty-fifth and Columbus. We found some blood on the sidewalk."

"So whoever it was threw him in the car and drove it to St. Patrick's?"

"Yeah. There's parking all night, from seven to seven. Whoever did it knew the car would be ticketed after seven, and we'd find out it was stolen. Obviously, they wanted the body to be found."

"And there's quite a statement in dumping a murdered Protestant corpse across from St. Patrick's."

"Yeah. These guys are real comedians."

"I'm afraid to ask, but what's the story on the gun?"

"It's too soon to know anything definite. But if I had to bet, I'd say it'll be traced to the IRA. Anyway, we're in contact with Scotland Yard. We'll know soon enough."

"When's the media going to find out?"

"We're breaking the story in about five minutes. I just wanted to give you a heads-up. I'm sure they'll all be calling you."

"Thanks, Howard. I really appreciate this."

"No problem. Just don't mention my name."

"You got it."

As soon as he put down the phone, Cross explained to Ninivassi that their meeting was off, canceled the rest of his appointments and dialed Jack Pender, repeating what Briggs had told him.

"The plot fucking thickens," said Pender.

"Someone really knows what they're doing," replied Cross.

"And once again it points back at you."

"You mean because I debated the guy?"

"Yeah. The two of you had some rough go-rounds. Christ, he was down the line with Paisley and totally against the Good Friday Agreement and the whole peace process."

"He really wasn't that bad. We actually got along okay."

"You better get ready for the media. This'll get more coverage than McGrath. Leaving the body outside St. Patrick's was a great PR move—Paisley's man lying dead in the shadows of the very symbol of Irish-American Catholicism. The media will fucking love it."

"I'm sure that asshole Spencer will love it even more."

"Are you going to put out a statement?"

"Yeah, I'll have to, right away, expressing my condolences to Williamson's family, condemning the media, and calling for a rededication to the peace process."

"When are you going to Washington?"

"As soon as the statement's ready, probably a half hour or so. Kevin can take all the calls; I'll return them when I get to D.C."

"What's your tone going to be?"

"Very aggressive. I can't seem at all defensive."

"Agreed. Sounds like the best approach. Good luck."

The news stories that evening and the following day echoed the ones on Frank McGrath's murder, only this time they were more intense. The St. Patrick's angle gave the story an extra edge. Cross got decent coverage, but Spencer got just as much—if not more—for his charge that "Each murder just raises more questions about what our congressman knew and when he knew it."

Things only got worse when the ballistics report came back, confirming that Williamson had been killed with the same gun used on Frank McGrath and Barry Kilpatrick. The *New York American* headline set the tone: "IRA SACRILEGE AT ST. PAT'S—Terrorists Blaspheme Cathedral."

Barclay Spencer held a news conference outside the FBI office in lower Manhattan, demanding that Cross immediately resign his seat in Congress and that the FBI investigate Cross's "links to international terrorism." The news conference was covered by nearly every New York television and radio station. Spencer also went on the *Mike Campbell Show* for two full hours, and it was hard to say who sounded more rabid. Cross gave interviews from Washington with virtually the entire New York media, each time attacking Spencer for being "a dupe of the evil forces who are carrying out murders on American soil and trying to destroy the peace process in Ireland."

Cross stayed on the offensive. Both he and Pender felt he was coming across much better than Spencer, but they didn't kid themselves. They knew the best Sean could hope for was to cut his losses. There was no way a congressman could gain votes while explaining why he had nothing to do with a string of murders.

Sean Cross had known Ronald Williamson for more than two decades. Williamson, who was seventy-two at the time of his death, had been born and raised in Belfast. Educated at Queen's University in Belfast and Cambridge, he was a hard-line unionist who'd been a close advisor to Ian Paisley throughout the 1960s and 1970s. An economist, Williamson came to the United States in 1980 to accept a teaching position at New York University, where he remained for ten years. Since 1990 he had been a professor at Columbia University.

Almost from the moment he arrived in New York, Williamson became the most visible and articulate spokesman for militant unionism. He was just finishing up his second semester at NYU when he began appearing on New York City television stations in the spring and summer of 1981 to denounce Bobby Sands and his fellow hunger strikers. Cross and Williamson first squared off in March 1985, when Cross was a very controversial grand marshall of New York City's St. Patrick's Day parade. They debated during a five-minute segment on the WCBS evening news, and neither gave an inch. Walking off the set, though, they exchanged innocent pleasantries and ended up in an amiable fifteen-minute conversation. And whenever they went up against each other after that—maybe once or twice a year—the pattern was the same.

Their most intense confrontations occurred in the aftermath of the 1998 Good Friday Agreement. Cross, of course, supported it. Williamson was strongly opposed. Cross began noticing a subtle but definite change in Williamson. It was almost as if Williamson realized his brand of unionism could not ultimately win. The best he and the Paisley unionists could do was delay and obstruct and fight a rear-guard action. But through it all, Cross and Williamson maintained cordial relations. They never socialized or even had a drink together, though Williamson did invite Cross to speak at several of his Columbia seminars, and Cross always accepted. But as far as the public knew, Cross and Williamson were bitter antagonists. And now Williamson was dead, murdered by a gun traced directly to the group whose cause Cross had long espoused.

Congress finished voting for the week on Thursday afternoon at four thirty. Cross was able to catch the five thirty Delta Shuttle to LaGuardia. Jack Pender was waiting in his black Buick.

"You're early. We should get to Clarke's in plenty of time," said Pender.

"When are the other guys getting there?"

"Doolan scheduled it for seven thirty."

"Frank Doolan, Mickey Brannigan, and Danny Lacy. This should be some fucking night," said Cross.

Yesterday afternoon Frank Doolan, the veteran defense lawyer in so many IRA gunrunning cases, had telephoned Cross after talking with Mickey Brannigan and Danny Lacy, a columnist with the *Daily News*.

"I smell a rat," Doolan had said. "Something's going on here that reminds me of a case I had in the '80s."

"What are we looking at?"

"Someone in our government is involved. I'm convinced of it."

P. J. Clarke's is a true New York City landmark. Built in the 1890s, this tough brick watering hole has served generations of New Yorkers and staved off endless creditors. With its dark wood walls and its crowded tables covered with red-checked cloths, Clarke's is the ultimate gin mill—which is why it was chosen as the setting for the booze film classic *The Lost Weekend.* Even today it has a regular clientele of hard drinkers whose taste in cuisine ranges from hamburgers medium rare to cheeseburgers well-done.

As Cross walked through the front doors and headed toward the back room, Pender at his side, he was greeted by the manager, Jack O'Connor.

"Good evening, Congressman. How ya holding up?" he asked in the rough accent of a retired New York City police detective.

"I'm doing fine," answered Cross. "So long as I'm standing, I've got nothing to complain about. Besides, who the hell would listen?"

"You're right. It could be a lot worse. You might have to work for a living."

"Since when does this joint have a comedy act?"

"Hey, I couldn't resist. Anyway, your guys are here," O'Connor said with a smile, pointing toward a corner table where Doolan, Brannigan, and Lacy were waiting.

Cross and Pender walked over and shook hands with the three men, who—defying the stereotypes—were all drinking Cokes.

"Christ, everyone's on time," said Cross, "even Mickey."

"Fuck you," rejoined Brannigan.

A waiter came and took their orders, and for the first few minutes, the conversation was light, focusing on the Mets and Yankees and their chances for yet another Subway Series, the fourth since 2000.

Moving on, Doolan then said he thought the Democrats would take the House in the November elections, and Cross told him he was delusional. Lacy said politics had become too plastic—no real people anymore. Things were better when ward heelers were running the show instead of image makers and pollsters.

The waiter returned with their orders, burgers all around. Doolan took a bite of his, paused for a moment, and said, "Sean, I'm glad you could make it in here tonight. It's important we talk over what's been happening, especially now, with Williamson's murder."

"Thanks for setting things up. I'd appreciate any thoughts you have. I think there's likely some intelligence link to this, and you're the one who's had dealings with that world."

"And I must say it wasn't very pleasant," replied Doolan.

"Pleasant enough to get your clients acquitted," interrupted Brannigan.

"I may have gotten them off, but it's never much fun to uncover the seamy side of your own government," said Doolan.

"Well, the Michael Farrell case certainly did just that," said Lacy.

Michael Farrell, an icon of New York's Irish-American community, was arrested by the FBI in the early 1980s and charged with gunrunning. The arrest was made in broad daylight on a Saturday morning, in full view of Farrell's Jackson Heights friends and neighbors. Farrell was seventy-nine at the time. Throughout the pretrial proceedings and the early days of the trial itself, the evidence against Farrell and his co-defendant appeared damaging and overwhelming. There were videotapes and audio recordings of Farrell buying machine guns and rocket launchers and arranging their shipment to the IRA. There was direct testimony from the FBI informants who'd set this sting operation in motion.

Then, with virtually no forewarning, Doolan unveiled a strategy that tore at the very heart of the government's case. Through solid evidence and clever questioning, he convinced the jury that the gunrunning operation had been conceived, planned, and coordinated by the CIA. The argument of CIA collusion and the verdict of acquittal brought howls of protest from the FBI and Justice Department and angry denials from the CIA. The Farrell case also raised troubling questions about CIA operations on American soil, which by law are absolutely forbidden, and whether the agency was operating against the foreign policy of our own government. Those questions remained unanswered.

"So you think the CIA is involved in killing McGrath and Williamson?" asked Pender.

"The CIA is a lot different now than it was then," said Doolan. "Certainly the World Trade Center tragedy made them bring in better people. But they're still not perfect. And, one way or the other, there has to be some sort of CIA involvement."

"Jesus, Frank," said Lacy. "Gunrunning twenty-five years ago is a helluva lot different from knocking two guys off in New York."

Cross sipped his pint of Harp, listening intently.

"I'm not saying I can prove it beyond a shadow of a doubt, but hear me out," said Doolan. "One thing I learned in the Farrell case was that the CIA is heavily involved in domestic operations—including infiltrating the Irish-American community. And interestingly the FBI had no idea what was going on, but MI6 sure as hell did."

"They're fucking partners in crime," said Brannigan.

"Another thing," Doolan continued, "was that it was almost impossible to trace the actual CIA agents involved. They go through so many layers of contractors and subcontractors that it's very hard to prove the connection."

"Then how do you prove it here?" asked Cross.

"Maybe I can't prove it factually," replied Doolan. "But I can prove it logically."

"Lay it out, then," said Lacy.

"Let's start with McGrath," said Duggan. "Only someone with access to the most sophisticated intelligence would know what Frank McGrath was up to, and that he would be in the United States. Only someone on the inside would have access to an IRA gun. Also the reality is that the Brits, the FBI and the CIA have been working so closely since the Twin Towers attack that no IRA guy like McGrath—who was actually a Brit agent—would have gotten in here without one of them knowing it."

"Couldn't that be the Brits?" asked Brannigan.

"I'm sure there's some Brit involved here," answered Doolan, "but it's not their M.O. to be knocking off Americans. Besides, it would be far too risky for them to be carrying out executions and moving bodies around in New York. They'd want a local for that."

"Couldn't they just hire some mick living in the Bronx or Queens to do the dirty work?" asked Lacy.

"Again, too risky. Remember, we're talking about national security-type information. Any Brit smart enough to have access to that level of intelligence is going to work with someone he trusts, someone who has a track record," said Doolan.

"Maybe this is moving too fast for me," said Pender, "but are we saying the CIA did this? The CIA director? The president? Or are we talking about some fucking nut out on the fringe, or one of those subcontractors you were talking about?"

"Sorry, Jack. I should've made that clear. I don't believe anyone at the top knows about this. And I doubt whoever's involved is actually on the government payroll. At the same time, it's not some nonentity, either. It had to be someone the Brits worked with and trusted."

"Frank, I'm going in circles," said Lacy. "If the CIA was helping send guns to Ireland twenty-five years ago, why are they trying to frame the IRA now?"

"Because the CIA never had any use for the IRA. They sent them the guns for two reasons—one, to counter anything the Russians might do in Ireland, which turned out to be nothing, and two, to have an element of control over the IRA. Believe me, the guys I came across in my investigation hated the IRA."

"How do you connect this to Kilpatrick?" asked Brannigan.

"Kilpatrick was definitely killed by the Brits," answered Doolan, "and it's obviously connected to McGrath and Williamson. Which goes back to my point that this is a very sophisticated operation. And it's being carried out by a hardcore who just can't accept that the IRA could never be defeated."

"I assume," said Lacy, "all of us believe the IRA had nothing to do with this, that it's all a setup attempting to kill the peace process."

"Sure," said Brannigan. "Why the hell would the IRA get involved in this stupid shit?"

Doolan, Pender, and Cross all nodded in agreement.

"Sean, you're the one on the front line here," said Doolan. "What do you think?"

"I agree completely that this is a very sophisticated crowd we're dealing with," said Cross. "And I'm sure there must be some American involvement. I just don't know if it's the CIA, even though they are a likely suspect. What I am convinced of is that there's Brit involvement. Whatever happens over here flows from that. The Brits're the ones who knew about Kilpatrick and McGrath, who placed the story about me in the *Telegraph*."

"How about Williamson?" asked Lacy.

"That was the easiest hit. Anyone could have shot him. Except that he was killed with the same gun that was used on Kilpatrick and McGrath. So, again, it goes back to the same source," said Cross.

"The bottom line here," said Pender, "is that Frank has made an overwhelming case for American involvement at some governmental level. We don't know whether it's the CIA or not, but sure as shit there's someone over here who knows what's going on."

"Jack's right," said Cross. "Let's all stay in touch, reach out to whatever sources we have and share any information we get."

"We'll stay in close contact," said Doolan. "So, Sean, what're you doing next?"

"The nominating convention's next Thursday," said Cross.

"Do you expect any problems?" asked Brannigan.

"No. It should go smoothly enough," said Cross, "and I'll get the official party designation. Of course, I'll still have the primary in September, but it always makes it easier to have the organization behind me."

"Mother of God, I never thought there'd be a day when I'd be praying for a Republican," said Doolan. "This must be the age of miracles."

"Then let's pray we can solve this damn case."

CHAPTER EIGHT

Early June

As he walked west along Forty-fifth Street in midtown Manhattan, Sean Cross took in the splendor of the beautiful spring evening. The bright sunset, the hint of warm breeze, the skyscrapers, and the incessant but somehow melodious honking of car horns. Walking beside Cross was Detective Brian Sullivan from the Special Investigations Bureau of the Nassau County Police. Cross and Sullivan were old friends, but Sully was here tonight on business.

The SIB's job was to evaluate threats against government officials and decide whether they were serious enough to warrant a security detail. Two days ago Cross had gotten a phone call from Matt Brady, the lieutenant in charge of the SIB.

"Sean, you've been keeping us pretty busy for the past few months," said Brady.

"It's part of my job, Matt. I want you to feel good about picking up that big paycheck of yours. What's up?"

"As you know, ever since McGrath was killed, threats against you have been coming in. For a while, we were pretty sure it was the usual harmless wackos and there was nothing to worry about. Since the Williamson murder, though, things have really stepped up. And the threats are different, much more serious."

"Are they organized?"

"No. But the guys behind them can be dangerous."

"Any particular group?"

"Not really—militia nuts, anti-Catholic bigots. That dirtbag on talk radio has them all worked up."

"Campbell?"

"Yeah. The crazier he goes after you, the more threats come in."

"How worried should I be?"

"We don't expect anything imminent. But the situation has to be monitored. We'll have patrol cars around your house and your district office on a twenty-four-hour basis, and there'll be a detective, usually Sully, with you everywhere you go."

"How about D.C.?"

"I called the Capitol police, and they agree with our evaluation. They'll give you protection whenever you're in town."

"How long do you expect this to go on?"

"Right now, I'd say at least until the primary. But you know what it's like. You've had protection before."

"Yeah, and you guys did a great job." Years earlier, Cross had been targeted by followers of Louis Farrakhan for investigating questionable federal contracts awarded to the Nation of Islam. "When does the detail start?"

"Sully should be at your office in a few minutes. The patrols are already under way."

"You don't waste any time."

"We can't afford to. Listen, let Mary Rose know we'll be sending some guys to your house tonight to install a special alarm system and panic device. If you suspect something's wrong, you can just hit the button. The cops'll be there in less than a minute."

"Christ, I hope we don't hit that button by mistake. It'll scare the hell out my neighbors, seeing SWAT teams breaking into the house."

"Yeah, that would be quite a show. So try to be careful."

"Don't worry."

"I understand you're having dinner with Clinton on Friday night."

"Yeah. At O'Neill's."

"We've been in contact with the Secret Service and the NYPD. So everything's coordinated."

"That's great. I wouldn't want to see Sully in a gun battle with the Secret Service in the middle of Third Avenue."

Though hemmed in by buildings on either side, O'Neill's stood alone, an outpost of rural Ireland in midtown Manhattan. A flagpole with an American flag jutted from the left side of the blue building. Located over the entranceway, it fluttered calmly above the throngs of passing pedestrians whose harried faces gave them the look of always being late for wherever it was they might be going. An Irish tricolor extended from the right side of the structure.

As Cross and Sullivan walked through the front door, they could see Kevin Stanton, the owner, standing anxiously just inside. He was wearing a dark blue suit, white shirt, and red tie.

"Jesus, Kevin, I barely recognized you with a suit on," said Cross as he shook hands with Stanton and introduced him to Sullivan. "You really didn't have to do this for me."

"I wouldn't do fuck-all for you," said Stanton, ostentatiously pulling at the cuffs of his well-tailored suit. "This is for the president."

"*Former* president," said Cross, smiling. "Remember, we have a Republican in the White House now."

"Sean, as far as I'm concerned, after what he did for Ireland, Bill Clinton will always be the president."

Cross had known Kevin Stanton since the mid-'80s. Stanton was now in his late forties. A Mayo native, Stanton had always been an outspoken supporter of the Irish republican movement, even during his early years in this country, when most immigrants from the south chose to remain silent on the plight of their compatriots in the north. Stanton had opened O'Neill's in the mid-'90s, and it was a success from the start. With its authentic Irish cuisine and dark wood decor, the bar's two floors were invariably filled to capacity.

Stanton was renowned for being glib and quick-witted. But when Cross called to tell him he'd be bringing Bill Clinton to dinner on Friday evening, Stanton was literally speechless.

Now Kevin stood with his hands deep in his pockets, looking nervously about the bar.

"Sean, I never thought I'd see a day like this. Mother of God, my brain is fucking wrecked. I hope everything turns out alright."

"I'm sure it will," answered Cross. "What time did the Secret Service say he'd be here?"

"He's due in about a half hour. There's agents here already. In fact, they've been in and out for the past two days, checking everything out."

"Where are you going to seat us?"

"Upstairs. I've set off the back half of the room for you. The front half'll be friends and cousins of mine who'll be doing some stargazing."

"Jesus, it'll be awkward knowing all those people are looking at me," said Cross.

"Don't worry, Sean. There won't be a fucking eye aimed at you all night. Come on, let me take you upstairs."

Stanton led Cross and Sullivan up the staircase and introduced them to the two Secret Service agents staking out the room. Cross saw one of the men press a hand to his earpiece. "Mr. Stanton," the agent said, "the president will be arriving in two minutes."

Stanton fixed his tie and adjusted his suit one more time, then went downstairs to greet Clinton. Cross stayed upstairs, watching the president's arrival from a second-floor window. A black car pulled up in front of O'Neill's and an agent jumped from the front seat. The back door opened. As Clinton stepped onto the sidewalk and buttoned his suit jacket, Stanton walked toward him and proudly shook his hand. Clinton smiled broadly. Photographers from the *Daily News*, the *American*, the *Irish Echo*, and the *Irish Voice* were there to record the event. As was Oistin McBride, the prize-winning photographer Stanton hired for the evening. Stanton escorted Clinton into the restaurant, where the first-floor customers shouted their greetings and approval. Clinton smiled, waved, and followed Stanton up the staircase.

Cross was waiting at the top. He greeted Clinton and the two men sat down at the table Stanton had reserved for them. Kevin asked if he could start them off with a drink. Cross ordered a pint of Harp, Clinton a diet Coke. *Nothing's changed there,* Cross thought. *Drinking's one vice Bill Clinton will never have.*

"Mr. President, it's great to see you. I really appreciate the opportunity to get together."

"Sean, it's my pleasure. You're a good friend. And besides, I'm really interested in what's happening. It's obvious someone's trying to destroy all the good we achieved in Ireland. We all worked too hard for too long to let that happen."

"We certainly did, Mr. President. Those were amazing days."

"They sure were," said Clinton, his voice trailing off.

CHAPTER NINE

November 1995–December 1996

As soon as Sean Cross sat down across the table from Gerry Adams, he could sense something was wrong. It wasn't the surroundings, the restaurant—the Sequoia in Georgetown—was first-class. Yet the look on Adams's face betrayed deep concern. Perhaps Cross should have seen it coming.

Throughout the summer and fall, the peace process had remained stalled. Even though the IRA scrupulously maintained its ceasefire, the Brits refused to begin peace talks with Sinn Fein, insisting the IRA must first start decommissioning its weapons. And the unionists were even more unyielding. Ian Paisley and his Democratic Unionist Party were still shouting "no surrender." As for the Ulster Unionist Party, its members had elected David Trimble as their new leader, a particularly uninspired choice. His only claim to fame was the victory jig he'd danced with Paisley that summer when British troops sided with unionists and forced Catholic residents to allow a Protestant march through their neighborhood.

"Sean, I'm worried," said Adams, sipping his glass of red wine. "Sometimes I wonder whether the Brits were ever interested in a ceasefire at all."

"They're not moving away from their decommissioning line?" asked Cross.

"Not in the slightest. If anything, their position is hardening."

"Are internal politics involved?"

"There's definitely some of that. Major's poll ratings get lower by the week. The Conservatives have lost every by-election in the past three years. Major needs the UUP more than ever."

"Is Trimble as hard-line as he seems?"

"I don't know the man at all. But nothing I hear is very encouraging."

"How has the White House been?"

"Sound as a bell. Tony Lake in particular. And the president, of course. They're doing all they can. But the Brits won't give an inch."

"And Bruton?" asked Cross, referring to John Bruton, who'd succeeded Albert Reynolds as Irish prime minister the year before.

"It can be frustrating dealing with him. Nothing in his background gives him any real understanding of the republican movement. Which makes it very difficult, when we're asking Bill Clinton to take more of a pro-Irish position than the prime minister of Ireland."

"What kind of reaction are you getting on the ground, from your own people?"

"It's not good. Some are very angry. All of them are very disappointed. There's been an IRA ceasefire for more than fourteen months now, and there's nothing to show for it. Nothing at all."

Adams and Cross continued their meal, discussing mutual friends and exchanging political small talk. When they had finished and were ready to leave, the usually stoic Adams looked directly at Cross and said, "Sean, we've shared the good times and the bad. I wanted to make sure we got together tonight in the event we should come on bad times again."

They shook hands and said good night. Taking a cab back to his Capitol Hill apartment, Cross reflected on the evening. *Gerry's exhausted and worn down from trying to deal with the Brits. That must be why he was so fatalistic—almost melancholy.*

It would be several months later—February 9, 1996, to be exact—before Cross would realize how completely he had misread Adams. How just the week before his dinner with Gerry, the IRA

Army Council had voted to end the ceasefire, a decision that would remain secret until the IRA decided when and how the world would learn that the war had resumed.

Another unsettling event that previous November was the meeting between the Ad Hoc Committee and David Trimble. This was Trimble's first visit to America since his election as leader of the UUP. It was also the first time any of the congressmen had met him. And the encounter did not go well.

From start to finish, Trimble was condescending, short-tempered, and ill at ease. What made Trimble's performance particularly perplexing was that the congressmen were conspicuously cordial toward him. Sid Gordon set the tone when he began the meeting by congratulating Trimble on his election, thanking him for his visit, and asking when Trimble thought Sinn Fein would be admitted to the bargaining table. Trimble responded by claiming that American congressmen were uninformed on the Northern Ireland issue, and he could not see his party sitting down with "Sinn Fein/IRA." Like questions from Dick O'Neill, Joe Kennedy, and Cross brought similarly worded answers.

As Trimble spoke, he rubbed his hands together constantly and his face brightened to a beet red. At no time was there even the barest hint of a smile. The extent of the verbal and emotional disconnect between Trimble and the congressmen was demonstrated when Jim Walsh, chairman of the Friends of Ireland Committee, sought valiantly to ease the tension.

"Mr. Trimble, I don't pretend to understand all the nuances of Northern Ireland politics. And I certainly don't think any of us believes we can resolve all the differences between the communities in the north. But don't you agree that political leaders in Northern Ireland should refrain from saying anything that would inflame religious bigotry or division?"

"No!" barked Trimble.

"No?" exclaimed Walsh.

Trimble then proceeded into a convoluted monologue, attempting to explain to the uninformed congressmen that actions perceived as examples of religious bigotry were more often political differences. That only the untrained eye saw bigotry where it did not exist.

The doubts and concerns from the Adams dinner and the Trimble meeting were soon overtaken, however, by President Clinton's triumphant tour of Belfast, Derry, and Dublin. When Air Force One landed at Belfast's Aldergrove International Airport on Thursday morning, November 30, and Bill Clinton walked down the stairway and onto the tarmac, he became the first incumbent American president ever to set foot in Northern Ireland. Clinton had flown to Belfast from London where he had a series of formal, very businesslike meetings with John Major.

Cross and a bipartisan delegation including Jim Walsh and Senator Chris Dodd of Connecticut had flown directly from Washington and arrived in Belfast several hours earlier. They'd gone immediately from the airport to the Dunadry Hotel on the outskirts of Belfast before taking a bus to the Mackie Steel Plant in West Belfast where Clinton would make his first speech.

Mackie's was situated on the Springfield Road at the so-called "peace line," a barrier that separated the Catholic and Protestant communities. The plant had been chosen not just for its location, but because it was known to employ both Catholics and Protestants. What was not advertised was that Catholic and Protestant workers used separate entrances. But that seemed a minor detail on a day when the president of the United States, leader of the most powerful nation in the world, was traveling the hard streets of West Belfast—streets very few Irish politicians had ever dared travel.

The congressional delegation pulled up at Mackie's about an hour before Clinton was scheduled to arrive. They were escorted to reserved seats near a stage that had been specially designed for this event. Looking around, Cross saw that the plant was already filled to capacity. Among the faces in the audience were a number of IRA and UVF paramilitaries he'd come to know over the years. Sitting near the congressional delegation were members of the president's entourage, including Tony Lake, Nancy Soderberg, and Susan Brophy. Closer to the front were local political dignitaries such as Sir Patrick Mayhew, who appeared to be trying to make the best of an uncomfortable situation. Cross scanned the crowd but couldn't spot Gerry Adams.

Shortly before eleven o'clock, the president arrived. He waited offstage, meeting with the plant manager and selected employees. After several minutes, a deep voice boomed through the sound system, "Ladies and gentlemen, the president of the United States." Clinton walked onto the stage, and the crowd rose to extend him a prolonged, roaring ovation. When the applause finally subsided, Clinton took a seat to the left of the podium and listened to two schoolchildren—a nine-year-old Catholic girl and an eleven-year-old Protestant boy—read messages of greeting. Clinton and many in the crowd were visibly moved by the girl's words. Her father had been murdered by loyalists.

Clinton got up to speak. He stood behind a podium emblazoned with the presidential seal. Behind him was a dark blue backdrop. Printed on that backdrop in gold letters was "Northern Ireland Welcomes President Clinton." Beneath that was a solitary word, "Peace."

Clinton's speech was neatly balanced and well delivered. He stressed the need for peace and reconciliation and pledged the continued support of the United States. The only discordant note came when, in an obvious reference to Sinn Fein and the IRA, Clinton said that those who have turned away from violence "are entitled to be full participants in the democratic process." The words had barely left Clinton's lips when a loud voice from the rear of the crowd shouted, "Never!" It was one of Paisley's people. Unfazed, Clinton continued his speech. When he finished, he received another sustained ovation.

The next destination was Protestant East Belfast, where the president would meet unionist political and community leaders at a forum at the Enterprise Center, a newly constructed industrial park. The motorcade traveling east on the Springfield Road extended for several blocks. The bus carrying the congressional delegation followed about a block behind the president's limousine. Looking out the bus window, Cross saw hundreds of children along the Springfield Road, laughing and jumping and waving toward the motorcade.

Behind them were their parents and grandparents, their faces etched with deep lines from too many years of suffering. Indeed, the stark walls of the buildings along the road were still adorned with defiant graffiti: "Brits Out," "Free Our Prisoners," "Disband the RUC," and "Up the IRA."

The Falls Road, the main thoroughfare in West Belfast, was a republican stronghold that over the years had come to symbolize IRA resistance to British rule. As the Codel bus approached the Falls Road intersection, Cross realized the motorcade in front of him had come to a halt. Media photographers jumped from their buses and ran toward the Falls. About ten minutes later, the photographers climbed back onto the media buses and the motorcade resumed its journey on to East Belfast. No explanation was given for the delay.

The crowds in East Belfast were considerably smaller and decidedly less enthusiastic than those in West Belfast. The format for the president's event with the unionists was a roundtable discussion held in a modest-sized meeting room in the industrial park. Clinton sat at the center of a horseshoe-shaped table, with four prominent unionists on either side of him. Behind him was a light blue sign with the lettering "East Belfast Welcomes President Clinton." The audience, seated on hard metal chairs, included the congressional delegation, the White House entourage, and local business leaders.

In his prepared remarks, the president pointed out that the East Belfast Enterprise Park had been financed through the International Fund for Ireland and then thanked Congress for continually appropriating money to the IFI. He also cited the importance of the cease-fire to continued economic growth. Clinton was great at these roundtable-type events, Cross knew, but here something was missing. The chemistry just wasn't there. Not like it was at Mackie's. Clinton was cordial to the unionists. And the unionists, even Paisley's deputy, Peter Robinson, were polite in return. But throughout the hour-long session the strain was evident to Cross.

Walking from the building to the congressional bus, Cross was approached by Gene Turner, a burly reporter from Belfast's *Irish News*, the local nationalist newspaper. Turner told Cross what had caused the ten-minute delay on the Springfield Road. Clinton had gotten out of his limousine to shake hands with Gerry Adams on the Falls Road. It was an event that obviously had been elaborately choreographed.

"Gerry was in McErlean's having a mug of coffee," said Turner, referring to the bakery and tea shop at 105 Falls Road. "As Clinton's limousine approached, Gerry walked out from the shop. When the limousine stopped, Clinton got out, and Gerry shook his hand."

"Could you hear what they said?" asked Cross.

"There was a lot of cheering from the crowd, but I definitely heard Gerry say, '*Cead Mille Failte*'—a hundred thousand welcomes."

"How about Clinton?"

"I couldn't make it out. But he had a smile from ear to ear. The two of them did everything but hug each other."

"It must have been some scene."

"Indeed it was. The crowd's roaring. Clinton's wearing his brown, bulletproofed trench coat. Tony Lake's standing to the side beaming, so he was. Richard McCauley's snapping pictures one after the other. And the Secret Service is all over the street, looking everywhere."

"Who'd have thought that Gerry and Clinton would have their first public meeting at the intersection of the Falls and Springfield Roads?"

"I wonder if the Secret Service knows it's called 'Hijack Alley,'" said Turner with a broad smile.

The remainder of the visit to the north went off without a misstep. The helicopter trip to Derry, where thousands of cheering people waving American flags lined the roads from the airport to Derry City and thousands more who had waited hours outside Guildhall Square roared their approval as Clinton and the First Lady stepped onto the stage with John Hume. The ceremony inside Guildhall, where Phil Coulter's heartfelt rendition of "The Town I Love So Well"—with their tanks and guns, my God what have they done?—moved many in the audience to tears. And the journey back to Belfast, where Clinton lit the official Christmas tree and addressed many thousands outside City Hall. Van Morrison sang his song of hope, closing with the words, "Oh, my mama told me, there'll be days like this." *That may be*, thought Cross, *but I never thought I'd see one.*

As Cross climbed onto the delegation bus leaving the Dunadry Hotel early the next morning, he was exhausted. The night before he and Susan Brophy and Chris Dodd and former New York Governor Hugh Carey had gone from a reception at Queen's University to Robinson's Bar on Great Victoria Street. Beers for Americans were on the house. In fact waitresses would resupply the Yanks as soon as their pint glasses even came close to hitting bottom. Cross lost track of the pints, and his last recollection was of turning off his hotel-room light at 3:30 A.M. Now he slept all the way to Aldergrove Airport, woke up long enough to go from the bus to the plane, and then slept again for the entire forty-five-minute flight to Dublin. When the C-137 landed at the Dublin Airport and Cross opened his eyes, however, he was wide awake once more. There was another historic day ahead.

Friday's central event was to be an outdoor speech at the Bank of Ireland building at College Green. Defying the dark rain clouds hovering ominously in the midafternoon sky, a crowd numbering in the tens of thousands stretched as far as the eye could see. Thankfully, the rain held off, and Clinton again hit all the right notes, assuring the crowd that "America will be with you as you walk the road of peace." Then there was a speech at the Irish Parliament and a stop-in at Cassidy's Pub. Clinton barely sipped his glass of Guinness but talked on and on—not just with the congressmen but with the fortunate locals who had squeezed themselves into the pub. Clearly, Clinton was reveling in the heady events of the past few days. And by then everyone knew that Clinton's picture with Gerry Adams was on page one of the *New York Times* and just about every paper in Ireland.

That evening there was a black-tie dinner at Dublin Castle hosted by Prime Minister John Bruton. John Hume was there. So, too, were Gerry Adams and former prime ministers Charles Haughey and Albert Reynolds. In his toast, Clinton quoted Seamus Heaney:

"'Now it's high water mark, and flood tide in the heart and time to go . . . It was a fortunate wind that blew me here.'"

Dining on rack of Royal Tara lamb and listening to tenor Finbar Wright, Cross was as hopeful about Ireland as he'd ever allowed himself to be. And it was not just the euphoria of the moment. All parties to the conflict were accepting America's diplomatic role. Britain was acknowledging that Northern Ireland had indeed become an international issue, and the unionists were realizing they could no longer ignore the diplomatic might of the United States. Indeed, on the eve of Clinton's arrival in London, John Major had yielded to American pressure and agreed to have former senator George Mitchell chair an international commission to resolve the IRA weapons issue so that all-party negotiations could begin by the end of February. *No,* Cross thought, *this time the effort won't fail. Not after all this.*

But it did fail. In a devastating and lethal manner. It was less than six weeks into the new year, 1996. Cross was sitting in his office in the Cannon Building on Friday afternoon, February 9, when Tom O'Connell put a call through from Ray O'Hanlon of the *Irish Echo.*

"Have you heard the news?" asked O'Hanlon.

"No. What?"

"The IRA just released a statement in Dublin. The ceasefire is over."

"Jesus Christ!"

"They're accusing Major of not responding to the ceasefire, of failing to schedule negotiations or talks."

"This must be their answer to Major's dismissal of the Mitchell report," said Cross.

"Apparently."

"Have there been any attacks?"

"Not yet. Just the statement."

"All we can do is hope and pray."

"I'm afraid you're right."

For the previous two months, George Mitchell had labored mightily to resolve the decommissioning impasse. Along with his two co-chairmen, General John de Chastelain, the retired head of the Canadian Defense Forces, who had been appointed by the Brits, and Harri Holkeri, the former Finnish prime minister, who had been designated by the Irish, Mitchell had met with John Major and all the significant party leaders, including Hume, Adams, Trimble, and Paisley.

Mitchell issued the commission's report on January 23. The report specifically rejected prior decommissioning and urged the start of all-party talks. The report did, however, suggest the parties explicitly commit themselves to democratic principles and "consider some decommissioning" during the talks.

The Irish government and John Hume endorsed Mitchell's report. Though not fully supportive, Gerry Adams called the report a "basis for moving forward." Not John Major, however. The very next day, January 24, Major went before the House of Commons. In Gerry Adams's words, Major "unilaterally dumped" the Mitchell report. And if he didn't actually dump it, Major interpreted the report so selectively as to render it meaningless. Specifically, he said if there was no prior decommissioning, then a special election demanded by Trimble would be held. And he failed to give any date for all-party talks. Clearly, John Major had decided to put the peace process on hold. And the peace did not hold beyond February 9.

Shortly after 2:00 P.M., about an hour after Cross had gotten the call from O'Hanlon, Gene Turner, the reporter from the *Irish News*, was on the line from Belfast.

"Sean, it's fucking terrible news. The IRA just bombed London."

"Christ. What did they hit?"

"Canary Wharf in the Docklands area."

"Any word on casualties?"

"Not yet. It's too early. But they bombed the shit out of the building. It must've been some fucking bomb."

As they were talking, Cross glanced at the television in his office. A CNN bulletin appeared, followed by the horrific scene of a bombed-out building spewing flames and smoke into the dark London night, sirens wailing in the distance. Cross said good-bye to Turner and hung up the phone.

He was crushed. He knew the IRA well enough to understand why they'd broken the ceasefire and set off the bomb. But he also knew how wrong they were. They'd been running and hiding in the shadows for so long, they had no idea how important international opinion was. Gerry Adams did, and Martin McGuinness. But not the IRA. Sure John Major was trying to screw them. Sure David Trimble couldn't be trusted. Sure Ian Paisley was a hateful bigot. But the British government and the unionist parties no longer had iron control over the destiny of nationalists and republicans. Not since Gerry's visa. Not since Clinton's visit to Belfast and Derry. Not since Mitchell's report. Ireland was now an international issue. Perversely, by breaking the ceasefire, the IRA was again allowing itself to be dominated by the Brits.

If he was upset by the IRA, Cross was enraged by Major and the Brits. After twenty-five years of carnage, the Brits had squandered a seventeen-month ceasefire. The IRA had taken the step toward peace, taken the daring risk, and gotten nothing. All because the Brits had insisted on decommissioning—a precondition neither meaningful nor attainable. The Brits were confusing a ceasefire with surrender. Or perhaps Gerry had been right back in November. Maybe the Brits had never wanted a ceasefire in the first place.

The casualty toll from Canary Wharf was two dead and almost $200 million in damages. The political cost for the IRA was incalculable. Countless editorials denounced them. Republican politicians across the United States ridiculed Clinton for being taken in. Some commentators charged that Adams had planned this type of attack all along.

Cross spoke to Adams on Sunday morning. Adams was subdued and somber but very much in control. He was doing all he could, he said, to put things back together again. It was important that friends in America get the message that, yes, the IRA was responsible for the bombing in London, but John Major was responsible for the breakdown in the peace process.

John Major said the IRA bombing would have no impact on British policy. The British were in no way responsible for the ending of the ceasefire, and they never yielded to terrorism. Then, on

February 28, Major and Bruton announced that all-party talks would begin on June 10. *Jesus Christ*, thought Cross, *if only Major had said that a month ago. Now it might be too late.*

Gerry Adams applied for a visa to visit the United States during the St. Patrick's Day festivities. Prior to Canary Wharf, approval would have been automatic. Now it was uncertain at best. Clinton had made a statement condemning the bombing and pledging his continued commitment to the peace process. But that didn't mean Gerry Adams had to keep his visa. And the pressure on Clinton would be great. Cross was particularly concerned that reaction against Adams by prominent Irish-Americans might scare Clinton off. Ted Kennedy, for instance, had already said he would refuse to meet with Adams until the IRA resumed its ceasefire. And then Senator Pat Moynihan—always somewhat of an Anglophile—said Clinton should revoke Adams's visa. *Shit*, thought Cross, *if the two most senior Irish-Catholic politicians in the country are turning away from Gerry, how can we expect a Southern Baptist to stick with him—especially in an election year?*

Cross called the White House switchboard, leaving the message he'd like to speak with the president about Northern Ireland. Cross wasn't even certain Bill Clinton would call back. In the event he did, Sean went over his case.

What the IRA did was terrible and inexcusable. But Major shouldn't have dismissed Mitchell's report the way that he did. Adams has been straight with us all along. If we take away his visa, we weaken his ability to influence the republican movement.

Cross had pretty much convinced himself of the persuasiveness of his argument. But then he realized how easily Clinton could say, "*Listen, you bastard. I put my ass on the line for Gerry Adams when the fucking Irish government wouldn't even talk to him. I stood up to our most important ally and took shit from John Major because I believed that bullshit you told me that the IRA really wanted peace. And now they're bombing the shit out of London, making me look like a dumb bastard and giving my opponents an issue to beat the shit out of me with during the election. Well, fuck you!*"

That would be an even more persuasive argument, Cross thought as he awaited the president's call.

He didn't have to wait very long.

"Sean, you called me about Ireland?"

"Yes, Mr. President. First, I have to thank you for staying so committed, even after the bombing. That was critical. But I also wanted to talk to you about Gerry Adams's visa and what Senator Moynihan said. I—"

"Thank you, Sean. I appreciate your support. I still think we can make this work. What happened here is that Mitchell was supposed to find a way to get the talks started. He did that and he put out his report. Then John Major says 'screw you' and the IRA blew up a building. What happened was terrible. But that only means we have to work harder. As for the visa, I'm not going to take it away. I realize Pat Moynihan doesn't speak for the Irish-American community on this issue."

"Thank you, Mr. President. I—"

"Would you do me a favor?"

"Sure, Mr. President."

"Would you tell Gerry I'll have to put some restrictions on his visa. After what's happened, I have to do something."

"I'm sure Gerry will understand, Mr. President."

"Thank you, my friend."

Fucking right, Gerry'll understand, Cross thought. *I hope the IRA realizes what a break they're getting.*

Adams was truly a man caught in the middle. Cross learned Adams had telephoned Tony Lake at the White House on February 9 just before the IRA bomb went off. Some Brits claimed that phone call proved Adams had been in collusion with the IRA all along. Cross didn't believe it for a minute. Cross did believe that Adams knew the IRA Army Council had voted to end the ceasefire. But Adams did not know where or when the IRA would strike, and to the very end was trying desperately to avert an attack.

Adams's visit to the United States, while more low-key than previous trips, was still productive. In Washington he made no effort to be invited to the Speaker's lunch or to the White House, but he did meet with the Ad Hoc Committee and many other House members. On the Senate side, Ted Kennedy wouldn't meet with him, but Chris Dodd did. In New York Adams attended the annual St. Patrick's Day mass at St. Patrick's Cathedral, celebrated by Cardinal O'Connor. Following mass, Adams met privately with the cardinal. Then it was onto Forty-fourth Street and Fifth Avenue, where Adams marched, Cross beside him, in the St. Patrick's Day Parade.

Marching up the Avenue, Adams was greeted by waves of cheers and applause all the way to 86th Street. Cross, looking carefully, saw no more than ten detractors along the entire route. Keeping with tradition, Cardinal O'Connor reviewed the parade from the steps of the Cathedral just south of 51st Street. Approaching the Cathedral, Adams and Cross left the line of march and walked up the Cathedral steps. O'Connor warmly greeted Adams and wished him well. As Adams returned toward the line of march, O'Connor clenched Cross's shoulder and said, "He's a very good man. We must help him."

The next several months were frustrating. The IRA launched several failed attacks in London, including one where an IRA man on a bus blew himself up with his own bomb. And John Major's political moves did nothing to bridge the gap with the republican movement. This seemingly insoluble impasse caused Cross for the first time ever to publicly criticize the IRA. In a series of RTE, BBC, and ITN interviews in mid-May, he made it clear Irish-Americans opposed this IRA campaign and strongly supported a restoration of the ceasefire. Cross made certain to condemn British policy and restate his support of Adams, but his main message was for the IRA.

The message was not well received. Friends in Belfast, who a year later would form the dissident Real IRA, accused him of being bought off by the Brits and swore never to speak to him again. Adams, in the closest he and Cross had ever come to a disagreement, told Cross he was "creating difficulties" for him.

May 30 brought a glimmer of hope. The election John Major had wanted and Sinn Fein had opposed was held that day. Its purpose was to create a proportionately representative forum for the all-party peace talks that George Mitchell would chair. Despite their opposition to the election, and even though their elected delegates would not be admitted to the forum without a ceasefire, Sinn Fein garnered its highest vote ever. Adams in particular received twice as many votes as his closest opponent.

The talks were scheduled to begin June 10, and the Brits seemed to be softening their stand, accepting a parallel negotiation on decommissioning. Desperate diplomatic efforts—with significant help from Tony Lake—were made to get the IRA to call a ceasefire. But then in a bungled robbery attempt in County Adare, an IRA unit murdered an Irish cop. It turned out the operation probably had not been authorized by the Army Council—killing police officers in the Republic was against IRA policy—but the damage was done. The ceasefire was not called, and Sinn Fein was not admitted to the talks on June 10. Gerry Adams and Martin McGuinness were stopped at the gates of Stormont Castle.

In mid-June, the president of Ireland, Mary Robinson, arrived in Washington for a state visit. She was Ireland's first female president, elected in a startling upset in 1990. More importantly, she'd captured the media's imagination and was enormously popular with the Irish public. This popularity enabled her to extend her influence beyond her constitutional powers, which were mainly symbolic. She made headlines on a visit to Belfast in the summer of 1994—before the IRA ceasefire—by shaking hands with Gerry Adams at a community festival. The Brits were outraged, and perplexed, since, prior to being elected, Mary Robinson had demonstrated unionist sympathies. Her meeting with Adams, however, demonstrated the iconoclasm that personified her presidency and made her popular.

Clinton had invited her to Washington when he was in Dublin the previous December and she readily accepted. Though Newt Gingrich wouldn't allow her to address a joint session of Congress, Clinton more than made up for it by hosting a gala state dinner in her honor at the White House on Thursday, June 13.

Prior to the dinner, Robinson met in the Capitol Building with a large assemblage of House members, including Sid Gordon, Dick O'Neill, and Cross. She was accompanied by Dick Spring, the Irish foreign minister. The meeting went well. To the extent Robinson could discuss the peace process and stay within her constitutional restrictions, she was hopeful. So, too, was Spring, who had no such limitations. It seemed as if it might only be days before the IRA would call a ceasefire and Sinn Fein would be at the talks.

The state dinner at the White House was a virtual who's who of Irish-America. As the guests milled about on the second floor of the White House during the cocktail reception, Cross had a few moments with Tony Lake. "It looks good," said Lake. "I think we're getting there." Niall O'Dowd from the *Irish Voice* was similarly upbeat.

After about an hour the guests lined up to go down the staircase to the first floor where they would go through the receiving line. Cross and Mary Rose took their place and inched forward over the next twenty minutes until they were at the head of the line. As Cross was shaking hands with Clinton, the President asked:

"What do you hear?"

"From all I can tell, it's going well. I think this might be it."

"Let's hope and pray," said Clinton.

The dinner went off perfectly. Robinson and Clinton were eloquent, stressing the links between Ireland and America and promising to stand together in the quest for lasting peace in the north. And after dinner, there was plenty of music, song, and drink, as well as joyful hope that peace was at hand.

That spirit was echoed the following night at a dinner at the Irish ambassador's residence. Though not as elaborate or ornate as the White House state dinner, it was just as uplifting and contained its share of heavy hitters. William Rehnquist, the Chief Justice of the Supreme Court was there. As was Louis Freeh, the FBI Director. David Rockefeller, the worldwide symbol of incredible wealth. And John Sweeney, the head of the AFL-CIO. Mary Robinson looked fatigued from the rigors of the past several days. But her spirit was as vibrant as last night. Seated at tables placed on the sprawling grounds behind the residence, the guests spoke of peace and a hopeful future. In a cab heading back to their apartment on D Street, Sean told Mary Rose, "This has to be it. There's got to be a ceasefire."

At eight o'clock the following morning, Mary Rose woke him from a deep sleep, her voice filled with emotion.

"The IRA set off a bomb!"

"What?" said Cross, rubbing his eyes and not believing what he thought he was hearing.

"I was just watching CNN. It sounds as if the IRA has blown apart half of Manchester. And the pictures are just horrible. Buildings blown to pieces. Bodies everywhere."

"And it was definitely the IRA?"

"Yeah. They put out a statement."

"What the hell is wrong with them?" Cross asked angrily.

The attack on Manchester was the largest the IRA had ever pulled off on the British mainland—a 3,300-pound bomb set off during the busiest shopping period. An entire square mile of the city center destroyed. More than two hundred people injured. Through some miracle, none were killed.

Mary Robinson, preparing to return to Dublin, broke down in tears when told of the bombing. President Clinton responded quickly, stating, "Such viciousness deserves universal condemnation." Cross, enraged by the attack, condemned the IRA in his strongest words ever: "There's absolutely no justification for it, morally or politically."

Cross worried that the Manchester bombing would weaken Adams's effectiveness. And sure enough, on Monday, June 18, *Newsday* quoted a "senior White House official" as saying, "Another of these, and the peace process will be finished. You have to wonder about Adams's leadership." In Dublin, John Bruton threatened to ban Adams and Sinn Fein from Irish television and radio.

Cross spoke with Adams twice that weekend. Of necessity, the conversations were guarded and indirect. Adams always assumed any phone he used in the north was tapped. As best Cross could decipher Adams's message, the Manchester bomb had not been approved by the IRA Army Council. It was the work of an active service unit cut off for security reasons from communication with the council. Almost all IRA members thus far canvassed, Adams said, supported a resumption of the ceasefire. His main focus was "to get the peace process on the rails."

Cross went on the offensive for Adams. "I hope the president realizes that without Adams, chances are very slim of getting anything done," Cross told *Newsday.* "If either Clinton or the Irish government cuts Adams off, that just plays into the hands of the people who want violence," he told the *Daily News.* And to the *Irish Times*, "Gerry Adams is more important now than ever. It would strengthen his hand with the IRA if they knew that Congress and the administration were still behind him and ready to play a supportive role in the all-party talks."

Clinton came through yet again. On June 20 the *Irish Times* reported "authoritative sources" as saying that "President Clinton believes the IRA bombed Manchester to undermine the efforts of Gerry Adams. 'Adams is the only game in town' and it would be foolish to cut contact with Sinn Fein at this stage."

During the next six months, there was still no ceasefire, but the IRA launched only occasional attacks. Most were ineffective, except for an operation in October that penetrated the main British military command post in Belfast, causing significant damage and carnage. America's attention shifted, focusing on the Clinton-Dole presidential race. Ireland wasn't even a blip on the political radar screen.

This suited Cross just fine. Any progress, he knew, would take place behind the scenes. The actual differences between the IRA and the Brits on decommissioning and entrance into all-party talks centered not on substance but trust. The republican movement wanted an absolute guarantee that an IRA ceasefire would get Sinn Fein into the talks by a precise date. With Tony Lake still playing an active role, the parties were inching closer, but not close enough to close the deal.

While they were engaged in this diplomatic maneuvering, all of them—the Brits, the Irish, and the republicans—had their eyes on the upcoming elections. By law, Major and Bruton would have to call national elections in 1997, and the odds were against either of them returning to power, John Major in particular. His Conservative Party had a razor-thin majority, was at rock bottom in the polls, and had lost one by-election after another. The Labour Party would be led by Tony Blair. He was young and animated and had rebuilt his party. John Bruton's situation was not as precarious, but his grip on power was slipping. Not only was his coalition government an odd grouping of ideologically divergent parties, but Bruton just hadn't captured the imagination of the Irish people. He always seemed a step behind in his dealings on the north, reluctant, almost, to advocate for the nationalists.

Bruton's opponent would be Bertie Ahern, who'd taken over the Fianna Fail party two years before when Albert Reynolds was forced to resign. In his mid-forties, Ahern was a blue collar populist with strong nationalist leanings. Clearly the republican movement would prefer Ahern to Bruton. In the few meetings Cross had with Ahern, he sensed that Ahern would be able to work well with Clinton and be on the same wavelength as Irish-America—two areas where Bruton was distinctly lacking.

So as 1996 wound to a close, political realities appeared to preclude the main players from taking any daring steps. John Major couldn't risk driving the Ulster Unionists from his government, which was already on life support. John Bruton's inherent caution and unionist leanings prevented him from taking any stand that Major might consider pro-republican. And the republican movement, still burned by the unreciprocated 1994 ceasefire, saw no need to reach agreement with an enfeebled British government it did not trust.

One dramatic occurrence during these months was an attempt by forces in the British power structure to smear George Mitchell's top assistant, Martha Pope, with a phony sex scandal. Martha had worked for Mitchell during his years in the Senate and was now a key player on Mitchell's staff in Belfast, where he was chairing the peace talks. Cross knew Pope well and trusted her implicitly.

The IRA's refusal to call a ceasefire barred Sinn Fein from the peace talks and precluded Mitchell and his staff from having contact with anyone in either organization. So Mitchell was blindsided on November 29 when Ian Paisley charged that "certain people in Mr. Mitchell's office are talking with the IRA." Paisley followed up at the DUP conference the next day by claiming that "people who work in Senator Mitchell's office are not to be trusted, for they're friends of leading members of the IRA."

Paisley named no names, but the Sunday tabloids proclaimed them with sordid details. The *Mail on Sunday* in London and the *Sunday World* in Dublin ran identical stories: Martha Pope was having an affair with Gerry Kelly, a former IRA man and prison escapee, now active in Sinn Fein. Separate photos of Pope and Kelly appeared in both papers. The story claimed that British intelligence services had provided detailed accounts of romantic liaisons between Pope and Kelly in the north and in the Republic. Monday's *New York American* joined the outcry, with the front-page headline "Sex Scandal Perils IRA Truce."

Clearly British intelligence had leaked the same information to Paisley and the tabloids. And it was all neatly choreographed—Paisley on Friday and Saturday, the British tabloids on Sunday, the New York tabloids on Monday.

The story was dirty, and it was damning. Unfortunately for the Brits, it was also untrue. And Martha Pope called their bluff. She had never even met Gerry Kelly. When she fought back and threatened a law suit, the story collapsed. The papers made retractions, issued apologies, and agreed to pay Martha a large settlement.

It was over as quickly as it had begun. But who, wondered Cross, had been behind it all in the first place? He noticed that in those first few days, the Brits never denied the story. Instead, the Northern Ireland Office had only encouraged it by saying, "We do not discuss matters of intelligence." And on Monday, when told by reporters that Mitchell was standing by Pope, Paisley had threatened, "He had better be careful when the MI5 paper appears."

So, had MI5 prepared a phony report? The tabloids and Paisley referred to such a document. The NIO alluded to "matters of intelligence." Cross saw the dirty hand of British intelligence and denounced MI5 for "attempting to destroy the peace process by smearing an innocent woman." Cross never wavered in his belief that MI5 was behind it. If anything, his conclusions were strengthened when, several years later, George Mitchell referred to elements in the British security service "working to sabotage the peace process by smearing Martin Pope."

And MI5 would have succeeded, Cross thought, *if Martha Pope had retreated the way they thought she would.* Instead, she hit back hard, and the peace process moved forward.

CHAPTER TEN

Early June

"I'd like another Diet Coke, please," said Bill Clinton as the waitress at O'Neill's removed an empty plate of potato skins from the table and served him his fish and chips.

"Certainly, Mr. President," said the waitress with her pronounced west of Ireland accent.

"But before you do that, make sure the congressman gets his meal," laughed Clinton. "We wouldn't want him passing out from starvation."

"There's no danger of that," replied the waitress with a smile. "Sean, would you like another Harp?"

"No, I have to keep my brain functioning. I'll switch to a Coke—regular, not diet."

As the waitress walked away, Clinton's face grew serious. "So, my friend, just how much have these shootings hurt your campaign?"

"More than I'd like. But I'm not surprised. People think, 'Where there's smoke, there's fire.' My job is to make sure I don't go into a free fall."

"You still have the organization with you, right?"

"Oh, yeah. The County Committee had its nominating convention last week in Levittown, and I was redesignated by acclamation."

"Can the organization still turn out the vote in a primary?"

"All things being equal, it would make the difference. But being implicated with murderers and international terrorists gives it a different wrinkle."

"But this guy Spencer's a real asshole."

"He sure is. I've beaten him bad the two times he's run against me. But he's got money and he's getting coverage on talk radio and in the *American.*"

"How about *Newsday*?"

"I never thought I'd see the day when I'd be counting on *Newsday*, but yeah, they're with me. They know the charges are bullshit, and they also know that Spencer is a fucking moron."

"How are your poll numbers?"

"Slipping. But more than that, the cross tabs show a softening of my support. There's real potential for trouble."

"How're you doing on money?"

"I should be okay. They're projecting I'll have almost two million for the primary."

"How about Spencer?"

"Unlimited. He can spend as much as he wants."

"Well, if you've got two million bucks, money won't be a problem. On the other hand, if you don't turn this story around soon, it might not matter how much money you have."

"We're on the same page."

"I suppose this is none of my business but did you give any thought to running against Hillary this time?"

"No. Not really. I think I would have had a shot the first time," answered Cross. "But the guys at the top didn't want it."

"I remember quite a few of the White House staff thought you'd be the toughest candidate back then. Especially after Giuliani dropped out."

"Who the hell knows? But the combination of supporting McCain and being pro-life was too much for the so-called leaders."

"Son of a bitch. That would have been one hell of an awkward campaign. I'm glad it never happened."

"It would've been difficult. That's for sure," said Cross with a shrug.

"Back to business," said Clinton, "what do you hear on the investigation?"

"My friends in the NYPD tell me they're getting nowhere. But they're really breaking their asses."

"What about Leonard Ellis?" asked Clinton.

"Like I told you on the phone, Ellis didn't deny that MI5 or MI6 was involved."

"He was probably being honest. British intelligence is much more independent than the CIA or the FBI. I wouldn't be surprised if half the time the prime minister—no matter who he is—has no idea what the hell they're doing. But I think it's significant that Ellis didn't rule it out. I'd say that means he has his suspicions."

"If they are involved, it'll be tough finding it out. They're supposed to be pretty good."

"Not as good as they think they are," said Clinton. "I can tell you for a fact no one in MI5 or MI6 had a clue about the first IRA ceasefire back in '94, or the breaking of the ceasefire in '96."

"Did you get a chance to talk to Blair about this when you were over there?"

"I had a terrific meeting with Tony, and we had dinner together as well. We covered a lot of issues, but we spent a good bit of time on Ireland."

"I hate to be parochial, but what did he say about these murders?"

"Like Ellis, it's more what he didn't say. He's very concerned about what's happening and thinks it's very well planned and coordinated. And he realizes whoever's involved has inside information."

"Sounds almost verbatim like my conversation with Ellis."

"When I asked him directly whether it could be MI5 or MI6, he said, 'We aren't yet in a position to make a final determination.'"

"That clearly leaves the door open."

"I'm sure that's what Tony intended. He knew I'd be meeting with you when I came back."

"You said Blair's concerned. Does he think there's any chance the whole peace process could collapse?"

"No. We're too far down the road for that. But it could set the process back a few years and cost a lot of innocent lives."

"There are still wackos on both sides."

"Tony seemed especially concerned about the remnants of the Real IRA."

"How many of them are still around?"

"He says only a handful. But they're deadly and have access to extremely sophisticated weapons and explosives."

"Does he think they have much popular support?"

"Fortunately not. Tony says whatever support they do have—and it's minimal—would be in the border areas—even though it seems like there's not much of a border anymore."

"Was Bertie Ahern at any of the meetings?" asked Cross. Ahern had been elected prime minister of Ireland just a month after Blair in 1997.

"Yeah. I had a great session with Bertie. He's the best. Tough as nails and a real straight shooter. He basically agrees with Tony."

"About MI5 or MI6?"

"He's convinced one of them is involved, maybe both."

"Any direct evidence?"

"No. Just his years of dealing with the British. He's convinced all this could be going on without Tony—or the top people at MI5 and MI6—knowing anything about it."

"I've always been amazed at how autonomous the British intelligence services are."

"The military's just as bad."

"So, what were Bertie's thoughts on the Real IRA?" asked Cross.

"He's really cracked down on them in the south, but he thinks that as few of them as there are, they still have enough firearms to fuck things up."

"They certainly devastated Newry two years ago, and Omagh back in '98."

"I'll never forget Omagh," said Clinton. "I couldn't believe the carnage. It seemed like those car bombs just blew out the whole center of town. And all those casualties . . ."

"Are you going over to Belfast at the end of the month?" asked Cross.

"For Mitchell's testimonial dinner?"

"Yeah."

"Sure. I wouldn't miss it. Are you?"

"Yeah. I'll be there. I understand there's also going to be a special recognition for you, Blair, and Bertie."

"It'll be a great time. Just about everyone from the old days should be there. Gerry, Martin, John Hume, Trimble—all of them."

"Do you get to see them often?"

"Individually, probably once every year or two. But it's seldom we can all get together at one time."

"Ten years ago you couldn't get them anywhere near each other," said Cross.

"Times certainly have changed."

Before Cross could reply, the waitress removed their dinner plates. After she had taken their dessert order, Clinton continued.

"Tony and Bertie both asked whether any agency from our government might be involved. Have you given that much thought?"

"You mean the CIA?" asked Cross.

"Or maybe the FBI."

"Actually, I have. Not the FBI. But definitely the CIA. I've been talking with a guy who represented some IRA gunrunners back in the '80s. He actually got them off by making a good case that the CIA was behind some of the gunrunning at the same time our government was supporting the Brits."

"Talk about being on both sides of an issue!"

"And he sees a lot of similarities with what's going on now."

The waitress served dessert and coffee. Clinton took a bite of cheesecake and sipped his coffee. He hesitated briefly and then said, "Sean, looking back on it, do you think I would have been able to move on Ireland the way I did if the World Trade Center had been attacked in 1991 instead of 2001?"

"No. And I've given that a lot of thought."

"The terrorism aspect?"

"Yeah. There was such an outcry against terrorism after the Twin Towers, it would have been almost impossible to distinguish the IRA from al Qaeda—even though to me there was no comparison."

"It would have been very tough."

"The IRA didn't hijack planes. They didn't use chemical or biological weapons. And although they fucked up too often, they didn't target civilians."

"And Gerry clearly was trying to take the political route."

"If there was any analogy to the IRA it would be the Irgun in Israel or the ANC in South Africa."

"Yeah, and Begin and Mandela went on to do okay for themselves."

"So did George Washington," Cross said with a smile. "But the average American wouldn't want to have heard that. And I really couldn't blame them."

"The Brits would've pounded away at me."

"That's for sure."

"So much depended on the political climate," said Clinton. "The Cold War had ended in '89. Gerry had brought the IRA right to the edge. There was nothing like the World Trade Center to scare people off. There was a window of opportunity."

"And you're the one who saw it and made it happen."

"Let's just be happy we were able to do it when we did."

CHAPTER ELEVEN

December 1996–December 1997

Behind-the-scenes maneuvering continued through the winter months. To maintain the fiction that they did not diplomatically engage with Sinn Fein, the Brits communicated with Adams through John Hume. In addition to verbal exchanges, there was also extensive correspondence between Patrick Mayhew, Hume, and Adams. The bottom line, however, was that the Brits were demanding an unequivocal IRA ceasefire while still refusing to specify a date for Sinn Fein's entry into the talks. Nor could the Brits give any assurance that the talks wouldn't drag on interminably. As Mayhew wrote to Hume, "Timetables cannot guarantee agreement."

Adding to the diplomatic stalemate was the removal of Tony Lake from the scene. Clinton had nominated Lake to head the CIA, and Nancy Soderberg was working on his Senate confirmation hearings. No one at the NSC had stepped in to take over the Irish issue. To help fill this void, Sid Gordon led a congressional delegation to Belfast, Dublin, and London in mid-February. Cross and Mary Rose were part of the group. The one-day stay in Belfast included a series of meetings at the Dunadry Hotel with representatives of each of the political parties in the north. Gordon skillfully scheduled Adams as the final speaker and then invited him to join the delegation at a news conference right after the meeting, giving Adams media exposure throughout the north and whatever credibility attached to being embraced by an American congressional delegation headed by the chairman of the International Relations Committee. At the news conference, Gordon and Cross affirmed their belief in Adams's veracity and called for Sinn Fein's entrance into the peace talks immediately after an IRA ceasefire.

When the news conference was over, Cross did a brief television interview with RTE before gathering briefly with Gordon and the other members of the delegation to review the evening's schedule: a meeting at Stormont Castle with Patrick Mayhew, followed by a helicopter ride down to Shannon Airport to spend the night at Adare Manor in Limerick. As the meeting broke up and Cross was heading for the hotel's front door and the bus that would take the delegation to Stormont, Mary Rose came up behind him and said, "Break away from these guys. I have to talk to you right away."

Cross followed her down a hallway into a room, and over to a men's bathroom. Richard McAuley was standing outside the bathroom door. "Gerry's inside. He has to see you," said McAuley.

Cross went into the bathroom as McAuley and Mary Rose stood watch outside.

Adams was leaning against the sink. "This will take but a minute," he said somberly.

"No problem, Gerry. What's up?"

"With Tony Lake gone, I have no high-level contact at the White House," said Adams, getting directly to the point. "We'll be coming into some very tense times, and I have to be able to talk to someone with access to our friend. I have to keep him updated."

"You know you're not going to be able to talk to the top guy until the IRA calls a ceasefire."

"I know that full well. But I need a line of communication with someone close to him, like I had with Lake."

"You're right. As soon as I get back, I'll call Jim Steinberg at the NSC. He's the one that'll be handling Ireland."

"That would be grand. And if you get the chance, could you tell our friend how much I need this contact?" asked Adams, referring to Bill Clinton.

"Of course."

"Thank you, Sean."

The conversation had been brief, but as Cross and Adams emerged from the men's room, Mary Rose looked harried, McAuley beleaguered.

"Some guy from the State Department has been running up and down the hallway looking for you," said Mary Rose.

"What did you tell him?" asked Cross.

"That I was looking for you, too," she answered.

"The poor man looked desperate," said McAuley. "How will he explain to his bosses in Washington that he actually lost a congressman?"

"The State Department might not be that upset about losing you," said Adams, laughing.

Just then the State Department man turned into the hallway.

"Congressman, we've been looking all over for you," he said.

"I'm sorry, but something came over me. I wasn't feeling well. I went into the bathroom to throw some cold water on my face."

"How are you feeling now?" asked the State Department man, looking back and forth between Adams and Cross.

"Much better," answered Cross, knowing the guy from State hadn't believed a word he said.

The meeting with Mayhew at Stormont went poorly. Just days before, an IRA sniper had killed a British soldier at a checkpoint in South Armagh. Mayhew was in no mood to placate the IRA or Sinn Fein or to listen to any lectures from their American sympathizers. Mayhew and Cross had a particularly rancorous exchange.

"How can you expect the IRA to call a ceasefire when your government won't even guarantee a date for Sinn Fein to enter into the peace talks?" asked Cross.

"The British government *has* guaranteed that Sinn Fein will be admitted to the talks as soon as an IRA ceasefire is called and we're sure it's unequivocal and real. But I must say these deplorable attacks by the IRA, notably this most recent and tragic murder of a young British soldier, engender serious mistrust," answered Mayhew.

"The last time the IRA called a ceasefire, your government did nothing for seventeen months," replied Cross. "That also engenders serious mistrust."

"You can always be counted on to take the side of the terrorists," rejoined Mayhew, glaring at Cross.

Before the encounter could get any more heated, Gordon stood up and said, "Sir Patrick, we greatly appreciate your hospitality and your willingness, as always, to take part in a lively discussion."

"It was my pleasure," said Mayhew through pursed lips.

On the helicopter ride down to Shannon, Cross thought to himself that Mayhew was one bastard he'd never be able to get along with.

After a night's sleep at the luxurious Adare Manor, the delegation was off to Dublin the next morning for another round of meetings. The Irish leg of the trip concluded with a reception hosted by Jean Kennedy Smith at the Ambassador's Residence at Phoenix Park. Cross expected this to be the standard diplomatic meet-and-greet nonevent. Drinks, music, handshakes, and small talk. There was some of that, but there were also intense conversations with Kennedy Smith, Sean O'Huiginn, Ireland's lead negotiator at the peace talks, and Martin Mansergh, Bertie Ahern's chief advisor on the north. All expressed frustration with the IRA and its failure to seize the diplomatic moment. These conversations heightened Cross's concerns that the entire process was in real danger of collapsing.

In London the following day, Cross checked in at the Churchill Intercontinental and then went downstairs to meet Martha Pope who was in town on a brief stopover from Belfast. He hadn't seen her since the Gerry Kelly imbroglio.

As always, Martha Pope was on time and on target. Seated at a corner table in the lounge, Cross ordered a cup of tea and Pope a glass of fruit juice to accompany their tray of finger sandwiches.

"Sean, I can't thank you enough for coming to my defense the way you did," said Pope. "It really meant a lot."

"It was the least I could do. It was obvious someone really wanted to destroy you."

"They sure tried hard enough."

"They just didn't count on you fighting back. Instead, they've made you a rich woman."

Cross finished a sandwich and sipped his tea, then asked, "Martha, where are the talks going?"

"They might not be going anywhere. Nothing can be done without Sinn Fein, and Sinn Fein can't get in without an IRA ceasefire. This can't go on forever. Besides, I think Mitchell's about to call it quits."

"What? When's this happening?"

"It's not definite yet, and don't say anything to anyone, but I think he's going to be leaving in the next few months."

"That could be disastrous. Who would take over?"

"I don't know. Whoever it is, I'd stay on until he's fully briefed. But the bottom line is it could be a whole new ball game."

Monday's meetings reminded Cross just how intractable the Conservative Party could be. First there was the morning session with Deputy Prime Minister Michael Heseltine at the Cabinet Office building. Then an afternoon encounter with Foreign Office Minister of State Nicholas Bonsor at the Foreign and Commonwealth Office. And finally a meeting with Defense Minister Michael Portillo at the Ministry of Defense.

At each meeting, the conversation was the same:

—Why won't the British government commit to a specific time for Sinn Fein to enter the talks after the IRA calls a ceasefire?

The British government will allow Sinn Fein into the talks when the British government decides the IRA ceasefire is genuine and the republican movement is committed to democratic, peaceful methods.—

—Since the British government stonewalled for seventeen months the last time the IRA called a ceasefire, why should the IRA trust the British now?

Democratic governments do not allow the terrorists to set the terms.—

In elaborating on their answers, the Brits displayed various levels of belligerence. Heseltine was haughty and patrician: "No gang of murderers has the moral right to question the good faith of the British government." Bonsor was smug and ignorant: "Our policy is our policy, and that will remain our policy." Portillo, who prior to the meeting had been very un-British as he slapped shoulders, shook hands, and said, "Hi, I'm Mike Portillo," now became every bit the enraged Brit as he pounded the table and shouted, "Those bastards will *never* tell the British government what we are to do. Who the hell do they think they are?"

So much for good faith, thought Cross. *The IRA may be blindly rigid, but these Brits are invincibly arrogant.*

That evening, entirely coincidental with the presence of the American delegation, a major debate was scheduled in the House of Commons. The Labour Party was seeking the impeachment of Douglas Hogg, John Major's agriculture minister, for mishandling the mad-cow disease crisis. The actual facts were largely irrelevant. And Labour knew it had no real hope of impeaching Hogg. Its sole purpose was to further wound the already terminal Major government.

When the delegation members were invited to watch the debate from the House of Commons gallery, Cross immediately said yes. Just being able to observe the thrust and parry of House of Commons debate up close and personal would be reason enough to attend. But Cross had an added motivation: he wanted to be there when Douglas Hogg suffered; he wanted to see his anguish. During his visits to Belfast in the early and mid-1980's Cross had developed a friendship with Pat Finucane, a Belfast solicitor who represented many IRA defendants. And represented them successfully. Finucane's extraordinary legal accomplishments would also cause his death. In January 1989 Douglas Hogg, then Margaret Thatcher's dutiful Home Secretary, publicly attacked "IRA lawyers who free IRA murderers." Everyone knew he was talking about Pat Finucane. Just weeks later, on a Sunday afternoon, Pat Finucane was shot dead in his home, in front of his wife and children. Loyalist paramilitaries had fired the bullets. Subsequent revelations showed that the paramilitaries had the assistance of the British security forces. As for the Home Minister, Cross strongly believed that Hogg had known full well that his irresponsible comments would trigger events that would kill Pat Finucane. Brian Feeney, the SDLP Councilor for North Belfast, had stated, "this cowardly act was a direct result of Douglas Hogg's remark." And Kevin McNamara, the Labor Party spokesman on Ireland, said Hogg "should be examining his conscience very carefully." Tonight's impeachment proceedings would cause Douglas Hogg nowhere near the suffering Pat Finucane endured when he was shot or the pain which Pat's family still endured but the fact that he would suffer at all was at least a form of justice.

Seated in the gallery directly opposite Speaker Betty Boothroyd, Cross and Mary Rose looked out over the historic House of Commons chamber, admiring its gothic style, its exquisitely designed wood, and its green leather rows of seating on either side of the center aisle. Moments later, the members entered the chamber, the government to Cross's left, the opposition to his right. Within minutes, it was standing room only. Hogg was seated next to John Major in the front row. Several seats away was Patrick Mayhew. As Cross was looking down toward the front bench, Mayhew glanced up the gallery. The two inadvertently made eye contact and nodded politely toward one another.

Cross found the debate even more of an event then he'd anticipated. The hooting and hollering, the shouting and heckling—it was what he'd seen on C-SPAN. But television didn't convey the true ferocity of the exchanges. As the debate wore on, it became clear the Conservatives had the votes and the motion would fail. But Major would pay a price. The ineffective and inefficient Hogg would be saved tonight, but only by the strictest party-line discipline.

The debate concluded, the members filed from the chamber to record their votes. Watching the more than six hundred members attempting to make their way from the chamber, Cross felt someone tap his right shoulder. Turning around, he was surprised to see Patrick Mayhew. Cross was even more surprised that Mayhew was smiling broadly and that his right hand was extended. Cross immediately stood and shook hands, as did Mary Rose.

"It was quite a pleasant surprise to see you here this evening," said Mayhew. "I'd just flown in from Belfast and had no idea you were to be here."

"Well, it's thoughtful of you to come up and say hello."

"My pleasure. Listen, we know full well how this vote will go. Why don't we go downstairs to the bar and enjoy a drink together."

"We'd be delighted to," said Cross, wondering if this was the same Patrick Mayhew he'd fought with so often over the past few years.

Mayhew led Cross and Mary Rose down to the members' bar of the House of Lords. It was what Cross thought a House of Lords bar would be—high ceiling, ornate dark wood, dim lighting, a large window overlooking the River Thames and London Bridge. They took a table in the back of the room, next to the large window.

As they waited for their drinks, they exchanged pleasantries for a few moments. Then Mayhew took over the conversation. And his tone and manner were different from anything Cross had ever seen from him.

"Finally, we have a chance to get together and chat in a relaxed setting," said Mayhew.

Cross smiled. "Yes, but I can't help feeling like I'm on *Masterpiece Theatre*," he replied, still not certain where Mayhew was going.

Mayhew soon came to the point.

"I wish there were a way to convince the IRA to call a ceasefire," said Mayhew. "I can't tell you how much the prime minister wants this to go forward."

"I wish the IRA would call a ceasefire, too," replied Cross, "but they're afraid it'll be like last time and nothing will happen."

"I can only tell you the PM will have Sinn Fein into the talks as soon as possible afterwards. Far more quickly than can be said publicly."

"And I guess far more quickly than you implied at Stormont the other night," said Cross with a smile.

"Ah, those briefings can be dreadful, with all of the posturing that has to be done."

"I always had the impression you thrived on those encounters."

"That just proves what a good actor I am. You might not believe this, but it truly bothered me that you and I had to have our row. But I simply saw no way around it. Anything I'd have said that indicated a softening of our position would have all sorts of ramifications here in Parliament and among the unionists. So much of this involves nuance, and that just wasn't the setting."

"I appreciate your candor. It's unfortunate the public lines get drawn so sharply," said Cross. "We met with some of your colleagues today—Heseltine, Portillo, and Bonsor—and they didn't seem very anxious to find an accommodation."

"Let me just say I'm the one who deals with the prime minister on Ireland, and I know what his thinking is."

They finished their drinks and ordered another round.

"Did I ever tell you my son is in the British army?" asked Mayhew.

"No, you didn't," answered Cross.

"And that he served in Northern Ireland?"

"No."

"Yes, in fact I was actually out on the street one day when he was on patrol. I had to laugh. When he saw me, he didn't know whether to salute or what to do."

Mayhew paused to sip his whiskey.

"Thank God my son finished his tour without any incident. But so many of them weren't so lucky. Nor were a lot of others. We must find a way to resolve this."

The conversation turned to electoral politics. Mayhew said, "Don't believe the papers. Major will win. He's tough, he's a fighter."

Cross listened politely but saw no way that Major could win. Even during tonight's impeachment debate, the Conservatives appeared dispirited, as if they were just going through the motions. Labor, however, was on its game. Carrying the debate. Launching attack after attack against the Conservatives, who seemed content to play defense.

Cross, however, was struck by what Mayhew had said about Ireland—and more so by the way he had said it. No patrician arrogance, no colonialist pomposity. Instead, he came across as sincerely interested in finding a way out of the morass, as someone several steps ahead of his party. A guy who needed his political adversaries to know he was acting honorably. Cross realized Mayhew's demeanor could be a clever ploy. But he doubted it. What could be in it for him? The IRA certainly wasn't going to call a ceasefire just because Sean Cross said that Patrick Mayhew wasn't such a bad guy.

If anything, Mayhew was leaving himself vulnerable to Cross, who could go public and make Mayhew look like an IRA sympathizer.

"Sir Patrick, I'm very glad we had this chance to see each other in a different light."

"Let's hope we have the opportunity to do it again," said Mayhew as he and Cross shook hands.

Cross was back in Washington several days later. He called Jim Steinberg at the National Security Council, and they met the following afternoon in Steinberg's first-floor office in the West Wing of the White House. Steinberg was relatively young, in his mid-forties, but he was very experienced in foreign policy, with close ties to top Democrats. Cross got directly to the point.

"Adams is working for a ceasefire. I think he could be close. But he's got to have a contact at the White House. Someone close to the president. Someone with authority to make quick decisions."

"How can you be sure about the ceasefire?"

"I'm not. It's just my sense of what's happening. Part of that's based on Gerry's body language. It's also based on Pat Doherty being with Gerry the whole time he was talking about a ceasefire."

"Pat Doherty?"

"A Sinn Fein vice president. He's considered very hard-line. That's a signal the militants are cooperating with Adams."

"We've been down that road before."

"I know."

"We've stuck by these guys, and it's cost us diplomatic credibility."

"Adams knows this ceasefire has to stick. That's why he wants to be sure everything's in place this time."

"You know the president is committed. I assure you we'll do everything we can. And I'll set up the line of communication for Adams. But Sinn Fein has to realize this is it. We can't go down this road again."

"I'll make sure they get that message."

"Stay in touch."

Dublin-born Mairead Keane had been running Sinn Fein's Washington office since it opened in 1994, soon after Adams got his first visa. She'd made herself a visible presence on Capitol Hill, lobbying, cajoling, and harassing any senator or member of Congress who evinced even the slightest interest in Ireland. She had a particularly close relationship with Cross's office, and it was not uncommon for her to stop by two or three times a week to brief Cross or Tom O'Connell on the latest development in the north. When Keane came to see Cross the Tuesday following his meeting with Steinberg, he decided the time had come for *him* to brief *her*. To tell her how much American support the IRA was risking by not calling a ceasefire.

Keane listened for a few minutes before interrupting.

"Would you do me a favor? Could you put all this in writing for Gerry and Ned Harlan? It's better if they get it directly from you."

"Sure. I'll get a memo together. It'll be ready in a few days."

Cross prepared a detailed memorandum and gave it to Keane on March 3. It was addressed to Adams and Harlan, who was Adams's closest political strategist. Cross realized there was little, if anything, he could tell Gerry and Ned that they didn't already know. The real purpose of the memorandum was to give others in the republican movement an indication of American thinking.

Cross began the memorandum by stating it was "based on the presumption that the republican movement has concluded that American diplomatic involvement will significantly advance the goals of Irish republicanism."

In other words, Cross was appealing to *realpolitik*, not righteousness or morality. He was not going to preach to them.

Cross detailed how, despite the efforts of so many Irish Americans for so many years, Ireland had not become a significant mainstream issue until Clinton granted Adams a visa. The visa made Sinn Fein and the republican movement respectable overnight. Gerry became the best-known Irish politician and was perceived as another Mandela or Walesa.

Cross stated how the breaking of the ceasefire—particularly the Manchester bombing—had drastically altered these perceptions. The average American now viewed Ireland as another Bosnia or Lebanon.

Cross emphasized the extent of Clinton's commitment. "Nevertheless," he wrote, "the reality is that the window of opportunity is closing. There is no political cry for the president to stay engaged on Ireland." Cross then cut sharply:

"If there is a feeling or mood in the White House right now toward Ireland, it is one of frustration and impatience—a feeling that Sinn Fein may not be ready for prime time. The clear consensus is that Gerry and Martin have been entirely honest with the administration and have great political skills in their public dealings. But the bottom line is that Sinn Fein was unable to keep the first ceasefire or deliver the second, despite the unprecedented extent to which the administration has committed itself. As Steinberg told me, the United States cannot continue to sacrifice its diplomatic credibility."

Cross disclosed that Mitchell intended to leave the talks in a few months and pointed out that, as with all second-term presidents, Clinton's power would continually diminish over the next four years.

Cross concluded his entreaty by saying that although he could offer no guarantee,

"I am extremely confident that if a ceasefire were called soon, Clinton would do all that he could to get Sinn Fein to the table by the time talks resume after the British elections, and the U.S. would be a guarantor of such talks. No one is asking you to trust the Brits. But we are asking you to trust the United States under Bill Clinton to act as an honest broker and guarantor. The opportunity will not be there much longer, and God only knows when it might come again."

On March 15, Jim Steinberg spoke by telephone with Gerry Adams, and the key line of communication between the republican movement and the White House was in place.

When John Major announced he was scheduling general elections for May 1, Cross realized there was no hope for a ceasefire until they were over and a new government was in place. To no one's surprise, Tony Blair and the Labour Party swept the elections. What was surprising was the margin of victory—Labour won a 179-vote majority, the largest of any party in more than a century. Not as surprising, but equally important, were the solid victories attained by Gerry Adams and Martin McGuinness. Although they'd made it clear they wouldn't take their seats in the British Parliament at Westminster, Adams recaptured his West Belfast seat by more than eight thousand votes and McGuinness unseated Paisleyite hard-liner Willie McCrea in Mid Ulster. Overall, Sinn Fein established itself as the third-largest party in the north, garnering more than 16 percent of the total vote. Then, just a few weeks later, Sinn Fein did even better in Northern Ireland's local council elections, getting almost 17 percent of the vote. Finally, in the Irish elections held on June 7, Bertie Ahern was elected prime minister by a close but solid margin, and Sinn Fein candidate Caoimhghin O'Caolain was elected to the Irish Parliament, leading the ticket in his Cavan/Monaghan constituency.

To Cross the stars were now optimally aligned. Major was gone. Bruton was gone. Blair, Ahern, and Clinton all wanted to make the process work. Sinn Fein would be able to negotiate from electoral strength. The only thing needed now was a ceasefire.

Blair moved quickly. As expected, he appointed Marjorie "Mo" Mowlam to replace Mayhew. Then he visited Belfast on May 16, stating, "We offer reassurance and new hope that a settlement satisfactory to all can be reached." His government conducted intensive behind-the-scenes talks with Martin McGuinness and Gerry Kelly. And one by one, the obstacles began to fall. George Mitchell decided to stay on as chairman. Mowlam announced the talks would be concluded by May 1998. She also made it clear there would be movement on paramilitary prisoners. Most importantly, on June 13 Blair transmitted a confidential written memorandum to the republican leaders, an *aide-mémoire*, pledging that Sinn Fein would be admitted to the talks within six weeks of an IRA ceasefire, without any weapons being handed over. This was what the republican movement had been holding out for all along. Everything was finally in place.

And then suddenly, it was all almost shattered.

On June 16, three days after the IRA and Sinn Fein had received Blair's communiqué giving them what they so desperately wanted, IRA men killed two RUC officers in Lurgan, County Armagh. Shot them at close range in the back of the head.

Cross was in his car on Sunrise Highway driving to his district office when the news came across the radio. *I can't believe it,* he thought. *This is fucking crazy.*

And after he arrived at his office, he got call after call asking the same question: what's wrong with these fucking guys? And almost all the calls were from hard-line IRA supporters, including two convicted gunrunners. The calls, e-mails, letters, and faxes continued throughout the week. Cross had never seen such a wave of revulsion against the IRA. And it was coming from everywhere.

That Friday, June 20, Cross was in his Washington office. Blair was in Denver for an economic summit with Clinton and other world leaders. Cross knew that Blair and Clinton would discuss Northern Ireland, and that couldn't be good for Sinn Fein. Blair had blasted the republican movement after the Lurgan killings, accusing them of "sickening cynicism and hypocrisy." Cross had told Mairead Keane just how strong the anti-IRA feeling had become among Irish-Americans. That afternoon Gerry Adams called Cross.

"Gerry, I've never seen it this bad. No one's supporting the IRA on this one."

"Mairead's told me how bad the reaction's been."

"We have to separate Sinn Fein from the IRA. Otherwise, I'm afraid there'll be no support over here for helping you in the peace process."

"Sean, do what you have to do in that regard. I'd also like you to get a message to the White House."

"What do you need?"

"It's important for them to know the shootings in Lurgan were entirely a local operation. The IRA unit that carried them out had no knowledge at all of Tony Blair's proposal."

"That is important, because of lot of people in the administration thought the shootings were a direct rejection of Blair's offer. Or that you were adding new conditions."

"Not at all. His offer is receiving the most serious consideration."

"How does it look?"

"Decommissioning's not yet sorted out, but we're very close. We know we can't get everything."

"Do you have a timetable?"

"Nothing precise. But it could well be sooner rather than later."

"Thanks, Gerry. This is reassuring. Let me try to get hold of Steinberg right away."

As soon as Cross hung up with Adams, he dialed the White House and left a message for Steinberg, who was traveling with the president in Denver. Late that afternoon Cross flew back to New York. He was at home in Seaford when Steinberg returned his call.

"What's up, Sean? You said it was important. I hope so. I've just come from a very rough meeting with Blair's people."

"How rough?"

"About as rough as it gets. As far as they're concerned, the prime minister made a fair and generous offer, and the IRA responded by murdering two policemen."

"Jim, that's why I called. I spoke to Gerry Adams today. He said unequivocally that Lurgan was not authorized by the Army Council and that Blair's proposal is being seriously looked at."

"They're not rejecting it?"

"No. He said there's still some 'sorting out,' as he called it, to be done on decommissioning, but they've accepted that they're not going to get everything."

"You're sure of this?"

"I'm sure that's exactly what he told me, and, for what my opinion is worth, I believe him. He's never lied to us."

"Okay. Let me get back in this meeting and tell this to the Foreign Office people. Otherwise, I'm afraid the whole thing could fall apart."

Fortunately, the Brits accepted Adams's assurances and progress continued at a rapid pace. The Northern Ireland Office confirmed to Martin McGuinness in writing not only that the IRA didn't have to decommission for Sinn Fein to participate in the talks, but Sinn Fein would not be ejected if the IRA failed to turn over any weapons during the course of them. The Brits also promised to expedite the requests of IRA prisoners in England seeking transfers to jails in the Republic. Perhaps most significantly, Mo Mowlam prevailed upon the Orange Order to reroute unionist parades away from nationalist neighborhoods on July 12, the date commemorating the 1689 victory of the Protestant King William over the Catholic King James.

Cross was in his Washington office on Tuesday, July 15, when Mairead Keane telephoned him from Dublin. She had been in Ireland since late June.

"I'll be back in Washington on Thursday," she said. "It's important I see you as soon as possible."

"How do things look?"

"Not so bad. But I have to talk to you in person."

"Come by whenever you can."

"*Slan*."

On Thursday afternoon, Cross was attending an International Relations Committee meeting with Eduard Shevardnadze, the President of Georgia, to discuss Russia's intrusion into Georgian politics when his beeper went off. It was Tom O'Connell. Cross went to the back of the room to return the call.

"I just spoke with Mairead," O'Connell said. "She'll be here in five minutes."

"I'll be right over," whispered Cross.

Cross left the meeting quietly and hurried back to the Cannon Building. When he got to his office, Mairead was already seated in front of his desk. He closed the door behind him, kissed her on the cheek, and sat down. Normally, they would banter and exchange lighthearted jibes. From the look on her face, he could tell this meeting would be all business.

"What's up?" he asked.

"Gerry Adams has asked me to give you a progress report on exactly where we are. I'm giving the same report to Ted Kennedy, Chris Dodd, and Dick O'Neill. Bruce Morrison has already been briefed."

"It sounds like there's movement."

"Considerable movement. The Dublin dimension—with the new government—has been very helpful. We've also had telephone contact with the Brits and have received the necessary clarification on decommissioning."

Mairead paused. Cross looked directly at her, waiting. She continued with the words Cross had been desperately hoping to hear.

"The elements are coming together for a ceasefire," she said.

"What's left to be done?" asked Cross, his voice betraying a hint of anticipation.

"Gerry and Martin intend to go to the IRA and recommend a ceasefire. But they can't go until they get certain assurances from the American government."

"What assurances?"

"When Sinn Fein deals with the government, we're not to be treated as second-class citizens."

"Give me specifics."

"On visas, no long delays and hassles."

"What else?"

"Direct access to the administration and the right to fund-raise."

"That shouldn't be a problem," said Cross, realizing that this merely restored Sinn Fein to where it had been during the first ceasefire.

"Also," Keane continued, "we'll need a generous statement from the president in the event of a ceasefire."

"I don't see any problem with that, either."

"Can you transmit all of this to the White House?"

"Sure. What's the time frame?"

Keane paused again. "This afternoon. Tomorrow morning at the latest."

Cross was silent. He knew what this meant. Tomorrow, Adams and McGuinness would be asking the IRA for a ceasefire. This was it.

Cross telephoned Steinberg right away, leaving a detailed message with an assistant. Steinberg returned his call early the following morning, saying the White House would deliver on all of Sinn Fein's requests if Adams and McGuinness delivered on the ceasefire.

Everything was in order on the American end; all that was left now was to wait.

At about 11:00 A.M. Cross received a telephone call from Martha Pope in Belfast.

"Sean, we're getting reports there might be a ceasefire. Have you heard anything?"

"Who'd you get this from?" asked Cross, stalling for time.

"A few reporters and some good sources on the ground. But we don't know for sure."

"Martha, I hate to play cute with you, but all I can tell you is that there could well be a ceasefire. Things are happening right now."

"Thank you. I understand what you're saying."

Shortly after noon, a letter from Gerry Adams came across Sean's fax machine:

> Martin McGuinness and I have provided a detailed political report and assessment to the IRA and urged them to restore the cessation of August '94. I have been told they will respond without undue delay.
>
> If this is secured, it is critical that the objectives of the peace process are advanced as speedily as possible and that this new opportunity not be squandered by the British government as happened before.

That does it, Cross thought. *There's going to be a ceasefire. Gerry wouldn't have met with the IRA in the first place if he hadn't been virtually certain he'd get it. And the letter cinches it.*

Within a few hours, the press calls began, from the United States and overseas. Adams had acknowledged meeting with the IRA. Giving the reporters no specifics, Cross commended Adams for his leadership, hailed Clinton for being so steadfast, and saluted Blair for having the courage to move forward. At about 5:00 P.M. New York time, Gerry Adams called from Belfast.

"Gerry, congratulations. This is a magnificent moment."

"Thank you, Sean," said a very subdued Adams.

"I'm glad the meeting went well."

"Yes, I'm very hopeful. And if the ceasefire does happen, we all have to take advantage of it.

"You're right. One thing that should help right away is that the president is ready to put out a favorable statement once the ceasefire's announced."

"That'll be very helpful indeed."

"I think it would also be helpful if you got some sleep. You sound like you need it."

"I'm afraid I do, and I intend to take your advice after I make a few more calls."

After he hung up the phone, Cross thought to himself, *That has to be the most exhausted man I've ever spoken to.*

Now everything seemed to move according to the game plan. On Sunday, July 20, the IRA announced its ceasefire and, as promised, Clinton issued a strong, supportive statement. On Monday, July 21, the talks adjourned for the summer. Six weeks later, on September 9, the talks resumed at Stormont Castle, and Sinn Fein took its place at the negotiating table.

Unfortunately—but not unexpectedly—little of substance was achieved over the next several months. Paisley and the DUP were boycotting the talks because of Sinn Fein's presence. Trimble and the UUP raised various procedural objections, attempting, unsuccessfully, to have Sinn Fein ejected. The UUP also refused to engage Sinn Fein directly, opting instead to communicate their positions through Mitchell as chairman. All of this was awkward and dilatory, but what mattered was that Trimble and the UUP had stayed in the talks. So long as Trimble remained, there was a real chance of a deal ultimately being reached. And the longer he stayed in, the harder it would be for him or the UUP to pull out. And the longer Sinn Fein was at the table, the more difficult it would be for the IRA to even consider breaking the ceasefire.

But, Cross realized, there was at least one ominous cloud on the horizon. A group of IRA hard-liners opposed to the peace process had broken away to form a splinter force labeling itself the Real IRA. The Real IRA was small in number, but it was lethal. From his sources at the Irish and British embassies, Cross believed the commander of this guerilla force was Marty McDevitt. Cross knew McDevitt, acknowledged to have been IRA quartermaster and a member of the Army Council. McDevitt played for keeps and would have access to the most sophisticated weapons and explosives.

Cross also knew McDevitt's wife, Fiona. In fact he'd known Fiona far better and considerably longer than he'd known McDevitt.

Fiona was the sister of Bobby Armstrong, a fabled IRA man who had been killed in an epic gun battle with British soldiers in 1981. Armstrong had attained legendary status among Belfast republicans during the late 1970s. As a unit commander operating out of the nationalist stronghold of Twinbrook on the outskirts of West Belfast, he had repeatedly outmaneuvered the Brits, inflicting heavy losses in a series of skillfully executed ambushes and hit-and-run attacks. Though he was the most wanted man in Belfast, he was able to evade capture by the Brits. That all ended on a Wednesday night in March 1981. Armstrong and his nine-man unit attacked a British convoy on Stewartstown Road leading into Twinbrook. The IRA men had rockets, grenades, and automatic rifles. As always, Armstrong had planned it down to the last detail. But what he had not counted on was an informer. The Brits had been tipped off about the attack. So just seconds after Armstrong and his men opened fire, heavy British reinforcements surged in. When the shooting stopped, the body count showed six Brits dead and three badly wounded; all nine of Armstrong's men were killed, and he himself was in a coma, where he remained until his death sixty-six days later. A torrent of grief was unleashed among the Irish people, surpassing anything since the death of Michael Collins almost sixty years before. And there were demonstrations of support from around the world. In Australia, silent marchers picketed in protest outside the British embassy and British-owned businesses. From Poland, union workers sent messages of solidarity. And on New York's docks, longshoremen refused to unload cargo from British ships.

In Belfast more than 100,000 mourners came to Armstrong's funeral. But Fiona was not among them. For more than five years, Fiona had been on the run from the Brits. Though never formally charged, she was wanted for questioning in a series of shootings in North Belfast. As much as she wanted to attend Bobby's funeral, she couldn't take the chance of being arrested.

Cross had met Fiona several months later in Dundalk during one of his fact-finding visits to Ireland. The two got on well. Though fiercely republican, her zealotry was leavened by an irreverent and self-deprecating sense of humor. They'd kept in touch over the years through phone calls and letters, and when Cross traveled to Ireland after his election to Congress in 1992, he stayed overnight at Fiona's new home just outside Dundalk.

By then she was married to Marty McDevitt. McDevitt was at least ten years older than Fiona. At first Cross found him to be soft-spoken, almost shy. More like a retired grammar-school principal than the IRA Army Council member he was reputed to be. But as they spoke late into the night, Cross could see just how determined and hard McDevitt could be. McDevitt despised the Brits and dismissed any notion of ever talking or meeting with them, other than to accept their surrender.

During the summer of 1996, Cross had called Fiona just to say hello and see how things were going. She ended the conversation abruptly, accusing Cross of selling out to the Brits by calling for an IRA ceasefire. And now, a year later, reports were that McDevitt and Fiona had broken away from Adams and Sinn Fein, and from the IRA and Army Council as well.

In November 1997 Sid Gordon led a large congressional delegation to Ireland. The delegation included Cross, Mary Rose, and Dick O'Neill. This time, however, there'd be no stop in Belfast, or anywhere else in the north. It was to be Limerick and Dublin, then on to Edinburgh. Cross and O'Neill agreed, though, that one way or the other they'd go north, without the delegation's knowledge. They decided to make their move the morning they landed in Dublin. They checked into the Berkeley Court Hotel with the rest of the delegation, went to their rooms, and unpacked. Then Cross and Mary Rose and O'Neill and his top aide, Bill Trangese, got a cab to the Connolly Street Station, where they took the 11:00 A.M. train to Belfast.

When they arrived two hours later, they were met by a Sinn Fein security team led by Gerry Adams's longtime friend Terrence "Cleeky" Clarke. Clarke got into the lead car while the other minders hustled the four Americans into other cars and drove them to Stormont Castle, where the talks were being held.

The afternoon was a whirl of meetings for Cross and O'Neill. Particularly useful was an extensive session with George Mitchell. Mitchell, as stolid as ever, was frustrated by the snail-like pace of the talks, but he still believed that progress was being made. After that, they met with Mark Durkan and Brid Rodgers of the SDLP, and then with Monica McWilliams, leader of the Women's Coalition Party. They, too, were hopeful that somehow things would work.

The final meeting of the day—with Adams and McGuinness—was the most significant. Walking into the office reserved for Sinn Fein, Cross was struck by the incongruity of seeing Gerry Adams and Martin McGuinness holding court in Stormont, the very symbol of unionist oppression. Though more subdued than the others, Adams and McGuinness showed at least a degree of cautious optimism.

"In the end it'll be up to Trimble," said Adams. "It's whether or not he wants to do a deal."

"What do you think?" asked Cross.

"It's possible, but only if the Brits stand up to him."

"Are you getting any signals on that?" asked O'Neill.

"Mo has been first-class, and Blair has said some very good things. But Trimble knows that whenever it comes time to make a decision, no British prime minister in this century has ever stood up to the unionists."

"All we can do is our best," said McGuinness. "And as this goes forward, we have to make sure that our grassroots are kept fully informed of what we're doing and where we're going. If the time does come that a deal can be done, there can't be any surprises."

"What about Trimble? From what I gather, he's telling his constituency he'll concede nothing."

"I'm afraid you're right," answered Adams. "All he keeps saying is 'No surrender,' which is just rubbish. He knows that one way or the other, he'll have to move off dead center."

"Even if he doesn't want to make a deal?" asked Cross.

"Yes," replied McGuinness. "Trimble has to know that no matter what comes out of these talks—even if there's no agreement—the six counties'll never be the same. At the very least, the Brits will have to reform the RUC and implement an equality agenda on housing and jobs. Mind you, that's certainly not enough for us, but it's far more than the unionists have in mind."

"Does Trimble realize he's boxing himself in?" asked Cross.

"I've no idea what Trimble's thinking," replied Adams. "But if I had to guess, I'd say he's just playing for time. There's no long-range planning involved."

When the meeting concluded, Adams and McGuinness walked the four Americans down to the carpark outside Stormont where Cleeky and his boys were waiting, their walkie-talkies in hand, the cars ready to take them to the station for the 6:10 train to Dublin. After the good-byes had been said, Cross asked Adams for a moment alone. He and Gerry walked toward the far end of the parking lot.

"From what I can put together," said Cross, "it seems like McDevitt is leading the breakaway group."

"I'm afraid you're right."

"How serious is it?"

"It's troubling. And there's no reason for it. McDevitt and Fiona were given the opportunity to make their case, and they were voted down. Any support they have is extremely limited. But any split is disturbing. That's why we made every effort to be sure we had widespread support before Martin and I asked the IRA to call a ceasefire."

"You don't think McDevitt'll get much support."

"No. But having said that, I also realize that he has a certain stature and credibility within the movement. So we'll have to watch the situation very carefully."

December was a month of peaks and valleys. A high point occurred when Gerry Adams and Martin McGuinness traveled to

London to meet with Tony Blair at Downing Street. They were the first Sinn Fein leaders to enter No. 10 since Michael Collins in 1921—although, as Blair reportedly pointed out in a moment of humor, the IRA had fired some rockets into the premises back in 1991. While nothing specific was agreed upon, it was a historic moment. So much so that the following day, the *New York Times* featured a front-page photo of Adams standing outside the door of No. 10.

The talks recessed for the Christmas season on somewhat of a down note—the parties couldn't agree on the agenda they'd pursue when they returned on January 12. Then, over the holidays, the INLA, a splinter republican paramilitary group that had not called a ceasefire, and a loyalist force, the LVF, engaged in a series of sectarian killings. There was fear the main ceasefires would break. But they held. So as 1997 ended, Sean Cross looked forward to 1998 as the year lasting peace might finally be reached.

CHAPTER TWELVE

Washington, D.C.
Mid-June

It wasn't Sean Cross's style to stand on ceremony or pull rank. Capitol Hill was replete with petty potentates who delighted in terrorizing their staffs and abusing those supplicants unfortunate enough to have to appear before their committees. Cross had nothing but contempt for these congressional despots.

But today Cross would be one of them. He had summoned Addison Bartlett III to his office in the Cannon Building. And Bartlett had been instructed to be there not a second later than 10:45 A.M.

Addison Bartlett was one of those eminences who strode about Washington as if he owned it. Now in his sixties, Bartlett had the quintessential WASP pedigree: scion of a New England family prominent in the highest society circles; graduate of Exeter, Princeton, and Yale; world-ranked polo player. He had also been an agent in the CIA, where he served with notable distinction for a quarter century.

For the past ten years, Bartlett had been the preeminent lobbyist for the defense industry. And with his finely tailored blue suits, silk ties, and neatly trimmed white hair, the fit and still athletic Bartlett cut an imposing figure in Washington's corridors of power.

Cross and Bartlett had developed a reasonably good relationship over the years. When Cross first came to Congress, Bartlett, though winding down his CIA career, was still a major player on the western Europe front. At first their meetings were sporadic and pro forma. But as Clinton and Tony Lake accelerated their dealings with Sinn Fein, Bartlett's meetings with Cross became far more frequent and intense. Always it was Bartlett doing the probing. And most always, the questions focused on the same theme. Who is Adams? Who is McGuinness? What exactly is the republican movement? What is the IRA's actual role? And Sinn Fein's?

Bartlett never revealed his personal feelings during these sessions, but Cross had no doubt Bartlett considered the Clinton-Lake overtures to Sinn Fein a colossal diplomatic blunder. It was written all over his face and permeated his body language. But, Cross mused, how could it be otherwise? Bartlett's people were the society crowd. The inbred country-club types whose names are parted in the middle and followed by Roman numerals. To these people, Gerry Adams and Martin McGuinness would always be street urchins trying to shoot their way onto the world stage. And besides, they were Irish and Catholic. Cross also knew that Bartlett had very close ties with the British foreign-policy establishment, particularly the Foreign Office. But through it all, Cross never detected any effort by Bartlett to sabotage or impede Clinton's Irish policy.

Bartlett's transposition from major CIA operative to defense-lobby heavyweight was virtually seamless. The defense industry welcomed him with open arms—and a very open checkbook. And Bartlett was effective. He knew all the players on Capitol Hill. He also knew what he was talking about, making reasoned and cogent arguments for the various weapons systems his clients manufactured and produced, and speaking with an air of authority and years of inside knowledge.

It was also no secret that Bartlett retained links to the intelligence community. Government officials could utilize Bartlett to pass on diplomatic messages or make discreet inquiries to his old contacts while still maintaining the diplomatic shield of plausible deniability. Now Cross wanted to send a very undiplomatic message—some might call it a threat—and he would be using Addison Bartlett to send it. Bartlett would be given no choice in the matter.

Cross's intercom rang at ten forty.

"Boss, Addison Bartlett is here," said Tom O'Connell.

"Tell him to wait," answered Cross, who went back to reading the *New York Times.*

When the wall clock read ten fifty-five, Cross got up and walked over to the coat rack in the corner of his office. Cross invariably worked in shirtsleeves. Particularly when meeting friends. Today he put on his blue suit jacket before opening the door to the waiting room.

"Good morning, Addison. I can see you now."

"It's a pleasure to see you, Sean. You're looking great," said Bartlett, shaking hands heartily.

Cross nodded. Bartlett entered the office and Cross closed the door behind him, asking Bartlett to sit down. Cross looked directly at Bartlett and spoke in a firm, deliberate voice.

"Addison, it's bad enough getting fucked in this business. But it's worse getting fucked by bastards in your own government. And that's what I think is going on here."

"Sean, I assumed this meeting would be about those dammed shootings. But I assure you I know nothing about—"

"Sure. Nobody knows a fucking thing about anything. That's what you fucking guys are all about. Everything's a fucking mystery."

"Sean, I swear to you—"

"Knock off the bullshit. I'm not saying you know anything about this. But what I am saying—and you know exactly what I'm talking about—is that some of your old buddies do."

"Sean . . ."

"Listen to me. This shit isn't just happening out of the fucking blue. It's an inside job, and it's getting close to me."

"I understand your anxiety."

"Believe me, it's a lot more than anxiety. I have fucking had it. So listen to me. You tell whoever you have to tell that, number one, this has to end, and end now. Second, I want answers."

"I'll do all I can. You know that."

"There's more. If I don't get what I want, your friends better hope to God I'm not re-elected. Because if I am and I become chairman of the European subcommittee, I'll make their lives fucking miserable. Believe me, they'll all be putting in their papers."

"I understand."

"There's something else you should understand. If you don't come through for me on this, then I don't see how I can ever trust you again. How I can ever have any faith in what you tell me about your clients who pay you so well to lobby people like me."

"It's extremely unfair to put me in that position."

"Unfair! Do you think what's happening to me is fair? What's happening to the whole fucking peace process?"

"I'll do whatever I can," said Bartlett, sighing slightly.

"I suggest you get started right away. Time is running out," said Cross with the same deliberate tone he'd maintained throughout the meeting.

"Very well," said Bartlett, rising from his chair and walking from the office.

Neither of them made any effort to shake hands or say goodbye.

A moment later, Tom O'Connell came into the office, closed the door behind him, and sat down in the chair Bartlett had vacated. Cross removed his suit jacket and threw it on the couch.

"That was mean shit," said O'Connell.

"You heard it all?" asked Cross.

"Every word. The speaker worked great. We got it all on tape," O'Connell replied with a laugh. "It's good to know we're talented enough to bug the CIA."

"Don't be too proud of yourself. I'm sure Bartlett was wired."

"You're probably right, but it gives us something to laugh about anyway."

"Christ knows we need that."

"How do you think Bartlett was reacting?"

"He's a tough guy, so I don't think he takes any of this shit personally. But I do think he believes I'm about over the edge and may flip out. I'm sure that'll get back to his friends at the CIA."

"Do you think he knows anything?"

"Probably not. Listen, I'm not sure myself whether the CIA's involved. But if they are, Bartlett's the guy who can find out."

"Will he say anything to the Brits?"

"Sure. He's about as close to them as he is to the CIA. It'll help if they think I've gone nuts, too."

"You're really sold on this idea, aren't you—acting crazy, I mean?"

"Nixon wrote about it in his memoirs. He said Syngman Rhee told him to always let your enemy think you're crazy."

"Look where it got Nixon."

"But he did make the history books."

CHAPTER THIRTEEN

January 1998–February 1998

Sean Cross would always remember the moment he heard the news. It was January 21, just after seven in the morning. He was at his home in Seaford, still asleep, when Mary Rose, already up and alert, came rushing into the bedroom.

"Sean, wake up. You'll never believe this—there's been an explosion in Washington!"

Jarred to his senses, Cross's immediate thought was that someone had set off a bomb, and the IRA somehow had something to do with it. Shielding his eyes from the bright light Mary Rose had turned on in her agitation, he said, "What are you talking about? Who exploded what?"

"No, no. It's all over the morning news—Clinton's been having an affair with some White House intern for the past two years. Monica Lewinsky. They're saying he perjured himself about it in the Paula Jones case and he might be forced out of office."

"Holy Christ!" said Cross as he pulled himself out of bed and hurried towards the den to watch the television newscasters and reporters describe the still unfolding scandal at increasing levels of hysteria and apoplexy.

Cross's first reaction was that something had gone on between Clinton and Lewinsky. Not the long affair that was being reported, but something. How could Clinton be so fucking dumb? To screw around with some starstruck bimbo. At the same time that he was being sued for sexual harassment.

While Cross thought Clinton had been dumb and irresponsible, he didn't see any grounds to impeach him. The Constitutional standard was a crime comparable to treason or bribery. That's what the Republicans had argued during Watergate. And consensual sex—even if the President lied about it or tried to cover it up—just wasn't on par with crimes of that magnitude. It might be a crime. But it wasn't a high crime. Not even close to it. Besides, opening a president's private life to public scrutiny with the potential for impeachment set a dangerous precedent. The allegations and investigations would never end.

That was Sean Cross's opinion the week the scandal broke. Over the course of that year, he would study the Federalist Papers, read Ken Starr's report, and watch the impeachment hearings. All of which just confirmed his original belief—none of it was impeachable.

Clinton delivered his State of the Union speech on Tuesday, January 27. The House chamber that evening was electric. Democrats standing and cheering the president with an almost maniacal frenzy. Republicans glaring and giving Clinton the most perfunctory and grudging applause. As Clinton stood behind the podium and looked about the chamber, luxuriating in the seemingly endless roars of approval from the Democrats, he glanced over to where the Republicans were located, made eye contact with Cross, smiled and nodded, and whispered in a voice loud enough to be picked up on television, "Hi, Sean." Cross nodded back.

Clinton delivered a masterful speech. Not so much for what he said but for how he delivered it under the most trying circumstances. Clearly he had no intention of leaving. Not without a struggle. A struggle of Herculean proportions and unknown consequences.

Clinton quickly divined that to survive he had to be seen as presidential. Somehow he had to position himself above the fray, show himself to be a leader on the world stage. The first opportunity would come the following week, when Tony Blair would be in Washington for his first visit as prime minister. All informed speculation was that he'd stand by Clinton, affirming his position as the tested leader of the free world.

Cross realized all too well that Blair's support at this most perilous moment would not only offer a dramatic boost to Clinton but indebt him to Blair for however long he was president. This could clearly impact the Irish peace talks, which were expected very shortly to enter their final stage. Cross had pretty much accepted that Blair wanted to do the right thing, that he had none of the bias, malevolence, or obtuseness of previous prime ministers. But, no matter how well intentioned, he was still a Brit. And he had a Foreign Office and a Northern Ireland Office run by career civil servants who still viewed Ireland through a colonial prism. Cross's fear was that when the negotiations reached crunch time, Blair would tilt toward the unionists and call in his marker with Clinton. Cross had to do something. He had no misconception about his status—there was no way he could match Tony Blair—but he could give it a shot.

Cross spoke with Gerry Adams. Adams and Sinn Fein were entirely behind Clinton. The president could count on them. Cross decided to communicate this support to Clinton before Tony Blair arrived in town.

Cross phoned the White House late Friday afternoon, January 30, and left the message he'd like to speak with the president, who was spending the weekend at Camp David. Cross thought he'd be lucky if Clinton returned the call by Monday or Tuesday. The next morning, Saturday, Cross left the house to buy newspapers and bagels. He was just pulling into the shopping center on Wantagh Avenue when Tom O'Connell called him from Washington on the car phone.

"The White House just let me know that the president's going to be calling you in the next half hour. So I suggest you get yourself home."

Cross was home in less than five minutes. Ten minutes later the phone rang.

"Congressman Cross?"

"Yes."

"This is the White House switchboard operator at Camp David. You can go ahead now."

"Hello, Mr. President," said Cross. "How are you, sir?"

"Just fine, Sean. I was told you called."

"I just wanted to wish you well as you go through this."

"Thanks. Have you seen the *New York Times*?"

"No. I—"

"Are you up in New York?"

"Yeah, but I'm at the house."

"It's on page one," said Clinton, apparently determined to make a point. "It shows that Paula Jones's lawyers can't find any other woman to come forward to testify. It also shows that Paula Jones's lawyers and Ken Starr's office are working together and co-operating with each other."

"Starr's really gone too far."

"It's important that Republicans like you talk to other Republicans and ask them just to wait a while."

"Mr. President, last night I was at a Lincoln Day dinner, and quite a few Republicans—who would disagree with you on almost every issue—told me they thought Starr was wrong and hurting the country. Anyway, I know that Chelsea's home and you've got more important things to do than talk to me, so I just wanted to mention the meeting you'll be having with Tony Blair. All this week I've been speaking with Sinn Fein, and with the British and Irish ambassadors. They're very concerned about what's going on. You're the linchpin of the whole peace process. There probably wouldn't have been a ceasefire without you. They want to be sure you'll continue your role as the talks move forward. It's important you know that when you meet with Blair."

"Thank you."

"We've got to get this resolved."

"I know."

"By the way, when this is over, both parties have to get together and find a way to stop the power of these Special Counsels."

"You're right. No one else should ever have to go through this. I appreciate your help."

"Mr. President, thanks for calling."

"Thank you, my friend."

* * *

The small group of senators and congressmen milled about in the living room of Blair House, the mansion located on Pennsylvania Avenue just across from the White House and used by foreign leaders visiting Washington. Sir Christopher Meyer, the newly appointed British ambassador to Washington, and other embassy officials engaged in polite small talk with the American politicos while they waited for Tony Blair to come down for breakfast.

As he engaged in light banter with Meyer, Cross couldn't help but reflect on the irony of it all. All the speeches he'd given off the back of flatbed trucks at demonstrations outside the British Consulate on Third Avenue in Manhattan. And all the faxed messages he'd received from the British Embassy condemning the IRA during his early days in Washington. Now, on Thursday morning, February 5, 1998, he was preparing to sit down for a breakfast meeting with the British prime minister himself.

The clear sound of footsteps could be heard on the staircase. Conversation ceased as Tony Blair entered the room. *He looks totally at ease*, thought Cross. *And distinctly nonpatrician.*

Blair stopped midway across the room, and the politicians instinctively lined up to meet him. Ted Kennedy was first, followed by Pat Moynihan, Dick O'Neill, and Cross. One by one they stepped forward to express their greetings.

"Prime Minister, this is Congressman Cross," announced Christopher Meyer.

"Ah, yes, Congressman, I've heard of you," said Blair with a friendly smile.

"It's a pleasure to meet you, Mr. Prime Minister. And I appreciate your inviting me."

"No. Thank you for coming. I'm very much looking forward to this meeting. I'm hopeful we can find common ground," Blair replied as the official embassy photographer clicked away.

The introductions complete, the group made its way into the dining room for breakfast. Blair led off with a ten-minute update on the peace process. He broke no new ground but impressed Cross with his strong grasp of details and nuances.

Blair asked for comments and questions.

Ted Kennedy commended Blair for his leadership, praising him particularly for his recent decision to reopen the Bloody Sunday inquiry.

Dick O'Neill pressed the point that any agreement must assure protection of nationalists' rights.

Cross said the talks could never succeed if David Trimble continued to refuse to engage with Sinn Fein.

Chris Dodd praised Mo Mowlam and asked about the release of paramilitary prisoners.

Pat Moynihan—out of nowhere—opined on what he called the "Council of the Celtic Fringe" and asked on behalf of his uncle, if the Isle of Mann would be included in the Council. (As best as anyone could determine, Moynihan was referring to a proposed Council of the Isles between Ireland and Britain.)

Blair's replies were reassuring. Any Northern Ireland Assembly would explicitly ensure the rights of nationalists. A successful agreement would have to provide for strong cooperation between the north and the south. And he expected movement on prisoners as the talks progressed. He gave no specific answer, however, to Cross's inquiry about Trimble.

The question and answer session concluded, Blair recounted his first meeting with Gerry Adams and the other Sinn Fein leaders at 10 Downing Street back on December 11.

"Gerry Adams sat down at the conference table directly across from me. From the look on his face I knew he was realizing the improbability of it all. After a few moments he looked at me and asked 'Tell me, is this the very same table where Michael Collins and Lloyd George sat in 1921?' Before I could answer, Mo Mowlam said, 'Yes, that's the same table, and that window behind you is the same one an IRA rocket came through seven years ago.'"

The room erupted in laughter at this gallows humor—with no one laughing harder than Tony Blair. *My God*, thought Cross, *the likes of Thatcher and Mayhew would have died before telling a story like that—or appreciating any of its ironic humor.*

Just then, as the laughter was subsiding, a searing tone ran through the room. It was the beeper of Carolyn McCarthy, the

Democratic Congresswoman from Long Island. As she frantically tried to extricate the beeper from her pocketbook and shut it off, Moynihan solemnly assured the Prime Minister: "Don't worry. It's not a bomb."

The breakfast ended, Cross walked up to Blair for what he expected to be a routine courtesy handshake.

"It was great to meet you, Mr. Prime Minister," said Cross.

"I think it went well," answered Blair. He paused for a moment, then continued in a low voice, "I heard what you said about David Trimble and Sinn Fein. If you're speaking with Gerry Adams, tell him we're trying to find a way to have Sinn Fein and Trimble engage directly."

"That's encouraging. I'll pass it on," answered Cross.

"It might take a bit of give on both sides, but I agree with you it's important and could be very helpful."

Leaving Blair House, Cross looked at his watch and realized the official White House welcoming reception for Blair was scheduled to begin in about forty-five minutes. He walked over to Tom O'Connell who was standing by his car, waiting to drive Cross back to Capitol Hill.

"So long as I'm down here. I might as well stick around for the whole show," said Cross. "Any votes coming up in the next hour or so?"

"The most there'll be is some procedural vote. Nothing major at all," answered O'Connell.

"Why don't you go back to the office. I'll hang out at the White House. It'll give me another shot at Blair and a chance to talk to Clinton," said Cross.

Only a handful of Congressmen and Senators made it to the ceremony. There was, however, a full compliment of Cabinet heads, NSC officials and State Department types. There was also the Marine Corps Band playing *Hail to the Chief*, *God Save the Queen* and the *Star Spangled Banner*. Then the welcoming remarks by Clinton and the response by Blair. Cross watched Clinton closely as Blair spoke. Clearly Clinton was pleased. Blair was saying what any British Prime Minister would be expected to say about the historic relationship between the two countries. But with body language and inflection he was going above and beyond the call of duty. He was making it clear that Bill Clinton was his friend and he was proud to be standing with him. Blair was giving Clinton what he desperately had to have with the Lewinsky scandal swirling about him—affirmation that he was the leader of the free world and that our allies needed him.

Minutes after the ceremony was concluded, the receiving line was set up. Senators and Congressmen were moved to the front where they would be greeted first by Clinton, Blair, Hillary Clinton and Blair's wife Cherie. As Cross approached Clinton, the President greeted him warmly:

"Sean, how are you?"

"Just fine, Mr. President. How are you?"

"I'm doing okay. I think I'll be okay. And I sure appreciate that call you made."

"Thank you Mr. President," said Cross.

"Tony, this is Congressman Cross."

"I know. We just had a breakfast meeting," said Blair.

"How did it go?" asked Clinton.

"I believe it went fine," answered Blair.

"Yeah. It was very positive," said Cross.

Then, as Cross started to move on to meet the First Lady, Blair grabbed his right arm and said: "I meant what I said about Gerry Adams and Trimble."

"Great. I'll pass it on."

Back in his office at the Cannon Building that afternoon, Cross spoke with Tom O'Connell.

"So, what'd you think of Blair?"

"The guy's okay. Very easy to get along with. None of that pompous British bullshit. More important, I'm convinced he wants a deal in Ireland."

"How far is he willing to go?"

"I don't know if he knows. I suppose a lot will depend on how it all unfolds over the next few months. But I'm sure he wants a political settlement."

"Will he push Trimble?"

"I think so. But the question is how far."

"Listen, you know as well as I do that when the money's on the line, no British prime minister has ever stood up to the unionists."

"You're right. But Blair might be different. He's done more in nine months than any other British prime minister has in history."

"How was Clinton?"

"Very friendly. Very upbeat. Blair certainly gave him a boost."

"Did he say anything about Lewinsky?"

"No. Just to thank me for the phone call. Also, one other thing, and I don't want to read too much into it, but when I asked him how he was doing, he looked a little pensive and all he said was that he thought he'd be okay."

"What do you think?"

"There's probably more there with Lewinsky than he's let on and after all the euphoria from the State of the Union and Hillary's appearance on the *Today* show, reality is starting to set in. I think he realizes he's got a tough time ahead of him."

"How about what Blair said about Adams and Trimble?"

"I'm not sure what it means. But it shows that Blair considers Sinn Fein a legitimate player. And that by itself is important. Anyway I'll tell Gerry about it."

CHAPTER FOURTEEN

Bronx, New York
Mid-June

It was early Saturday afternoon. The day was overcast and gray. An occasional raindrop flecked the windshield of the black Ford crossing the Throgs Neck Bridge, headed for the Bronx.

"Traffic's not too bad," said Cross from the front passenger seat.

"Thank God there's not a fucking Yankee game today, or we'd never get there," said Jack Kilbride in his typically hard-edged style.

Kilbride was a plainclothes sergeant in the NYPD. He still sported the same almost totally bald crew cut he'd gotten in Marine boot camp almost forty years before.

"Jack, these names are great," said Cross, reading over the typewritten sheet Kilbride had prepared for him. "Just what I'm looking for. You're sure all this shit's on target?"

"Every fucking word. I've got good sources."

Kilbride had been on the job more than thirty years and would be retiring sometime in the next six months. Ever since Cross had been elected to Congress, Kilbride had been available to help, donating hours of volunteer time virtually every week. Just last month, he'd arranged with Howard Briggs to work on the McGrath and Williamson cases. Today, though, he and Cross were on their own time. This one would be off the books.

Kilbride paid the bridge toll and turned onto the Cross Bronx Expressway, heading for the Major Deegan and on to Gaelic Park at the north end of the Bronx.

Gaelic Park was an antiquated—some would say dilapidated—structure used for decades by generations of Irish immigrants to stage their hurling and football matches. As befits most Irish locales, Gaelic Park had a bar, just next to the playing field.

Kilbride parked down the block. "You think this fucking mick is going to show up?" he asked, turning off the ignition.

"Yeah. Liam Naughton might be a prick, but he wouldn't duck out," answered Cross.

Kilbride reached down and pulled up his right pant leg, just enough to adjust his ankle holster and pistol. Then he reached back under his loose-fitting sport jacket to the small of his back, where he adjusted the .45 Glock automatic.

"Let's get started," said Kilbride.

He and Cross got out of the car and walked toward the bar.

Cross first met Liam Naughton in 1984, soon after Naughton had arrived from Belfast and settled in the Bronx. Like so many northern Irish Catholic men who came of age in the '60s, Naughton had grown up under the unyielding yoke of loyalist intimidation and British oppression. Liam's home was a cold-water flat in a Catholic ghetto on the lower Falls Road in West Belfast, where he was raised with his five brothers and three sisters. His father, though a skilled carpenter, was almost always out of work. Liam's mother died when he was fourteen. The following year Liam dropped out of school and for the next decade, when he could find work at all, went from one odd job to another—usually as a barman, occasionally as a docker.

Neither Liam nor anyone in his family had ever been political. They'd come to accept injustice as their fate. When Catholics began a peaceful civil rights movement in 1968 and 1969, Liam took no part in it. To the extent he thought about it at all, he thought it might improve their lot. Certainly, conditions couldn't get any worse.

But they did. Much worse. Outraged by what they deemed Catholic impudence, armed loyalist gangs—with police acquiescence and indeed encouragement—rampaged through Catholic neighborhoods, brutally battering all those in their way and burning down block after block of Catholic houses. Liam's home was one of them. His father and each of his brothers and sisters grabbed whatever they could of their meager belongings and moved in with aunts, uncles, and cousins throughout Belfast.

Four days later, Liam's youngest brother Colm, who had barely turned twelve, was standing in his aunt's living room when a bullet crashed through the first-floor window and struck his throat, killing him instantly. Those who knew Liam over the years said he was never the same after Colm's murder.

Liam's first act was to join the IRA—defunct for years but now hastily regrouping in a desperate attempt to protect the besieged Catholics. And Liam was a brutally effective soldier, killing loyalist paramilitaries. And police officers. And then British soldiers.

Liam struck quickly and in the dark of night. There was never any evidence linking him to the shootings. Still, word got back to the Brits. In May 1972 a British paratrooper unit raided the Belfast flat where Liam was living. He was taken to the Interrogation Centre, where for weeks he was brutally tortured. But Liam gave them nothing.

After that, the Brits shipped Naughton to Long Kesh prison camp in Lisburn, just outside Belfast. In those years the IRA had virtual POW status at Long Kesh. Conditions were harsh, but the IRA ran its own compounds, known as cages. Lasting friendships were formed there. Much of the leadership that would guide the republican movement over the next quarter century—men like Gerry Adams and Richard McAuley—spent time in the cages.

But Liam Naughton took no part in the joking or political discussions. Colm's murder and the brutality Liam suffered had changed him forever. When he was released about two years later, his friends on the outside knew straightaway that he was entirely different from the easygoing, good-natured guy they'd knocked around with over the years. Now he was distant, remote. And lethal.

Reporting back to his IRA unit, Naughton was more effective than ever. And still the Brits could pin nothing on him. They would periodically lift him and brutalize him some more. But he was impervious to it all. Until he married Delia in 1981 and they had their first son, Colm, named after Liam's murdered brother.

On a November night in 1983 Naughton was returning to his home in Lenadoon. It was a few minutes past midnight, and Naughton was taking the long way around the rear of the housing estate. He'd seen the British Army patrols at the estate's front entrance. *No point in needless confrontation*, he thought.

Liam was about two blocks from home when flames shot into the dark sky. Instinctively he knew what had happened. Running as fast as he could, Liam turned the corner to see his house engulfed in fire. But what he was looking for was Delia and Colm. The street was already flooded with neighbors.

Filled with panic, his eyes darted about the crowd until he saw them. He breathed a sigh of relief. Delia, wearing a light robe, was holding Colm tightly to her. He was wrapped in a blanket, crying hysterically. Liam embraced them both.

"Thank God I was still awake. I was sitting up for you in the living room," said Delia. "I heard the upstairs window smash, and just a second or two later, some sort of firebomb came flying through the front window. Fortunately, the wee child had fallen asleep next to me on the couch. I was able to grab him and be out the door in seconds. Otherwise, we'd have been dead, so we would."

As Delia broke into sobs, Liam held her tight. He knew straightaway this had been a professional job. One firebomb in the bedroom. The other in the living room. It was a miracle Delia and Colm had survived.

"There were two cars," he heard a neighbor say. "As soon as the bombs were thrown, the cars raced away. Right through the front of the estate."

Those bastards. That's what those Brits were doing at the entrance, thought Liam. *They were covering for the fuckers that threw the bombs.*

Over the next few days, Liam and the local IRA commanders pieced together what was happening. It confirmed Naughton's first instinct: the Brits were working in concert with the UVF to get him. And if necessary, they'd murder his family to do it.

It was the toughest decision he'd ever made. But he decided he had no choice. And the IRA agreed. That week Liam left for New

York, taking Delia and Colm with him. The morning he left, two UVF commanders were incinerated by car bombs.

Naughton settled in the Bronx and, like thousands of other Irish illegals, went underground. The network was in place, and Liam got phony papers—Social Security card, work visa, driver's license—so he could find a job and rent an apartment. For his first years in New York, he was Patrick Regan from Sligo.

Naughton could have remained in the shadows forever. But he was still an IRA member, and he still had a job to do. Actually, he had several. One was to brief trusted Americans on what was happening at home. Since Sinn Fein members, and, of course, IRA members, were still barred from the country, Liam's briefings were particularly helpful. It was at one of these that Cross first met Naughton. They continued to meet one-on-one every few months for the next several years.

Cross's reaction to Naughton was mixed. Obviously, the guy knew his stuff and was wired to the top people. He expressed himself well. But there was the steel-hard look in his eyes. The lack of humor—or any feeling at all. And, of course, the mementoes of his long nights in the interrogation centres—the crushed left jaw, the deep scar below his right eye, the crooked nose.

Naughton's other job was to acquire guns. Any guns he could, however he could. From what Cross heard, Naughton quickly established a well-coordinated supply line of weapons and explosives from the Bronx to Belfast.

As times began to change—the Adams visa, the IRA ceasefire, the Good Friday Agreement—Cross's contact with Naughton became virtually nonexistent. And, over time, Naughton had managed to legalize his status. He got his green card and started his own construction company. It wasn't a big one—primarily sidewalk curbing—but he did pretty well.

About a year after the Good Friday Agreement was signed, Cross began to hear reports that Naughton was opposed to taking the political route. "Gerry Adams has sold us out," he'd say to anyone who'd listen. But Cross paid him no attention. The guys against the agreement were yesterday's men. By 1999, the only ones left were

Marty McDevitt and his Real IRA, and they'd lost all support after the massacre at Omagh. But with Trimble and the unionists throwing repeated roadblocks in the way of the peace process and the Brits refusing to confront Trimble often enough, McDevitt's movement managed to stay alive. Naughton went back to his old job of shipping weapons to Ireland—this time to Marty McDevitt. The supply line was nowhere near as effective as it had been in the '80s, but enough got through to cause some trouble. But now the Real IRA was on life support. The World Trade Center tragedy in 2001 had brought cooperation among Sinn Fein, American law enforcement and British intelligence to an unprecedented level. The primary targets were Islamic fundamentalism but the Real IRA was cut off as well. Naughton was lucky if he could get a bullet or two through. Still, he was McDevitt's man in America, and that's why Cross wanted to see him today.

Kilbride opened the front door of the bar. He let his eyes adjust to the darkness, looked around, and nodded to Cross that it was okay. Sean was wearing jeans, a light blue shirt, and a dark blue nylon jacket.

"Your man's at the end of the bar," said Kilbride, looking toward the wiry, white-haired man sitting on a stool, whiskey glass in hand, talking to the bartender. Naughton was the only customer in the room.

"It's show time," answered Cross.

"I'll sit here," said Kilbride, pointing to a table just inside the door. "It gives me a clear view, and I'll be out of earshot."

Cross walked toward Naughton, who turned to greet him.

"Hey, Sean, how're you keeping?" asked Naughton as he extended his hand.

"I've been better. But there's lots of others doing worse," answered Cross, shaking Liam's outstretched hand and sitting on the stool beside him.

"What'll it be, Sean?" asked the bartender.

"Jameson's on the rocks, Paddy," said Cross.

The bartender quickly poured Sean's drink, then walked to the opposite end of the bar.

"Well, Sean, it's not every day I get to meet with a congressman. Certainly not with one as distinguished as yourself. How can I help you?"

"Don't fuck with me, Liam. You know why I'm here. Your friend McDevitt."

"Marty's a good man."

"He's a fucking psycho."

"At least he doesn't sell out his people."

"Listen, Liam, you and McDevitt have lost the debate, so I don't give a shit what either of you thinks about Ireland."

"So why're you taking up my time?"

"Because I think McDevitt was involved in knocking off McGrath and Williamson, and probably Kilpatrick."

"That's an awful lot of work for a psycho with no support for what he's doing."

"Working with the Brits—or the CIA—and God knows who else—might make his job easier."

"Now you're fucking dreaming."

"Liam, I'm not here to argue with you. I'm here to tell you to tell McDevitt to knock this shit off. And since you're his fucking friend in America, he'll listen to you."

"And why should I do anything you tell me to do?" asked Naughton with an ice-cold stare.

"Because if you don't, I'll fucking destroy you."

Naughton fixed his eyes on Cross and put down his drink.

"Fuck you, Congressman. It's time for me to go."

"No, Liam. Fuck *you.* You're going nowhere." Cross removed the list Kilbride had given him from his shirt pocket.

"Liam, how's your business doing?"

"Fucking great. I make a lot more than some fucking congressman."

"Well, I hope you've put enough money aside to pay all the back taxes and penalties and fines you're going to get hit with."

"What the fuck are you talking about?"

"Well, on this list alone, I see fifteen illegals who've been working for you in the last six months. They have phony Social Security numbers. Probably half their pay is off the books."

"You fucking bastard."

"Shit, by the time the IRS is finished with this, your company'll be in fucking mothballs and you won't have a nickel left."

"I always knew you were no fucking good."

"And Liam, don't try anything crazy. Otherwise, another one of your dark secrets might get out."

Naughton stared blankly.

"Remember Seamus McCoy? Your old friend in the Real IRA. The guy I met with in Dundalk three years ago who got blown up. You know, the meeting the *Telegraph* wrote about."

"Seamus was a good man."

"He also had a big mouth. He told me you were running the operation over here. And that you didn't have to raise money the old way—the dinners and passing the hat in the bars and all that."

"This is fucking madness," said Naughton, lighting a cigarette.

"No, madness is getting involved in drug deals with those Dominicans in Washington Heights and cutting in on the Colombians in Queens."

"You can't prove any of that," snapped Naughton, betraying anxiety to Cross for the first time ever.

"Liam. I know it's true and you know it's true. But I don't have to prove it. If Mickey Brannigan or Danny Lacy writes a column on your drug escapades—and your gunrunning and your IRS problems—it's curtain time for you. Because if the FBI doesn't get you, then Immigration will. And if the Dominicans don't get you, the Colombians will."

"You'd sell out one of your own . . ."

"Spare me that shit. It's up to you. You can talk to McDevitt or—you get fucked!"

For a long moment Naughton was silent. Then he said "I'll see what I can do. I'll see what I can do."

"Do it," said Cross, getting up from the stool and walking from the bar with Kilbride.

CHAPTER FIFTEEN

March 1998

The five weeks following Blair's visit to Washington saw little progress in the peace talks. Cross relayed Blair's message to Adams, and Gerry was hopeful. But things went nowhere. Trimble continued his refusal to engage or even acknowledge Sinn Fein, offering not even a hint of any concession. Masterfully, George Mitchell had managed to keep all the parties at the table. But there had to be a limit even to Mitchell's patience, thought Cross. The stalemate couldn't be allowed to drag on forever.

It was against this dreary backdrop that St. Patrick's Day festivities began on Friday evening, March 13. There was the *Irish-America Magazine* annual gala at the Plaza Hotel in Manhattan. The event honored the "Top 100" Irish Americans, including Sean Cross, and attracted many well-to-do members of the Irish-American community. For the past several years it had also attracted players from the Irish peace process. This year Gerry Adams and Martin McGuinness were there. They were accompanied by Rita O'Hare, a feisty Belfast-born redhead who would be taking over for Mairead Keane as Sinn Fein's American representative.

When Adams and McGuinness spoke, they received larger and more sustained ovations than anyone else. But Gary McMichael from the loyalist Ulster Democratic Party (UDP) was there as well. His father, John McMichael, was thought to have been behind the assassination attempt on Gerry Adams back in

1984. The IRA had subsequently killed him. This night McMichael spoke from the stage just minutes after Adams had concluded his remarks. McMichael seemed pleasantly surprised by the cordial response he received from this audience of Irish Americans, thanking him for demonstrating the courage and leadership David Trimble so sorely lacked.

Throughout the evening, Cross sat in the front row alongside Adams and McGuinness. Several times Cross turned and looked around the ornate Plaza ballroom. And each time, he saw the faces of rich, high-society Irish Americans who until just a few years ago would have looked upon Gerry Adams with absolute contempt and been unaware that Gary McMichael or his late father even existed. But now these rich micks were on board. And that's what counted.

The program ended just before eleven o'clock. Now it was time for Adams, McGuinness, and Cross to return to their true base—the Towerview Ballroom in Woodside, where a packed crowd of more than six hundred was patiently waiting. Howard Briggs, who headed the security detail whenever Sinn Fein leaders were in town, walked over with three guys from his squad.

"Sean, we'll take you guys down the back stairs. We've got a motorcade set up on Fifty-ninth Street. We'll be able to get you over the bridge and out to the Towerview in less than twenty minutes."

"I still feel a bit uncertain, being driven about in police cars," said Adams with a wry smile.

"You've no choice, Gerry," said McGuinness. "Your adoring public anxiously awaits."

The Towerview Ballroom was a ramshackle two-story building located at Sixty-first Street and Roosevelt Avenue in the Irish enclave of Woodside, Queens. Situated just beneath the el, the walls of the Towerview would literally quake when the IRT train lumbered along the overhead tracks. There was nothing upscale or elite about the Towerview, but it was solid and dependable. And so were the people who frequented it. They had been there for the republican movement and never wavered, even during the bleakest days.

Now, entering the Towerview's lobby, Adams, McGuinness, and Cross were welcomed by Tom Manton, who represented Woodside in Congress. The NYPD detectives led them up the staircase to the second floor, where they waited outside the ballroom door while the NYPD Emerald Society Pipe Band tuned their pipes and prepared to escort them in. As the pipers began to play the stirring rebel song "A Nation Once Again," the doors to the ballroom were opened.

At the first sight of Gerry Adams and Martin McGuinness, the crowd was on its feet, applauding and roaring its greeting. And when Adams and McGuinness stepped onto the stage, the roar became deafening. Cross and Manton knew enough to stand to the side. This night was for Adams and McGuinness. It was as if they were being welcomed home.

Cross and Manton gave brief speeches, each urging loyalty to Sinn Fein in the climactic weeks ahead. McGuinness then spoke to the crowd. Yes, Sinn Fein realized a united Ireland was not attainable at this time. Yes, Sinn Fein would compromise to reach a fair agreement that provided the framework for eventual unification. But no, Sinn Fein would never compromise on principle. It would never yield to pressure—no matter how strong or from what source—to sign an agreement that did not guarantee human rights and establish an all-Ireland dimension.

When Adams was introduced, the assemblage again cheered loud and long. But as the Sinn Fein president began his remarks, the crowd fell silent. Just then, the walls began to quake and the No. 7 train rumbled by overhead. Adams smiled, looked toward the window, and quipped, "That must be the peace train. Someone should tell David Trimble."

The crowd erupted into laughter. As soon as the laughter subsided, Adams turned deadly serious.

"Once before," he said, "the British government squandered an IRA ceasefire, with disastrous consequences. That must not be allowed to happen again. David Trimble must not be allowed to set an agenda of no compromise and no surrender. The British government must not allow itself to be dictated to by David Trimble and the Ulster unionists. Today Ireland has within its grasp the opportunity for a true and lasting peace for all its people. This would never have happened were it not for the United States—President Clinton, members of Congress, and most of all, you yourselves. I implore you to continue to stand with us during the perilous days and weeks ahead. And if you do, we will prevail."

It was late in the afternoon on Sunday, March 15. Sean Cross stepped off the elevator on the sixth floor of the Phoenix Park Hotel in Washington, D.C., walked down the hall, and knocked on the door of Gerry Adams's room.

"Sean, come in. It's grand of you to come by," said Adams.

"Thanks for seeing me," answered Cross. "We really didn't have a chance to talk the other night in New York."

"No. There certainly was a lot of running about. The crowds were brilliant, though. Especially at the Towerview."

"How are the talks looking?"

"Very dicey. I wasn't exaggerating the other night when I said Trimble's not giving an inch. It's hard to see how much longer this can go on."

"Any chance the ceasefire will break?"

"No. There's no worry of that for now. But the longer this goes on with nothing getting done, the greater the chance that something will go wrong."

"McDevitt's group?" asked Cross.

"Yes. They're certainly capable of doing something disruptive. But the loyalist paramilitaries could start in as well, killing some innocent Catholic. Then there might be retaliation. But there's no need for any of this. The Brits just have to put the pressure on Trimble."

"Do they have that kind of leverage?"

"I believe they do. But Trimble is convinced they'll never use it."

"Is it possible Trimble's just playing the tough negotiator and plans to make a deal in the end?" asked Cross.

"Maybe, but the danger is he's boxing himself in. He's taken such a hard line the unionists will be outraged if he makes any compromise at all."

"Which is why it's so helpful you've been preparing your own people. Letting them know you won't be getting a united Ireland this time around."

"That's only common sense. There's no point in making an agreement if it's not acceptable to your own community."

"When are you meeting the president?"

"Tomorrow at the White House. Just before the Ireland Fund Dinner."

"When's Trimble meeting him?"

"I believe on St. Patrick's Day, the night of the White House party."

"Did Sandy Berger or Steinberg hint at what Clinton's going to bring up?"

"They told me to expect nothing in particular. I'm on the same page as he is, though. Sinn Fein wants a negotiated settlement. It's Trimble who's out of step."

"I just hope Clinton's mind is on the meeting."

"What do you mean?"

"Tonight on *60 Minutes*, Kathleen Willey is going to claim that Clinton attacked her in the Oval Office."

"Oh, yeah. I heard about that. Do you think it'll have much impact?"

"I have absolutely no idea. So far, I've been wrong all along. The more that comes out against Clinton, the more popular he gets. But I guess that could just as easily turn around."

"Is Clinton going to survive?"

"Like I said, so far he's doing great. But I don't know what's going to happen by the time it's all over. Also I don't know what the hell the problem is with this guy. It's like he's got a death wish. And no matter how the whole thing turns out, it could tear the country apart."

It was just after noon on Monday, March 16. Sean Cross, Mary Rose, and Jack Pender entered the British Embassy on Massachusetts Avenue for the Brits' second annual St. Patrick's Day party. Unlike last year's event, however, Gerry Adams would be in attendance. Drinking a ginger ale, Cross walked about the main dining room during the cocktail reception preceding the lunch. In a single glance he was able to spot all the party leaders participating in the peace talks. *Christ,* thought Cross, *they're all here. It's St. Patrick's Day. The most important time of the year in Ireland. And they're all celebrating it here in America.*

Cross said a polite hello to David Trimble, who smiled briefly. He then shook hands with John Alderdice, head of the small but respected Alliance Party. As he turned from Alderdice, Cross heard a very distinctive, highly irreverent female British voice, one he had come to know well.

"Hey, mate. Happy St. Patrick's Day."

"Mo, it's great to see you. Have you settled this yet?" asked Cross.

"You know fucking well I haven't settled a fucking thing, so don't be giving me a hard time," replied the Rt. Hon. Marjorie "Mo" Mowlam, the British secretary of state for Northern Ireland.

"I can see the talks have done nothing to improve your disposition."

"Talking with you does even less for it."

Mo Mowlam was one of a kind. *Sui generis,* the Jesuits would say. She was a rough, streetwise politician who didn't know how to back away from a fight. Anyone who spoke to her for more than a minute realized that she couldn't have even an ounce of patrician blood in her.

She was fiercely loyal to Tony Blair, but Sinn Fein trusted her. The unionists—including David Trimble and Ken Maginnis—showed nothing but undisguised contempt for her. But no one despised Mo more than the British bureaucrats—particularly those in the Northern Ireland Office. During the previous ten months, they'd constantly worked against her, leaking internal memos to the unionists, anonymously telling reporters how unsuited she was for her job. But Mo let neither the bureaucrats nor the brain tumor she'd been battling for the past year deter her even in the slightest. The frustration, however, of seeing the talks going nowhere was wearing her down, which was what Mo now wanted to discuss.

"Sean, do you have a moment to talk?"

"Sure."

"How about a bit of a walk in the garden?"

"Let's go."

Cross opened the glass door, and he and Mo walked out into the beautiful, sunny spring day.

"You're looking much better, Mo. How're you feeling?"

"Terrific. I truly am. I've all my energy back."

"How are the talks going?"

"Not so terrific. They're stuck on dead center."

"Can anything be done?"

"I'm convinced there's never going to be any movement unless we impose a deadline."

"How does Mitchell feel about that?"

"He's for it. How do you think the Congress will react?"

"You won't find much opposition. In fact, Adams and McGuinness have been asking for a deadline since day one. When do you think the announcement'll come?"

"Probably in a week or so."

"Will that get Trimble to move?"

"I don't know if anything can move Trimble. But the Shinners have to be ready to move as well. Because once the talks get going—if they get going—they're going to move very quickly."

"I think Sinn Fein's up to it. They've been preparing for this moment for years," said Cross.

"I fucking hope you're right," answered Mowlam.

The Great Hall of the National Building Museum, located on Washington's F Street, was filled to capacity for the annual Ireland Fund dinner. The cocktail hour was ending, and many hundreds of men in black tie and women in evening dress were finding their way to their tables, located around a large fountain in the center of the hall and amidst the eight colossal Corinthian columns, which reached seventy-five feet to the ceiling dome. The surroundings might have been Italian Renaissance, but the atmosphere was entirely Irish. The strains of "Danny Boy" were in the air, and talk of the peace process was on everyone's lips.

Cross and Mary Rose, as well as Jack Pender and his wife, Laura, were guests of Irish-American insurance executives who bought a table of tickets every year. Their table was to the left of the dais and adjacent to the fountain.

"You better watch your drinking, Jack," laughed Cross, "or you'll end up underwater."

"That'd be better than listening to you go off again on the chances for the Irish peace process," answered Pender.

"Seriously, Congressman, is there any hope?" asked Sean King, the president of Shamrock Life Insurance Company.

"That's just what I asked Mo Mowlam this afternoon," said Cross. "It's the question everyone's asking."

"Well, what do you think?" asked Tom McShane, Shamrock's senior vice president.

"If I had to bet, I'd say yes," answered Cross. "But they've got to set a deadline. Blair will have to lean on Trimble. And—I think this is the most important thing—Clinton's got to stay engaged. He's got to stay on top of it."

"Do you think he will?" asked King.

"From everything I've seen so far—yeah," replied Cross. "But I'll get a better idea when I talk to Gerry. He was meeting with Clinton tonight."

"What time?" asked McShane.

"About five thirty," said Cross.

"Christ, it's almost seven forty-five," interjected Pender.

"Yeah, I thought he'd be here by now," said Cross. "Maybe the meeting started late."

The evening's honoree was Jean Kennedy Smith, who'd be stepping down as ambassador in a few months. Speaker after speaker, including her brother Ted, hailed her great work. Bertie Ahern, in a not so subtle dig at the State Department Anglophiles, pointed out that "like Frank Sinatra, she did it her way." Ahern went on to say that the talks were entering their most critical phase ever and it was time for all parties to move away from outdated positions and negotiate honestly for a real peace. Cross looked across the fountain to where David Trimble was seated. It was a considerable distance away and the lights were dim. But Cross could see that Trimble's face was flaming. He could also see that Adams and Richard McAuley had arrived. They were seated about ten tables away from Trimble.

The speeches concluded and, the main course finished, Cross edged around the fountain and worked his way to Adams's table.

"Your meeting must've gone on for quite a while," said Cross.

"It did indeed," answered Adams, "and the president was dead on. He knows that Trimble's the only one who's not moving."

"He knows everything that's been going on at the talks," McAuley jumped in. "His grasp of detail is amazing."

"As well as his grasp of the larger picture," said Adams.

"Did he mention anything about Lewinsky?"

"Nothing specific, of course. But he let us know he thinks he's under siege from the Republicans," said Adams.

"The last few days have been rough," Cross agreed. "I'm sure the Kathleen Willey interview didn't help."

"How damaging do you think it was?" asked McAuley.

"Not as bad as most people expected it to be."

"You don't feel she was believable?" asked McAuley.

"Not completely," answered Cross. "And that's the way it always seems to be with Clinton. Whether it's Gennifer Flowers or Lewinsky, or now Willey, you get the impression they're not telling the full truth. But neither is Clinton."

The events on St. Patrick's Day itself went smoothly for Adams and Cross. The morning began in Cross's office with a reception. More than thirty members of Congress showed up to eat soda bread, drink coffee, and get a chance to speak with Adams. To each of them his message was clear and direct: time is running out. Trimble must begin to negotiate seriously.

No one disputed Adams's analysis.

At five of twelve, Adams and Cross entered the Rayburn Room for the annual Speaker's lunch. Standing about fifteen feet inside, Mary Rose and David Trimble were engaged in cordial conversation. Seeing one another, Adams and Mary Rose warmly exchanged

St. Patrick's Day greetings. Then Adams extended his right hand toward Trimble and, in a pleasant tone, said, "Hello, David. How are you keeping?"

Ignoring Adams's outstretched hand, Trimble placed both his hands in his pockets, said nothing, and walked away toward the far side of the room.

"Not very promising," Cross said ruefully.

Adams just smiled and shook his head.

During the next ten minutes or so, the remaining invited guests arrived. Combined with the media, it made for wall-to-wall people. Then someone gave the signal. Seconds later, the blare of bagpipes could be heard from the outer hallway. Shortly after that, the pipers made their grand entrance into the Rayburn Room, leading the way for Bill Clinton, who was flanked by Bertie Ahern and Newt Gingrich.

When Clinton spotted Adams, he walked right over to him, shook hands, and placed his hand on Gerry's shoulder. The cameras flashed furiously.

"Gerry, I think our meeting went well last night."

"It was very positive indeed, Mr. President. I appreciate all the time you gave us."

"This is very important to me, Gerry. We just can't lose this opportunity. We can't."

"Your involvement means so much to us."

"Well, I'll be with you all the way. Believe me, I'll do whatever I can."

Moments later, Cross saw that Clinton and Trimble were alone at the far corner of the room. Clinton was doing virtually all the talking. He appeared calm but insistent. Trimble said little, his face growing increasingly red. When Trimble did speak, Clinton listened intently, slowly stroking his chin with his left hand. As Trimble concluded, Clinton said only a few words. Then the president lightly touched Trimble's left shoulder and slowly walked away. There was no handshake. The president's lips were pursed.

Leaning toward Adams, Cross whispered, "How's that for bad body language?"

"I'd say there's no peace agreement yet," answered Adams.

The guests were soon seated at their assigned tables. The formal program was unremarkable. Gingrich was polite and cordial as he welcomed Clinton and said the Republican Party would stand with the president in the search for peace. Clinton thanked the Speaker and again urged the Irish parties not to let this best hope for peace slip from their grasp. And Bertie Ahern thanked the Americans for all they'd done, and were still doing. But despite the pleasantries, there was an underlying tension in the room that had nothing to do with the peace-talks impasse. St. Patrick might have driven the snakes from Ireland, but his spirit was not formidable enough to drive the specters of Monica Lewinsky, Kathleen Willey, and presidential impeachment from the Rayburn Room. The festivities concluded, the guests slowly made their way toward the door. Cross stood near the rear of the room, waiting for Adams, who was accommodating every photo request. Clinton walked toward Adams and motioned Cross to join them. Putting his hand on Adams's shoulder, Clinton lowered his head and drew them close to him.

"Everyone is where they should be," said the president. "Everyone except Trimble. I don't know what I can do. But I'm meeting with him tonight before the party and I'll try again."

Tom O'Connell inched his black Jeep Cherokee through the various security checkpoints, drove through the opened iron gate, and pulled into the parking area at the east entrance to the White House. Sean and Mary Rose stepped from the sturdy vehicle into the crisp early evening air.

"Thanks for the lift," said Cross. "I'll see you in the morning."

"Have a good time," answered O'Connell. "But remember not to drink all the booze. You're not shanty Irish anymore."

"At least I'm not supposed to be," replied Cross.

It was quarter past six. The reception was scheduled to begin at six thirty. Yet the walkway was already crowded with early arrivals. *This is the first Irish event I've ever seen where anyone's been on time, never mind early*, thought Cross. *Maybe this is the age of miracles.*

Identifying themselves to the security man, who checked off their names on the appropriate lists, Cross and Mary Rose walked through the gate and up toward the east entrance, where they were greeted by the sound of bagpipes. Once inside the White House, they strolled down the spacious first-floor corridor and up a marble staircase.

It wasn't yet six thirty, but the second floor was more than half full. Not surprisingly, the most crowded room was the State Dining Room, where the food was located. There was a bar there as well. To the extent that Irish cuisine exists, it was laid out in the State Dining Room. Smoked fishes with horseradish, poached salmon with cucumber salad, Irish cheeses with soda bread. And the Irish-American staple, corned beef and cabbage.

Not being a gourmet, Cross went right for the corned beef and a bottle of Harp. Mary Rose contented herself with poached salmon and a glass of white wine.

As Mary Rose struck up a conversation with Pauline Hennessey, the wife of the Irish Embassy's political counsellor, Cross spotted John Hume in the adjacent Red Room and went over to greet him.

"Happy St. Patrick's Day, John."

"A happy St. Patrick's Day to you as well."

"Any word?"

"No. The president's been meeting with David Trimble for some time."

"It's still going on?"

"As far as I know."

"Let's hope Clinton can move him."

The formal program—Irish entertainment and speeches by Bill Clinton and Bertie Ahern—had been scheduled to begin at seven thirty. It was now ten minutes past nine. There was no sign of Clinton or Ahern, or Trimble. Cross was with Mary Rose in the East Room, where the program would be held. Gerry Adams and Martin McGuinness came up to him. To override the din of the crowd, Adams spoke directly into Cross's left ear.

"I understand the meeting's finally ended," said Adams.

"Who told you?" asked Cross.

"Jim Steinberg."

"Did he say how it went?"

"Just that there was a 'frank exchange of views.' "

"I guess that means Trimble didn't move."

"Yes, but neither did Clinton. That's critical."

As Adams stepped back, six military officers came into the East Room and began moving the packed throng away from the center of the room.

While the Irish suffer from a congenital inability to be orderly, they generally try to be cooperative. So within two or three minutes a path had been cleared and roped off by the military. Then there was a blare of bagpipes, and at the end of the second floor a lone piper began leading the president and Hillary Clinton down the Grand Staircase. They were accompanied by Bertie Ahern and his partner, Celia Larkin. From his vantage point in the East Room just in front of the stage, Cross had a clear view of the Clintons and Ahern and Celia Larkin as they slowly made their way down the hallway. Cross was struck by the irony that Catholic Ireland paid no mind at all to its still-married prime minister escorting his "partner" about the world while the supposedly sophisticated United States was tearing itself apart over a presidential affair.

Once under way, the program moved smoothly. The Celtic band, the step dancers, a Protestant-Catholic youth chorus from Armagh, an Irish tenor, and a reading by *Angela's Ashes* author Frank McCourt entertained the crowd and induced a temporary calm. That calm was obliterated, however, when Clinton stepped to the microphone. The almost frantic applauding, cheering, and roaring went on for minutes.

When the tumult finally subsided, Clinton began speaking.

He's a bit off his game, Cross thought. *The meeting with Trimble really must have been rough.* Cross detected a tightening in Clinton's jaw and noticed that his hands, usually so expressive, were fastened to the lectern. He was also reading more from his prepared text than usual. But as Clinton got into his speech, urging compromise, calling for courageous leadership, the crowd reacted enthusiastically and Clinton responded. His jaw loosened, his hands moved with forceful emphasis, and his voice resonated with rich fervor. He exhorted all the parties to seize this moment in history.

"When I heard the wonderful songs up here and all the eloquence of Irish passion and pain and joy come flooding out of the performers, young and old, I was reminded of that great line from Yeats: 'In dreams begin responsibility.' All the Irish are dreamers. In the next few weeks, if Irish responsibility measures up to Irish dreams, next year's celebration here will be the greatest in the history of this great house."

As Clinton concluded to a tumultuous ovation, Cross thought, *He's ready for the fight. This is going to be a hell of a few weeks.*

It was about a half an hour later that Cross and Mary Rose were approaching Clinton for their formal receiving line photo op. As the military ceremonial officer announced "Congressman Cross and Mrs. Cross," Cross stepped forward and extended his right hand toward Clinton. Instead of shaking hands, however, Clinton made an elaborate display of bowing toward Cross as if Sean were some sort of Irish potentate. Caught off guard, Cross froze for a moment until Clinton broke into a loud laugh and began shaking Cross's hand. Just as suddenly Clinton's face turned dead serious.

"Sean, I tried everything with Trimble. The meeting went on for so long and I tried everything I could think of," said Clinton.

"Do you think you got anywhere?" asked Cross.

"I just can't tell. He's so hard to read. But he has to know how serious we are. After that meeting he has to know."

CHAPTER SIXTEEN

April 9, 1998
Holy Thursday

It was late morning. Sean Cross was in his Massapequa Park office, signing letters and clearing his desk. In a few hours he and Mary Rose would be taking the shuttle from LaGuardia to Washington, D.C. That evening they'd be joined at their apartment by Danny and Kara, who were driving in from Notre Dame. It was to be a quiet, relaxing Easter weekend. At least that's what Mary Rose had in mind when she set the plan in motion back in February.

But since George Mitchell had announced on March 25 that the absolute deadline for peace negotiations was Holy Thursday, no one knew what Holy Week would bring.

The talks were still stalemated. Bertie Ahern and Tony Blair had become directly involved in the negotiations. Indeed, Ahern's mother had died earlier in the week and was buried yesterday in Dublin. Yet the Taioseach had helicoptered back and forth to Belfast for his meetings with the prime minister. And George Mitchell was working literally around the clock.

The huge imponderable was still David Trimble. Did he even want a deal? He certainly didn't appear to be conditioning his people for any concessions or compromise. Just two days before, he had summarily rejected a proposal from Blair and Ahern that, in his eyes, gave too much power to the Irish Republic. The fear was that Trimble would reject anything but a surrender by the nationalists and republicans.

Mitchell had structured the negotiations along three lines, or strands. The first related solely to the six counties of Northern Ireland. Because the unionists were a majority there, Trimble advocated the creation of a Northern Ireland Assembly with strong powers. Adams and Hume saw this as a return to the discredited, unionist-dominated Stormont Parliament. The second strand focused on the creation of cross-border institutions linking the north and the south. To Trimble, this was too much of a united Ireland policy. The third strand centered on a newly created intergovernmental council representing the whole of the British Isles, including Northern Ireland, Ireland, England, Scotland, Wales, and the Isle of Man. This was generally viewed as a harmless sop to unionism.

At about ten forty-five, Anne Kelly told Cross, "Mo Mowlam is on the phone."

Cross wasn't expecting this call. It was midafternoon in Belfast, and Mo was immersed in the final day's negotiations.

"Mo, how are you? How are things going?"

"Sean, we're up against the wall. Time is running out on us."

"How's Trimble?"

"The same as he always is: silly, awkward, and childish. But it's the Irish I'm worried about."

"What's wrong?"

"First off, let me tell you that Bertie Ahern is doing a great job. He truly is."

"Then what the hell's the problem?"

"The Irish negotiators are getting nervous. Did you see that ad by those Irish Americans in today's *Irish Times*?"

"You mean the one placed by the hard-liners?"

"Yes, the one that accuses Ahern of selling out."

"Mo, that ad is bullshit. No one over here's paying any attention to it."

"That may be. But it's having an impact here. The Irish negotiators are afraid they'll be undercut by the Irish Americans."

"Mo, believe me. There's nothing to it."

"Well, then, please do me a favor. Could you ring Bertie and tell him that directly?"

"Sure, Mo, I'll be happy to. But Christ, he is the fucking prime minister. I don't see how I can make that much of a difference."

"It's important he hears from Irish Americans. That's why I'm asking you," said Mowlam in an uncharacteristically somber tone.

"I'll do it right away."

"Thank you, Sean. You can reach him at 522259."

"Good luck, Mo."

"Thank you, mate. We'll bloody well need it."

As soon as Cross hung up with Mowlam, he telephoned Ahern. Ahern was in negotiations, but a secretary took Cross's number. About ten minutes later, Jack Pender told Cross that Dermot Gallagher was on the line. Gallagher was now the Irish government's chief negotiator at Stormont.

"Sean, I see you rang the Taioseach."

"Yeah. Mo said he was concerned about the ad in the *Irish Times*. I told her it was bullshit, but she wanted me to tell him personally."

"Are you sure it's bullshit?"

"Absolutely. I can guarantee you if there's an agreement, and Gerry and Martin sign on to it, 99 percent of Irish Americans will support it."

"That's reassuring. I'll tell it to the Taioseach straightaway."

"Are you going to get an agreement?"

"We're making headway. But it's going very slowly. The unionists are dead set against any meaningful cross-border institutions. And those institutions are essential if Sinn Fein are to be on board."

"And what time is it over there?"

"It's just after four."

"Christ, time really is running out."

Sean Cross looked anxiously at his watch. It was 4:20 P.M. He and Mary Rose looked out the window of the US Air jet at the runway, where they had been sitting since three o'clock.

"Looks like the rain might be letting up," he said to Mary Rose.

Before she could answer, the pilot announced that the flight would be taking off in about ten minutes.

The hour-and-a-half delay was agonizing enough for Cross. But even more excruciating was the fact that he'd lost contact with the outside world. The storm had blocked the plane's airphone system, and he had no idea what was going on in Belfast, where it was now about nine thirty—just two-and-a-half hours before the Mitchell deadline.

The plane landed in Washington at five twenty. Tom O'Connell was waiting at the gate, a harried look on his face.

"I thought you'd never get here. You've got a shitload of calls you have to return right away. We better use the pay phones. Cell phones aren't that reliable from out here."

"What do you hear?" asked Cross as they walked toward the pay-phone area.

"It doesn't look too good," answered O'Connell, handing Cross a full sheet of typed messages.

Cross scanned the page. There were the press calls from *Newsday*, ABC's *Nightline*, BBC, the *Daily News*, and Reuters. But the message that jumped out at him was just above the center of the page:

> Niall O'Dowd
> Rita O'Hare told him Sinn Fein was getting screwed (about 3:50 P.M.)
> Please call

"Shit. What did Niall say?"

"Sinn Fein feels they're getting fucked. The Brits and Dublin are making one concession after the other to Trimble."

"Any details?"

"You'll have to talk to O'Dowd, but basically it looks like the Assembly will be powerful, while the cross-border bodies will barely exist."

Cross tried O'Dowd three times. Each time the line was busy. So he started in on the media calls, not knowing exactly what the situation was. But he thought he knew enough to wing it:

—No. Sinn Fein could not be expected to endorse any agreement that did not contain meaningful all-Ireland provisions.

—Yes. He was very concerned by reports that nationalists and republicans were being sacrificed to appease Trimble.

—Hopefully, there was still time to get the negotiations back on track.

As O'Connell drove him and Mary Rose to their apartment, Cross called the White House and spoke to Bill Parsons, Jim Steinberg's assistant at the National Security Council.

"Bill, I was stuck on a plane for two-and-a-half hours. What's happening?"

"It's going well. I think they're close to wrapping it up."

"I heard there might be some problems."

"Well, they obviously won't be able to get all the details fixed by midnight, but they'll just extend the deadline a few hours."

"I heard Sinn Fein feels they're getting screwed, that Strand Two is being totally watered down."

"No. We're hearing all the problems are being worked out."

"That's odd," Cross said quizzically. "I hope you're right."

"This'll be a tremendous foreign-policy achievement for the president."

"If they get the agreement, it certainly will."

"This will have to go to a referendum in the north and the south in about four to six weeks' time. We should organize a presidential visit with congressmen and senators right after it's ratified."

"Bill, if this works, I can't think of a better idea."

Cross and Mary Rose walked into their apartment. O'Connell followed a few minutes later, after parking his car. Cross looked at the clock. It was six thirty—only a half hour to go before it would be midnight in Belfast.

"I don't know what the hell's going on. Parsons acts like it's all wrapped up. O'Dowd says it's falling apart. This could be a long night," said Cross.

"Why don't I go get some Chinese?" asked O'Connell.

"That'd be great," answered Cross. "I'll get started on the calls."

Cross dialed Niall O'Dowd again. This time he got through. Debbie McGoldrick, Niall's wife and senior editor of the *Irish Voice*, answered the phone.

"Niall's out right now. But I know he was trying to get hold of you. It doesn't look good at all."

"That's the message I got. But I was just talking to Parsons at the NSC, and he says everything's good."

"Obviously, somebody's got this screwed up. I have a number for Ned Harlan—760027. Why don't you call him directly. He should know exactly what Gerry and Martin are thinking. That's the direct line into the Sinn Fein office at Stormont."

"Thanks, Debbie. I'll call him right away."

Cross looked at the clock as he dialed Ned Harlan. It was now eleven forty-five in Belfast. He dialed Ned Harlan—Gerry Adams's closest advisor—at 011-44-1-232-760027.

"Hello," said a female voice with a pronounced northern Irish accent.

"Hi, this is Sean Cross in Washington. Who's this?"

"Ah, Sean, it's Mary Nellis. How're you keeping?"

"I'm doing great. It's you guys I'm wondering about. Could I speak to Ned?"

"You can indeed."

"Hello, Sean."

"Ned, what's happening? I'm getting conflicting reports."

"It's not going well, Sean. Not well at all."

"What's the problem?"

"Trimble's getting what he wants with the Assembly, and there's nothing firm about the cross-border bodies. They just keep weakening them more and more."

"Ned, this isn't what the White House is telling me."

"Then they're not getting the true story. I'm telling you what's happening."

"I believe you. Let me call the NSC right away."

"Thank you, Sean."

O'Connell arrived with the Chinese food. Cross put sweet-and-sour chicken and fried rice on a plate, took a few bites, and dialed Bill Parsons at the White House.

"Bill, I'm afraid there've been some mixed signals."

"What do you mean?"

"Sinn Fein tells me it's going badly. All they see are concessions to Trimble."

"Well, there are always last-minute concessions in any negotiations."

"Bill, from the way Sinn Fein is talking, these concessions are deal breakers. They've been playing ball all along. Trimble doesn't do shit, but he comes in at the end and walks away with the prize."

"Congressman, I really don't think it's that bad. But we'll check it out."

Cross put down the phone and sat silent in exasperation. Mary Rose and O'Connell were sitting on the couch, eating Chinese and looking intently at the television screen. C-SPAN was televising the live BBC feed from outside Stormont. It was after midnight in Belfast, but the floodlights from scores of television stations and camera crews illuminated the Stormont grounds. The BBC announcer said that tension was "approaching fever pitch." Just then the phone rang. Cross picked it up on the first ring. It was Ned Harlan.

"Sean, the situation is very serious. Now Trimble is carrying on about decommissioning."

"I thought everyone had forgotten about that."

"They had—until just now."

"What does this mean?"

"I don't know for certain. But I wouldn't be surprised if Sinn Fein walked out. That's the mood right now. We might be left with no choice."

"You realize how serious that would be?"

"I do indeed, and believe me it's not something we want to do. Not after coming this far. But, as I said, we may have no choice."

Cross hesitated for a moment. "Ned, I'll just say this once so you'll know where I'm coming from. If you have to leave the talks, I'll support your position. Sinn Fein has been straight throughout this process, so you're entitled to that."

"Sean, you've your own interests to look after, and we'll understand any decision you make. But we'd certainly appreciate your support."

"Let me make some calls, and we'll hope for the best."

Cross ate a few more mouthfuls of Chinese food and sipped Coke from a glass.

"What's going on?" asked O'Connell.

"I don't know for sure," answered Cross, "but I think the Brits, and to some extent the Irish, want to put together a deal with Trimble and then present it to Sinn Fein as a fait accompli."

"So Gerry and Martin will be boxed in. It's literally the last minute. They'll have nowhere to go," said O'Connell.

"Ned Harlan tells me they'll go out the door," replied Cross.

"Would they do that?" asked Mary Rose.

"Yeah. If they think it's a bad deal, they'll have to."

"Even though they'll take the blame?" asked O'Connell.

"Yeah. These guys are in for the long haul," said Cross.

"And you told Harlan you'd stick with them?" asked Mary Rose.

"Yeah," said Cross.

"Well, that'll end your days at the White House," said O'Connell. "Looks like you're back on the outside again."

Cross's smile was grim. "Guess I was just meant to be shanty Irish. But while I'm still in the game, let me try something," he said, picking up the phone.

"Who are you calling?" asked O'Connell.

"The Irish government. The media. But first the White House. Maybe I'm naive, but I don't know if the NSC is getting the full story."

Cross dialed the White House and was put through to Jim Steinberg.

"Congressman, Bill Parsons tells me you've been concerned. We really think it's moving okay."

"Jim, I'm hearing just the opposite. I'm hearing the whole thing could crash."

"I don't see how."

"Believe me, Jim, I'm not trying to argue with you and I hope you're right. But I was just talking to Ned Harlan. He's—"

"I know who Harlan is. Gerry's top guy."

"Right. He tells me Sinn Fein is on the verge of walking out."

"Walking out?"

"Yeah. And he seemed pretty serious."

"I'll try to check that out."

"Great."

"One way or the other though, Congressman, if we get an agreement, all of us here need to support it."

"Jim, if Sinn Fein's not on board, I don't see how I can."

"It's important that you do."

"We'll have to see."

As Cross put down the phone, O'Connell said, "From what I heard, you're definitely going to be out in the cold again."

Cross then called Pat Hennessey, the political counsellor at the Irish Embassy, and told him what he'd told Steinberg. In true diplomatic fashion, Hennessey said he would pass the information to the appropriate party.

It was now nine thirty—two thirty in the morning Belfast time—when the telephone rang. It was BBC Radio.

"Congressman Cross, we understand you might have some idea of what's going on in the talks."

"I know a little, but I'm not sure how much," replied Cross.

"Well, our station's broadcasting live from Stormont. Would you be willing to do a live interview in a minute or so?"

"That would be fine," said Cross, wondering if Harlan had put BBC up to the call and realizing this would be one way to communicate directly with all the parties.

"Grand. Just give us a few seconds to switch this to the control room."

Cross was on hold when he heard the call-waiting signal. He quickly pressed the dial-tone button.

"Sean, this is Dermot Gallagher. I'm at Stormont. I understand you've heard there's a problem."

"Yes, Dermot. But I'm about to do a live interview with BBC. Can I get right back to you?"

"Of course."

"Are you at the same number as before?"

"Yes."

"Fine. I'll talk to you in a few minutes."

Cross pressed the button and heard a female voice with a British accent at the other end.

"Congressman Cross?"

"Yes."

"I thought we'd lost you."

"Sorry. It's a very busy night."

"It is indeed. Are you ready?"

"Yeah."

"Grand. Our presenter will be Elizabeth Frammingham."

"Fine."

"Congressman Cross," said Frammingham, "the midnight deadline passed more than two hours ago and nothing has been heard from any of the talks' participants. Can you tell us anything?"

"Yes, I can. I've been talking with Sinn Fein, and they're very concerned about the deterioration of the talks."

"Because the deadline has passed?"

"No, because it appears one concession after the other is being made to the Ulster Unionists at the expense of Sinn Fein and, more importantly, the nationalist community."

"Just how serious are their concerns?"

"Serious enough . . ." Cross hesitated. "Serious enough that Sinn Fein is considering walking out of the talks."

"Walking out! Do they realize what that would mean?"

"Yes, they do. And they're very reluctant. But they feel they're running out of options."

"Well, thank you very much, Congressman."

"Thank you."

"As you have just heard, Congressman Sean Cross from the United States has told BBC that Sinn Fein is considering walking out of the talks. This is Elizabeth Frammingham, BBC News."

When Cross finished with BBC, he telephoned Dermot Gallagher and relayed what Ned Harlan had said.

"Sean, I'm glad you've told me this," said Gallagher. "We can't afford to lose Sinn Fein."

"Can you do anything?" asked Cross.

"We'll try to firm up the language in Strands One and Two for them. Also, we've been holding back on the prisoners. I think we can offer them something on that."

Not long after ten, *Nightline* phoned Cross to cancel his appearance that evening because no agreement had been reached. Several New York and Washington reporters called to trade information—they didn't have much—and to speculate. Cross watched C-SPAN's live BBC coverage from Stormont but learned nothing new. Everyone was still behind closed doors. Finally, around 1:00 A.M., Cross decided to go to bed.

Just before he turned off the light, Mary Rose asked, "Well, what do you think?"

"I hope I'm wrong, but I don't think it's going to work."

As soon as his head hit the pillow, Cross fell sound asleep. The next thing he heard was the insistent ringing of the telephone. He pulled himself out of bed to pick up the phone. He didn't know how long it had been ringing. He glanced fleetingly at the clock and saw it was 6:45 A.M.

"Congressman Cross?"

"Yes," said Cross, rubbing his eyes.

"This is Mr. Steinberg's office. Mr. Steinberg would like to speak with you."

"Fine."

"Sean, good news. It was like I told you last night. Everything worked out. There's an agreement."

"Jim, that's great news. Congratulations."

"Actually, the president deserves the congratulations. He made several calls in the middle of the night."

"He did?" asked Cross, wondering why Clinton had to make middle-of-the-night calls if everything had been going so smoothly.

"Yes. He spoke several times with Gerry and Trimble."

"This really is terrific news. When's it going to be announced?"

"In a few hours. Trimble's still meeting with his people. But it's done."

"Great job, Jim."

Cross immediately dialed the Sinn Fein office at Stormont. Mitchell McLaughlin, the party's national chairman, answered the phone.

"Mitchell, how are you?"

"As you can imagine, we're all pretty tired. It's almost noon and not one of us has slept a wink."

"I hear there's good news."

"Yes, there's an agreement. It was a very close call. But in the end, we believed there was enough in it for us to go ahead."

"Can you give me any details?"

"Believe it or not, the actual text of the agreement is being written right now. I'd suggest you ring again in a few hours or so and Ned can explain it all to you."

"Thanks, Mitchell. And good luck."

"All the best, Sean."

Cross quickly updated Mary Rose on what Steinberg and McLaughlin had told him, turned on the morning news—they were reporting "rumors of a dramatic breakthrough in the Irish peace talks"—took a fast shower, and walked over to his office in the Cannon Building.

It was just past eight o'clock. Cross telephoned the Sinn Fein office at Stormont and asked for Ned Harlan.

"Hello, Sean."

"Ned, how are you?"

"Sean, this is Gerry."

"Gerry! You caught me off guard. Tell me what's been happening."

"I've had to swallow an awful lot. More than I thought I would," said Adams. "And it's important you know this. I only did it—we only did it—because of the personal assurances I received from President Clinton."

"Any particulars?"

"No. All the details are in the agreement, and Ned can brief you on that in a moment. The assurances—and I spoke with the president twice—were that United States would stay engaged until the entire agreement is implemented."

"It must've been a long night for you."

"It was difficult, but I believe we've done the right thing—so long as America remains involved."

"Gerry, I'll make sure I get that word out. And good luck."

Ned Harlan then got on the phone to explain the details of the agreement. Under Strand One, the unionists would get their Assembly, but for legislation to pass, it would have to be approved by majorities of both communities. This would prevent unionist domination. The government would be run by an executive of ten ministers, and Sinn Fein would get two of those ministries. Strand Two would establish a North-South Ministerial Council consisting of the ten northern ministers and their counterparts in the Republic. It would cover at least twelve areas, including agriculture, education, and health. This was the all-Ireland element essential to Sinn Fein. To prevent unionist obstruction, the Assembly could not exist unless there was a North-South Council. Strand Three, which was uncontested, set up the British-Irish Council to "promote harmony" among all the governments in the British Isles. Significantly, there was to be reform of the police and the criminal justice system. Institutions would also be set up to ensure equality and the upholding of human rights.

"What about decommissioning?" asked Cross. "How'd you take care of that?"

"Each of the parties pledges to do all they can to bring about decommissioning by May of 2000."

"So there's no actual requirement to decommission?"

"No. And to be honest with you, Sean, if everything's in place and up and running in the next few months the way it should be, I don't see decommissioning being an issue in two years."

"How about prisoners? Dermot Gallagher mentioned that to me."

"They're all to be released by the summer of 2000. A number of them will be getting out straightaway."

"That should be a good psychological boost."

"It should indeed. And Sean, thanks for your help last night."

"Thank you for keeping me in the loop."

It was noon in Washington, five o'clock in the afternoon in Belfast. Sean Cross fixed his eyes on the office television as CNN showed all the parties taking their places around the large conference table as George Mitchell announced that an accord had been reached. The talks for which he had set a Holy Thursday deadline had been consummated in the Good Friday Agreement, an agreement that just hours before had seemed unattainable.

Cross believed the Good Friday Agreement was a fair one, acknowledging and protecting the legitimate rights and aspirations of both communities. From the nationalist and republican perspective, it ended unionist hegemony and provided the road map to a united Ireland. But Cross fully agreed with Adams. Continued American involvement was essential. Otherwise the unionists and the Brits could walk away from the agreement and reimpose their stranglehold on the Catholic community. Little wonder Clinton's intervention was so meaningful.

Over the next several days Cross would learn the full extent of that intervention. Clinton had telephoned Adams at 12:50 A.M. Washington time, and again at 5:00 A.M. The first conversation went on for twenty-five minutes, the second not as long. Clinton also spoke with Blair, Mitchell, and Trimble during the early morning hours. All this after the White House had said everything was under control.

Cross would later learn that Tony Blair had given Trimble a private letter assuring him that Sinn Fein would not be allowed into the executive until the IRA decommissioned—even though nothing in the agreement provided for this. Also Paisley and elements of the Ulster unionists had pledged to block the agreement in every way possible, as did the so-called Real IRA.

But for now, in the euphoria of Good Friday and the overwhelming approval of the referendums in both north and south on May 22, there was real hope and the prospect of joy for the Irish people after centuries of suffering and heartbreak.

CHAPTER SEVENTEEN

Belfast
Late June

The Europa Hotel, located on Great Victoria Street in Belfast, was once acknowledged to be the most bombed-out hotel in Europe. Throughout the '70s and '80s—during the height of the Troubles—this was where the reporters stayed when they were supposed to be covering the war. Too often, these reporters spent more time at the hotel bar than on Belfast's hard streets. And far too often, nationalists would contend, these journalists were content to accept British press handouts as the basis for their "frontline" reporting.

But that was the past. Belfast was now a dynamic business center, and the Europa was at its very heart.

Tonight's gala banquet was sponsored by the Belfast business community to honor George Mitchell's Herculean efforts in bringing about the Good Friday Agreement. It also commemorated the start of the Stormont peace talks in June 1996. All the major players of the past decade would be there: Blair and Ahern. Hume and Mallon. Trimble. Adams and McGuinness. And, yes, Bill Clinton, who'd flown in that morning. Many other political and community leaders would be there as well. Cross, who'd arrived the day before, would be sitting at a table with the leaders of the West Belfast Community Redevelopment Association.

The president of the WBCRA was Bernadette Hanlon. It had been almost a quarter century since Cross first met Bernadette, but she was still a woman of classic beauty: shoulder-length auburn hair, silky skin, finely sculpted cheekbones, a magnificent body. Bernadette Hanlon was as striking as a woman could be. And as strong and determined.

Cross and Bernadette had met in the early 1980s when Cross was in Belfast observing the notorious supergrass trials. Bernadette's husband, Dermot, was an IRA man on trial for a murder he didn't commit. The only evidence against him had been the testimony of a single informer, an alcoholic psychopath whose testimony was riddled with obvious lies and inconsistencies. But the informer had said what the Brits wanted him to. And that was enough for the unionist judge, who did what the Brits told him. Dermot Hanlon was found guilty and sentenced to life imprisonment.

The informer—the supergrass—was Frank McGrath, whose dead body had been found in a dumpster behind a saloon in Sunnyside less than three months ago.

Before Dermot's arrest, Bernadette had been decidedly nonpolitical. Her older brother Rory had been in the IRA and was killed when a bomb he was setting detonated prematurely and blew his body into small pieces. Afterward, Bernadette wanted no part of the IRA or Sinn Fein. As for Dermot's IRA activities, she simply blocked them from her mind. She'd created her own world within war-wracked Belfast, consisting of her children and a few streets around her small home in Andersontown.

But Dermot's arrest and the murder of a neighborhood girl by British soldiers radicalized Bernadette to an extent she could never have envisioned. She found herself leading public opposition to the supergrasses. Organizing the family members of republican defendants. Leading street demonstrations. Appearing on radio and television. Bringing in international observers from America, Europe, and South Africa. And conducting a speaking tour of the United States, where she raised interest and money.

At the end of the day, the Appeals Court threw out the convictions of Dermot and all the other defendants. And, most importantly, the Brits never used supergrasses again.

Cross had gotten to know Bernadette well during that time, both in Belfast and New York. And he'd stayed in touch with her over the years. Bernadette remained a devoted wife and mother but never again retreated into her own private world. She continued to be an active force in the community, canvassing for Sinn Fein, working with released prisoners, and then, after the Good Friday Agreement, heading the WBCRA, encouraging investment, creating jobs, promoting art festivals, and helping families adjust to peace after decades of war.

It had not always been easy for her. In 1991 her son Brendan was wounded in a gun battle with British troops and sentenced to twenty years in jail. This caused Dermot—who'd never flinched when he himself was arrested or tortured—to fall into a two-year battle with depression and alcohol. It was during this dark time that Bernadette confided in Cross her deepest secret.

Cross had just been elected to Congress and had flown to Belfast to meet with Adams and McGuinness. The next evening he met Bernadette at the Hunting Lodge pub in Lenadoon for a drink.

"These must be trying times for you," he said.

"In some ways it's even worse than when Dermot was in jail," she answered. "Sometimes I think I'm going out of my mind."

"Bernadette, I know what you went through during Dermot's case. And somehow I know you're going to make it through this, too."

Bernadette dragged deeply on a cigarette. She looked around the room. Then she leaned forward and whispered to Cross, "Sean, you don't know everything that went on, all that I did. And sometimes I think God is punishing me now for what I did."

Cross was surprised that after all these years, the worldly Bernadette still saw God as a brutal avenger.

"There's no need for you to be telling me anything," answered Cross.

"Sean, please, I have to talk to someone about it. Everyone else who knows is dead."

"Bernadette, you can tell me whatever you want. And no one will ever know."

That night Bernadette told Cross how when Dermot was in jail she had executed Harry Hamilton, a Catholic politician who'd been informing to the Brits. How the IRA had selected her precisely because no one would suspect her. How she had come up behind the unsuspecting Hamilton as he was getting out of his car one evening on the deserted Falls Road and blew his skull apart, splattering his brains onto the sidewalk.

Cross sat silently while Bernadette spoke. When she had finished, all he said was, "I'm sure you did what you thought you had to."

Bernadette dragged on her cigarette and took a sip of her white wine. She looked at Cross with a ghost of a smile. And neither of them ever mentioned that conversation again.

Dermot overcame his struggles with depression and the bottle. Brendan was released from Long Kesh in 1999 as part of the Good Friday Agreement. They were both working for community organizations helping ex-prisoners and their families. Bernadette had gone to college at night and received a degree in community planning. She was now a major player in postwar Belfast.

When Bernadette learned Cross would be in Belfast for the Mitchell testimonial, she phoned him in Washington, and they arranged to have dinner at the McCausland Hotel the evening before the Europa event.

McCausland's was clearly a first-class operation. Cross was greeted at the entrance by the maitre d', Tom Sarsfield, a former IRA prisoner and hunger striker Cross had also befriended in the early '80s.

"Christ, you've come a long way," laughed Cross as he touched the lapel of Sarsfield's dinner jacket.

"Not as far as you might think," quipped Sarsfield. "They just haven't caught on to me yet."

"Well, if nothing else, it looks like you've more than made up for your hunger strike," said Cross, pointing to Sarsfield's ample paunch.

"There's just no substitute for peace and prosperity," said Sarsfield, leading Cross to a secluded corner table where Bernadette was already seated.

Bernadette was sipping white wine. She greeted Cross with a wide smile as he leaned over and kissed her cheek.

"I'm sure the two of you have a lot to talk about. I'll make sure you have some peace and quiet," said Sarsfield.

"So, Sean, how're you keeping? You're looking well," said Bernadette.

"Not as well as you. Apparently, this community work really agrees with you."

"Ah, it's grand, so it is. It's been a long haul. But we're really making progress. You could almost say we're leading normal lives," she said with a broad smile.

"Jesus, when you think back, did you ever imagine you'd actually see peace? That there wouldn't be Brits on the street? That everyone would be out of jail? That people would have jobs?"

"I certainly didn't. And, thanks be to God, we're making the best of it. But Sean, let me ask you this—did you ever think all these years later that Frank McGrath would still be fucking things up? Even after he's dead."

"No. He was one problem I thought was gone and forgotten."

"I couldn't believe it when I saw the news about them finding his body."

"How did you feel when you learned he was dead?"

"To be honest, I had no feeling whatsoever. As far as I was concerned, once he walked off the witness stand in Dermot's case, he was dead. He gave his body and soul to the Brits. Frank McGrath was an unfortunate excuse of a man to begin with."

"So you don't believe the IRA had anything to do with the killing?"

"God, no. You can be sure of that. And they had nothing to do with Barry Kilpatrick, either. That type of thing simply isn't on anymore."

"That's what everyone's been telling me."

"But how is your campaign going? That last time we spoke, you said you were hurting a bit."

"Things could be better. I was on the phone this afternoon with my pollster, and he says I've dropped another five points."

"And when's the election?"

"The primary is in mid-September. About eleven weeks from now."

"What do you think'll happen?"

"Hard to say. The committeemen going door to door getting my petitions signed tell me they're getting some flack."

"Surely they're not blaming you for Frank McGrath's murder."

"No. But there's something about it they don't like. And there's the professor who was murdered outside St. Patrick's. Plus that story in the *Telegraph* about me being involved with Seamus McCoy and the Real IRA. It's all too close for comfort."

"Jesus, the Real IRA. Marty McDevitt. What a bunch of fuck-ing headers they are."

"That's the truth."

"Do you have any clue who's behind all this?"

"There's all sorts of theories. Frank Doolan, the lawyer who handled all the IRA cases in New York, thinks it could be someone involved with the CIA. Some guys in the Dublin government say it could be MI5 or MI6. And, then, of course, there's McDevitt's crowd. But I just don't know."

"You told me you've done some checking on your own?"

"Yeah. I tried to put some heat on a former CIA guy in Wash-ington and on McDevitt's man in New York."

"Liam Naughton?"

"That's the one."

"What did you learn?"

"The CIA guy swears up and down that the agency has no in-volvement. But he does admit that some of their old 'contract em-ployees' might be involved for reasons of their own."

"Do you believe him?"

"For the most part. But I'm sure the CIA could at least narrow down who those guys might be."

"Do you think that's what they're doing?"

"Probably. But they won't be telling me. They'll probably try to resolve it on their own."

"And Naughton?"

"That was interesting. About a week after we met, he told me McDevitt assured him they had nothing to do with McGrath's or Williamson's murder in New York. Their rule is no operations in the U.S."

"But he didn't deny the Real IRA was trying to get McGrath. Or Kilpatrick."

"No."

When they had finished eating, Bernadette leaned across the table and spoke to Cross in a soft whisper. For a moment he thought of that night in the Hunting Lodge so many years ago.

"Sean, after tomorrow's dinner would you be able to go to your room and change into something casual and then wait across the street in front of Robinson's Bar?"

"Sure. What's up?"

"Dermot and I will collect you and take you out to Twinbrook."

"What's in Twinbrook?"

"Vera Toomey."

"Who's she?"

"Frank McGrath's old girlfriend."

The predinner cocktail reception was nearly over. Everything was going well. Conversations were pleasant and the mood decidedly upbeat. Cross, nursing a straight Bushmills, had spoken with Adams and McGuinness, exchanged greetings with Tony Blair and Bertie Ahern, and congratulated George Mitchell. He even had a few words of polite conversation with David Trimble. Now Cross was talking with Bernadette, who looked particularly beautiful in a tight-fitting, low-cut black cocktail dress.

"So you'll be able to meet us outside Robinson's after dinner?" she asked.

"Yeah, it shouldn't take more than a few minutes to change into jeans and a sweater," answered Cross.

"That'll be grand, Sean. We don't want to be attracting attention by having a Yank walking about Twinbrook all dressed up in a suit."

"Do many people know that she was his girlfriend?" asked Cross, careful not to mention any names.

"As far as I'm aware, almost no one. We didn't know ourselves until just a few days ago."

"How'd you find out?"

"She contacted Dermot. Apparently, Dermot's sister and her sister went to secondary school together. She heard you'd be over for the dinner and sent word she wanted to meet you. She's very nervous about it, though."

"Afraid someone'll find out?"

"Aye. Being an informer's girlfriend is worse than being a whore."

"Don't worry. I won't say a word to anyone."

Just then Bill Clinton came walking over, a glass of Diet Coke in his hand.

"Good evening, Mr. President. How are you?" Cross asked.

"I'm doing just fine," answered Clinton, who was talking to Cross but looking at Bernadette.

"Mr. President, this is Bernadette Hanlon, an old friend of mine."

Clinton grinned expansively and shook Bernadette's hand. "It's a pleasure to meet you, Bernadette. Now I know why Sean spends so much time in Belfast."

"It's an honor to meet you, Mr. President," replied Bernadette. "None of us would be here tonight if it weren't for your work."

"If I'd known Belfast had such beautiful women, I would have done a lot more," said Clinton, still holding Bernadette's hand.

"Bernadette is very active in community renewal, Mr. President. She's head of the largest organization in West Belfast," said Cross.

"I've always believed more should be done to help organizations like yours," said Clinton. "To help real peace, there has to be a sense of confidence at the grassroots level. A sense that hard work and democracy are better than the bullet and the bomb."

"That's what we've been working for," said Bernadette.

"I'd be delighted to help you in any way that I can," said Clinton. "If you want, I can meet with your organization when I'm in Belfast again."

"That would be just grand," said Bernadette.

"And you can always get together with me when you're in the States, especially if it's Washington or New York."

"That's very thoughtful of you indeed," said Bernadette.

"You can reach me through Sean. Or you can contact me directly," said Clinton.

"I'll be sure to follow up," said Bernadette.

"I'm looking forward to working with you on this."

As Clinton walked off to talk with Tony Blair, Bernadette looked at Cross, smiled, and said, "Now I know what they mean when they talk about the Clinton charm."

"Yeah, he certainly is in a class by himself," laughed Cross.

Cross walked out the front door of the Europa and crossed the street to Robinson's. It was a few minutes past eleven. The dinner had ended about fifteen minutes before. Wearing a blue cotton sweater and jeans, Cross had been standing in front of Robinson's for less than a minute when a gray Opel drove up. Dermot was at the wheel, Bernadette in the backseat. Cross opened the front door and slid in.

"How're you doing, you ugly bastard?" said Cross, shaking Dermot's hand.

"Not so bad. And, unlike you, I'm making an honest living," retorted Dermot.

"Will you eejits stop your nonsense long enough so we can talk about Vera Toomey?" said Bernadette.

"Keep that attitude up, and I'll tell your charming husband here about your new boyfriend," said Cross.

"Who's that?" asked Dermot, feigning outrage.

"Bill Clinton," answered Cross.

"Ach, that's no bother at all," said Dermot. "He's not even in my class."

"That's the truth," said Bernadette with undisguised sarcasm.

"Okay, enough of the bullshit," said Cross. "What can you tell me about Vera Toomey?"

"She's a very unfortunate soul who's paying a huge price for her sins," said Bernadette.

"Vera's about forty years of age," said Dermot. "She moved to England in the early '90s, and that was the last I heard of her until about two months ago, when she moved back in with her mother and father in Twinbrook."

"Then she rang Dermot at the house last week," Bernadette jumped in.

"What did she want?" asked Cross.

"She just asked if she could stop by that evening to speak with Dermot."

"How'd that go?" inquired Cross.

"It'd been so long since I'd seen her—and I hardly knew her to begin with—that I barely recognized her," replied Dermot. "But she acted as if we were old friends, so she did, saying how much it meant to her to be able to talk with me."

"Is she from a republican family?" asked Cross.

"Her older brother Mick was in the IRA, but I never had any real contact with him," answered Dermot. "Anyway, she sat down, and Bernadette gave her a cup of tea."

"And then I left the room," said Bernadette. "It was obvious she wanted to speak privately with Dermot."

"As soon as Bernadette closed the door, Vera started talking," said Dermot. "Straightaway she told me she'd been living in Birmingham for the past ten years with Frank McGrath."

"That must have shocked the shit out of you," said Cross.

"I couldn't believe my ears," answered Dermot. "All these years and I'd never heard a word about that fucking tout. Suddenly, out of nowhere, I hear he's been found dead in New York, and then his girlfriend appears in my living room."

"What did she tell you?" asked Cross.

"Not as much as she's going to tell you. You're going to get all the details. What she did say was that Frank always felt bad about what he'd done to me and the other lads. That the Brits made him do it. That he told her how delighted he'd been when the Appeals Court threw out all the convictions. Apparently, that eased his conscience a bit. He was a very lonely man, though. Living with a totally new identity in a strange city for all those years. Always looking over his shoulder, always afraid someone would recognize him despite the plastic surgery and the voice lessons to disguise his West Belfast accent."

"Apparently, he didn't look over his shoulder often enough," said Bernadette.

"I guess he felt he was safe in New York," said Cross.

"Maybe Vera can tell you more about that," said Dermot.

"Did she give you any idea of what she wanted to talk to me about?" asked Cross.

"No. Just that it was important," answered Dermot.

Dermot turned left off of Stewartstown Road into Twinbrook estate, a nationalist enclave on the periphery of Belfast. Once inside, Dermot turned right and then circled around to Summerhill Road, parking his car in front of the third house on the left.

"How are we going to work this?" asked Cross.

"I'll go inside with you," said Dermot, "and stay there until you're finished."

"What about Bernadette?" asked Cross.

"I'll take the car down to my cousin Brigid's. She lives at the other end. I'll wait there until Dermot rings me. Then I'll come back and collect you."

Dermot and Cross got out of the car and walked quietly toward the front door. Dermot gently pressed the doorbell. A moment later, the door opened. The blonde woman inside beckoned them into a dimly lit vestibule and shut the door behind them, locking it in three places.

"Vera, this is Congressman Cross," said Dermot.

"It's a pleasure indeed to meet you, Congressman," said Vera.

"I appreciate the opportunity," answered Cross. "And please, call me Sean."

"Why don't you step into the living room?" said Vera.

"I think I'll just wait in the kitchen," said Dermot, "so you two can talk freely."

The living room was small, heavily wallpapered, and very well kept. Cross sat down on the couch. Vera closed the door, poured him a cup of tea and sat down in an armchair, dragging heavily on a cigarette. She wore tight black leather pants and an equally tight red blouse with the top three buttons undone. Her hair was platinum blonde with dark roots, her lipstick bright red. She was wearing rings on almost every finger. Her face, though heavily made up, was attractive and her figure good. The guys in Cross's neighborhood would have pegged her as an easy make. But as she began speaking, Cross saw there was more to her than that.

Her eyes had the tired look of a woman who'd seen too much. When she put her cigarette down, she rubbed her hands together. And when she crossed her legs, her right ankle shook incessantly. This obvious anxiety, however, could not conceal her fierce determination or her sense of loss.

"I assume Dermot's told you that Frank McGrath was my boyfriend," said Vera.

"Yeah, he did. But that's all he told me," answered Cross.

Vera looked hard at him, her eyes searching. "No one, including my own mother and father, knows what I'll be telling you now."

"Go ahead."

"I left Twinbrook in the early '90s to find a job in England. The situation here was just desperate—all the shootings, so many being lifted, Brits everywhere, no jobs. I just wanted to get away. Away from all this fucking madness."

"How'd you end up in Birmingham?"

"First I went to London and stayed there a few months. Then I heard there were jobs in Birmingham. A week or so after I got there, I found a job with an insurance agency."

"Did you know Frank then?"

"God, no. He'd left Belfast years before. I just knew his name. That he'd been a fucking tout. Everyone in West Belfast knew that. I was in Birmingham about two years before I met him."

"Where was that?"

"At a pub."

"One of those Irish pubs?"

"No. It was working-class all right, and Irish went there. But there were a lot of Brits as well. Frank would never have gone to a real Irish place for fear of being recognized. As it was, he was taking a bit of a chance."

"Had the Brits done much to change his looks?"

"Aye. Later on, after I was living with him and he trusted me, he showed me pictures of himself when he was in Belfast. He'd had a good bit of plastic surgery, and his hair was totally different as well."

"Could someone have recognized him?"

"If one of his mates was looking for him and looked carefully enough, I'm sure they'd've made the connection. But to pass him on the street or see him in a pub—no, I don't think so."

"So, how'd you meet him?"

"I was at the bar with some women from work. We were having a drink and, before you know it, Frank was looking at me. He told me his name was Bill Arnold."

"The name on the passport the cops pulled from his body was Edward Barrington."

"That was the alias he used in America."

"Did he have a Belfast accent when you met him?"

"No. Not a trace. It was definitely English."

"Working-class?"

"No. It was more middle-class. Actually, when I say there was no trace of a Belfast accent, that's not entirely true. Later, when I got to know him much better, the Belfast accent would occasionally come out. But I never heard it with anyone else."

"How long did you know him before he told you who he was?"

"Jesus, it was almost a year. The two of us hit it off pretty well from the start. And I moved into his flat after about three months."

"Did he say where he was from, or even that he was Irish?"

"Aye. He told me he'd been born in Belfast, but his family moved to Birmingham when he was a young lad. And since he was more than ten years older than me, there was really nothing we'd have had in common that I'd've asked him about."

"How did he tell you who he really was?"

"I'll never forget it, so I won't. We were in his flat, just the two of us, watching the telly. He had a pint of beer in front of him, but he'd barely taken a drop. He seemed as if something was on his mind. But I didn't give it much bother. I just thought it was something from his job."

"What was his job, anyway?"

"He was a carpenter. And a skilled one."

"He wasn't a carpenter when he lived in Belfast, was he?"

"No. The Brits trained him. That was all part of his new identity. Anyway, several times that evening, he started to talk, and then he'd hesitate and just mumble something. After a while, I began to think maybe he had another girlfriend or some carry-on like that. So I asked him, 'Is there something you're trying to tell me?' And he just blurted it out. First, I couldn't believe what I was hearing. Then I thought I'd pass out. Here I was, someone who never had a political thought in her life, living with the most hated man in all of Belfast."

"What exactly did he say?"

"He said, 'Did you ever hear of Frank McGrath?' And I said, 'Everyone's heard of that fucker.' And then Frank says, 'Well that's me. I'm that fucker.' I said nothing. I just looked at him. And he kept talking."

"Was he nervous or awkward at all?"

"No. Once he started, it all just came pouring out. He told me how right after he'd finished testifying at that terrible trial—the one where Dermot was convicted—the Brits'd taken him to England, where they hid him away for almost two years. During this time, they taught him how to be a Brit—how to talk, how to act. They taught him his trade. They gave him his new identity, Billy Arnold, with all the papers he needed. Finally, when they thought he was ready, his minders got him a flat and a job and gave him money beyond whatever his salary was."

"These minders—who were they?"

"Special British intelligence agents. Experts at psychological operations."

"MI5?"

"I guess that's who they were. I don't think they ever really told Frank. But they were definitely spooks."

"So he just kept talking?"

"For some time he did. Until I stopped him and asked how he could've done what he did to his mates."

"Did he admit his testimony was all lies?"

"Oh, aye. All he said in defense of himself was that some of them had committed other crimes. So, it wasn't like he was betraying innocent men."

"What did you say to that?"

"Before I could say anything, he told me he knew his excuses were no good. He'd done the worst thing possible by becoming an informer—the most hated type of bastard throughout Irish history."

"Did he say why he did it?"

"Aye. He was scared. Just petrified, so he was. He'd had a drinking problem. The Brits had evidence of some serious crime he'd committed which didn't involve the IRA at all. They'd also had enough evidence to convict him of membership in the IRA, which would've gotten him at least four or five years inside."

"Wouldn't that have been easier than spending the rest of his life on the run?"

"You'd have thought so. And maybe that's what he would've done if the Brits hadn't scared the shit out of him with something worse than jail."

"What?"

"They told him that if he didn't testify as a supergrass, they'd let him go but convince the IRA he was an informer. And, Jesus, nothing could be worse than what the IRA would've done to him after that."

"Did Frank think the IRA would believe it?"

"He didn't want to chance it."

"So, he agreed to recite a script in court against thirty-five of his friends."

"Aye. And not a of word of it was true."

"Dermot told me you said Frank was happy when the Appeals Court threw out the convictions."

"Oh, aye. He said it made it much easier to live with himself. There'd always be the shame of being an informer, but at least he knew there was no lasting damage to his mates."

"What kind of life did he lead?"

"He told me that for the first five years or so, he stayed entirely in the shadows. He avoided people as much as he could, just going to work and then back to his flat every night. And checking with his minders every few days."

"How would he do that?"

"Usually, they'd meet for a few minutes in a shopping center or a park. Places where no one would take any notice."

"How long did that go on?"

"Right up to the end. Except the meetings became much less frequent. For the past few years, he'd meet them maybe once every two or three months. But he always had an emergency telephone number he could ring at any time of the day or night."

"After the first five years, it got better for him?"

"Aye. It was never perfect, of course, or anything like normal. But he established roots in Birmingham and people there accepted him as a hard-working, decent sort of bloke."

"So he stopped looking over his shoulder?"

"Not completely. The fear was always there. There was always a chance someone would come in from the outside and recognize him. But he was fairly sure the people he worked with and the people in his community accepted his new identity. But no, Sean, he could never truly relax."

"From the way you're talking about him, it seems as if Frank was a pretty solid guy. I hate to hurt your feelings, but I was at the trial, and as far as I was concerned, he was a really bad guy. He drank. He lied. He beat up old ladies. Besides ratting on his closest friends."

"Don't worry, Sean. You're not hurting my feelings at all. Frank himself told me he'd been a waster during that time. He drank too much, and he had serious emotional problems. But the whole time I was with him, I never saw any of that."

"What caused the change?"

"I think it was the years of living almost alone in Birmingham, of living in such fear and with such shame and guilt. He could either collapse altogether or put his life back together. And, with tremendous willpower, he made himself a new person."

"How did he feel about the Good Friday Agreement and all the changes in the north?"

"I met Frank just a month before the first ceasefire. And then when the Agreement was signed, I remember him just being over the moon about it. He said every Irish man should be happy there'd finally be peace. He hoped it would bring peace to him as well."

"Did he ever reach out to anyone in Belfast?"

"No. Not at all. He never had contact with anyone from his past life."

"Did he have any relatives?"

"There are two sisters still living. His mother and father died just a few years after he left Belfast."

"And he never spoke a word to any of them?"

"No. Not from the day he left Belfast."

"They never knew if he was dead or alive?"

"No. No one could be trusted. Remember, Frank was an informer."

"What about when he was killed?"

"I was told the relatives were notified after he was buried."

"Who buried him?"

"The Brits."

"Where?"

"I haven't a clue. It's an unmarked grave somewhere. That's what Frank told me would happen. That he'd still be a nonperson even after he died. He just didn't think it would be so soon."

"Tell me—why did he go to America?"

"His minder told him to. It was back in January that they came to him. And he was in America within a month."

"Why did they want him to leave? And why the States? Was there a problem in England?"

"It happened all of a sudden. One day Frank came home and he was obviously distraught. He said he'd met his minder for a routine get-together. Usually, they were over in fifteen minutes. But this time the meeting lasted about three hours. Basically, what it came down to was that the intelligence people got information that the IRA had found out about Frank and were arranging for a special unit in England to get him."

"Did Frank believe that the IRA would risk everything by going after him after all these years?"

"At first, he didn't. He told the minder it made no sense. But the minder said they knew it for sure. Besides—and this is what upset

Frank the most—the minder said Frank had to do whatever they told him to do. He also told Frank he was to say nothing to anyone about this. Not even me.

"He'd have to start all over again. With a new name. A new job. Only this time he'd be living in America. And he'd be without me."

"How could the Brits protect him in America?"

"Apparently, it was all worked out with the CIA."

"I thought Frank wasn't supposed to tell you."

"He wasn't. But it was too much for him not to say anything. To just leave me forever. He knew it would've driven me mad for him to be gone one day without so much as a goodbye."

"Did the Brits give him any kind of a cover story?"

"Aye. He was to tell me he was going to Brussels for about six months on some huge construction project. That would get him out of the country without causing any trouble. And then he'd just disappear."

"I'm getting the sense you didn't think Frank believed the Brits."

"No. And this was very difficult for him. Jesus, for all those years, like them or not, the Brits had kept their word. That's a hell of a long time. In many ways Frank had become a Brit. Of course, underneath it all he still saw them as the enemy. But all along what'd given Frank confidence was that it was in the Brits' interest as much as his own that he be kept alive."

"Yeah. It would've been a tremendous psychological victory for the IRA to have been able to take out the Brits' prize informer."

"And that's why Frank didn't fully trust his minder this time. During all the years when the IRA was at full strength and the war was raging, the Brits had been able to protect Frank. Now the war's over and the IRA's virtually nonexistent, and the Brits have to take him out of the country and send him all the way to America?"

As Vera recounted her story, her voice, though tinged by emotion, was strong and resolute. So, too, her nervous tics had ceased. And after she'd finished her first cigarette, she didn't light another. As she spoke, she leaned forward and fixed a steady gaze on Cross.

"How about the Real IRA?" asked Cross. "Were they a threat?"

"I suppose they could have been. After all, anyone with a gun is. But I go back to my point. If the Brits were able to protect Frank from the full might of the IRA when the war was at its peak, how could they let this handful of stragglers drive him from the country?"

"Did you ever meet the minder yourself?"

"No. And, as far as they know, I never had any knowledge there was a minder. Frank'd never told them that I knew who he really was. Frank did tell me, though, that his minder had changed."

"He got a new one?"

"Actually, he got an old minder back. Last fall, the minder Frank had had for the past five or six years was replaced by a guy who'd been his minder over ten years ago."

"What do you know about him?"

"His name is Walter Marley. He'd spent a lot of time on the northern issue over the past twenty-five years or so. I'd never heard of him until he reappeared last year."

"Did Frank say anything about him at the time?"

"I didn't pay it much mind, but, yes, he showed some concern. He said of all the minders he'd had over the years, Marley had the harshest edge. And Frank thought he seemed even harsher now than ever."

"Anything in particular?"

"No. And I didn't pursue it. I didn't believe it was that important. Frank just got the impression that Marley didn't believe the peace process was as promising as everyone thought it was."

"What about in January?"

"Again, Marley didn't give specifics. When Frank asked him for more details on the threats, Marley just said all this optimistic talk about peace was crazy. That the situation was as dangerous as it ever was."

"What did he mean by that?"

"I don't have a clue. But it didn't seem right to me, or to Frank."

"So what did you decide to do?"

"Frank wanted me out of England before he left for New York."

"What did he tell Marley?"

"That I would stay with some cousins in Cork while he was in Brussels."

"Did Marley ask for any details?"

"No."

"Did they know you were originally from Belfast?"

"They must have. They knew everything. That's why I'm scared to death."

"I can understand that. Especially with all that's gone on."

"Anyway, I flew to Dublin. Stayed in the south for a week or so. And then came here to Twinbrook as quietly as I could."

"Did Frank have any way of contacting you?"

"Yes. Before I left Birmingham, I was able to get the telephone number of a bakery shop in Andersontown that's owned by a friend of my da. Frank was to ring me at that number after he got to New York."

"Did he?"

"Aye. He rang me about a week after he arrived. And then every ten days or so after that."

"How would he call you?"

"It was always from a pay phone, and from a location where he thought he wouldn't be noticed. I know several of the calls were from the Underground, or subway, as you call it."

"What did he tell you?"

"He was always very careful about what he said, in case anyone was listening. But he did tell me he'd met the CIA man."

"Did he tell you the guy's name?"

"Charles Webster."

"Did he say anything about him?"

"Only that he was a Yank in his late forties or early fifties and acted like he was in one of your gangster movies."

"For all we know, he may have been a gangster."

"Why do you say that?"

"For one thing, the CIA isn't allowed to operate in the U.S. It's against the law. So either Webster is a criminal or he's an imposter."

"Anyway, he gave Frank all the papers he needed—passport, driver's license, everything. He was officially Edward Barrington. Then he got a good-paying job on a construction site in Manhattan and an apartment in Queens. Actually, in the Woodside section of Queens."

"And Webster did all that for him?"

"Every bit. Frank just had to show up where Webster told him to."

"Did he meet anyone else who was supposed to be from the government?"

"No. Only Webster."

"What did Frank do? Had he gotten to know anyone?"

"He just went to work and back to his apartment. He didn't spend time with anyone. He said it was very much like his first years in Birmingham."

"Do you know anything about Barry Kilpatrick? Did Frank mention him to you?"

"When I read he was killed in London, I recognized his name, of course. He was the only informer almost as hated as Frank. The only mention Frank ever made of him was that he assumed Kilpatrick was in the same type of protection program."

"But he didn't know where Kilpatrick was?"

"Not a clue. Frank didn't even know if he was still alive."

"When did you hear about Kilpatrick?"

"He was shot a few weeks before Frank, but it wasn't reported in the press until after Frank was murdered."

"Did Frank tell you anything else at all?"

"Not really. He did seem surprised that Webster wasn't saying more."

"Did he have any more contact with Marley?"

"Just Webster telling him that Marley was doing his best to monitor the IRA unit that was supposed to be after Frank."

"You must've been devastated when you got the news."

"I read it in the papers, like everyone else. I was shattered, so I was. And to make it worse, there was no one I could talk with. My own family had no idea I was with Frank McGrath. And, Jesus, all the terrible things I heard people say about Frank, it just broke my heart."

"Are you worried for your own safety?"

"As I said, I'm scared to death. I can't trust anyone. The Northern Ireland police that we have now are better than the RUC, but they still work with Scotland Yard and all their intelligence services."

"MI5 and MI6?"

"Aye. And I'm embarrassed to tell any of my neighbors, not just for myself but also for my mother and father. Can you just imagine how they'd feel if they found out their daughter was an informer's whore? They'd . . ."

And that was as far as Vera could go. Her composure collapsed. And she broke into uncontrollable sobs.

CHAPTER EIGHTEEN

August 1998–September 1998

The political heat on Bill Clinton was searing by late August 1998. Throughout the summer months, Clinton's denial of a sexual affair with Monica Lewinsky had become less and less credible. On August 17, he became the first president ever required to testify under oath before a grand jury. That evening, just hours after his testimony, President Clinton went on national television and admitted to the American people that he had indeed had an affair with Monica Lewinsky.

The day after Clinton's apologia, he and Hillary and Chelsea flew off to Martha's Vineyard, where they spent the next two weeks in virtual seclusion. From the moment the President and First Lady crossed the White House lawn to the Marine helicopter that would take them on the first leg of their journey, there was an icy tension between them. Neither would look at or even acknowledge the other. And from news reports and leaks, things remained that way throughout the vacation.

Now, at about two thirty in the afternoon on Monday, August 31, Sean Cross was sitting in Air Force One on the tarmac of Andrews Air Force Base. He and the other legislators and Cabinet officials were awaiting the President and First Lady. As soon as they arrived, the presidential jet would take off for a two-day stint in Moscow. Then they'd be off to Belfast, Dublin, and Limerick for three more days before returning to Andrews the following Saturday night.

In an apparent fence-mending gesture to Cross, Newt Gingrich had asked him to represent the House Republicans in this mission. Now as he waited, Cross engaged in friendly conversation with Steny Hoyer, the Democratic congressman from Maryland representing the House Democrats, and Senators Pete Domenici and Jeff Bingaman, both from New Mexico, representing the Senate Republicans and Democrats respectively.

The mood among the four was light and the banter pleasant. But there was also undeniable apprehension. *This could be a helluva long flight*, thought Cross. *It's bad enough being around a married couple that's fighting. But to be locked in a plane for nine hours with the main players in a national soap opera could be a real bitch.*

Just then Cross heard cheerful voices and playful laughter. The Clintons had arrived. There they were, laughing, holding hands, wearing smiles that didn't look the slightest bit forced.

"Well, you guys certainly look comfortable," said the First Lady.

"This should really be a great trip," said the president. "And it's very important. This situation in Russia is really serious. After Hillary and I get settled, I'd like to come back and talk to you about it. Probably in about a half hour or so.

"That'd be fine, Mr. President," said Domenici, the elder statesman of the group and a true Senate gentleman.

"The situation's much more critical than most people realize," said Clinton. "And, Sean, we're going to have a terrific time in Ireland. Things are going well there."

Hand in hand, still smiling broadly, the President and First Lady walked up to their compartment near the front of the plane.

"Can you believe that?" asked Domenici. "I suppose if you live long enough, you see everything."

The President was right about Russia. Its financial markets were in free fall, resulting from an inherently unstable and corrupt economy and a massive Asian financial crisis. As for Ireland, Cross was as excited as the President about going there. But he was concerned that the Good Friday Agreement wasn't being implemented. Yes, prisoners were being released and elections for the new Assembly had been held, with both Sinn Fein and the SDLP doing very well. But the Executive and the cross-border bodies still hadn't been set up. And Trimble was saying they wouldn't be until the IRA began decommissioning—something not required by the agreement. Again the process was stalemated.

Clinton had said he'd be back in a half hour. But more than two hours went by and there wasn't a sign of him. This was going to be a nine-hour flight. So Cross and the other three decided to take sleeping pills and get some sleep. Hoyer found himself a comfortable spot on the floor while the others pressed their chairs almost completely back. All were sound asleep within minutes.

After about a half hour, though, Cross was awakened by an excited voice exclaiming, "The stock market's fallen five hundred points!"

Cross, uncertain whether he was having a nightmare or had been committed to an insane asylum, forced his eyes open and saw Bill Clinton standing above him. He was dressed in jeans, a sport shirt and sneakers.

"This is all because of Russia," said Clinton. "And they're just a pissant economy. They shouldn't be having such an impact on us."

Hoyer rolled over and, from his position on the floor, asked the President if he'd gotten any sleep.

"No, I've been following this market news all afternoon. Man, five hundred points! Those damn Japanese won't get off their asses," said Clinton. "But you guys really look tired. Why don't we have a detailed meeting about an hour before we land in Moscow."

"That'd be great," answered Domenici, who immediately fell back into a deep sleep.

It took Cross a few minutes to get back to sleep. As he lay back with his eyes closed, he could still hear Clinton talking. This time it was to Strobe Talbott, the Assistant Secretary of State and Clinton's Russian guru.

"We've been working on this for a year," said Clinton. "But no one realizes all we've been doing for the economy."

"This isn't the end, Mr. President," answered Talbott.

"No, it's a new chapter," replied Clinton.

And with those words Cross was again sound asleep.

Domenici woke Cross up at about 6:15 A.M. Moscow time.

"We should start getting ready. We'll be landing in about an hour and a half and the President said he wanted to meet with us," said Domenici.

Cross pulled his chair upright and then pulled himself up from it. By seven o'clock the four jet-lagged legislators had just about returned to a functioning level. Then the stewards served a hot breakfast and the four engaged in small talk as they ate. Cross particularly enjoyed Domenici's talks about his exploits as a pitcher in the Brooklyn Dodger farm system during the 1950s.

At about 7:45 the pilot announced they would be landing in a few minutes at Moscow's Vnukovo Airport. After the plane had landed and come to a stop at its appointed location, Cross and the others got up from their seats and walked along the long hallway on the left side of the plane which led to the front exit door. Protocol demanded that no one exit Air Force One before the President. And the door to the President's compartment was closed. After a few minutes the compartment door opened and the President emerged looking well rested and fresh. He and the First Lady appeared not to have a care or a worry in the world.

"Oh, I was supposed to meet with you guys this morning," said Clinton. "I'm sorry. I was just so tired I overslept."

"No problem," said the always agreeable Domenici. "You have a busy day ahead of you."

"Well, let's get the show on the road," said Clinton, as he and Hillary walked toward the front door.

The two days in Moscow were a blur of meetings, conferences, receptions and banquets—much of it ceremonial, but some informative.

Cross was most struck, however, by the Wednesday news conference which Clinton and Yeltsin held at the Kremlin. On the Russian side, Yeltsin appeared bloated and unsteady. Very dismissive and condescending toward the media. On the United States side, Clinton was barraged by Lewinsky questions from the American reporters. *Jesus,* Cross thought, *I figured they'd let up on this shit when he's in a foreign country.* Clinton answered the questions but obviously was not pleased. Suddenly it ended. Yeltsin arbitrarily announced the news conference was over, stood up and walked off—leaving the media gaggle at least temporarily mute.

Clinton's approach in Russia was very businesslike. But that all changed Thursday morning when Air Force Once landed at Aldergrove Airport in Belfast. If Russia was his job; Ireland was his vocation.

The first stop was Stormont Castle for a reception with the elected members of the new Assembly. Waiting at Stormont was the congressional delegation headed by Jim Walsh, which had arrived a few hours earlier. The reception was held in the ornate Long Gallery. The Assembly members were lined up by party, with Paisley's DUP and Sinn Fein placed a considerable distance apart. Clinton began on the DUP side, Blair on Sinn Fein's.

One of the first to greet Blair was Gerry Kelly. The same Gerry Kelly that British intelligence—MI5—had tried to link with Martha Pope. The same man who was a convicted bomber and who the Brits had long said was a very high-ranking IRA leader. But here were Gerry Kelly and Tony Blair warmly shaking hands and exchanging good-natured jibes, neither one showing the slightest discomfiture or unease. Blair and Cross exchanged cordial greetings, and Cross watched Blair work his way toward the center of the room, shaking hand after hand until he passed Clinton, who was working his way down from the other end. When Clinton neared the Sinn Fein delegation, Gerry Adams said, "Mr. President, have you met Sean Cross, the Sinn Fein member of Congress?"

"It's funny you should say that, Gerry," Clinton replied, laughing. "That's what Paisley's people just told me."

"I'm sure that's not all they said to you," quipped Martin McGuiness.

"You're right. They also told me it was wrong for me to attack terrorists in Afghanistan and the Sudan and still deal with Sinn Fein."

"How'd you handle that?" asked Cross.

"I told them the IRA was like the PLO. They genuinely wanted peace. And we deal with the PLO."

After the handshakes were concluded and the photo ops completed, the next stop was Waterfront Hall, a magnificent, state-of-the-art convention center recently constructed in Belfast's prestigious Lanyon Place development. The thousands who filled the main auditorium were keen with anticipation that today might yet prove historic. No, the Executive still had not been set up, but it appeared progress was being made. The parties had gone ahead and designated the First Minister and the Deputy First Minister, who would preside when the Executive was formed. Not surprisingly, the unionists elected Trimble as First Minister. In a somewhat unexpected move, however, John Hume stepped aside and the nationalists chose Seamus Mallon as Deputy First Minister. Then just yesterday Sinn Fein took two dramatic steps. First it announced that Martin McGuinness would represent the republican movement at the decommissioning panel set up pursuant to the Good Friday Agreement. Then in an article in the *Irish Times*, Gerry Adams had written, "The violence we have seen must be for all of us now a thing of the past, over, done with, and gone." Now the vast assemblage in Waterfront Hall—and millions throughout Ireland and around the world—awaited a reciprocal response from Trimble, who would be speaking along with Clinton, Blair, and Mallon.

Clinton and Blair were good, stressing the need for cooperation and progress. Mallon was brilliant. Making his debut on the international stage, the silver-haired schoolteacher, now in his late sixties, soared to heights of rhetorical brilliance. The speech had it all—forgiveness, trust, vision—with no hint of rancor or begrudgery.

But as much as Mallon surpassed even the most hopeful expectations, Trimble fell that far short. Simply stated, his speech was a total failure. No acknowledgment of the McGuinness appointment or the Adams statement except for the patronizing remark that he welcomed any move by those "crossing the bridge from terror to democracy."

The man is just incapable of any generosity of spirit, thought Cross.

Following Waterfront Hall, the delegation moved on to Springvale College in West Belfast for the dedication of a new campus. All went well at Springvale, but the arid tone of Trimble's Waterfront remarks cast a lingering pall over what should have been an entirely festive occasion.

After Springvale, a chartered bus took the congressional delegation directly to Armagh City for a massive outdoor rally. The Clintons and the Blairs, however, would not go directly. Instead, they would helicopter to Omagh and walk through the bomb-ravaged city center to demonstrate solidarity with Omagh's residents, devastated so terribly just three weeks before.

Omagh. The blood-drenched legacy of the Real IRA, and of its driven leader, Martin McDevitt.

Saturday, August 15—a beautiful day, the sun shining, the air clean and clear. The center of Omagh was filled with shoppers—Catholics, Protestants, and tourists—when a bomb went off, causing the crowd to flee—in the direction of another, more powerful bomb. Bodies were blown apart. Blood and bits of flesh were everywhere. So, too, were the sounds of anguished screams. The final toll was horrific: twenty-nine dead, more than two hundred injured. It was the worst carnage in the history of the Troubles.

For McDevitt and his ilk there could never be peace. The war must go on. But even McDevitt must have been surprised by the reaction to Omagh. Cries of outrage and revulsion came from everywhere. Not just from Trimble and the unionists, or Hume and the SDLP, but unequivocal denunciations from Adams and McGuinness and grassroots republicans all over Ireland—north and south. It was soon clear that the Real IRA stood for no one but a handful of psychopaths.

On this day, September 4, by appearing in Omagh, Bill Clinton and Tony Blair made it clear that the civilized world stood against the Real IRA, thus ensuring it would never attain any popular support. It also ensured that Marty McDevitt and the Real IRA would go further underground, and become capable of even more desperate acts.

The event that evening on the mall in Armagh City was magnificent—the weather ideal, the crowd mammoth, spirits exuberant. Clinton and Blair were eloquent, pledging again their governments' commitment to see the process through, for as long as it might take.

About ten minutes before the program was to conclude, military escorts came up to Cross and to each member of the congressional delegation, escorting them behind the stage and across the street to a sturdy but unimposing three-story house. Inside, Cross saw Hillary Clinton and Mo Mowlam, Sandy Berger and Jim Steinberg, various Secret Service agents, and several men he recognized as members of Blair's staff. Cross realized this was the governmental equivalent of a safe house. He smiled, thinking of the thousands of people who would walk past this anonymous building tonight, not knowing it contained the two most powerful leaders in the western world and their entourages.

"Great excitement out there on the mall, mate," said Mowlam.

"It was terrific just being there," answered Cross. "Especially after Omagh."

"All that devastation," said Hillary Clinton. "I can't believe anyone would do that."

"And if it's that bad today," said Mowlam, "imagine what it was like the day the bombs went off."

Just then, a door at the rear of the building opened and Tony Blair stepped in. He shook hands with a number of congressmen before greeting Cross.

"Sean, it's been a marvelous day."

"It certainly has, Prime Minister."

"Do you mind if we speak for a moment?" asked Blair, indicating a vacant area of the dining room.

"Of course not," answered Cross, following Blair toward the corner.

"This Real IRA has me quite concerned. How much support do they have in America?"

"None. Except for some isolated individuals who have no following themselves."

"That's reassuring, because we can't have another Omagh."

"Prime Minister, let me put it as bluntly as I can. I know most of the people the Real IRA would go to for weapons, and believe me, they're supporting the Good Friday Agreement. They're entirely behind Adams and McGuinness."

"I believe Gerry wants peace. We have to find a way to resolve the decommissioning issue—"

As Blair was in midsentence, a voice behind Cross interrupted.

"Tony, I think we should get started in the other room."

Who the hell's interrupting us? wondered Cross. Turning around, he realized it was Bill Clinton.

"Mr. President, with all the noise, I didn't recognize your voice," said Cross.

"It's been some night, hasn't it? Tony and I are going to speak to the delegation in the side room over there."

As they trailed behind Clinton, Blair said to Cross in a low voice, "Tell Gerry we want to resolve this. We'd welcome any ideas."

"Thank you, Prime Minister."

Clinton and Blair positioned themselves at the front of the room, with Mowlam just off to their side. Clinton spoke first and again expressed solidarity with Blair. Blair began by referring to his conversation with Cross.

"As Sean and I were just discussing, we can't allow the Real IRA to get any sort of foothold. I ask all of you to do whatever you can to keep them from gaining any support in America."

Cross, concerned that all this talk about the Real IRA would give it an undeserved legitimacy, interjected, "Prime Minister, as we discussed, 99.9 percent of the Irish-American community supports the Good Friday Agreement. And they were outraged by Omagh. But, most importantly, none of the characters who might possibly be involved in supplying weapons will have anything to do with McDevitt or the Real IRA. My worry is that by focusing too much attention on them, we're going to give the Real IRA a credibility they don't deserve."

"It's very gratifying to see how united we all are on this issue," said Blair.

Less than an hour later the Congressional delegation was on a Nighthawk helicopter heading toward Dublin, where they would land in Phoenix Park and then travel by bus to the Berkeley Court Hotel in fashionable Ballsbridge.

The leading event on Friday was to be the luncheon hosted by Bertie Ahern at the Royal College of Surgeons located in the center of Dublin. All the talk that morning, however, leading up to the luncheon concerned what was happening in the Senate back in Washington, D.C. Democratic Senators Joe Lieberman, Pat Moynihan and Bob Kerry had assailed Clinton for the Lewinsky scandal and that's what the media bombarded Clinton with at his news conference with Ahern. *Dammit*, thought Cross, *couldn't those guys in the Senate at least have waited until Clinton was back in the country?*

The luncheon was lavish. Not only were Ireland's leading politicians in attendance, so too were noted talents such as Nobel Prize winning poet Seamus Heaney. All seating was assigned. Cross was three tables away from the President and Taioseach. Among those at Cross's table was Dr. Walter Empey, Archbishop of the Church of Ireland, who was one of Ireland's leading Protestant clergymen.

About halfway through the lunch, Clinton got up and walked over to Cross's table. A sly smile on his face, Clinton shook hands with the Archbishop and said:

"Archbishop, you'll really have to earn your money today. This guy sitting next to you—Congressman Cross—really needs help. It will be difficult. If you can help *him*, you really are doing God's work."

"Mr. President," answered the Archbishop with mock seriousness, "I truly thank you for letting me know he's such a sinner. I'm sure I'd have found out on my own sooner or later. But thank you indeed for saving me the time."

"Mr. President, I want to thank you as well," said Cross. "I certainly can use whatever help I can get."

"I'm just trying to do my job, Sean," said Clinton. "Just trying to do my job."

As Clinton sauntered back to his table wearing a huge smile, Archbishop Empey leaned toward Cross and said:

"He looks as if he's the most relaxed man in the world. I don't know how he does it."

"I don't think anyone knows," said Cross.

Later in the afternoon Clinton and the delegation traveled out to the American Embassy where Clinton gave a speech to the embassy employees. After the speech, which had been delivered outdoors under a tent, the Congressmen were invited into the embassy to watch the President tape his weekly national radio address. Following the radio speech, they all went into an elaborately decorated room off the dining area. The President sat in a large, heavily cushioned chair. A fireplace was just behind him. Cross sat on a couch to the President's left along with Dick O'Neill and Martin Meehan, a celebrated reform-minded Congressman from Massachusetts. Others sat randomly in chairs throughout the room.

Clinton and the First Lady were flying to Limerick that night. The delegation would be flying there tomorrow. Now the President had about forty-five minutes of what was supposed to be "down time." He used the time to give an update on his Russian trip.

—Clinton was surprisingly pessimistic about Yeltsin. "He doesn't seem strong enough to run the country."

—Over the years "Yeltsin had drunk enough whiskey to float this building." But Clinton didn't think he was drinking now.

—Even though he wasn't drinking, "Yeltsin is able to function for only a few hours a day."

—General Lebed, recently elected as Governor of Serbia, "had a strange look in his eyes."

—Clinton just didn't see "much chance for short term economic or political improvement in Russia."

—Switching gears, Clinton said, "Japan's decline is actually more serious than Russia's."

—To impress on the Japanese the need to revive their economy, Clinton wanted to put together a Congressional delegation to visit Japan in November or December after the elections.

It was about seven o'clock when the President got up to leave for his flight to Limerick. As Clinton left the room, O'Neill said to Cross:

"The guy didn't look at a note the whole fucking time. He's too much."

Cross would never forget the day in Limerick City. His mother's family—the McNamaras—was from Limerick and when

Cross got off the Air Force jet that morning many of the McNamaras were there to greet him. So too were his son, Danny, who'd flown over from Notre Dame's London campus where he was studying for his MBA, and his mother and sister, Barbara, who'd come over from New York for the occasion.

The White House had arranged to have Cross's family travel with the delegation. So they took the Congressional bus into Limerick City, attended the VIP reception with Jean Kennedy Smith and then sat in the reserved area just to the left of the stage. The Limerick sky had been ominously dark and gray the entire morning and showers had fallen intermittently. But none of that deterred the tens of thousands of Limerick men and women who filled O'Connell and Thomas Streets for as far as the eye could see. And then, just minutes before the President was to emerge from the holding area behind the stage, the bright sun broke through and drove the clouds from the sky. When Clinton and the First Lady, along with Bertie Ahern and Celia Larkin, stepped onto the stage, the reception was thunderous and seemingly unending. Limerick, a city never known to be particularly generous in its praise of anyone, was according Bill Clinton a reception as tumultuous and heartfelt as any he would receive in his presidency.

And Clinton didn't disappoint. Playing the crowd as if he'd lived in Limerick his entire life, Clinton struck responsive chord after responsive chord with the usually hard-edged people of Limerick. He touched all points. The unprecedented opportunity for peace in the north. The vision and leadership of Bertie Ahern. The limitless contributions which the Irish have made to America. The proud tradition of Limerick. Then, without any signal, Clinton acknowledged Cross and the McNamaras and asked them to stand. It certainly was a moment the McNamaras of Limerick had never envisioned. Clinton then concluded his speech:

"Standing here on these streets on this fine, late summer day, we cannot possible know all the changes the new millennium will bring. But I believe at the end of another 1,000 years, Limerick and Western Ireland will still face out toward and reach out toward America. And I know America will never turn away.

"In an old Irish tale, Finn MacCumbal says, 'The best music in the world is the music of what happens.' What happens here today is quite wonderful. Never let the music die in your heart, and it will always play out in your lives. And America will be there every step of the way."

As in Armagh, one of the President's men came up to Cross just before the end of the program. But this time it was just for Cross and his relatives. The White House man led them through the crowd and then behind the stage into the Bank of Ireland building. Minutes later the President came bounding in asking, "Okay, where are all these relatives?" He then hugged Cross's mother. "How are you, mom?" Asked Danny how London was. And then shook hands, joked and posed for pictures with Barbara and all the cousins. The cousins repeatedly thanked Clinton for all he had done for Ireland. Clinton suddenly became serious:

"When I became President and looked at Ireland, I realized something had to be done. I also realized that the United States could play a real role. That's why it was so important for me to give Gerry Adams a visa. But Tom Foley, who was our Speaker—and a Democrat—opposed the visa so much. But not Sean. He has supported me all the way."

Clinton paused for a moment before saying, in a very emotional voice, "I love this man" as he threw his arms around Cross and hugged him.

Air Force One was smoothly making its way over the Atlantic. The plane was about three hours out of Shannon, and it was nearly one o'clock in the morning Irish time. The lights were dimmed and the other members of Congress were sound asleep. Cross, however, was only half dozing when he heard a steward say, "He's over by the window, Mr. President. I think he's still awake." Cross looked over and saw Clinton—in jeans, sport shirt and sweater—starting to climb across the seats to get to him. Cross stood up, pointing to an open area where they could meet. Clinton nodded. Cross got up and walked over to a small vestibule type area between where the Congressmen were seated and where the Secret Service agents were situated.

"Mr. President, I can't thank you enough for what you did for my family today. I'll never forget that."

"I enjoyed it, Sean. They're really good people. I could tell that. Listen, I think we've got some good news about the north."

"What's that?"

"Gerry Adams and David Trimble will be meeting in a few days."

"That is great. It'll be their first direct meeting."

"I hope they make some progress. I really think Gerry's gone as far as he can on decommissioning."

"What did you make of Trimble's speech?"

"Trimble reminds me of an accountant who is suddenly put in charge of a political party at a key point in history and isn't sure what to do. That speech in Waterfront Hall was basically a 'Fuck You' speech."

"Do you see any hope on decommissioning?"

"I was thinking there might be a way around the decommissioning issue. The IRA could announce a schedule for decommissioning, and then Trimble could form the Executive—with Sinn Fein in it—before the IRA actually decommissions any weapons."

"That could have possibilities. I'll pass it on."

"Fine. I had just a great time in Ireland. I really love it. When I'm not President anymore, I'd love to come to Ireland for three weeks or so."

"How'd your private meetings with Yeltsin go?"

"I actually have a good personal relationship with Yeltsin so I could talk frankly with him. I told him he's 'pissing away his legacy' and making a mistake by not meeting with members of the Duma. In my own case"—Clinton paused for a moment before continuing—"despite my self-inflicted wound I still come to the office every day and work continually."

"Last night at the Embassy you mentioned General Lebed and said he had a strange look in his eyes. I saw that same look when he was talking to me. When I saw him look at you that way, he seemed like he was trying to intimidate you."

"He's not going to intimidate me," said Clinton defiantly.

"I'm sure he didn't, but I think he was trying," said Cross.

"Lebed's a funny guy," said Clinton who was now smiling. "When I congratulated him on his victory in the election, he said in a real cold voice—'It won't be my last.'"

"I thought it was wrong for the American reporters to be asking you so many personal questions during the news conference in Moscow. No matter how they feel, they should confine that shit to the United States."

"I think I understand why they do it," said Clinton, sounding bemused and somewhat detached. "For four years they weren't able to prove anything against me and that made them very frustrated. Now because of my self-inflicted wound, they have something to use against me and they want to make the most of it."

"That could be it."

"Well, I'm going to try and get some sleep. This has really been a terrific trip."

"Thanks again for being so good to my family, Mr. President."

"My pleasure."

Clinton then walked quietly back to his compartment. The conversation had lasted about twenty minutes. Throughout the conversation Clinton had held an unlit cigar. Cross went back to his seat and fell dead asleep.

CHAPTER NINETEEN

Belfast
Late June

The phone rang in Sean Cross's room at the Europa. It was his 6:00 A.M. wake-up call. As it turned out, Cross didn't need it. He'd been lying awake since five thirty making sure he had everything straight that Vera Toomey had told him the night before.

By six thirty Cross had showered, shaved, and gotten dressed. He was ready for what had to be done. First, he placed a call to President Clinton's room.

"Good morning, Sean."

"Mr. President, I'm sorry to bother you this early."

"That's okay. I've been up for a while."

"I know you're going to London later today, but I've got to talk to you before you leave. It's very important."

"How long will you need?"

"About twenty minutes."

"How about right now?"

"I'll be there in two minutes."

The Secret Service agent waiting at the door greeted Cross and escorted him into the president's private suite before retreating into the outer room, closing the door behind him.

"Sit down, Sean. Make yourself comfortable. There's plenty of coffee, juice, and toast, so take whatever you want."

"Thanks," said Sean, pouring himself a cup of coffee.

"Whatever's on your mind, let me have it."

Cross proceeded to tell Clinton everything Vera Toomey had shared with him in Twinbrook the night before. He also told him about his contacts with Bartlett, the ex-CIA man, and Naughton, McDevitt's man in New York. Clinton immediately grasped the implications.

"You told Vera Toomey you'd be talking to me about this?"

"Yeah."

"And she had no problem with that?"

"No. She honestly feels the only people she can truly trust are those at the very top. Anyone in between could, as far as she knows, be part of whatever operation is going on."

"Is she telling the truth?"

"Unless she's some MI5 agent sent to put one over on me, I believe her. She sounded authentic, and I don't see any reason for her to lie. In its own way, her story fits together. And it doesn't contradict anything Bartlett or Naughton told me."

"How would you sum it up?"

"Someone in British intelligence with MI5 or MI6, but probably MI5, still can't accept that the British government made an agreement with the republican movement. They want to bring down the Good Friday Agreement and everything that's flowed from it. And somehow they've linked up with McDevitt. By killing McGrath and Kilpatrick and Williamson, and using a gun that could be traced to the IRA, they hoped to provoke a reaction from the loyalist paramilitaries."

"We're talking about British intelligence. But two of the murders occurred in New York," said Clinton. "Plus, Toomey told you that McGrath met with a guy in New York who was supposed to be CIA. Whether he was or not, there's an American connection. And both operations were pretty sophisticated. We're not talking about some militia wacko."

"You're right. These guys knew what they were doing."

"We have to make sure that we don't add two and two and get five here. Vera Toomey could be a liar. The IRA could have a wing trying to disrupt the process. I don't think that's what's happening, but we've got to be careful."

"I agree."

"On the other hand, we have to do something. I'm supposed to see Tony this afternoon just before I leave for Rome. I'll relay what you heard last night, but I won't mention Vera Toomey's name. In fact, I won't say it even came from a woman."

"I think that'd be the best way to handle it. You're going right to the top, with a minimum of risk to Vera."

"You're really worried about her."

"Yeah. But I agree with her that it's too risky to go to the police."

"Even after all the reforms?"

"There are still a number of hard-asses hanging around. And all you'd need is one of those bastards to tip off MI5, or whoever the hell is involved."

"So what are you going to do?" asked Clinton.

"I'm meeting a guy in about an hour who was a pretty active IRA man in the old days. Now he helps recruit Catholics for the cops and is a member of the local policy planning board. I'm hoping he can help."

"Even someone who was involved with an informer?"

"I don't think he'll hold it against her. My experience has been that the guys who've been through the most—on both sides, IRA and loyalist—realize that everything's not always black and white."

"I hope it works out. But let me give you some free political advice."

"You're the expert," said Cross.

"Watch yourself with those IRA guys. Remember, you're in the middle of a tough election. The last thing you need are news stories about you running around Belfast with terrorists. Those talk-radio nuts will turn this into a big fucking conspiracy. Believe me, you don't need it."

"I'll keep the meeting very low-key."

"And you can trust this guy to keep you out of whatever he does?"

"Yeah. I trust him completely."

Two hours later, Sean Cross stepped out of a cab on Colligan Street in the heart of West Belfast. Indeed, it was just down from the Springfield Road, where Bill Clinton and Gerry Adams had their historic handshake in 1995. The sky was filled with clouds, but there was only the barest hint of moisture in the air. Cross was wearing a sport jacket and jeans. Opening the door of the Colligan Sandwich Bar, he spotted Joe McNamara sitting at a table, his back against the wall.

"Hey, Sean. How's things?"

"I'm doing okay. How about you?" asked Cross as he shook McNamara's hand before sitting down.

"Not so bad."

Joe was sipping a cup of tea. Cross ordered coffee.

Cross first met Joe McNamara more then twenty years ago during the supergrass trials when McNamara was a Sinn Fein activist and community worker in Ballymurphy, a particularly strong republican area. Cross never asked McNamara whether he was in the IRA. The Brits claimed he was. So, too, did much of the media. And Cross assumed it was true. But he didn't really care. McNamara fought hard for his community, whatever the issue—be it the lethal use of plastic bullets, the abuse of republican prisoners, or the supergrass show trials.

There were always reports that McNamara was about to be charged or that his arrest was imminent. But the Brits never quite managed to collar Joe. And once the Good Friday Agreement was signed, it was too late. Like the other Shinners, he became a legitimate political player. He concentrated on police reform and delighted in tormenting the RUC.

For almost five years the Brits had resisted real reform. But their resistance slowly crumbled and by now needed reforms had been implemented. One of them was the creation of local commissions to oversee police conduct. Joe McNamara sat on the West Belfast Police Commission.

As a member, McNamara closely monitored police practices to ensure there were adequate safeguards against the brutality and human-rights violations that had permeated the RUC. Joe also urged the increased hiring of Catholics to make the new police more acceptable to the nationalist community and encouraged

Catholics to join the police service. Nationalists hailed his efforts. Unionists conceded his industriousness and honesty. Sean Cross saw Joe as the man who might be able to provide Vera Toomey with security and peace of mind.

"Joe, I appreciate your seeing me on such short notice."

"Ah, Sean, I knew you wouldn't be asking if it weren't important."

"Is it safe to talk here?"

"Aye. The owner is dead on, so he is. And our lads swept the place, so there shouldn't be bugs or any of that carry-on."

"Jesus, I almost forgot. You're running the show up here," said Cross with a laugh.

"Not quite, Sean. Not quite. But we're sure as hell trying," answered Joe with a wide grin.

Cross then reconstructed Vera Toomey's story. When he had finished, Joe sat quietly for a moment before responding.

"Frank McGrath. Jesus, he was a rotten fucker. A lying bastard, so he was. You remember. You were here for that trial."

"McGrath was bad. There's no doubt about that. But Vera had nothing to do with Frank then, and, to be honest with you, my only concern is for her safety. If her story is true, I think it's just a matter of time before MI5 or MI6, or whoever the fuck is behind this, murders her. She knows too much."

"Twenty years ago, maybe ten, I'd've stiffed Frank McGrath without giving it a thought. But the past few years? No. If I'd come across him, I'd probably have walked right by him. There's enough fucking problems today without reliving old ones. As for Vera Toomey, she'd nothing to do with Frank when he was a tout, so I've no feeling against her. And I certainly don't want the Brits killing her."

"Can you help her?"

"First of all, you were right to come to me rather than the police. We're slowly weeding them out, but there's still some of the Special Branch bastards left. They know they've lost, but they won't let go."

"You can't trust them at all?"

"Ach, no. Remember, it was the RUC's Special Branch that was involved in the dirty tricks with MI5, MI6, and the police Special Branch in England. They were in collusion with the UVF and UDA, killing innocent Catholics. And it was the RUC Special Branch that worked with the supergrasses until they snuck off to England, or wherever they went."

"So what can you do?"

"Community policing is working. The police lads patrolling Twinbrook, for instance, are almost all from West Belfast. Some are actually from Twinbrook. They can be trusted."

"You'll talk to them?"

"Aye. Directly, so I will. There'll be no official report. Nothing in writing. Nothing the Special Branch hangers-on can put their eyes on. It'll be 'off the books,' as you Yanks say."

"Are you going to coordinate this with Vera?"

"I'll arrange to meet with her today, and then I'll work it out with the lads."

"Are you going to tell them what it's about? Why she needs protection?"

"No. I'll just say it's a special project. And they'll ask no more. Vera will have around-the-clock protection."

"Thank you, Joe. I knew you'd come through."

At seven o'clock that evening, Cross walked into the Europa's main dining room. Seated at the bar was another old friend from the supergrass days, Richard Lee Manning, the renowned barrister who had represented Dermot Hanlon, among many other IRA defendants over the years. Even though Hanlon had been convicted, Manning's defense had been brilliant, particularly his cross-examination of McGrath. Manning lost the case because it was fixed. But Manning had built such a strong trial record that the Appeals Court had no choice but to reverse. And Dermot Hanlon became a free man.

Dick Manning had worked hand-in-glove with Pat Finucane, an equally skilled solicitor. Their talents fitted perfectly. Finucane preparing the defense, Manning presenting the evidence in court.

That ended in 1989 when Finucane was murdered at home in his kitchen in front of his wife and children. It was loyalist paramilitaries who fired the shots, but nationalists believed there was Brit collusion. Cross knew that Dick had never fully recovered from Pat's murder, even though Manning was still Belfast's preeminent courtroom performer.

"Sean, it's a pleasure to see you," said Manning as he stepped forward to shake hands. "Your call took me a bit by surprise, but I'm delighted you rang."

"I'm just glad I was able to get hold of you. You're always so damn busy."

"Not at all. This works out just grand. I've got a few days before my next trial, and Laurie's away in Dublin for the night. Can I order you the usual, straight Bushmills?"

"That'd be terrific. I see your memory's still working," said Cross with a laugh as the bartender poured the whiskey.

"Most of the time, anyway," answered Manning. "And how's Mary Rose keeping?"

"She's doing fine. Thanks for asking."

"Sean, I know we've important matters to discuss, so why don't we take our drinks to the table, where we'll have some privacy?"

"Good idea."

Cross and Manning sat down about twenty feet from the bar.

"Sean, when you rang this afternoon, you said you wanted me to tell you all I knew about British intelligence and what they're capable of."

"Yeah, Dick. For your sake and mine, I can't tell you the source of my information, but I've got evidence that MI5 or MI6 might be involved in the McGrath and Kilpatrick murders, as well as the unionist professor in New York."

"Forgive my attempt at humor, Sean, but from what I read in the papers, your political opponents are blaming *you* for the murder."

"Not quite," laughed Cross, "but almost."

The waiter took their orders.

"How's your election going? I assume none of this is helping."

"It's not. That's for sure. But it's not wrecking the campaign either. There's just slow but steady attrition. About a point or two at a time."

"Christ, it sounds like death by a thousand cuts."

"Don't worry, it's not that bad. But to use your metaphor, I would like to stop the bleeding."

"How do you do that?"

"By showing that the IRA had nothing to do with any of this—because in the public eye, I'm being identified with them."

"Which, I assume, is why we're having this conversation."

"Yes. That and your unique wit and charm."

For the next hour, Dick Manning educated Cross on decades of British intelligence operations in Ireland. He began by recapping the basics, comparing MI5 with the FBI, and MI6 with the CIA. MI5 and MI6, he continued, were supposedly monitored by the Intelligence and Security Committee, consisting of MPs and lords appointed by the prime minister, which met secretly every week in a secure room in the Cabinet Office.

MI6 should have had no involvement in Northern Ireland because its mandate as defined by statute was to "obtain and provide information relating to the activities or intentions of persons outside the British Islands." Yet there had been an ongoing turf battle between MI5 and MI6 for jurisdiction in the north.

Cross then detailed for Manning the events of recent months, including what he had learned from Vera Toomey.

"Sean, what you've described brings to mind past British operations."

"Give me some examples."

"I can think of two straightaway. During the '70s the Brits had two brothers, the Littlejohns, rob banks in the Republic and blamed it on the IRA. The Brits also had loyalists set off bombs in Dublin and Monaghan in 1974, killing many people, all of them innocent civilians, so that the Dublin government would adopt repressive legislation, fearing the war was moving south."

"Didn't that special legislation apply to loyalists as well as republicans?"

"Yes. But since there were no loyalists in the south, it only hurt the IRA."

"They are clever bastards. So, who's been worse—MI5 or MI6?"

"They've both been rotten. But I'd have to give MI5 the edge. They'd even go against their own people."

"I remember they ruined the top MI6 man during the turf wars in Northern Ireland by revealing he was gay."

"Yeah, poor Maurice Oldfield. MI5 treated him worse than the KGB ever did. MI5 even tried to overthrow Harold Wilson when he was prime minister."

"In the States, we have to keep an eye on the CIA and the FBI, but there's never been anything like that."

"Even the cops were afraid of them. Back in the '90s the chief constable of Devon and Cornwall said, 'MI5 operates like a cancer.'"

Cross hesitated for a moment before asking, "What about Pat Finucane?"

"Pat was a magnificent lawyer. He was my closest friend. And I've no doubt he was murdered by RUC Special Branch and MI5 working with the UDA. No doubt at all. Also—and this I'm not certain of even though several sources have told it to me—MI5 may actually have forwarded their plans to target him to the oversight committee back in London."

"Pat's death was a tragedy. I knew him pretty well."

"It was a tragedy not only for Pat and for his family, but for the republican movement as well. He was such a brilliant solicitor. He drove the Brits mad. That's why he had to be killed. And that's where it all came together for me—MI5, the RUC, and the UDA. And maybe even the British government itself."

"I guess you could say Pat's murder was a microcosm of what the Catholics were up against all those years."

"And that's why I'll never forgive those bastards."

"It's incredible that with all they had going for them, MI5 never was able to defeat the IRA."

"That's because they were good at torturing poor Catholic bastards coming home from the pub after a few pints, and murdering lawyers. But they missed most of the big stuff."

"Yeah. Clinton told me MI5 never knew about the IRA ceasefire or the breaking of the ceasefire."

"Let me tell you something that'll really give you a laugh. They didn't know about the 1916 Easter Uprising in Dublin, either."

"What about MI6?"

"Don't misunderstand what I say about MI6. They've indulged in more than their share of brutality and treachery. But for whatever reason, MI6 always seemed to have more of an interest in a political solution, setting up local contacts in the republican movement. That was especially true during the hunger strikes in '81."

"You mean that guy they called 'Mountain Climber'?"

"That's the one. Michael Oatley. He was involved on and off in Ireland for about twenty years. From the brief ceasefire in 1975 to the key one in 1994."

"I remember the attacks on him when he defended Adams and McGuinness over decommissioning back in '99."

"That was your friends at the *Telegraph.* They hammered him, so they did. But the *Telegraph* can always be depended upon to do MI5's work."

"If MI5 is behind all this, do you think it could go right to the top, like Pat's murder may have done?"

"Maybe five or six years ago. The World Trade Center and the war against bin Laden changed all that. Blair really asserted himself. He wanted MI5 and MI6 modernized from top to bottom. They got rid of a lot of their deadwood—those old fuckers who just hung around to satisfy their old vendettas and even old scores. So my guess is it's just a small element that's behind this—maybe one or two guys who've never given up the fight."

"That's at least somewhat encouraging."

"Yes and no. It's a good thing not all of MI5's involved. On the other hand, if it's just a few guys, it could be like finding a needle in a haystack, as you Yanks say. The old MI5 may not have been the best at gathering information, but they were excellent at secrecy and deception."

"Dick, I can't thank you enough. You've been tremendously helpful."

"Sean, I'm delighted to have been of some help. The only other thing I'd suggest is speaking to as many sources as you can. But don't divulge anything to anyone you can't trust implicitly. These bastards play a deadly game."

CHAPTER TWENTY

December 1998–February 1999

The fall of 1998 had been a Lewinsky whirlwind. The Starr Report was released the week following Clinton's return from Ireland. In a style almost adolescent in its prurience, Starr explored the depths of intimacy between the President and his intern in excruciatingly graphic detail. This was followed several weeks later by the national telecast of Clinton's videotaped August 17 testimony to the grand jury.

To the talking heads and other political movers, these disclosures portended political doom for Clinton. But with each disclosure, Clinton's favorable ratings soared. As did the Republicans' unfavorables. By election day in November the rout was complete. The Republicans, who on Labor Day had confidently predicted gains of between thirty and forty House seats, lost seats. On election night, commentators solemnly pronounced the demise of impeachment.

Republicans plummeted farther into the night of the long knives. Newt Gingrich was the first to go. Facing a challenge from Appropriations Committee chairman Bob Livingston, Newt Gingrich surrendered just days after the election, announcing he would step down as Speaker and then resign from the House altogether. As Bill Clinton surveyed the American political terrain, his foes were vanquished and he stood unchallenged. Impeachment would never come to a vote. Or so he thought.

Just weeks later, all that had changed. By December 7, the date of the White House Christmas Ball, Bill Clinton was scrambling to survive.

As Cross explained it to Susan Brophy that evening in the Red Room as the Marine Band played "Silent Night," "It was there all along, but we never saw it coming. But DeLay did and you've got to give him credit. He knew what he was doing."

Cross was referring to Tom DeLay, the Republican Congressman from Texas and the Majority Whip. What DeLay had realized was, yes, the country was overwhelmingly against impeachment. And, yes, the majority of voters in most of the Congressional districts were against impeachment. And maybe even a majority of Republicans in many districts were against impeachment. But to get elected, Members of Congress first have to be nominated by their party. That's done in primaries and who votes in party primaries?—maybe 15 percent of the registered party members. Only the most dedicated. The most hard-core true believers. And the Republican hard-core despised Clinton. Most Republican Members of Congress would have preferred that the cup of impeachment pass from them. But Tom DeLay would not give them that option of avoidance. He would force a vote on impeachment. DeLay's efforts received an unexpected boost when Clinton's lawyers submitted a series of legally obtuse answers to eighty-one questions that had been asked by the Judiciary Committee. And suddenly Bill Clinton, who such a short time ago was luxuriating in what he thought was his ultimate political triumph, was staring at the abyss of his political extinction.

When DeLay first made his move in late November, Cross thought there would be 35 to 40 Republican votes against impeachment. And since only 15 to 20 votes would be necessary to thwart impeachment, Cross thought the margin comfortable. But one by one DeLay peeled off the votes. That's why, when Cross walked through the Presidential receiving line with Mary Rose, he was not surprised that Clinton's face appear flushed and worried. The look of a man wracked by tension and getting little sleep. Cross tried to sound hopeful.

"Mr. President, this isn't over. I was just talking to Amo Houghton upstairs," said Cross, referring to the respected veteran Republican Congressman from upstate New York, "and he's coming out against impeachment tomorrow. He's announcing it in an op-ed piece in the *Times*."

"That's good news, Sean. I think I can hold the Democratic defectors to less than five, if you can hold the Republicans."

"I'll do what I can, Mr. President," answered Cross, not certain when he went from being a guy trying to help out, to a guarantor of Republican votes.

On Tuesday, December 8, Cross attended a lunch at the British Embassy in honor of John Hume and David Trimble, who'd just been awarded the Nobel Peace Prize. In fact, they'd be leaving for Oslo that evening to receive their awards.

When the Nobel Committee had made its announcement, Cross's reaction was typical of most observers of the Irish peace process. Certainly, Hume deserved it. He had been the champion of peace and justice for thirty years. But Trimble? It was as if he'd won the lottery without ever having bought a ticket. Because of Trimble's obduracy, there was still no Executive and the process was stalled. And how could the Nobel Committee have ignored Gerry Adams? But to have said anything publicly would have come across as begrudgery. So Cross's announced position was that by honoring Hume and Trimble, the Nobel judges were acknowledging the outstanding work of the many people in both communities working so hard for peace.

The luncheon was a typical high-powered British Embassy extravaganza peopled with political heavyweights, syndicated reporters, noted authors, and other assorted breeds of opinion makers. So, too, were most of Northern Ireland's political leaders in attendance. Adams was the exception. He had decided not to go, a benign expression of disapproval of the Brits' failure to lean on Trimble to do the right thing.

Even at the British Embassy, however, impeachment trumped Ireland as the topic of the day. The Brits and the Irish were bewildered it had actually gone this far. So were most of the Americans.

That evening Cross attended a reception for Al D'Amato, who had lost his re-election bid. At Sean's request D'Amato came out against impeachment. Then Cross took a cab to the Omni Shoreham

Hotel in northwest Washington. He arrived just as the National Democratic Institute dinner was getting under way. The NDI, a nonpartisan think tank, was honoring the eight Northern Irish leaders who had signed the Good Friday Agreement, including Hume, Trimble, and Adams. As Nobel Peace Prize honorees, Hume and Trimble were the principal guests. Bill Clinton was the featured speaker.

Cross edged his way to his assigned table as the invocation was being given. Gerry Adams was seated there, as were Susan Brophy, Margaret Carlson of *Time* magazine, and Mary McGrory of the *Washington Post.* Again the talk was of impeachment, with Carlson saying the most obscene phone calls she'd ever received were ones she'd gotten over the past few weeks from members of the Christian Right self-righteously condemning Bill Clinton's immorality.

During the evening, Susan Brophy went up to the dais to talk with Clinton. When she returned, she whispered to Cross, "The president would like to talk with you later."

The dinner ended just after ten. Cross and Brophy said goodnight to the others, except for Gerry Adams, who'd already left. They ducked behind the podium and out into a long hallway lined with Secret Service agents and White House staff. The only room along the hallway was on the right. A Secret Service agent outside the door told Cross the president was busy inside.

Cross nodded. He and Brophy stood quietly against a wall. The only sounds were the hushed whispers of agents and staffers. To Cross the scene was eerily reminiscent of a hospital waiting room.

After about ten minutes, Cross asked an agent whom the president was meeting with.

"Gerry Adams. The First Lady's in there as well."

"Gerry Adams?"

"Yes, sir. You want me to advise the president that you have a time problem?"

"No, no. Mr. Adams can have all the time he wants," said Cross with a wide smile.

At about eleven o'clock the door opened and the First Lady came out.

"Sean, how are you?" said Hillary Clinton, throwing her arms around him.

"I'm doing fine," answered Cross, kissing her on the cheek.

"We had a great meeting. I'm sure I'll see you soon," said Mrs. Clinton as a group of Secret Service agents escorted her down the hall.

Through the doorway, Cross saw Clinton and Adams exchanging an obviously friendly handshake. Off to one side, Richard McAuley and Rita O'Hare were speaking with Jim Steinberg. As the Irish contingent was leaving, Cross shook hands with them and said he'd stop by Gerry's room after his meeting with Clinton.

Only the president, Cross, and Brophy remained. The door was closed. Clinton and Cross sat facing each other in the center of the room, mere inches apart. Brophy sat just off to the side.

"Sean, I'm sorry to have kept you waiting so long."

"Mr. President, after all the years it took to get Gerry into the country, it doesn't bother me a bit."

"The meeting went very well. Gerry's always thinking. And I really believe we can break this decommissioning impasse."

"I hope so."

"If the issues that are important to republicans, such as making Irish language programs available, could be resolved, I'm sure there'd be some decommissioning. But nothing would be tied together. It would just happen."

"Mr. President, I've heard Blair's really mad at the way Trimble's delayed everything. He thinks Trimble's screwing him. Do you think Blair could lose interest?"

"Tony will stay involved, especially since he has such a large majority in Parliament. That gives him a lot of flexibility."

"How about Trimble?"

"I asked Gerry if he thought Trimble might be more willing to implement the Good Friday Agreement once he came back from Norway with his Nobel Peace Prize."

"What did Gerry say?"

"Maybe. But he didn't know."

Clinton paused for what seemed to be a very long moment. "Sean, what do you think we can do on impeachment?"

"Believe me, I've been thinking about it."

"By the way, thank you very much for Al D'Amato's statement. Did Al do it for you?"

"I did ask him to do it as a personal favor. But he has a high regard for you. I promised him that if he did make the statement, I'd pass this message to you: 'Tell your friend in the White House I'm doing this for him even though he came into New York four times against me.'"

Clinton laughed uproariously before continuing. "I always liked Al. I met him during the '92 campaign. It was at some Jewish event in Brooklyn. I always got along with him. In fact I told him back in 1994 when he started investigating Whitewater that this would only be trouble for him. He was getting bad information from people he shouldn't believe."

"I'd strongly suggest that you call Al tomorrow and thank him. That could motivate him to start calling other members of the New York delegation."

"Good idea. I will."

"As far as the overall vote, I think it's still in play. But you have to find a way to reach out to undecided Republicans. The combination of DeLay pushing as hard as he is and the impression that you were defying the Congress with your eighty-one answers is making this much more difficult for you."

"Sean, those eighty-one answers were honest," said Clinton in a very emotional tone. "For instance, they asked about my grand jury testimony. They asked whether my answers were true and complete. They weren't. They were true and misleading which is not a crime. And that's not all . . ."

"Mr. President," Cross interrupted, "with all respect, I know you believe what you're saying. But most members of Congress thinks it's bullshit. Whether it's fair or not, the reality is that the undecided Republicans think you're trying to screw the Congress and you must accept that. Mr. President, you have to contact as many undecided Republicans as you can, find out what they want you to say and then decide whether or not you can say it. I can't emphasize enough that you're probably only going to be able to make one statement. So you have to make sure that statement will get you the votes you need."

"Don't these people in Congress realize what I've been going through the last three months?" said Clinton, again becoming emotional and grabbing Cross's knee. "Do they think this has been a fucking walk in the park? I'm not just trying to save my ass. Just because I come to work every day and keep my head up doesn't mean this isn't tearing me apart. I have to act that way because I'm the President."

"Mr. President, I know this must be a very rough time for you but I can't stress enough to you how important it is that you contact the undecided Republicans."

"Listen, Sean, I'm concerned if I start making phone calls, some Republicans would claim I'm trying to interfere with them. I trust you completely and I'd tell you anything. But I just know some of those guys would go public and say they were being threatened."

"If you have any doubts about any of them, give the names to Susan and I'll let you know what I think."

"Fine. Also be sure to let me know what you think we can do to move the Irish situation along."

"I certainly will, Mr. President."

"I understand that Larry Flynt is going to make disclosures about Republicans, including members of the Judiciary Committee."

"Yeah. I heard that too. That about ten or twelve will be named."

"That's the number I heard. That would be terrible. I don't want anyone else to go through what I've gone through."

"I'm really afraid where this is all leading."

"Believe me, I am too. Will you stay in touch with Susan?" asked Clinton, as they got up to leave.

"Sure. By the way, Mr. President, I should have mentioned this to you're earlier but Tim Russert told me at Al D'Amato's party that he thinks you have enough votes to win."

"That guy's awful tough on me for a guy from south Buffalo," said Clinton, shaking his head. "Has Hillary gone back to the White House?"

"Yes, sir," answered one of the agents.

"Sean, there's some good football games on this Sunday."

"There sure are."

"Man, isn't Doug Flutie great?" asked Clinton, referring to the Buffalo Bills quarterback.

"He sure is. Good night, Mr. President," said Cross.

"Good night Sean."

When the meeting was over, Cross looked at his watch. It was just past midnight. He took an elevator to Adams's room on the sixth floor and knocked on the door. Richard McCauley answered it.

Adams was sitting on the couch, his tie removed, his shirt collar open, his shoes off. Rita O'Hare sat in a club chair, smoking a cigarette.

"Can I get you a beer?" asked McAuley.

"Thanks, Richard. A Bud would be great," answered Cross.

"It was a long meeting, Sean," said Adams.

"It certainly was," said Cross, popping the beer can and taking a long swig.

"I couldn't believe how focused he was on Ireland during our meeting," said Adams.

"He was brilliant," added O'Hare, puffing on her cigarette.

"But all this talk of impeachment has to be driving him mad," said Adams.

"I'm sure it is," said Cross. "He's very concerned."

"I hope he makes it, for his sake," said Adams. "And Ireland's."

Cross had been on record for several months as opposing impeachment. It hadn't received much attention because the prospect had seemed so remote. Now it was imminent, if not inevitable. And media attention focused on Cross. Would he stand against virtually his entire party by supporting the president?

Cross saw no reason to change his vote. He determined that the best way to resist the pressure was to go on the offensive. He answered every question that every reporter threw at him. And appeared on every television and radio show that invited him.

That decision soon took on a life of its own. He was the only anti-impeachment Republican willing to argue his case in the media. On straight news shows such as *Meet the Press* and *Face the Nation*, in hard-edged debate formats such as *Hard Ball* and *Crossfire*, and in the cauldron of right-wing talk-radio shows such as *Mike Campbell.* At the height of the impeachment frenzy, it was not unusual for Cross to be doing six or seven national television shows a day. One morning there were two camera crews knocking on the front door of his Seaford home at five-thirty in the morning. One was from NBC's *Today Show*; the other from ABC's *Good Morning America*. NBC set up in the living room; ABC in the den. *Today* interviewed Cross at 7:05; *Good Morning America* at 7:35.

Cross noticed the phone calls still coming into his office in torrents were now about 60-40 in Clinton's favor. But, one by one, the undecided House Republicans were breaking against Clinton. Before leaving for Israel on Friday, December 11, Clinton made a statement from the Rose Garden. This was the statement aimed at the undecided Republicans. But neither Clinton nor his staff had coordinated it with any of the Republicans he was trying to win over. All he said was that he was "profoundly sorry" for misleading "the country, the Congress, my friends and my family." It fell short. And impeachment loomed larger.

On Sunday evening, December 13, at seven twenty-five, the phone rang in Cross's Seaford home. Cross picked up the extension in the kitchen, next to the refrigerator.

"Congressman Cross," said the voice at the other end, "this is the White House switchboard. The President would like to speak with you."

Cross looked quickly at the wall clock and realized it was two twenty-five in the morning in Jerusalem.

After about a minute, Clinton came on the line. "Sean, I really appreciate what you've been doing. You must be going through hell. I'm thinking of you."

"Thank you, Mr. President. I'm doing what I can."

"I've been going over the names. I think I can hold the Democratic losses to three or four. I believe I need fifteen Republican votes. But I'd like to get eighteen."

"That's not going to be easy, Mr. President."

"Let me give you some names."

"Sure."

"Charlie Barron."

"Charlie's very moderate and has a real regard for a lot of your policies. But," Cross hesitated, "he told Al D'Amato the other day he was concerned you'd be getting away with perjury, something other people would be indicted for."

"I never committed perjury," insisted Clinton, his voice rising slightly. "Tell Charlie I have a number of experts—former Republican prosecutors—who are convinced I didn't perjure myself. Plus, I ran very well in his district. I carried it by seven points."

And so it went, Clinton suggesting names, Cross reluctantly saying why Clinton really couldn't count on them. And Clinton giving his precise margin of victory in each district. There was the Congressman who would reluctantly vote for impeachment because DeLay wouldn't allow a censure vote—and the Congressman who faced losing his Committee Chairmanship and the other Congressman who was threatened with being stripped of his leadership assignment if he voted against impeachment. The reality was that Cross was not able to offer him one positive bit of news on any of the names Clinton gave him. But Clinton persisted in focusing on each member of Congress individually, never acknowledging the clear trend that was obviously emerging against him.

Not wanting to create false hope but attempting to conclude the conversation on a much more upbeat note, Cross said, "Mr. President, a reporter from *USA Today* called me about an hour ago and gave me the numbers on the polls they're releasing tomorrow."

"What are the numbers?"

"The Republicans' 'highly unfavorable' number has gone from 15 percent to 21 percent in the past two months."

"That's high."

"It certainly is. Even when the government was shut down in January '96, our numbers never went above 14 percent."

"I'm not surprised."

"Another good number for you is that 58 percent favor censure over impeachment—"

"Those numbers are wrong," Clinton interjected. "My polls show that 70 percent want censure."

"I'm sure your numbers are right," said Cross, seeing no need to argue the point.

"Sean, getting back to the perjury issue, I think it might be helpful if I spoke to some of the members who aren't lawyers and explain my testimony to them."

"Mr. President, that certainly couldn't hurt."

"Sean, thank you very much. This conversation has been very helpful."

"You're welcome, Mr. President. Get some sleep."

As Cross hung up the phone, he looked at the clock. It was seven forty-six. And in his mind he envisioned Bill Clinton sitting in his hotel room in Jerusalem in the middle of the night, still thinking that somehow he would prevail over the forces of impeachment.

"That was the saddest conversation I've ever had," said Cross to Mary Rose. "He's definitely reaching out. Grasping for anything. And there is nothing there. I couldn't tell him anything good."

"Doesn't he realize how bad it is?"

"No. He won't let himself. That's why it was so sad. And it's only going to get worse."

Cross was right. Republicans Clinton had counted on announced they were voting for impeachment. And the undecided Republicans continued their cascade toward impeachment. The Republican leadership announced the impeachment schedule. The debate would be on Thursday, December 17, the vote Friday, December 18.

Cross flew to Washington on Wednesday morning, December 16. He would be interviewed at noon by ABC's Ted Koppel for that evening's *Nightline*. Flying down on the US Air Shuttle, Cross received no shortage of advice. "Come on, Congressman, you gotta impeach that guy." "You're doing the right thing. Don't let them wear you down." But a bit surprisingly, there was little anger or intensity. Those dispensing the advice were subdued. As if they realized all that could be said had been said. Or maybe it was just too early in the morning for them to get too excited.

As Cross exited the terminal and opened the door to the waiting car, Tom O'Connell greeted him with, "Have you heard about Iraq?"

"No. What?"

"We're supposed to start bombing any minute. It's about Saddam and the U.N. inspectors."

"What's the reaction on the Hill?"

"The Republicans are going fucking nuts. They're saying Clinton's doing it to put off impeachment."

"Christ," replied Cross, "just when you think it can't get any worse."

The lights were in place and the camera set up when Cross walked into his office in the Cannon Building. Stepping over the sound adapters and wiring strewn about the floor, Cross was greeted by Koppel who seemed a bit perplexed.

"Congressman, it's a pleasure to meet you. Sorry we had to tear your office apart like this."

"It's good to see you Ted. And don't worry about the office. I'm used to it with you TV guys."

"Thanks for the vote of confidence. Listen, I have no idea which direction the show is going in tonight. It was supposed to be impeachment. After all this is the first impeachment in 130 years. But now it looks as if we may be at war. Which is also a fairly important story."

"We're certainly living in interesting times."

"So we'll do your interview exactly the way things are. We'll assume that you don't know whether you're going to be confronted by impeachment, by war or by both."

And so for the next 20 minutes Cross answered questions about impeachment and war. His answers tried to strike a balance.

- Yes. Republicans have an obligation to make sure the President is not bombing Iraq to divert attention from impeachment.
- No. Republicans should not say or do anything that would weaken the President in carrying out his duties as commander-in-chief.

Sure enough, Clinton did order bombing attacks on Iraq. So did Tony Blair. The reaction was immediate—Democrats demanding that impeachment be put off until hostilities were finished, Republicans charging that Clinton was starting a phony war to delay the impeachment vote until after January 1, when there would be a new Congress with more Democrats and a drastically reduced Republican majority.

That evening at six o'clock, the Republicans held an emergency meeting in HC-5, a stark, cavernous room in the bowels of the Capitol Building. Bob Livingston, the Speaker-elect, had scheduled the meeting after Clinton phoned him that afternoon, asking that the impeachment schedule be pushed back one day. Livingston, who was from the old school, acceded to the president's request. Now he had to sell it to a roomful of avaricious zealots.

Cross arrived a few minutes early. The room was filling quickly. A television had been set up so the Republicans could see Bill Clinton's address to the nation, which was scheduled to begin in the next ten or fifteen minutes. By six o'clock every seat was taken and the doors closed. The hallway outside the room was jammed with reporters.

Before Livingston could speak, the chant of "Vote! Vote! Vote!" filled the room. Finally, Livingston calmed them enough so he could be heard. The first thing he did was remind his members that the national media could hear every outburst through the doors. So no matter how they felt about Clinton, he was the president and there would be no booing or hissing or laughing during his speech.

For a moment Cross thought he was in St. Teresa's Grammar School in Woodside, with some nun instructing the third-graders how to act during assembly.

Clinton appeared on the screen. He delivered a brief speech. Iraq wouldn't allow the arms inspectors required by the UN. Clinton had no choice; he had to attack. He thanked our allies, particularly the British, for standing with us.

The presidential address had barely concluded when many of the Republicans began howling and yelling and renewing the chant of "Vote! Vote! Vote!" It reminded Cross of the old *Morton Downey, Jr. Show*. Again, Livingston was able to restore calm, making it clear he had decided the president of the United States was entitled to a one-day delay. Cross was struck by Livingston's firmness. It made him wonder why Livingston had allowed Tom DeLay to set party policy on impeachment over the past three weeks.

As Cross was leaving, Luke Christian, an introspective Republican who had been leaning against impeachment, approached Cross and whispered, "Sean, you still going to vote no?"

"Yeah, Luke, I am."

"Has anyone told you about the files over in the annex?" asked Christian, referring to the building where the Judiciary Committee secured its impeachment files.

"No. What files?"

"They showed me files with evidence against Clinton going back to 1979."

"Evidence of what?"

"Sexual abuse of women. Including a rape."

"Was any of this brought out at the hearing?"

"No. And it's not part of any of the four articles of impeachment. But this'll come out in a month or two, and it'll look as if we defended a rapist. You might want to consider going over there and at least looking at what they have."

"Listen, Luke, I appreciate what you're saying. But if it doesn't relate to the four articles, then screw it. It's not relevant, and I'm not looking at it."

"Are you sure?"

"If they feel that strongly about it, they should put it in an article of impeachment and get it out in the open. I'm not going to impeach a president based on secret evidence."

"Okay. I just didn't want you to get blindsided."

There was one procedural vote late Thursday morning. With nothing scheduled for the rest of the day, Cross decided to fly back to New York. Mary Rose had come down with pneumonia. The doctor attributed it directly to the stress of impeachment. Cross thought he would serve some purpose by talking with her and keeping her company. It was just after three when he walked into the house.

"How're you feeling?" he asked.

"A little better. How was the trip?"

"Not bad. Except for some guy in a pickup truck on the Cross Island giving me the finger."

"The voice of democracy," she said, smiling weakly.

"The calls to the office are actually more encouraging than that guy in the truck. So far this week, they're coming in about 2–1 against impeachment."

"When are you going back?"

"I'll catch a plane out first thing in the morning. I'm supposed to be speaking sometime in the afternoon."

"Any chance Clinton can win?"

"No. It's all over but the counting."

About 6:15 Sean and Mary Rose were sitting in the den watching the local news when the phone rang. Cross picked it up.

"This is Brannigan," said the grizzled reporter.

"Mickey, how're you doing?"

"Lousy. They're sending me to Washington to cover you fucking clowns."

"When're you leaving?"

"Tomorrow morning. First thing."

"I'm getting an early flight, too. Maybe I'll see you."

"That's something to look forward to."

"Mickey, could you hold a minute? I've got call waiting."

"Yeah. Go ahead."

"Hello," said Cross.

It was ABC TV news reporter Lynn Duncan. "Sean, what can you tell me about Livingston's affair?"

"What?"

"We're going with it as our lead story at six thirty. Livingston's admitting he's had an affair."

"I don't know anything about it."

"It was on the Roll Call Web site," she said, referring to Capitol Hill's insider paper. "Livingston's supposed to be announcing this right now at your party's conference."

"Christ, I skipped that to come home. I figured it'd be the same crap as last night."

"That's the story of your life. Wrong place at the wrong time. Anyway in about ten minutes you'll see me reporting at the top of the show and find out what you missed by leaving Washington."

"Thanks Lynn. I'll recognize your blazing red hair."

Cross hit the dial-tone button.

"Mickey, you still there?"

"I could fucking die of old age."

"That was Lynn Duncan at ABC. She's reporting that Livingston's had an affair. This is fucking crazy."

"You guys deserve it. You're doing it to yourselves. You start this and it comes back to bite you in the ass."

"The shit must really be hitting the fan. I'd better get back tonight."

Brannigan grunted and slammed down the phone.

Cross told Mary Rose about Livingston and took off for another trip to LaGuardia Airport.

As Cross was coming onto the Grand Central Parkway, less than five minutes from the Delta Shuttle at the Marine Air terminal, his cell phone rang.

"Sean? "

"Yeah."

"Danny Lacy."

"What's up?"

"I'm heading to Washington tonight. What plane are you catching?"

"I should just about make the 7:30."

"The earliest I can get is the 8:30."

"I'll meet you down there."

"Where?"

"How about the Dubliner?"

"Great. Between 9:30 and 10:00 okay?"

"Terrific."

"Some crazy shit going on, heh?"

"Crazier by the minute."

"See you soon."

By nine fifty, Cross was seated in the Dubliner's "snug" with Danny Lacy and a pint of Harp. Lacy used a teaspoon to twirl the ice in his Diet Coke.

"I wonder where this fucking thing is going," said Cross. "In two days we're going to impeach the president of the United States for having an affair. Tonight that president is bombing the shit out of Iraq. And our new Speaker is caught having his own affair. I feel like I'm trapped in an insane asylum."

"Once the shit starts, it doesn't stop. What's the story tomorrow?"

"The House'll open about ten. The main thing'll be the reading of the four articles of impeachment."

"There's perjury and obstruction of justice on the Lewinsky deposition and on the grand jury testimony, right?"

"That's it. After they read them, the rest of day will be the debate."

"When are you speaking?"

"Early afternoon."

"How long?"

"They've given me two minutes."

"Any idea what you're going to say?"

"No."

It was shortly after one o'clock on Friday that Ray LaHood, Cross's good friend and the Speaker pro tempore, recognized Cross for his two minutes. Cross stepped to the lectern in the well of the House, glanced at the notes he had scribbled on small pieces of memo paper, and began speaking.

"Mr. Speaker, I rise today in opposition to the articles of impeachment. My opposition to impeachment has nothing to do with Bill Clinton, but everything to do with the office of the presidency.

"By setting a standard that goes beyond the Constitution, we are continuing our spiral toward a government subject to the whims of independent counsels and based on the frenzied politics of the moment, rather than a government of immutable principles and transcendent institutions.

"This is not a decision that came easily to me. It is not a position which I particularly enjoy. But I feel I have no alternative. I strongly believe that for a president of the United States to be impeached, for an election to be undone, there must be a direct abuse of presidential power, a crime comparable to treason or bribery.

"But there is an even larger issue here: where we going as a nation? We are a nation consumed by investigations, by special counsels. We are a nation consumed by scandal. We are driving good people from government.

"In this case, the president's conduct was illegal, it was criminal, it was immoral, it was disgraceful. But it doesn't rise to the level of treason or bribery.

"This is a sad day for our country. It is a sad year for our nation, because of the conduct of our own president, and also because I believe that as Republicans, we failed to rise to our obligations. As a matter of conscience I must vote against impeachment and I rue this day."

Pounding his gavel, LaHood decreed, "The time of the gentleman has expired." Cross walked from the well of the House, up the center aisle, and out into the hallway on the east side of the Capitol building. Jack Pender was waiting. As were Mickey Brannigan and Danny Lacy. Despite the historic events swirling around them, they engaged in only the barest, pedestrian small talk as they made their way down to the Members Dining Room on the first floor. It was as if the moment spoke for itself.

After living off adrenaline for the past three weeks, Cross could feel all energy draining from him. Lars-Erik Nelson from the *Daily News* and Mary McGrory from the *Washington Post* joined the table but added little to the conversation. The mood was not one of sadness—or even anticipation—but almost benign disinterest. Perhaps it was the final realization that while the crisis was historic, its genesis was so tawdry and insignificant. So the conversation was more the minutia and detail than substance.

—How long would the debate go?

Almost until midnight and it's not really a debate. Just one speech after the other with no reference being made to the speech before it.—

—Any change in the votes?

No.—

—What's the agenda for tomorrow?

We'll have the wrap-up speeches in the morning. Probably Livingston for the Republicans and Gephardt for the Democrats.—

—Any votes besides the four impeachment articles?

Yeah. The first vote will be a motion by the Democrats to allow a censure vote.—

—Any chance that'll pass?

God no. Even Republicans who are voting against impeachment will vote against that.—

—Why?

It's treason to go against your party on procedural votes.—

—How about you?

I'll vote for it. That's the whole issue. If they allow a vote on censure, there'll never be impeachment.—

—Isn't that treason?

Fuck it. At this stage what's the difference?—

It was late morning, Saturday, December 19. Cross was sitting just off the center aisle. On the Republican side—but "just barely," as Danny Lacy would write it. Bob Livingston was speaking. Cross always thought highly of Livingston—solid guy, straight shooter. He also knew that Livingston had never thought much of impeachment. So when Livingston was elected Speaker in mid-November, Cross was convinced impeachment was dead, that Livingston would work out some sort of censure compromise. But instead he had just stepped back and let Tom DeLay drive the impeachment train. Even if that train was taking the Republican Party over the political cliff. Thursday night's admission by Livingston that he had an affair explained to Cross why he'd been so deferential to DeLay. Livingston must have realized he couldn't risk having any involvement in an impeachment based on sex. But now his own scandal was out in the open. So far the Republicans appeared willing to stand with him.

Livingston's speech this morning was surprisingly partisan. And when he demanded that Clinton resign, the Democrats responded with jeering and catcalls: "You resign! You resign!" *This is going from bad to worse*, Cross thought. Just a few moments later, he realized how much worse.

Bob Livingston announced his resignation.

Cross felt as if he were in a political wind tunnel. Nothing was structured or rooted. The president of the United States was about to be impeached because of a sex scandal. Then the Speaker of the House was resigning because of a sex scandal. Who would be next? What would happen next? Cross had experienced this sense of political vertigo only once before, when he was much younger. In November 1963. President Kennedy was shot to death on Friday. And his assassin, Lee Harvey Oswald, was shot to death on Sunday. Now, thirty-five years later, sex was substituted for bullets.

For a long moment the air went out of the House chamber. The shrieking Democrats fell still. Republicans sat motionless. Reporters sitting up in the gallery, behind where Livingston was speaking, stood up and craned their necks to get a better view of the melodrama unfolding beneath them.

Livingston went back to his speech. And when he concluded, the Republicans applauded loudly. As did the Democrats.

But none had heard a word after they heard "resign." Nor were any of the succeeding speakers—Gephardt asked Livingston to stay on; DeLay called him a great man—paid any heed. It had all been said.

The first vote was on the Democratic request for a censure alternative. Cross was one of two Republicans to vote with the Democrats.

The impeachment votes began at about ten past one. Each time, Cross voted no, one of only four Republicans to do so. Two articles passed. Two were defeated. And Bill Clinton was the first president in more than 130 years to be impeached.

The Republicans had finally gotten Bill Clinton. After all the years and all the investigations. But fate prevented them from having even a moment to savor their victory. Instead they filed down to HC-5 to elect a replacement for their second fallen Speaker. When Cross walked into the room, he saw DeLay and Gingrich huddling. Unlike Wednesday evening, there were no shouts or cheers. The mood was somber. Almost dark. Not out of any realization of what damage they had just done to the Presidency, but because Livingston's demise prevented them from luxuriating in their impeachment triumph. Gingrich spoke briefly and recommended Denny Hastert as the next Speaker. Most heads nodded yes. There was little debate. The official vote would be in January. But Hastert would be the man. Cross thought it was a good choice. Denny was a thoroughly decent guy. The Republicans had finally done something right this day.

When Cross landed at LaGuardia Airport, it was just after 4:30. There was a camera crew there from Channel 11 to interview him. He said he regretted that the President had been impeached and was hopeful the Senate would acquit him. But there was no edge or emotion to his voice. Just a tired resignation.

The holiday traffic wasn't as bad as he thought it would be; so Cross was back in his Seaford home before six. He was sitting at the kitchen table with Mary Rose trying to make sense of the day's events when the phone rang. It was the White House. The President wanted to speak with him. The voice he heard was Betty Currie, the President's much besieged secretary.

"Love and kisses from the Oval Office," she said in an unusually festive tone.

"Same to you Betty."

"Be sure to wish your family a very Merry Christmas. The President will be right on."

"Sean?"

"Mr. President, how are you doing?"

"I'm doing fine," answered Clinton in a particularly strong voice. "I just wanted to thank you for what you've done for me."

"You've always been there whenever I needed you. So whatever I did for you, you deserve it. I just wish it worked out better."

"I hope you don't get hurt."

"I think it'll work out okay for me. How are the First Lady and Chelsea doing?"

"They're doing a lot better. I thought your speech on the House floor was very good. You were right when you said the Republicans wouldn't be doing this if it was a Republican President."

"You're my friend. But I would have voted against those articles even if my worst enemy was President. Bob Livingston's resignation is an example of where all this is going."

"It's awful. I asked Bob to reconsider. He shouldn't have to go out this way."

"There's rumors there might be more to this than what's come out so far."

"I don't know anything about that."

"It doesn't matter anyway. The way things are today once a rumor starts, everyone believes it and it might as well be true."

"This is what I've gone through for seven years. I have to tell you I was very disappointed that some of the Republicans I was counting on turned against me in the end."

"Mr. President, I was surprised by some of the guys who switched but you probably still don't realize how many Republicans actually hate you. You couldn't have believed the meeting we had Wednesday night."

Cross detailed some of the goings-on at the meeting where Livingston announced the one-day delay. Clinton then continued:

"I heard that some undecided Republicans were shown raw files during the week to sway their vote."

"That's true. Luke Christian told me on Wednesday they showed him charges against you going back to 1979."

"Sean, if there was anything there, don't they think Starr would have gone after it?"

"Mr. President, what's most important is that the Senate trial is over with as soon as possible. We have to end this."

Cross then handed the phone to Mary Rose. Clinton asked if she was feeling better and said he had sent her a note. She told him to give her best to the First Lady and Chelsea. Cross got back on the phone.

"Thank you, man," said Clinton in a voice which seemed subdued and perhaps emotional.

"Mr. President, I'll always be there for you."

"Thank you," said Clinton in a very low voice, hanging up the phone.

Cross got up early Sunday morning. He was going to pick up Kara and go into Manhattan to do Christmas shopping since Mary Rose still wasn't well enough to leave the house. Before he left, he opened *Newsday* and turned to Mickey Brannigan's column. It was headlined *Alone on the Hill.*

> Each time that card went into the counter it said, no, he was not for impeachment, he would not wound a country that let him rise from a cop's family in Brooklyn and Sunnyside. And when Sean Cross caught the Shuttle back to Seaford last night, he brought with him a record that will live forever and be admired everywhere by people who know what it means to stand up.

Good old Mickey, Cross thought as he picked up the phone to dial Brannigan.

"Mickey, I just read the column. Thanks a lot. It was great."

"I had nothing else to fucking write about. Good-bye."

"Good-bye, Mickey."

The Senate impeachment trial began in January. The Republican senators, unlike their House counterparts, made it clear from day one they wanted impeachment over and done with at the earliest possible date. That date came on Friday, February 12, when the Senate acquitted Clinton on both counts. The votes took place in early afternoon. About half past two, Clinton addressed the nation from the White House Rose Garden and asked for healing.

At about three o'clock the White House operator called Cross at his Massapequa Park office, where he was in a meeting with a delegation of Irish republican women from South Armagh. When Cross picked up the phone, Betty Currie was on the line.

"Betty, how are you doing?"

"Congressman, I'm doing fine. In fact I'm going to have one or two glasses of wine this evening."

"In that case I'll have two or three."

"That sounds great to me. Here's the President."

"Mr. President, congratulations."

"Thank you, Sean."

"That was a great victory in the Senate. The fact they couldn't get a majority on either article shows how weak the charges were. Your speech was great. It struck the right tone."

"Thank you, man," said Clinton in a very low tone. "I'll never forget that you stuck with me even after your vote didn't count anymore."

"Like I told you before, you've always been there for me."

"Sean, did you see that story in today's *Times*?" asked Clinton, referring to a piece saying the president was plotting revenge against individual Republicans.

"Yeah, I did."

"That was bullshit. All I intended to do is campaign for Democratic candidates in 2000 and they call that revenge."

"Mr. President, we have too much important shit to deal with in this country."

"We certainly do."

"And I think Denny Hastert will work with you."

"Well, I want to work with him. Could you tell him that?

"Sure. Speaking of important work, I was just meeting with a group from Northern Ireland, and they're telling me how much your input is needed."

"I know the peace process has hit a snag. Tony's been all over me to get it going again. If you have any ideas, will you let me know?"

"Of course."

CHAPTER TWENTY-ONE

July

Side Tracks was an Irish bar and restaurant located on the south side of Queens Boulevard, in the shadow of the massive concrete el.

Cross and Jack Pender were at a corner table in the very rear of the restaurant, with Frank Doolan, Danny Lacy, and Mickey Brannigan. They were all eating steaks. Brian Sullivan, the Nassau County detective protecting Cross, sat at a nearby table, his eyes scanning the room.

"Sunnyside Gardens used to be right down the block from here," growled Brannigan. "On the corner of Forty-fifth."

"For a small club, they sure had some great fights," said Cross.

"Best fight I ever saw was at Sunnyside," said Brannigan. "Two guys most people never heard of. Heavyweights. Joe McFadden and Nino Valdez."

"I remember Valdez," said Cross. "He beat Ezzard Charles."

"That was a good fight," said Brannigan. "But McFadden and Valdez, that was fucking unbelievable. Eight knockdowns in six rounds before Valdez finally took him out. I never saw anything like it. Now there's a fucking hamburger joint there. The whole fucking world's falling apart."

"Let's hope that doesn't include the peace process," said Doolan. "Sean, you've given me some of what you heard in Belfast. Why don't you give us the full story."

Cross then recounted Vera Toomey's story. The others listened intently. When Cross concluded, Lacy was the first to speak.

"Guess you were right, Frank. Looks like the CIA is involved.

"Assuming Vera's legit, and it sounds like she is, they certainly could be," said Doolan. "Or maybe just someone who had dealings with them."

"That's pretty much what my source in Washington told me," said Cross, referring to Addison Bartlett. "He said it might be a CIA contract employee."

"What kind?" asked Lacy.

"Someone who agrees to give information. Like a bar owner in an Irish neighborhood. Or a gun-store owner who did some IRA gunrunning. Maybe even someone who knows his way around and provides safe houses for guys the CIA wants to hide," replied Doolan.

"So this guy wouldn't be carrying a badge or be listed on some civil service list," said Cross.

"No, nothing like that. But whoever he is, he's obviously had past dealings with MI5. Enough dealings that the British guy who calls himself Walter Marley could hand McGrath over to him and McGrath would get all his papers, a job, an apartment—"

"And a fucking bullet in the head," interrupted Brannigan.

"But you don't think there's any CIA direction on this from the top," said Lacy.

"That's unlikely," answered Doolan. "The CIA has really been cleaned up since the attack on World Trade Center. The only official involvement would be if some CIA guy in New York took a look at this and figured one of his contract employees is the perp. Then he might try to cover it up to protect the agency."

"That's why I haven't told any of this to my CIA contact," said Cross.

"So, what the hell do we do now?" asked Lacy.

Doolan turned to Cross. "Sean, is Howard Briggs still the lead detective on the case?"

"Yeah, he is. I'm meeting with him tomorrow. I've already told him what I got from my CIA guy."

"Be sure to tell him not to give Vera Toomey's name to anyone. Including the FBI and the Brits. There's too many potential conflicts of interest here," said Brannigan.

"I won't give him anything that could help identify her," said Cross.

"Will Briggs go along with that?" asked Doolan.

"Sure. He's a good guy, and we know each other well," replied Cross. "If it turns out I'm wrong, I'll deal with it then. But I don't foresee any problem."

"Briggs'll do fine," said Doolan. "Probably better than my investigators on the Farrell case, because he's got police power. He'll question McGrath's landlord, talk to the owner of the construction company where he was working, check into any local rent-a-spooks the CIA might have contacted."

"Any word from Clinton?" asked Lacy.

"Yeah, he passed the information I gave him on to Blair, and Blair was having his top security man check it out, whoever that is," answered Cross. "I assume someone'll contact me if anything turns up."

The July 4 recess was over and Cross was back in his office in the Cannon Building when his private line rang.

"Cross?"

"Yes."

"Ellis here."

"Sir Leonard, how are you?"

"Very well indeed."

"This is a pleasant surprise."

"Life is full of surprises. Can we get together tonight?"

"Tonight? Where are you?"

"D.C., at the embassy."

"When did you get in?"

"Just last night. I'd very much like to get together with you this evening."

"Tomorrow night's actually a lot better for me. But if it's important . . ."

"The PM thinks it is."

"Oh. I understand. Where can we meet?"

"1789 satisfactory?"

"You're the boss. What time?"

"Half past seven."

"See you there."

"Cheers."

A two-story townhouse tucked away on a quiet residential street in Georgetown, the 1789 restaurant had an air of refinement. So much so, it could be British. Indeed, during the halcyon days of Reagan and Thatcher, when Anglo-American cooperation was at its zenith, 1789 was reputedly the favorite locale of MI6 agents the American government allowed to operate with impunity in Washington.

Ellis certainly chose the appropriate setting, thought Cross.

He entered 1789 through the doorway on Thirty-sixth Street at seven twenty-five. The maitre d' was waiting just inside.

"Congressman, would you mind following me?"

He led Cross up the old wooden staircase. At the top of the stairs, he opened the door to a private dining room. Ellis was standing inside, a martini in hand. He greeted Cross warmly.

When their server arrived, Cross ordered rack of lamb and a glass of sparkling water. No booze tonight, he had decided. He and Ellis were genuinely pleased to see one another, but Cross realized Ellis was here on assignment. So he got to the point.

"I assume you have some information for me."

"Yes. Your friend spoke to the prime minister as he said he would. The PM asked me to make an inquiry and inform you of my findings."

"I was told the prime minister had given this to his top security man. You always said that wasn't your field."

"Circumstances change."

"So I gather."

"Let me assure you the prime minister takes this matter very seriously. And what you've given us is extremely troubling. I've not finished my inquiry yet, but I've confirmed enough to know we have a significant problem on our hands."

"How significant?"

"You gave us the name Walter Marley?"

"Yes."

"Walter Marley retired from the service years ago."

"Which service?" asked Cross, attempting to project a calm veneer.

"MI5," answered Ellis after a brief hesitation.

"Years ago?"

"Yes. About a year after the Good Friday Agreement."

"And he did serve in the north?"

"Yes."

"Can you tell me what field?"

"Special operations. Some might call it 'dirty tricks.' "

"If he'd left MI5, how could he have been McGrath's minder?"

"He wasn't. The agent assigned to McGrath was Marcus Stockman."

"How did Marley get involved?"

"We don't know."

"What happened to Stockman?"

"That I can tell you, though we don't know all the circumstances."

"What do you mean?"

"Stockman was killed last October."

"Killed?"

"By a hit-and-run driver. It was on a Saturday night in the East End of London. Outside a place called the Crescent Bar. That's all we know of it."

"And it was in October that Marley first contacted McGrath."

"That's what you told Clinton."

"Wouldn't MI5 have been suspicious?"

"MI5 didn't know Marley had made contact with McGrath. Stockman wasn't to see McGrath again until April. So a new agent would have contacted him then. In the meantime, Marley knew how to operate so he wouldn't be detected."

"So Marley contacted McGrath, posing as his minder, and made sure Frank was out of the country before the new guy even had a chance to meet him."

"Exactly."

"What about when Stockman was killed—wasn't MI5 suspicious?"

"Anytime an MI5 man is killed there are suspicions, but this appeared to be your standard late-night hit-and-run."

"The fact that Stockman was a minder for an IRA informer didn't set off any bells?"

"No. For one thing, very few people would have known of Stockman's involvement with McGrath. Also—and I can tell you this now—our people had an understanding with the IRA that supergrasses were no longer targets."

"And you took their word?"

"Yes. Whatever anyone thinks of the IRA, they have a very rugged type of honesty. They keep their word."

"Was the killing investigated at all?"

"Of course. The police gave it their standard procedure. But they hadn't a clue Stockman was MI5. They accepted the cover that he was an antiques dealer."

"How about MI5?"

"They conducted a very discreet investigation at the time. And nothing turned up."

"Any idea where Marley is now?"

"No. And that's an additional problem. All of Marley's personnel records are missing. As you might imagine, MI5 keeps track of its operatives even after they've left the service. Everything's been removed or deleted."

"So you have no idea where he's been or what he's been doing since 1999?"

"No. It's almost as if he never existed."

"Shit."

"But all isn't lost. I personally went to MI5 headquarters the other day. Which by the way is something I'd prefer to avoid."

"Why?"

"Very depressing. A very arid atmosphere."

"What do you mean?"

"Actually the location is charming. The Thames House on Millbank. Just north of Lambeth Bridge. But inside—it is the ultimate mind control setting."

"How so?"

"All these icy gray desks lined up one after the other. Not the barest hint of individuality. And the offices all divided by frosted glass. I'm amazed an original thought has ever emerged from there."

"Did you find anything?"

"I reviewed our Northern Ireland files. Everything was standard except for one particularly interesting matter. From the fall of 1997 until July 1998 there was considerable contact between Marley and Marty McDevitt."

"What was the supposed reason for that?"

"Intelligence gathering. And there's enough in the files to make it appear legitimate. But knowing what we now know, it raises the most serious questions."

"July '98. That was the month before Omagh. Anything in the files to indicate Marley knew about it?"

"Not a word. In fact, to read Marley's reports, McDevitt was just an independent-minded chap who had honest political differences with Adams and McGuinness. Which is why I'm convinced his reports were a cover. Marley was too good an intelligence man not to know what McDevitt was up to."

"Any idea who his CIA contact in New York might be?"

"Not a hint. But if I can give you some free advice?"

"Sure."

"I've never had dealings with the CIA regarding actual operations. Just some policy-level meetings for the PM. So I've no idea how they'd deal with MI5 or MI6 on domestic operations in the United States, or if they've even had such dealings, since I know it's illegal for the CIA to operate in the U.S."

"I understand," said Cross, now realizing that Ellis did indeed know of such operations and how they were coordinated.

"They'd probably be intelligence-gathering and sharing-type jobs," said Ellis. "And whoever the CIA would be using would have no formal connection to the agency. Someone who'd give the CIA complete deniability if anything went wrong."

"What kind of guy would that be?" asked Cross.

"Often some borderline type of character. Someone just barely on the right side of the law, most of the time anyway."

"Where do we go from here?"

"I'm quite concerned about the safety of whoever gave you this information. Obviously, this person was close to McGrath. And Marley would be able to figure that out. I understand your reluctance to identify your source, but I am concerned."

"If you can't figure out who it is, how could Marley?"

"Because the file on McGrath has also been removed, and we believe Marley has it."

"I see what you mean."

"Anyhow, I would very much like to deal with the police detective heading the investigation. Considering my position with the prime minister, that could be very dicey unless you clear the path for me."

"The detective is an old family friend. I'm sure there'll be no problem. He already knows everything I've told you. Obviously, his main job right now is to locate the CIA guy."

"Is he having any success?"

"Not so far."

"I'd like to fly to New York in the next day or so to meet your detective."

"I'll work it out."

"Thank you, my friend."

"Charlie, I've got to give you credit," said Cross. "You were the first guy to suggest our own government might be involved."

"I'm not going to kid you and say I knew for sure, but yeah, I did think it was a possibility," said Charlie Rice, the Notre Dame law professor, who was in Washington to testify before the House Judiciary Committee on pending anti-trust legislation.

"I'm really glad you could stop by."

"Listen, when you called and told me what's been going on, I had no choice."

"I know you have to be out of here in twenty minutes, so why don't you just lay out the invaluable Rice wisdom."

"I'll use small words to make it easier for you."

"I appreciate that."

"All I know about what MI5 and MI6 did in Britain or Ireland is what I read in the papers. But I do have some knowledge of what they did over here, primarily MI6. But I think the M.O. would be the same for both."

"Go ahead."

"Like any other foreign intelligence agency, it's always been illegal for MI6 to spy in this country. But for many years during the '80s and '90s our government looked the other way. After all, the CIA still has a guy sitting on the Joint Intelligence Committee in Whitehall."

"Dick Manning told me that the Joint Committee might have had prior knowledge of Pat Finucane's murder."

"That could be," said Rice. "Anyway, the Brits had spooks attached to the British Embassy. They did no diplomatic work at all. Their main job was to gather as much intelligence as possible. That gin mill where you hang out—"

"The Dubliner?"

"Yeah. That was filled with Brits. Getting down every word that was spoken. So I hope you didn't say anything particularly stupid."

"No more than usual."

"Good. Anyway, they didn't just keep this information for themselves. They shared it with the CIA. Which was how the CIA got around the prohibition on domestic spying."

"What about guys the CIA's hired over here—would they work with the Brits as well?"

"You mean whoever knocked off McGrath and Williamson? If I had to bet, this was a guy on CIA retainer, some holdover from the old days who was supposed to make things easier for the Brits over here. Probably nothing very dramatic. Just arranging to get them into certain bars or dinners. Maybe getting them papers if they needed them."

"But nothing really illegal?"

"Nothing like murder. This sounds like a private deal, way off the reservation. And chances are the guy has some connection in the Irish community—probably some kind of business. International intrigue is pretty tricky, though. So nothing would surprise me."

"Thanks, Charlie. I appreciate your input."

"Are you still getting police protection?"

"Yeah, but nothing heavy. I have one cop with me in New York. Here in Washington the Capitol police keep an eye on me. A few cranks've been making phone calls."

"Well, keep your head down."

CHAPTER TWENTY-TWO

March 1999–June 2000

Impeachment was history. Bill Clinton could again focus on being president. Particular energy was invested in alleviating the still stalemated Irish peace process.

Trimble remained inflexible, insisting that the Executive would not be formed until the IRA began decommissioning its weapons. Adams claimed Trimble was violating the Good Friday Agreement, which had not stipulated prior decommissioning. The Brits agreed that Adams was technically correct but called on the IRA to show good faith by beginning decommissioning anyway. Adams replied that the continued ceasefire in the face of Trimble's provocation was demonstration enough of the IRA's good faith.

Clinton repeatedly attempted to devise a diplomatic solution that would finesse the impasse and allow all sides to declare victory. He tried during the 1999 St. Patrick's Day festivities. He tried with trans-Atlantic calls during the frantic Holy Week negotiations, which failed to replicate the previous year's success. He tried in conversations with Blair during the Kosovo war. But he couldn't break the logjam.

Clinton asked Cross to fly with him to Whiteman Air Force Base in Missouri on June 11 to help welcome troops home from Kosovo. Seven other members of Congress were on board. The President came back to talk with the congressmen about a half hour after Air Force One had taken off from Andrews Air Force Base. As always with Clinton, the meeting more resembled a graduate seminar. The conversation—which he dominated—ranged from the Balanced Budget Act to teaching hospitals to the successful effort in Kosovo. Clinton, Blair, Chirac and Schroeder had been great. He also said Yeltsin had been very helpful but "if the Russians think they'll control any zone in Kosovo, they must be smoking something." Clinton then asked Cross to step off to the side.

"I was just talking to Tony," said Clinton, "and he was very enthused about Kosovo. But I told him we can't lose Ireland."

"How did he react to that?"

"He's very nervous. There's just no progress. Do you think the IRA really does intend to decommission?"

"I think so. But it has to be done voluntarily, and in the context of the entire agreement being implemented."

"I've got a proposal I'm going to make to Tony. Tell me if you think it can work."

"Sure."

"Blair would set up the Executive. Blair, Ahern, and Trimble would say there has to be significant decommissioning within four months or both governments would withdraw support for the Good Friday Agreement. In return for those statements, Trimble would enter the government. Gerry wouldn't have to say anything at all. That takes away decommissioning as a precondition."

"That sounds as good as anything I've heard. It might have possibilities. I'll pass it on to Gerry."

"That'd be great. And you can call me any time of the day or night on this."

"Thank you, Mr. President."

"And remember that Gerry won't have to say anything publicly. Not a word."

Over the next several weeks, a variation of Clinton's proposal emerged as the basis of discussion at the talks in Stormont. Basically, Blair and Ahern would agree to the formation of the Executive, the IRA would say nothing, Sinn Fein would publicly urge decommissioning, and Trimble would enter the Executive. On June

28 Clinton was interviewed on BBC, urging the formation of the Executive and reaffirming America's commitment to the Good Friday Agreement. Rita O'Hare told Cross Sinn Fein was pleased by Clinton's statement and asked him to pass that along to the president. Cross spoke to Clinton by phone that evening.

"Mr. President, Sinn Fein wants you to know how much they appreciate your efforts. They're on board. Their only concern is that Trimble would go too far in his public statements."

"Sean, I understand now it's a matter of theology to the IRA that they can't decommission prior to the Executive being formed. My message to the unionists is that they should back Trimble. If Trimble thinks he has a good-faith agreement with Gerry on decommissioning, he should enter into the Executive because he always has the power to bring it down if Sinn Fein reneges."

"It's impossible to know what Trimble's going to do."

"I'd like to be able to say that if the IRA doesn't decommission by next May, then Trimble or the British and Irish governments have the right to take the Executive down. Can I go that far?"

"My understanding is that Sinn Fein could accept that type of statement so long as they could keep quiet on it. They would not, however, agree to keep quiet about any statement that allows Sinn Fein to be ejected if decommissioning doesn't take place, because the Good Friday Agreement doesn't provide for it. Bringing down the entire Executive is very different from kicking out a single party."

"Thanks. It's important I know I can say the government could be brought down."

Weeks later Blair and Ahern established the Executive. Hopes were high but then dashed when Trimble refused to enter it. Seamus Mallon was so angered by Trimble's obduracy, he resigned as Deputy First Minister. Again the process appeared to be at the precipice. And again George Mitchell stepped in to save it.

By early November, he appeared to have succeeded. In a carefully orchestrated sequence of events, Sinn Fein issued a statement recommitting itself to the Good Friday Agreement and saying the

IRA should begin decommissioning as soon as possible. The IRA followed with a statement of its own, saying it supported Sinn Fein and would appoint a representative to the international decommissioning panel. Then David Trimble was supposed to say that progress toward decommissioning had begun and the Executive could be formed.

Trimble followed the game plan, but only to a point. When he went before the Ulster Unionist Party council to get formal approval to enter the Executive, he added an unscripted proviso. He pledged to leave the government if the IRA did not turn over weapons by February 1. This undercut the essential premise of Mitchell's skillful handiwork—that all actions be voluntary. By setting a deadline, Trimble was again imposing a precondition on the IRA, a term of surrender.

Trimble gave Adams no advance notice he would be moving the goalposts. Gerry was in bed recovering from the flu when he heard the announcement on television. Nor did Trimble warn the Brits. Peter Mandelson, Mo Mowlam's replacement, also saw the news on BBC. His immediate reaction was to ring Adams.

"Gerry. Did you hear what Trimble just said?"

"I did indeed," said Adams.

"What do we do now?" the British secretary of state anxiously inquired of the man the British government had vilified for more than two decades as a brutal terrorist.

"I suggest we just go forward and make the best we can of this."

"Thank you, Gerry."

"You're welcome, Peter."

The IRA made no response to Trimble's statement. Adams and McGuinness went ahead as if the original deal was on. So, too, did the British and Irish governments. And Trimble. The Executive was to be set up in Belfast on Thursday, December 2, along with the North-South Ministerial Council. Trimble's February 1 deadline was temporarily forgotten.

Under the unique selection system the parties had agreed upon, Sinn Fein received two ministerial posts—Education and

Health. Unionists realized just how much their world had been shattered when Martin McGuinness assumed the title of Education Minister. The man they'd accused of being IRA Chief of Staff during the bloodiest days of the fighting would now be in charge of their children's education. The Health slot went to Bairbre de Brun, a longtime Sinn Fein activist slightly less controversial than McGuiness but equally committed.

Cross was invited by Adams to attend the opening ceremonies. He took an Aer Lingus flight to Dublin, where he met Dick O'Neill, who'd flown in from Boston. They had a quick breakfast before catching the eleven o'clock train to Belfast.

As the Enterprise pulled out from Platform 2, Cross and O'Neill took window seats facing each other. O'Neill showed Cross the headline on the *Irish Times:* "Direct Role in North Due to End at Midnight." Just under it was a color photo of Martin McGuinness seated behind his ministerial desk.

"It's a new world," said O'Neill.

"Too bad Trimble's always doing something to fuck it up," said Cross.

When the Enterprise pulled into Belfast's Central Station, Cleeky Clarke's boys were waiting at the top of the staircase. Talking into their radios, the minders led the two congressmen to waiting cars, which took them to the nearby Hilton Hotel on Lanyon Place. Thoroughly modern, the newly constructed Hilton was just across the road from Waterfront Hall, where Trimble had delivered his infamously uninspired speech fifteen months before.

Cross and O'Neill barely had time to put their luggage in their rooms before the minders had them back in the cars, taking them to Stormont Castle, where everything was scheduled to happen tomorrow. Today, the Shinners were making final plans and ensuring everything was ready to go.

Parking their cars behind the Parliament Building, the minders led Cross and O'Neill into the massive building and up the staircase to the second floor. Cross and O'Neill entered Room 264, Gerry Adams's office. Adams was seated behind his desk. On the wall to his left was a portrait of Bobby Sands, the famed IRA hunger striker. Standing next to Adams were Richard McAuley and Ned Harlan. After handshakes and congratulations had been exchanged, Cross and O'Neill sat down, and Adams's tone turned serious.

"Trimble has created a massive problem for us all, including himself."

"Any chance of something happening by February 1?" said Cross, being intentionally obscure.

"Decommissioning is not on," said Adams. "Trimble knows that and Mandelson knows that."

"We're heading toward a massive train wreck," said Harlan. "Unless someone performs a miracle."

"Still, nothing should be allowed to diminish the significance of this moment," said Adams.

Just then Martin McGuinness entered the room. Adams immediately stood up and asked with mock seriousness, "Have you all met the minister of education?"

"Just call me 'Your Lordship'," said McGuinness, and the room erupted in laughter.

Just how improbable it all truly was struck Cross the next day. It was twenty past noon. He was standing at the top of the marble staircase leading to the rotunda of Stormont's Parliament Building. Sinn Fein's news conference was to begin momentarily—the "victory" news conference, as the media had dubbed it.

Looking down at the rotunda, Cross saw a phalanx of camera crews and reporters crowded in behind an ornate red rope. They were waiting for the moment when Sinn Fein would stride down the palatial staircase and change Irish history. The mood was electric. Looking around him, Cross saw the faces of men he'd known over the years. Men who'd been shot. Who'd been in jail, and on the run. Adams. McGuinness. McAuley. Harlan. Gerry Kelly. Alex Maskey. Now they were respectable. And they'd done it on their terms.

"Gerry, they're all set. We're ready to go," said McAuley, checking his watch.

"Where's Bairbre?" asked Adams, looking around for Bairbre de Brun.

"She's stuck in traffic," answered McAuley. "But we have to get started. The whole bloody world is waiting."

"We've waited more than eight hundred years. Five more minutes will do no harm."

The minister of health finally arrived, and at twelve thirty-four, Adams led his delegation down the staircase and into history.

The news conference went well. While the speeches were going on, Cross happened to glance up toward the second-floor balcony. There, standing alone, his shoulders sunk as he leaned forward on the marble railing, was Ian Paisley. Cross couldn't help wondering what was going through Paisley's mind as he watched his world being turned upside down.

Unfortunately, the euphoria of early December was overtaken by the dark reality of January and February. Rewriting history, Mandelson now accepted Trimble's February 1 deadline as if it had been agreed to all along. As the deadline drew closer, Cross had separate phone conversations with Adams and Jim Steinberg. And with Christopher Meyer, the British ambassador. No progress was made by February 1, but White House involvement kept the talks alive into the following week. Then, late Friday morning, February 11, Cross got a phone call from Rita O'Hare.

"Sean, listen, I was just talking to Gerry. There may've been a breakthrough. The IRA's made a proposal to de Chastelain." De Chastelain was the retired Canadian general heading the decommissioning panel.

"What did de Chastelain say?"

"That it had promise. It's worth pursuing."

"What about Mandelson?"

"Gerry met with him this morning. He sounded positive. He's getting back to Gerry this afternoon."

"This is the first good news in weeks."

"It is, indeed. But it's vital that we keep up the media coverage as soon as this gets going. So we'd appreciate you doing whatever interviews you can."

"Sure. No problem."

"Good. I'll be back to you soon."

Less than an hour later, Cross received a phone call from WCBS Radio. *The media campaign must be beginning*, thought Cross. What he didn't realize was that it was already over. The Brits were ignoring de Chastelain.

"Congressman Cross, we'll be on the air in about forty-five seconds. As you've probably guessed, it's about Ireland," said the reporter.

"Yeah. The IRA proposal."

"I don't know anything about that. I'm talking about the British decision to bring down the government in Belfast."

"What?"

"It was announced just minutes ago. Okay, we're going on the air now."

Cross quickly decided he had to go on the offensive.

"Congressman Cross, British officials have just announced they are stripping all power from the new government in Northern Ireland because the IRA has refused to turn over a single gun or bullet. The question now is, when will the IRA live up to its agreement and begin decommissioning?"

"Let me first disagree with your premise. The British have absolutely no legal or moral right to bring down the government in Northern Ireland. There was never any agreement to have weapons turned in by February 1. The British government has disgracefully caved in to pressure from David Trimble and the unionists."

"The Good Friday Agreement says all weapons must be decommissioned by May 1. Will the IRA comply with that date, at least?"

"Again, I must disagree. The IRA did not sign the Good Friday Agreement, Sinn Fein did. And, like all parties to the agreement, Sinn Fein agreed to do all it could to bring about decommissioning. Which it has. But the British and the unionists are not complying with their obligations under the agreement and are making it very difficult for Sinn Fein to convince the IRA to move unilaterally."

"What promises of the Good Friday Agreement have the British failed to comply with?"

"For one thing, the Executive was expected to have been formed by September 1998. This would have given Sinn Fein almost twenty months to show the IRA that democratic institutions can work in Northern Ireland. Instead, the Executive wasn't set up until last December—a fifteen-month delay. Additionally, there are now more British troops in parts of Northern Ireland than there were before the Agreement. Plus, police reform, human-rights reform, and criminal-justice reform have not been enacted, even though they were required by the Agreement. And on top of that, there are 150,000 so-called 'legal guns' that the British allow the unionists to possess."

"Congressman Cross, we're out of time. But it looks like the next few months will be very tense."

On Thursday morning, April 6, Cross was sitting in the White House West Wing, waiting for his eight o'clock meeting with Jim Steinberg. That evening Cross and Mary Rose would be flying to Dublin for the Sinn Fein Ard Fheis, the party's annual convention. His official purpose was to address the delegates. But he'd be meeting privately with Adams and McGuinness as well, and he wanted to see if Steinberg had any proposals to pass along. A secretary escorted Cross to Steinberg's NSC office.

"Jim, I appreciate your taking the time."

"You know how important this is to the president. We want to take advantage of every opportunity."

"I'll be seeing Gerry and Martin."

"What's their mood?"

"From what I can tell, not good. They negotiate a deal in November, and Trimble's able to overturn it. They convince the IRA to make an offer in February, and Trimble's able to veto that. They're wondering what sense there is in having negotiations if Trimble always has the last word."

"We can see why they feel screwed. I believe the Brits boxed themselves in, and in the end had no choice. I think the Brits realize that as well."

"So, there's a chance to get this moving?"

"I think so. More importantly, if an agreement is reached with Sinn Fein, the Brits, and the Irish, then all three governments—London, Dublin, and Washington—will support Sinn Fein and the government will be reinstated."

"No matter what Trimble says?"

"Yes."

"That would be terrific. That's what they're looking for. What's expected from Sinn Fein?"

"There's a few things. Generally, there has to be an overall sense of confidence from the IRA. I think the IRA can do this by clarifying what they mean when they tie decommissioning to the conditions of the Good Friday Agreement being implemented—otherwise that could mean no decommissioning until there's a united Ireland," said Steinberg with a laugh.

"I see your point," answered Cross, smiling.

"They have to give some idea of a time frame—even if it's tied to events rather than specific dates. And there has to be something up front, even if it's words."

"Jim, obviously I don't know all that's gone back and forth with all of you but this sounds like it could be workable."

"I appreciate your giving it a try."

Sinn Fein held its two day Ard Fheis at the Royal Dublin Society, an imposing structure of impressive design always called the RDS. The RDS was in Ballsbridge—a particularly upscale section of Dublin often referred to by its postal zone "Dublin 4." Cross appreciated the irony of Sinn Fein choosing the RDS as its venue since no residents of Ireland had more disdain for Sinn Fein then the residents of Dublin 4. But for the next two days the west Brits of Dublin had no choice but to grin and bear it as Shinners by the hundreds from all over Ireland descended on Ballsbridge and filled the RDS beyond capacity. Arriving at the convention complex early Saturday morning, Cross immediately recognized not just today's main players but faces from the past. There were hunger strikers, ex-prisoners, relatives of kids murdered by plastic bullets, and at least two guys who were on the run.

The mood in the hall was friendly but tentative. Cross was confident Adams and McGuinness and the Sinn Fein leadership had convinced their grassroots—even the hard-core—that the war had run its course. That it was time for politics. If the Brits didn't rig the system against them. If the unionists didn't claim some inalienable right to arbitrarily move the goalposts.

In his presidential address delivered on Saturday afternoon, Adams was greeted with enthusiasm. But the delegates were silent when he discussed the peace process. No applause. But no hostility or antagonism either. They trusted Adams, but the essence of his strategy depended on reciprocal action by the Brits. And they weren't sure the Brits could be trusted.

That evening Cross and Mary Rose attended a dinner hosted by Adams at Kites, a Cantonese restaurant a short walk from the RDS. McGuinness was there, as were much of the Sinn Fein leadership and several Irish-American business leaders. No connoisseur of Chinese food, Cross ordered his staple of sweet-and-sour chicken.

As Cross was finishing his meal, Adams came over and asked if they could talk privately. They moved to an empty table in a secluded corner of the restaurant, where McGuinness joined them moments later.

Speaking in a low voice, Cross detailed what Steinberg had told him over the phone. Adams and McGuinness listened carefully.

"The key point is that Trimble can't be allowed to determine the pace and the conditions," said Adams.

"Gerry's right. If this continues, we could lose the Army," said McGuinness. "It would be the beginning of the end of the Adams and McGuinness leadership."

"We had a good meeting with Bertie," said Adams. "He understands how serious this is."

"We've also been told by sources in the Irish government that Blair thinks Mandelson made a balls of it in February, so he's sending in Jonathan Powell," said McGuinness, referring to Blair's top political operative.

"That's a good sign," replied Cross. "If Blair's going to use Powell, he's looking at this as a political issue that has to be resolved."

"That's our analysis as well," said McGuinness. "Blair realizes there's no more time for messing about."

Cross addressed the Ard Fheis on Sunday afternoon, just after the lunch break. In the first half of his speech, Cross made the requisite attacks on Trimble and the Brits. It was wrong for David Trimble to unilaterally impose conditions. It was wrong for the British government to go along with those preconditions, and to suspend the institutions. The remainder of the speech, however, dealt with the issue Cross considered more pressing and significant—affirming American solidarity with Adams and McGuinness. "If you continue to stand with your leadership, we, in Congress, the White House and throughout America, not just Irish-America, will stand with you as long as it takes, until victory is yours." The delegates responded with strong applause. *Not because the words were particularly eloquent or the delivery especially articulate*, thought Cross, *but as an outlet to demonstrate their solidarity with Adams and McGuinness.*

Leaving Dublin on Monday morning, Cross was sure Gerry and Martin were secure for the moment. But he knew full well that at the first indication of weakness, Marty McDevitt would make his move.

It was a few minutes before six on Friday evening, May 5. Cross was in his car pulling away from his Massapequa Park office when his cell phone rang.

"Hello?"

"Sean, Rita here," said Rita O'Hare.

"You still in Dublin?"

"Aye. I've very positive news."

"What?"

"The IRA is ready to issue a statement saying they'll put their weapons beyond use."

"That's wonderful. Is everyone on board?"

"Aye. Blair and Ahern should be releasing a joint statement shortly. Then the unionists. Then Gerry."

"And the IRA?"

"Tomorrow morning."

"How are they defining 'beyond use'?"

"The Army will show arms dumps to international inspectors—no Brits—and they'll certify the weapons can't be used."

"And that's acceptable all around?"

"Aye."

"Any problems at all?"

"There's some suspicion the Brits may mess about with RUC reform. But we have the commitment from Blair—face to face with Gerry and Martin—that they're going ahead with implementing Patten."

"When will the Executive be back up?"

"Within weeks."

"Does Trimble have to get approval from his council?"

"Aye. But he says he can do it."

"No last-minute cute maneuvers?"

"No."

"Thanks, Rita. This is good news."

"I'll ring you tomorrow."

Cross was at home in Seaford when Tom Russell, the Irish Embassy's political counsellor, called to read him excerpts from the statement being put out by Blair and Ahern that evening. The two leaders said they believed the Good Friday Agreement would be fully implemented by June 2001 and the British government would issue "the necessary order to enable the Assembly and the Executive to be restored by 22 May 2000." They went on to say that the governments "believe that paramilitary organizations must now, for their part, urgently state clearly that they will put their arms completely and verifiably beyond use. In response the British government would take further substantial normalization measures by June 2001." In an accompanying statement, the Brits agreed to implement the Patten report on police reform by November 2000.

There it was. After all the rancor and debate. Each party was getting what it was legitimately entitled to. Trimble would be assured IRA weapons couldn't be used. The IRA was not handing over any weapons to the Brits. The request for the IRA to put its arms beyond use was coupled with the British pledge to demilitarize. And the Good Friday Agreement would be fully implemented.

The IRA responded the following day. "For our part, the IRA leadership is committed to resolving the issue of arms. The IRA will institute a process that will completely and verifiably put IRA arms beyond use. . . . The contents of a number of our arms dumps will be inspected by agreed third parties who will report to the Commission on Decommissioning. The dumps will be re-inspected regularly to ensure that the weapons have remained silent."

Within hours Mandelson called the IRA statement "a jump forward." Trimble said it did "appear to break new ground." Adams hailed the IRA statement, adding, "The onus is very much on David Trimble, but the onus is really on Tony Blair to honor his commitment."

The choreographed statements issued, the arms inspectors were now designated. All that remained was for Trimble to get approval of his party council, with no strings attached. Unfortunately, reports were already surfacing that Trimble would attempt to link restarting the Executive with watering down the Patten Commission's proposed RUC reforms.

That Sunday afternoon, Rita O'Hare telephoned Cross at home.

"Sean, it looks as if Trimble's up to his usual tricks."

"Patten?"

"Aye. He says his council just can't accept the reforms."

"Blair told you he's sticking with Patten, right?"

"Aye. He told it directly to Gerry and Martin last Thursday night at Hillsborough. But the Brits may have Blair play the good cop while the embassy does the dirty work in Washington."

"It's important for the White House to stay strong on this."

"It's critical. When will you be seeing Clinton?"

"Tomorrow. He's flying to New York for Cardinal O'Connor's funeral."

"Will you get a chance to talk with him?"

"Probably. I'll be flying back to D.C. with him on Air Force One."

"Be sure to remind him that this deal never would have happened without him. His continued interest's what did it for the IRA."

"If I get the chance, I'll tell him."

The following day, Cross and Sid Gordon and nine other members of the New York Congressional delegation were aboard Air Force One, discussing how moving the funeral ceremony had been, when Bill Clinton emerged from his compartment to join them. He stood in the center of the group, controlling, as always, the topics of conversation: trade with China, strengthening Social Security, visas for highly skilled immigrants. As the discussion wound down, Clinton turned to Cross.

"Sean, I think it's going to work."

"That agreement is so important, Mr. President, and you should know—Sinn Fein has told me this—that it wouldn't have happened without you."

"Blair and Ahern worked so hard to get this deal."

"I'm sure they did, but the IRA wouldn't have signed on if it weren't for you. The republican movement trusts you."

"It's good to know that some republicans trust me," Clinton said, laughing. "Now we have to make sure Trimble does his part."

"What do you think?"

"I called him yesterday. I actually tracked him down at a wedding reception outside Belfast. I told him he had to do it. The IRA's done its part. Now it's up to him."

"What did he say?"

"He brought up the RUC, but I told him Gerry's gone further than anyone could have expected. The Patten Commission's already a compromise. The time has come when Trimble's got to end it."

"Sinn Fein says Blair promised Adams and McGuinness there'd be no backing down on Patten."

"Gerry told me that as well. And I believe him. That's what I was told all along. Besides, it's the right thing."

Despite Blair's pledge to Adams and McGuinness, the Brits did try an end run. First, by the embassy. And then Blair himself, in two phone calls to Clinton. As the *Irish Times* reported on May 25:

> The famously close relationship between Mr. Bill Clinton and the British Prime Minister came under strain last night as it emerged that the President had refused two successive pleas for help from Mr. Tony Blair.

> In what one highly-placed source described as "an extraordinary and unprecedented event," Mr. Clinton rebuffed Mr. Blair during two phone calls to the White House. The Prime Minister asked Mr. Clinton to lean on the Irish government and Sinn Fein, to urge them to compromise on the proposed name change of the RUC.
>
> Clinton told Blair straight: "Not every issue is negotiable." Mr. Clinton stressed his belief that the Patten report should be implemented in full "as it was written."
>
> The President's rebuff of Mr. Blair came after an all-out effort by the British Embassy in Washington to persuade US opinion formers to understand the unionist case on the RUC. But Mr. Clinton made it clear the onus was on the unionists to compromise. The episode is the first known clash between the two leaders, who have made much of their closeness.

Trimble got the message. After a week's delay, the UUP met on Saturday, May 27, and ratified Trimble's entry into the Executive. The margin was narrow but decisive. Still lacking any generosity of spirit, Trimble commented to reporters that he hoped Sinn Fein was "housebroken." Within days the Executive, the Assembly, and the North-South Council were reinstated. It had been a tortuous path. And the journey was far from completed. But Ireland had indeed changed utterly.

CHAPTER TWENTY-THREE

Early August

"Sean, I hate to be ringing you so early," said Joe McNamara, "but I think it's important enough to wake you up."

"Don't worry, Joe. It's six fifteen over here. I had to get up early anyway. I have campaign stops this morning. What's up?"

"There's been a development. You recognize the name Cormac Morrow?"

"Yeah. Wasn't he Marty McDevitt's hit man?"

"Aye. Still is. We spotted him yesterday in Twinbrook."

"Twinbrook!"

"Aye. By your friend's house on Summerhill," said McNamara, referring to Vera Toomey.

"One of your guys recognized him?"

"Aye. Morrow was just strolling about, so he was. Very casual."

"You're sure it's him?"

"Oh, aye. And we got some long-range photos as well."

"Any confrontation at all?"

"Nothing. As far as we can tell, Morrow hasn't a clue he was sighted."

"How long was he there?"

"No more than five minutes. He walked past her house twice, then got back in his car."

"Where'd he go?"

"Back to his flat in North Belfast. Nothing out of the ordinary."

"What's next?"

"We'll put a tail on Morrow and increase the protection for your friend. But until Morrow actually tries something, there's nothing we can do against him."

"It's that new police service of yours," said Cross, his tone ironic. "If you had the powers the RUC used to have, you'd have tortured a confession out of him by now."

"Ah. It almost makes me long for the good old days. Except we were the ones being tortured."

"How confident are you that you can protect her?"

"I think we can do it. She's easy to work with, very cooperative. We'll just have to stay on constant alert."

"I was talking to Detective Briggs yesterday, and he says he's working well with you."

"He's very good himself, so he is. We share everything."

"How's the arrangement with Ellis working out?"

"It's a bit cumbersome, that's for certain. Ellis still has no idea I'm involved. And I want to keep it that way. I know he's your mate, but he's still a Brit. Which means he can be trusted only so far. I don't want him turning on any of my lads tomorrow or the next day."

"So Briggs gives your information to Ellis?"

"Aye. And Ellis gives his to Briggs, who passes it on to me. When will you be seeing him?"

"Briggs? Tomorrow night in the city."

"Tell him hello for me."

It was a hot, humid summer evening in Manhattan. Sean Cross and Brian Sullivan, his detective bodyguard, were walking north on Park Avenue, headed for Bobby Van's Steakhouse, a New York classic located in the Helmsley Building on 46th Street.

Cross and Sullivan were barely through the door when they were greeted by Joe Smith, a Belfast man who was the proprietor of the establishment.

"It's grand to see you, Sean," said Smith. "How's things?"

"Not so bad. But I'll let you know for sure after the primary in five weeks."

"Your guests are already seated. Will Sully be joining you as well?"

"No. I'll sit here at the bar and keep my eye on things," answered Sullivan.

Smith led Cross to the table where Howard Briggs and Jack Kilbride, the veteran NYPD sergeant, were waiting. Like Kilbride, Briggs was in his late fifties. Unlike Kilbride, who was almost totally bald, Briggs had jet-black hair, combed straight back. Both had the gritty look of street-smart cops. Briggs was drinking a martini, Kilbride scotch on the rocks.

Briggs raised his glass. "We're off duty," he said with a smile.

"Me, too," said Cross to the waiter. "Could you give me a Manhattan?" He turned to Briggs. "Thanks for coming by."

"No sweat. I brought Kilbride along because he understands you donkeys."

"Thanks for the vote of confidence," said Kilbride.

"We've gotten a break in the case, and I wanted you to know about it right away."

"Howard, you've got my attention," said Cross.

"Then let me get to the point," said Briggs, "because this is finally starting to come together. We got nowhere on fingerprints, nowhere on eyewitnesses. We did get some interesting leads from McGrath's landlord, and from the guy who owned the construction company where he worked. But they seemed to be dead ends."

"What do you mean?"

"They both told us the same story. Years ago, they had a deal with a government agency, maybe the Justice Department—they didn't know for sure. A guy would call. But he said his name was Mike. Nothing's turned up on a Charles Webster. But I'd bet anything 'Mike' was Webster's alias."

"I agree," said Kilbride.

"Anyway," continued Briggs. "They never saw 'Mike.' He'd tell them he had a guy that needed an apartment and a job. They'd take care of it and get cash in the mail. Enough to cover their costs. Plus 10 percent."

"It came in the mail?"

"Yeah. Inside a magazine. And it always arrived on time. Like clockwork," answered Briggs.

"When did this go on?"

"Almost fifteen years ago. And it lasted about five years."

"Was it mostly Irish guys?"

"No. There were a few micks. But there were also Central Americans—Nicaraguans, Salvadorans, Guatemalans—and Bosnians and Albanians as well."

"But it ended ten years ago?"

"Yeah. There were no problems or anything. It just ended."

"And I guess these guys never asked any questions?"

"No. What the hell did they care? They got their money. And nobody bothered them."

"When did they first hear about McGrath?"

"They didn't. As far as they knew, his name was Edward Barrington. Anyway, sometime in February, each of them got a call from 'Mike.'"

"Did the landlord and the construction guy know each other?"

"No. The landlord's an Irish guy, John Paul Sweeney, originally from Dublin. Owns a few apartment houses. The contractor's a big Italian guy, John Tucci, who does a lot of work here in the city and in Nassau. As far as we can tell, they've never met each other."

"What did 'Mike' tell them?"

"That Edward Barrington would be coming over soon. That it was important to the government he be taken care of. And it would be the same arrangement as before—cash up front, plus 10 percent."

"Anything else?"

"No other details. But Webster had everything in order. McGrath appeared on the scene with all his papers intact, identifying him as Edward Barrington. And everything went along normally until he got whacked. Since then, neither one's heard a word."

"Have you contacted the feds?"

"Yeah," answered Briggs.

"And?"

"No federal agency has any record of placing jobs with contractors or finding apartments for foreigners. And they denied ever having heard of a guy called 'Mike.'"

"So, a dead end."

"Yeah. But then we got a break, and that's where Jack comes in."

"I was checking all the usual shit and came up dry," said Kilbride. "Then, by a fluke, I came across arrest records from a raid on a bookie joint in Jackson Heights a few months ago. In May."

"A bookie joint?"

"Yeah. It was a bunch of Colombians. Nothing big-time. Mostly nickel-and-dime shit. But the guy running the show panicked and started running his mouth so he could make a deal for himself."

"What did he give?"

"That these guys were all illegal. Which is no surprise. Also no surprise, most of them had phony papers. The perp—Carlos—said if the cops let him off, he'd give up the guy they got their papers from."

"And the cops made the deal?"

"Sure. It was a fucking no-brainer. You let off a low-level bookie for a guy who's supplying phony passports, driver's licenses, Social Security cards—all that shit."

"So what happened?"

"Carlos said the guy's name was Edward Tyler."

"Tyler? This isn't Webster, is it?"

"No. But we think he works for Webster. Tyler's in his early fifties. Owned a printing operation in Manhattan for almost twenty years. And has worked part-time in a gun shop in Flushing for quite a while."

"Did the cops grab him?"

"No. This was a federal matter, so the actual collar would be made by the feds. But NYPD did all the preliminary investigations. Tracked down where he lived, where he worked. Had him under surveillance for a few weeks."

"Any photos?"

"Some good ones."

"So NYPD gave the case to the feds?"

"Gift-wrapped. All the evidence the feds could possibly need."

"What happened?"

"Not a fucking thing. The vice squad gave the case to the special task force on immigration crimes. INS, the FBI, the Border Patrol—they're all coordinated through the Justice Department. When I checked, not one of them would say a fucking thing about it. They claim there's no record of Tyler."

"Shit!" exclaimed Cross.

"It gets fucking worse. Tyler's gone from his apartment, gone from his company, gone from the gun shop."

"Any idea where he went?"

"None. All we know is, last time anyone saw him was two days after the case was turned over to the feds."

"Did you do any background on Tyler?"

"Yeah. We found some shit that's a little unusual," answered Kilbride.

"Like?"

"He was in the army just after Vietnam. And got a 'less than honorable' discharge. Something was fucked up."

"Anything else?"

"During the late '90s he was very involved with the Rocky Mountain Militia, a wacko group in Montana."

"They must really be nuts if Kilbride thinks they're wackos," interjected Briggs.

"Believe me, they are," said Kilbride. "And this guy had a hell of an expensive lifestyle—great apartment in Forest Hills, place in the Hamptons. And just yesterday I found out he has a condo in Tribeca."

"Does NYPD still have the photos?"

"Yeah. I've got guys on the street showing them around. We can still grab him on the gambling rap."

"Do you have any contacts in the Justice Department or the U.S. attorney's office that could help us out on this?"

"I've called everyone I know," said Briggs, "and I'm getting nowhere. It's a goddamn brick wall. Especially the U.S. attorney's office."

"Those motherfuckers," said Kilbride. "They go after every poor son of bitch who's ten cents short on his taxes, and they let this dirtbag Tyler just disappear."

"I've got no use for those fucking prosecutors either," said Cross. "But if there's a fix, it must come from somewhere higher up."

"You're probably right," said Briggs. "The only time I've even seen a curtain like this come down was in an espionage case I stumbled onto about twenty years ago. Some Russian got killed in Coney Island, and before I knew what was happening, the FBI was in and the case disappeared."

"So, Sean, what're you thinking?" asked Kilbride.

"Based on everything I've heard, I'd lay my money on someone in one of the national security outfits—most likely the CIA. And odds are that Tyler is Webster's hit man, but I don't think I should tell any of this to my CIA contact," said Cross, referring to Addison Bartlett.

"You're right," said Kilbride. "I wouldn't trust him."

"This scares the living hell out of me," said Briggs. "We're trying to track down a murderer, and people in our own government could be working against us."

"And let's not forget the Brits and MI5."

CHAPTER TWENTY-FOUR

Labor Day Weekend

When it happened, it happened fast, and without notice. Cross had spent all of August campaigning hard. The beaches and parks. The temples and churches. All the veterans' groups. The Hibernians and the Sons of Italy. Thousands of handshakes. The county organization was flexing its muscle, and the building-trades unions were going all out. So were the cops and firefighters.

But Cross could sense it slipping away. Barclay Spencer's multimillion dollar campaign blitz was taking its toll. Television ads, radio commercials, countless mailings, all implying Sean Cross was tied to the murders of Frank McGrath and Ronald Williamson.

Just last Wednesday, John O'Laughlin had confirmed the accuracy of Cross's instincts. O'Laughlin's poll, taken over the previous two nights, had Cross at 44 percent, Spencer at 38 percent. But the momentum was all Spencer's. And as O'Laughlin told Cross: "when we push the undecideds, they lean toward Spencer."

The primary was a week from Tuesday, and Cross dug in for the final stand. He was on the phone, trying to raise every dollar he could for a last-ditch media effort. He met with Mondero and the labor guys and told them this was it. They had to go all out. Cross would fight with everything he had until the final bell. But he knew the odds were against him and he needed a break.

It came on Friday, a few minutes before midnight. Cross and Mary Rose had just come in from a day of campaigning that had begun at six thirty that morning at the Hicksville train station. As he walked through the front door, the phone rang. He picked up the extension in the bedroom.

"Sean, it's Howard Briggs."

"We just nabbed Edward Tyler."

"Holy Christ! Where?"

"Bensonhurst. In a furnished room."

"How'd you find him?"

"One of our street informants recognized the picture we were passing around."

"Did Tyler put up a fight?"

"No. We broke in and caught him totally off guard. And we got evidence."

"What'd you find?"

"The gun he used to kill McGrath and Williamson. Plus photos of both guys."

"Christ, how'd you find that?"

"It was easy. The gun was in the top drawer of his dresser and the photos were in a folder right under the gun."

"Did Tyler say anything?"

"For a second or two, he seemed startled. But the guy's a pro. He didn't say a word."

"Does he have a lawyer yet?"

"Some guy from Court Street. Rich Rosenfeld. Nothing shady about him."

"What's the courtroom schedule?"

"He'll be arraigned in Queens Supreme tomorrow for McGrath and then Tuesday in Manhattan for Williamson."

"Do the reporters know?"

"They will in the next fifteen minutes. I wanted to give you the heads-up."

Despite the late hour, Cross immediately phoned Jack Pender and told him the news.

"What a gift!" was Pender's immediate reaction. "Let's maximize this and destroy that fucking Spencer. But you have to make sure it's your spin."

"It's too late for tomorrow's papers," said Cross.

"Yeah. But you can do radio all day tomorrow and television tomorrow night. And then you should be all over the fucking Sunday papers."

"I've got to make sure I get some of the credit for nailing this bastard. Otherwise Spencer could say that Tyler was working for me."

"Briggs'll have to say he got key leads from you and that you were working with the NYPD."

"Should I go anywhere with the CIA or MI5 angles?"

"Not yet. I'd just say that there's reason to believe international forces are involved who want to destroy the peace process. That should be enough for now."

Saturday went as planned. The NYPD and the Queens district attorney issued statements hailing Cross for his efforts in securing Tyler's arrest. Throughout the morning and afternoon, Cross never left home. There were telephone interviews with every New York City and Long Island radio station, plus BBC, RTE, and Reuters as well. Then there were the television reporters lining up one after the other for sound bites. The tone of the questions was exactly what Cross and Pender had hoped for.

"Congressman Cross, do you feel vindicated now that this arrest has been made?"

"I'm just pleased that justice is being done."

"Will you be demanding an apology from Barclay Spencer for all his attacks against you regarding the murders?"

"As I said, my main interest is that justice is served. I hope Mr. Spencer would agree. As to whether he'll apologize, that's between him and his conscience."

"Do you think Mr. Tyler acted alone, or were these killings part of a conspiracy?"

"Mr. Tyler is entitled to a fair trial, and we shouldn't prejudge him. But it's difficult to believe a single person is behind all this. 'Conspiracy' is probably too strong a word, but there could well be international forces involved."

"What kind of international forces?"

"Individuals or groups here and abroad who oppose the Irish peace process."

"How do you think this arrest will affect your primary next week?"

"It's really not appropriate to discuss politics at a time like this."

Cross was up by six o'clock the following morning to read the Sunday tabloids. At a glance, he saw they'd taken their lead from Saturday's radio and television newscasts. The headlines emblazoned across the front pages of *Newsday* and the *Daily News* read like Sean Cross campaign brochures.

N*ewsday* headlined it:

ARREST IN IRISH MURDERS

NYPD Credits Congressman Cross With Breaking the Case

While the *Daily News* said:

COPS NAB HITMAN IN IRISH KILLINGS

Hail Rep. Cross for Uncovering Key Leads

Even the *New York American* gave Cross grudging recognition:

COPS COLLAR SHOOTER IN IRA CASE

L.I. Rep Cited for Aiding Probe

It was barely six thirty when Pender called. "Did you see the headlines!" he exclaimed. "It doesn't get any better."

"That's the truth. The best part about it was that beautiful little line in each of the stories: 'Cross's opponent, Barclay Spencer, was unavailable for comment.'"

"What the hell can he say? He gets screwed every which way."

"Good. I hope he fucking suffers," said Cross.

"That's very Christian of you on a Sunday morning. What are you doing today?"

"I'm back on the campaign trail. Mostly parties and barbecues at the beach and Eisenhower Park. But I've got to be in the city by five."

"What's up?"

"Live news shows. CNBC at five and Fox at six."

"I'll skip the handshakes, but I'll go with you to the city."

"Great. I'll pick you up at three thirty."

CNBC went well, Fox News even better. As Cross walked off the Fox set into the green room, Pender handed him his cell phone and said, "Mary Rose called while you were on the air."

"Anything important?"

"Could be. She said Joe McNamara needs to talk to you immediately."

The station manager led them to a small office down the hall, where Cross could make his call in privacy. As Pender closed the door behind them, Cross dialed the Belfast number Joe McNamara had given Mary Rose.

"Joe, Sean here."

"Thank God you called. There's been a major development."

"What's that?"

"Cormac Morrow's been shot dead. Just after ten o'clock tonight."

"What happened?"

"Our lads got him, so they did. In Twinbrook. It was a fierce gun battle. It started outside Vera's house, and it didn't end until he was shot dead on Laburnum Way."

"Joe, I'm going to put you on speaker phone. I want Jack Pender to hear this, too. Give us all the details."

"Early this afternoon, less than an hour after the news about your man Tyler was on the telly, we spotted Morrow surveying Vera's house. We increased his tail and doubled our stakeout. We were able to get her out of the house without anyone spotting us."

"So, Vera's okay," interrupted Cross.

"She's grand. Just before ten o'clock, Morrow's car drove through Twinbrook, made a U-turn in front of her house, and stopped. Morrow got out of it. We had ten officers waiting. He must have spotted one of them, because he started firing, jumped back in the car, and took off. There was a chase. Shots were fired. And then the car careened into a lightpost on Laburnum Way. Morrow was slumped over the steering wheel, dead. A bullet in his head, one in his back. Another in his arm."

"Did you find anything on him?"

"No. We searched his flat as well, and there was nothing there either."

"Joe, I can't thank you enough. Give my best to Vera."

"You're very welcome indeed. I'll ring you straightaway if anything else should develop."

* * *

It was ten after nine on Labor Day morning. As Cross got up from the kitchen table to answer the phone, he almost knew what to expect.

"Cross?"

"Yes."

"Ellis here."

"Hello, Sir Leonard," answered Cross, struggling to contain his apprehension.

"I thought you might be interested to know that Walter Marley's body was found less than an hour ago."

"Where?" asked Cross reflexively, with a morbid sense of déjà vu.

"Just off Trafalgar Square. In a parked car. An apparent suicide. It seems he put a revolver in his mouth and blew his head apart."

"Any note?"

"None."

"What will the government say?"

"There's no need for Her Majesty's government to say anything. Mr. Marley was an art dealer despondent over severe business losses. I'm informing you of his demise as a courtesy. And I've told you all I know."

"Sir Leonard, I—"

"Sean, I really must go," said Ellis as he put down the receiver.

The courtroom in the Criminal Court Building at 100 Centre Street in lower Manhattan was filled to capacity. As Sean Cross looked around the room, he spotted virtually every major New York reporter: Mickey Brannigan, Danny Lacy, Jimmy Breslin, Michael Daly, Pete Hamill, Jack Newfield, Terry Golway. Even the movie director, Terry George, and media magnate, John Feehery.

The proceedings were brief. Charles Weiss, the Manhattan assistant D.A., said the defendant was being charged with murder in the second degree and should be held without bail. Defense attorney Richard Rosenfeld entered a plea of not guilty for his client and asked that bail be set. "Edward Tyler is innocent, and that will be proven when the entire story of this matter comes out at trial."

Ignoring Rosenfeld's argument, Supreme Court Justice Jerome Scharoff granted the D.A.'s request and ordered that Tyler be held at Riker's Island until trial.

Following the arraignment, Cross, Brannigan, and Lacy accepted Frank Doolan's invitation to his nearby Duane Street office for coffee and rolls.

"Well, Frank, you've been right from day one," said Cross as he stirred cream into his coffee.

"The key was getting Tyler," replied Doolan. "Once McDevitt heard about that, he knew he couldn't afford to wait any longer. So he gave Morrow the order to kill Vera Toomey. Once Morrow was killed, Marley knew it was only a matter of time. So he did what he thought he had to do and killed himself—or someone higher up had him killed."

"Are you surprised by what that Brit told Sean?" asked Brannigan. "That the guy was an art dealer!"

"No. Not at all," answered Doolan. "MI5 is a secret organization. That's why Marley had a cover of being an art dealer. Art, antiques, that's standard for those guys. In case something like this happens. I'm amazed Ellis has told you as much as he has."

"What do you think of Tyler?" asked Lacy. "He seems like a pretty cool customer. Didn't look a bit nervous."

"I'm sure he's concerned. But he's also been waiting for something like this to happen," answered Doolan. "That's why he kept the murder weapon and the photos of McGrath and Williamson. Sure, it's evidence against him. But it's also evidence against the CIA. And I'm sure he's got other evidence hidden away. Remember no one's found Webster yet. Tyler's betting—and we'll find out soon enough whether he's right or not—that the feds'll use whatever pressure they can to keep this from ever going to trial."

"What about McDevitt?" asked Brannigan.

"It'll be like Omagh and Newry," said Cross. "Everyone knows he did it, but no one can prove it. By the way, McNamara called me this morning and told me Morrow was in England the day Kilpatrick was shot."

"Jesus, they had it planned perfectly," said Lacy. "Thank God they didn't get away with it."

"We might not be so lucky the next time," said Brannigan. "And Webster, whoever he is, and McDevitt are still out there. And there could be a Brit who knocked off Marley. I think someone should lay out everything that happened so those bastards don't try it again."

"You're the writer," said Cross.

The next day, *Newsday* ran Mickey Brannigan's column as its lead news story.

Murder Without End?

New Yorkers have reason to be proud of their cops for tracking down the lowlife who executed two people in cold blood on the streets of our city. Edward Tyler didn't just murder an IRA informer and a Northern Irish professor, he almost brought down a fragile peace process that has saved countless lives. And he also almost ended the career of a good congressman.

But before we put too much effort into congratulating ourselves, we better do something. And we better do it quickly. Because we might not be so lucky the next time. And I think there will be a next time. Unless we realize now that Edward Tyler is just one part of a much larger picture. A picture that includes powerful people doing horrible deeds.

Edward Tyler is in jail in New York. Cormac Morrow is being buried today in Belfast. Who was Cormac Morrow? He was an IRA fanatic. A member of a gang of psychos that styles itself the "Real IRA." These guys hate peace. They're not happy unless they're killing some poor bastard. They don't want the Irish peace process to work. A few months ago Morrow executed a pathetic character in London. Then on Sunday night Morrow was killed when he tried to murder the person who had the goods on a Brit who was one of the masterminds of this evil plot.

And the Brit. He couldn't accept that Tony Blair had decided to give the Irish a fair break. The Brit worked in the shadows and back alleys of his own government. They call it intelligence work. I call it a license to kill. And to inflict pain and suffering on the streets of our city, the Brit reached out his bloody hand to sinister men who operate in the shadows and back alleys of our own government.

The Brit? They found him dead. In his car. In London. They say he ended it all with a gun that he put in his mouth.

That's what they say.

CHAPTER TWENTY-FIVE

September 12
Garden City, New York
Primary Election Night—10:15 P.M.

By ten fifteen on primary night, it was all over but the shouting. Sean Cross had known for days that he would win the primary. He'd sensed it the day the Edward Tyler story broke. John O'Laughlin had confirmed it with last Thursday's poll results: Cross 71 percent, Spencer 15 percent, Undecided 14 percent. "I've never seen such a turnaround," O'Laughlin had said.

As for Barclay Spencer, he'd been in hiding for the past ten days. And Mike Campbell, the talk-show zealot, was taking a previously unscheduled vacation.

The polls had closed at nine o'clock. Just five minutes later, Anne Kelly phoned in the first results, from Cross's own election district in Seaford: Cross 182, Spencer 4. Five minutes later, he got the first results from Old Brookville. That was Spencer's home area. Cross 140, Spencer 32.

Now Cross was backstage at the Garden City Hotel. Mary Rose, Danny, and Kara were with him. About half the votes were tallied. Cross 11,820, Spencer 856.

"Those numbers are unbelievable," said Jack Pender.

"That's over 93 percent, and some of your best areas aren't in yet," said Tom O'Connell.

In the ballroom a band played, and supporters were crowded wall-to-wall, cheering each new result as it was tabulated. Then Joe Mondero arrived, flashing Cross a big grin.

"Sean, I'm going out onstage. I'll give a brief warm-up, and then I'll introduce you. This is your night."

"Thanks, Joe. Thanks for everything."

Mary Rose, Danny, and Kara gathered around Cross. The band stopped playing. Cross could hear Mondero begin his speech.

"Tonight, we're here to celebrate a great victory for a great Republican."

The crowd erupted with loud applause and boisterous cheers.

Jack Pender's cell phone rang. Cross heard Pender say, "He's right here. I'll put him on."

Pender handed Cross the phone. "It's Howard Briggs."

Mondero had begun speaking again. "He faced the toughest odds any candidate could ever face."

Holding the phone in his right hand, Cross said, "Howard, this is Sean."

"I just got a call from Rikers."

In the background, Cross could hear Mondero faintly, barely audible over the roaring crowd. He pressed the phone closer and covered his other ear.

"Rikers?" asked Cross.

"Yeah. Tyler's dead. They say it's suicide."

Cross was stunned. After a long pause, Briggs continued.

"Both wrists were slashed. And he had a deep puncture wound in his stomach."

"But he was supposed to be under twenty-four-hour watch," said Cross.

"Sean, I just heard this five minutes ago. I'll call you as soon as I hear more."

Cross pressed the "End" button absently and handed the phone to Jack Pender.

"Let's go, Sean," said O'Connell. "Here's your moment."

"Ladies and gentleman," said Mondero. "Let's hear it for our great congressman—Sean Cross!"

Cross led Mary Rose, Danny, and Kara up the steps. The band broke into the Notre Dame "Victory March." Balloons—red, white, and blue—fell from the ceiling. The crowd roared its support as he took center stage.

And Sean Cross smiled. For this moment at least, he would savor the sweet taste of victory.